HARLEQUIN A VERY SEXY CHRISTMAS COLLECTION

It's time to turn up the heat this holiday season!

It all starts when these couples are tempted by a few sexy surprises under the tree. Whether it's being stranded with that superhot guy, reuniting with the one who got away or even assuming a different identity, these couples are reveling in their steamy, *private*, gifts.

This will be one sizzling Christmas they won't forget...especially when they discover that being naughty can be very, very good.

Indulge yourself with this special 2-in-1 collection of classic stories that brings the sexy into Christmas.

If you enjoy these stories, be sure to look for more red-hot reads in Harlequin Blaze.

TAWNY WEBER

An avid reader, neurotic writer and die-hard shoe fanatic, *New York Times* and *USA TODAY* bestselling author Tawny Weber has been writing sassy, sexy stories for Harlequin since her first book hit the shelves in 2007. When not obsessing over deadlines, she's watching Johnny Depp movies, scrapbooking or hanging out on Facebook and Twitter. Come by and visit her on the web at tawnyweber.com or on Facebook at facebook.com/tawnyweber.romanceauthor.

Be sure to look for other books by Tawny Weber in Harlequin Blaze—the ultimate destination for red-hot romance! There are four new Harlequin Blaze titles available every month. Check one out today!

New York Times Bestselling Author

Tawny Weber
and
Joanne Rock

UNDERCOVER
FESTIVITIES

HARLEQUIN® A VERY SEXY CHRISTMAS COLLECTION

Recycling programs
for this product may
not exist in your area.

ISBN-13: 978-0-373-60966-6

Undercover Festivities

Copyright © 2014 by Harlequin Books S.A.

The publisher acknowledges the copyright holders of the individual works as follows:

Sex, Lies and Mistletoe
Copyright © 2011 by Tawny Weber

Under Wraps
Copyright © 2010 by Joanne Rock

Printed in U.S.A.

CONTENTS

SEX, LIES AND MISTLETOE
Tawny Weber

To all the wonderful people who read my books.
You bring untold joy to my life. Thank you!

PROLOGUE

"I'VE MADE THE ARRANGEMENTS. Everything is in place."

As the assurance echoed through his speakerphone, Tobias Black leaned back in his Barcalounger, shifted an unlit cigar between his teeth and grinned.

"That was fast. I didn't think you'd pull it off."

A lie, of course.

He'd known once the challenge was issued, it'd be impossible to resist. Just as he'd known that the person he'd challenged had the power to make it happen. Tobias Black only worked with the best. Even when the best's main goal in life had once been to arrest him.

Tobias looked at the pictures framed and fading on his study wall. A gap-toothed trio of schoolkids with wicked looks in their golden eyes and hair as black as night.

Damn, he missed them. All three had turned their backs on him eight years ago. Caleb because he rejected what his father stood for. Maya out of disappointment. And Gabriel? Tobias gave the photo of his middle child, his youngest son, a worried frown. Gabriel in fury, determined to prove that he was twice as good and twice as clever as his old man.

They'd all felt justified in leaving.

And Tobias felt justified in bringing them back. A

man spent his life building a legacy, he needed his children to hand it down to.

"You're sure you can handle your part?"

Tobias laughed so hard the cigar fell from his lips. Him? Handle a part? That was like asking if the sun was gonna rise in the morning.

"I'll play my part like Stevie Ray Vaughan played guitar."

Silence. Tobias rolled his eyes. Maybe it wasn't so far-fetched to ask if he could handle the part if he could so easily forget who he was talking to. "Let me rephrase that. I'll play my part like Babe Ruth hit the ball."

"If you're not careful, cockiness could be your downfall."

Tobias almost brushed that away like an irritating bug. Then he sighed. Only a stupid man ignored a fair warning.

"There's a fine line between confidence and cockiness. I'll watch my step." He glanced at his eldest son's photo. "Caleb will take the bait. He won't want to come home, but he will. Loyalty is practically his middle name."

"You think he's loyal to you after all these years?"

"To me? Absolutely not." And that hurt like hell, but it was the price Tobias paid for ignoring his kids to feed his own ego. "But he's loyal to Black Oak."

Tobias was gambling everything on Caleb caring about Black Oak. A small town in the foothills of the Santa Cruz Mountains, Black Oak was in many ways the same as when it'd been founded a hundred years ago. A quaint and friendly community.

And now it had a drug problem. Tobias might have no problem skirting the law—or hell, laughing in its face—but he was a man who had zero tolerance for drugs. Especially when those drugs were being dealt in a way that conveniently pointed the finger his way.

It would be smarter to let the locals deal with the drug problem. If the evidence kept pointing at Tobias, they could be more easily…influenced. Because the sad truth was, there were still a few outstanding crimes that Tobias could be arrested for, with the right evidence. And there were hints that whoever was pulling off this drug ring had access to the right evidence. So bringing the feds in was a huge risk.

Someone was framing him. And they had enough dirt to do the job well. And it looked as if they were planning it all here in Black Oak.

That little bit of info he wouldn't share with the feebies.

Because he knew he had to offer up a big enough lure to get the FBI's attention, but not so big that they'd insist on coming in and playing it their way.

He wanted control of this venture.

"This is a huge undertaking, Black. All indications are that the drugs moving into Black Oak are yours. And now you're planning to play your family, who know you well enough to see the game. You're talking about playing a townful of people, many of whom depend on you. And more important, you're going to have to play the FBI, who, as a general rule, want nothing more than to arrest you."

He wanted to point out that he'd played them all, quite successfully, many times before. But bragging was rude. More important, ego was the first nail in the coffin of a good con.

"And your point is?" he asked instead.

"My point is, you're not as young as you once were. And you've been out of the game for a while." There was a pause, then a soft sigh that made Tobias's smile drop away. "You've got a lot on the line. Are you sure you're willing to risk it all? Because if this goes bad, the FBI is going to reel you in and toss your ass in jail for a good long time."

Tobias rolled the cigar between his fingers, staring at the unlit cylinder.

He considered what he'd built here in Black Oak. After a lifetime of running cons, he'd settled down and gone legit five years ago. He'd been quietly making reparations over the years, but paying back a few hundred grand wasn't going to stop the FBI from nabbing him if they had a chance. He could opt out, let someone else take point. The risks were huge.

But then, so were the stakes. And every good con knew, it was the high-stakes games that were worth playing.

"I can handle it."

"And your kids?"

Tobias sighed, pushing to his feet and pretending his bones didn't protest at stretching quickly in the damp winter chill. He tossed the cigar on his desk and strode over to stand before the pictures.

Caleb, Maya and Gabriel.

Smart kids. Good-looking, shrewd and nimble-fingered, even as little punks. Once, they'd thought he'd spun the sun on the tips of his fingers and carried the moon in his back pocket. Once, they'd believed in him. Once, they'd been in his life.

Now? Now he'd settle for one out of three.

"I can handle it," he repeated.

And before this game was through, he'd know who was behind the drugs, who was trying to set him up. Whatever fledgling crime ring was forming would be busted.

If he won, his kids would be a part of his life again.

And if he lost? At long last, his ass would be locked up in the federal pen.

But Tobias Black didn't lose.

CHAPTER ONE

Damn sex. It ruined everything.

"I can't believe I'm back in Black Oak." Pandora Easton's murmur was somewhere between a sigh and a groan as she dropped a dusty, musty-smelling box on the floor behind the sales counter.

"No guy, no matter how good in bed, is worth losing your job, your reputation or your self-respect for," she muttered to herself as she looked around Moonspun Dreams. The morning light played through the dance of the dust motes, adding a slightly dingy air to the struggling New Age store.

Sometimes a girl just needed to come home. Especially when she didn't have a choice.

Even if that home was falling apart.

Two months ago, she'd been on top of the world. An up-and-coming pastry chef for a well-known bakery in San Francisco, a gorgeous boyfriend and a strong belief that her life was—*finally*—pretty freaking awesome.

Then, *poof,* everything she'd worked so hard for the last several years was gone. Destroyed. Because she'd fallen for a pretty face, been conned by a smooth line and, worst of all, been ruined by a good lay.

Nope. Never again.

Pandora was home now.

Which was *really* just freaking awesome.

With a heavy sigh, she poked one finger at the box she'd rescued from next to a leaking pipe in the back room. It was unlabeled, so she'd have to see what was inside before she could figure out where to put it.

To disguise the musty scent, she lit a stick of prosperity incense. Then Pandora rubbed a speck of dust off a leaf on the braided money tree she'd brought in this morning to decorate the sales counter, and tidied a row of silken soy wax candles with embedded rose petals.

"Not a bad display from a recently fired bakery manager," she commented to Bonnie.

Bonnie just cocked her head to one side, but didn't comment. Since she was one of the two store cats, Pandora hadn't expected much response. Probably a good thing, since the last thing Pandora's ego needed was anyone, human or feline, to point out all the crazy reasons for her thinking returning home to start her life over was going to work.

The cats, like the rest of Moonspun Dreams, were now Pandora's responsibility. She was excited about the felines. But the jury was still out on the quirky New Age store that'd been in Pandora's family for decades. The very store Pandora had wanted to get away from so badly, she'd left town the day after she'd graduated high school.

Before she could settle into a good pout, the bells rang over the front door. Bringing a bright smile and a burst of fresh air, Kathy Andrews hurried in. One hand held a bakery bag, the other a vat-size cup of coffee.

"I'm here to celebrate," Kathy sang out. She stepped over the black puddle of fur that was Paulie the cat sunning himself on the braided carpet, and waltzed across the scarred wooden floor.

"What are we celebrating?"

"That you're back in Black Oak. That you're taking over the family store. Not just for the month your mom is in Sedona for that psychic convention, but for good. And, more important, we need to celebrate the news that your best friend had some really great sex last night."

Pandora exchanged looks with Bonnie. There it was, sex again. But this was Kathy's sex. It wasn't as if that could mess Pandora's life up.

"I'm not so sure having to come home because I failed out there in the big bad world is an excuse to party," Pandora said with a rueful laugh as she took the bakery bag and peeked inside. "Ooh, my favorite. Mrs. Rae's éclairs. I thought she'd retired."

"Mr. Rae's off competing in some pumpkin-carving contest until next Saturday, leaving Mrs. Rae home alone for their anniversary week. Cecilia said her mom dropped off four dozen éclairs this morning with notice that she'd be making pies, too."

One of the joys and irritations about living in a small town was knowing everyone, and everyone knowing your business. In this case, both women knew Mrs. Rae's irritation meant cherry pie by dinner.

"Cecilia seemed surprised when I mentioned I was coming here," Kathy said, not meeting Pandora's eyes as she took back the bag and selected an éclair. "She said she thought Moonspun Dreams was doing so bad, your mom had given up keeping it open on weekends.

I know I should have given her a smackdown, but the éclairs smelled too good."

While Kathy dived into her éclair with an enthusiastic moan, Pandora sighed, looking around the store. When she'd been little, her grandmother had stood behind this counter. The store had been filled with herbs and tinctures, all handmade by Grammy Leda. She'd sold clothes woven by locals with wool from their own sheep, she'd taught classes on composting and lunar gardening, led women's circles and poured her own candles. Grammy had been, Pandora admitted, a total hippie.

Then, when Pandora had been thirteen, Granny Leda had retired to a little cabin up in Humboldt County to raise chinchillas. And it'd been Cassiopeia's turn.

Her mother's intuitive talents, the surge of interest in all things New Age, and her savvy use of the internet had turned a quirky small-town store into a major player in the New Age market. Moonspun Dreams had thrived.

But now that the economy had tanked and New Age had lost its luster, it was almost imploding. Leaving Pandora with the choice of trying to save it. Or letting it fade into oblivion.

"Cecilia was right. Things are really bad," Pandora said. "No point in risking the best éclairs in the Santa Cruz Mountains over the truth."

"And now Moonspun Dreams is yours. Are you going to give up?" Kathy asked quietly, holding out a fingerful of the rich cream for the cat. They both watched Bonnie take a delicate taste while Pandora mulled over the slim choices available.

Her mother had said that she'd run out of ideas. She'd told Pandora before she left to be the keynote speaker at the annual Scenic Psychics conference that the store was hers now. And it was up to her to decide what to do with it.

After sixty years in the family, close up shop and sell the property.

Or fight to keep it going.

Her stomach pitched, but of the two, she knew there was only one she could live with.

"I can't give up. This is all I have, Kath. Not just my heritage, given that Moonspun Dreams has been in the family for four generations. But it's all *I've* got now."

"What are you going to do? And what can I do to help?" Both questions were typical of Kathy. And both warmed Pandora to the soul, shoving the fears and stress of trying to save a failing business back a bit.

"I don't know. I've been racking my brain, trying to figure something out." Her smile quirked as she gestured to the small table in the corner. Rich rosewood inset with stars and moons, part of the table was covered by a brocade cloth and a handful of vividly painted cards. "I've finally reached the point of desperation."

Kathy's eyes widened. Pandora had sworn off all things metaphysical back in high school, claiming that she didn't have the talent or skill. The reality was that Cassiopeia was so good at it, nothing Pandora did could measure up. And she'd hated knowing she'd never, ever be good enough.

"What'd the reading say?"

"Tarot really isn't my forte," she excused, filling her mouth with the sweet decadence of her éclair.

"Quit stalling. Even if you don't have that psychic edge like your mom, you still know how to read."

That psychic edge. The family gift. Her heritage.

Her failure.

"The cards weren't any help," she dismissed. "The Lovers, Three of Swords, the Tower, Four of Wands and the Seven of Swords."

The éclair halfway to her lips, Kathy scrunched her nose and shrugged. "I don't understand any of that."

"I don't, either." Pandora's shoulders drooped. "I mean, I know what each card means—I was memorizing tarot definitions before I was conjugating verbs. But I don't have a clue how it applies to Moonspun Dreams. It doesn't help me figure out how to save the business."

Yet more proof that she was a failure when it came to the family gift. Handed down from mother to daughter, that little something extra manifested differently in each generation. Leda, Pandora's grandmother, had prophetic dreams. Cassiopeia's gift was psychic intuition.

And Pandora's? Somewhere around her seventeenth birthday, her mother had decided Pandora's gift was reading people. Sensing their energy, for good or bad. In other words, she'd glommed desperately onto her daughter's skill at reading body language and tried to convince everyone that it was some sort of gift.

Despite popular belief, it hadn't been her mother's overdramatic lifestyle that had sent Pandora scurrying out of Black Oak as soon as she was legally able. It'd been her disappointment that she was just an average person with no special talent. All she'd wanted was to get away. To build a nice normal life for herself. One where she wasn't always judged, always found lacking.

Then she'd had to scurry right back when that nice normal life idea had blown up in her face.

"You're going to figure it out," Kathy said, her words ringing with loyal assurance. "Your mom wouldn't have trusted you with the store if she didn't have faith, too."

"The store is failing. We'll be closing the doors by the end of the year. I don't think it's as much a matter of trusting me as it is figuring I can't make things any worse."

Pandora eyed the last three cream-filled pastries, debating calories versus comfort.

Comfort, and the lure of sugary goodness, won.

"These are so good," she murmured as she bit into the chocolate-drenched creamy goodness.

"They are. Too bad Mrs. Rae only bakes when she's pissed at her husband. Black Oak has a severe sugar shortage now that she's retired." Kathy gave her a long, considering look. "You worked in a bakery for the last few years, right? Maybe you can take over the task of keeping Black Oak supplied with sweet treats. You know, open a bakery or something."

"Wouldn't that be fun," Pandora said with a laugh. Then, because she was starting to feel a little sick after all that sugary goodness, she set the barely eaten éclair on a napkin and slid to her feet. "But I can't. I have to try to make things work. Try to save Moonspun Dreams. Mom was hoping, since I'd managed the bakery the last two years, that maybe I'd see some idea, have some brilliant business input, that might help."

"And you have nothing at all? No ideas?"

Failure weighing down her shoulders, Pandora looked away so Kathy didn't see the tears burning in her eyes. Her gaze fell on the dusty box she'd hauled in earlier.

"We've got a leak in the storeroom," she said, not caring that the subject change was so blatant as to be pathetic. "Most of the stuff stored in that back corner was in plastic bins, so it's probably seasonal decorations or something. But this box was there, too. It's my great-grandma's writing, and from the dust coating the box, it's been there since she moved away."

"Oh, like a treasure chest," Kathy said, stuffing the éclairs back in the bag and clearing a spot on the counter. "Let's see what's in it."

Pandora set the box on the counter and dug her fingernail under one corner of the packing tape. Pulling it loose, she and Kathy both winced at the dust kicking them in the face.

She lifted the flaps. Kathy gave a disappointed murmur even as Pandora herself grinned, barely resisting clapping her dirty hands together.

"It's just books," Kathy said, poking her finger at one.

"My great-grandma Danae's books," Pandora corrected, pulling out one of the fragile-looking journals. She reverently opened the pages of the velvet-covered book, the handmade paper thick and soft beneath her fingers. "This is better than a treasure chest."

"Oh, sure. Piles of gold coins, glistening jewels and

priceless gems is exactly the same thing as a box of moldy old books." Still, Kathy reached in and pulled a leather-bound journal out for herself, flipping through the fragile pages. Quickly at first, then slower, as the words caught her attention.

"These are spells. Like, magic," she exclaimed, her voice squeaking with excitement. "Oh, man, this is so cool."

A little giddy herself, Pandora looked over at the book Kathy was flipping through. "Grammy Danae collected them. I remember when I was little, before she died, people used to call her a wisewoman. Grammy Leda said that meant she was a witch. Mom said she was just a very special lady."

"Do you think she really was a witch?" Kathy asked, glee and skepticism both shining in her eyes.

"I'm more inclined to believe she was one of the old wives all those tales were made from." Pandora laughed. "Despite the rumors, there's nothing weird or freaky about my family."

She wanted—desperately needed—to believe that.

"But wouldn't it be cool if these spells worked? Say, the love ones. You could sell them, save the store."

"It's not the recipe that makes a great cook, it's the power," Pandora recited automatically. At her friend's baffled look, she shrugged. "That's what Grammy always said. That words, spells, a bunch of information… that wasn't what made things happen. Just like the tarot cards don't tell the future, crystals don't do the healing. It's the intuition, the power, that make things happen."

"I'll bet people would still pay money for a handful of spells," Kathy muttered.

"They'd pay money for colored water and talcum powder, too." Pandora shrugged. "That doesn't make it right."

"Maybe you can offer matchmaking or something," Kathy said, studying the beautifully detailed book. "People would flock to the store for that kind of thing."

For one brief second, the idea of people believing in her enough to flock anywhere filled Pandora with a warm glow. She wanted so badly to offer what the other women in her family had. Comfort, advice, guidance. And a little magic.

Then her shoulders drooped. Because she had no magic to share. Even the one little thing her mother had tried to claim for her had been a failure.

"I'd let people down," she said with a shake of her head. "Hell, when it comes to love stuff, I even let myself down."

"You can't let that asshole ruin your confidence," Kathy growled, lowering the book long enough to glare. "It wasn't your fault your boyfriend was a using, lying criminal."

"Well, it was my fault I let him dupe me, wasn't it? If I was so good at reading people, I'd have seen what was going on. I wouldn't have let the glow of great sex cloud my vision."

Just thinking about it made her stomach hurt.

She'd thought she was in love. She'd fallen for Sean Rafferty hard and fast. The bakery owner's son was everything she'd wanted. Gorgeous. Funny. Sensitive. Her dream guy. She'd thought the fall was mutual, too. Great sex with an up-and-coming pharmacist who seemed crazy about her. He didn't care that she didn't have any special gift. And she hadn't cared that she couldn't seem to get a solid read on his body language. He'd said plenty. Words of love, of admiration.

Then Sean had been busted in an internet prescription scam. And, as if her shock of misreading him that much hadn't been enough, they'd informed her that she was under arrest for collusion. Apparently, her own true love had run his scam using her computer IP address, and then told the police it was all her idea. It'd taken a month, a pile of lawyers' fees and the word of one of Sean's colleagues shooting for a plea deal to convince the cops that she'd been innocent. Clueless, gullible and stupid, but innocent.

His mother firing her had been the final straw. Whether she fit in or not didn't matter, Pandora had needed to come home.

"What's that book?" Kathy asked, clearly trying to distract her from a confidence-busting trip down memory lane.

Pandora gave an absent glance at the book in her lap. Faded ink covered pages that were brittle with age. Some of the writing she recognized as Grammy's. Some she'd never seen before. Then, a tiny flame of excitement kindling in the back of her mind, she flipped the pages. "It's a recipe book."

"Oh."

"Make that *Oh!*" Pandora angled the book to show her friend the handwritten notes above the ingredient list. "These are recipes for aphrodisiacs. Better than love spells, these don't rely on a gift. They just require a talent for cooking."

"Oh, I like that. Maybe you can whip up a tasty

aphrodisiac or two for me?" Kathy said with a wicked smile. "I'd be willing to pay a pretty penny for guaranteed good sex."

"Hot and fresh orgasms, delivered to your door in thirty minutes or less?" Pandora joked.

"Sure, why not? Maybe your éclairs aren't quite as amazing as Mrs. Rae's, but you're still a damn good cook. So why not use that? Use those recipes? Put the word out, see what happens. If nothing else, it'll stir up a little curiosity, right?"

It was a crazy idea. Aphrodisiacs? What the hell did Pandora know about sex, let alone sexual aids? The last time she'd seen Sean, he'd been behind bars and, probably for the first time in their relationship, honest when he'd told her that she'd been easy to use because she was naive about sex.

So unless it was a how-to-survive-and-thrive-alone, a do-it-yourself guide to pleasure on a budget, Pandora had very little to offer.

But could she afford to turn away from such a perfect idea? Her mother would say she'd found this box, this idea, for a reason. Could she take the chance and ignore fate?

Pandora puffed out a breath and looked around the store. This was her heritage. Maybe she didn't have a gift like the rest of the women in her family, but couldn't this be her gift? To save the store?

While her brain was frantically spinning around for an answer, she paced the length of the counter and back. On her third round, Paulie lifted his black head off the carpet to give her the look of patience that only cats have.

"I guess we should do some research," she finally said.

"Don't you have all the recipes you need in that book?"

"I'm sure I do. But I need to find out what kind of food is going to lure in the most customers. Then I can use the recipes to add a special dash of aphrodisiac delight."

As she reached under the counter to get a notepad and pen so she and Kathy could brainstorm, she had to shake her head.

Wasn't it ironic? It was because of sex that she'd had to run home and now sex was going to be the thing that saved that home.

Two months later

"I NEED A FAVOR… A sexual favor, you might say."

The words were so low, they almost faded into the dull cacophony of the bar's noise. Pool cues smacking balls and the occasional fist smacking a face were typical in this low-end dive. Sexual favors were plentiful, too, but usually they involved the back room and cash in advance.

Caleb Black arched a brow and took a slow sip of his beer before saying, "That's not the way I roll, but Christmas is coming. Want me to slap a bow on the ass of one of those fancy blow-up dolls and call it your present?"

Hunter's dead-eyed look didn't intimidate, but it did make Caleb hide his smirk in his beer. Caleb was known far and wide as a hard-ass dude with a bad attitude. But when he was around Hunter, he came off as sweetness and light on a sugar high.

The man was a highly trained FBI special agent swiftly rising in the ranks thanks to his brilliant mind, killer instincts and vicious right hook.

He was also Caleb's college roommate and oldest, most trusted friend. Which meant poking at that steely resolve was mandatory.

"Okay, crossing blow-up doll off my shopping list," Caleb decided. "But you should know that my sexual favors don't come cheap."

"From what I've heard, dirt cheap is more like it."

Caleb's smirk didn't change. When a man was as good as he was with women, he didn't need to defend his record. Knowing Hunter would get to the point in his own good time, Caleb leaned back, the chair creaking as he crossed his ankle over his knee and waited.

Always quick on the uptake, Hunter pushed his barely touched beer aside and leaned forward, his hands loose on the scarred table between them. Even in the dim bar light, his eyes shone with an intensity that told Caleb the guy was gonna try to sucker him in.

But Caleb had learned suckering at his daddy's knee.

"You're coming off a big case, right?" Hunter confirmed.

Not quite the tact he'd expected. But it wasn't his game, so Caleb just nodded. And waited.

"Word is you've hit burnout. That you're taking some time off to consider your options."

The smirk didn't shift on Caleb's face. But his entire body tensed. He wasn't a sharing kind of guy. He hadn't told anyone he was burning out except his direct superior, who'd sworn to keep it to himself.

"Word sounds like a gossipy, giggling teenager," was all Caleb said, though. "Who's the gossip and when did you start listening to that kind of crap?"

"It's amazing how much information you can pick up through speculation." Hunter sidestepped. "So while you're considering those options, maybe you might be interested in doing a friend a favor?"

"I'm more interested in lying on a beach in Cabo with half-naked women licking coconut-flavored oil off my body," Caleb mused, taking another swig of beer.

"What if I used the owe-me card?" Hunter asked quietly, his gaze steady on Caleb's. Intimidation 101.

Last week, Caleb had faced down a Colombian drug lord who'd preferred to blow up the building he stood in than be arrested when he found out his newest right-hand man was actually DEA.

It would take a lot more than 101 to make Caleb squirm.

Then again, he did owe Hunter. Back in their first year of college, Caleb had been a better con than a student. Overwhelmed by the realities of college life, he'd cheated on his midterm psych project. Hunter had caught him. He didn't threaten to turn him in. He didn't lecture. He simply threw Caleb's own dreams back in his face until he'd cracked, then helped him pull together a new project. He hadn't snagged the A he'd hoped for, but Caleb had found a new sense of pride he'd never known.

Shit.

Caleb hated unpaid debts. Especially sappy emotional ones.

"Cut the bullshit and get to the point," he suggested.

Realizing he'd won, Hunter didn't gloat. He just leaned back in his chair and took a sip of his own beer. "You're from a small town in the Santa Cruz Mountains, right? Black Oak, California."

It wasn't a question, but Caleb inclined his head.

"You still have family there."

"Maybe." Probably. He knew his sister was living just outside of San Francisco, playing the good girl. And who the hell knew where his brother was. A chip off the ole block, Gabriel was probably fleecing some rich widow of her wedding ring. But their father's family had founded Black Oak, and while Tobias Black hadn't ever gone for the political game, he'd always kept his fingers on the strings of his hometown.

But Caleb hadn't lived there since he'd left for college twelve years before. And he hadn't been back at all since he'd graduated and joined the DEA.

Eight years before, two months before Caleb had graduated, they'd had one helluva family brawl. Ugly accusations, bitter recriminations and vicious ultimatums.

Tobias Black had raised his three kids alone when his wife had died, keeping the family tighter than peas in one very conniving pod. But with that explosion, they'd all gone their separate ways. Caleb had grown up with an almost smothering sense of family. These days he was more like an orphan.

Just as well. Spending time with Tobias was an emotional pain in the ass at best, a conflict of interest at worst.

"It's an interesting little town. Quaint even. Your maternal aunt is the mayor, but word is that it's actually your father who runs the town. Tobias Black, a known con artist with a huge FBI file and no convictions. Estimates of his take over the years is in the millions. And even knowing he was behind some of the major scams of the century, they've never gathered enough evidence to convict him."

Arching his brow, Hunter paused. Caleb just shrugged. So his dad was damn good at what he did. Maybe it was wrong to feel pride in the old man, given Caleb's dedication to the law. But you had to admire the guy for his skills.

"Five years ago, for no apparent reason, Tobias Black pulled out of the con games. He reputedly went straight, focusing his attention on his motorcycle shop and the small town he calls his own."

"You're saying a whole bunch of stuff we both know. Why don't you get to the part where you fill me in on the stuff I don't."

"For the last few months, we've been getting reports of a new drug. Some new form of MOMA."

"Ecstasy?" Caleb pushed his beer away since they appeared to be getting down to business. "What's new about it?"

"It's been refined. Higher-grade ingredients, some obscure herbs that counteract a few of the side effects."

"Herbs? Like, what? Holistic shit?"

"Right. Not a major change, really. Enough to give

sellers the 'healthier choice' pitch, but that's about it. The problem stems from the addition of pheromones."

Eight years in the DEA had told Caleb that just when he'd thought he'd seen and heard everything, some clever asshole would come up with a new twist to screw with the human body. He sighed and shook his head. "So not only does it give the user a cheap sexual zing, but they can drag unsuspecting suckers down with them?"

"Pretty much. As far as the labs can tell, it's not a high enough grade to classify as a date-rape drug, but the potential is there."

The potential to make things worse was always there. Once upon a time, Caleb had figured he could make a difference. But he'd been wrong. After years of fighting drugs in the ugly underbelly of society, Caleb was pretty much done waging the useless battle. He'd turned in his resignation two days ago, but his boss had refused to accept it. Instead, he'd told Caleb to take some time off. To go home, visit family, come out of deep cover for a few months and reconnect with himself before he made any major decisions.

The only piece of that advice Caleb had planned to take was the time off.

He noted the rigid set of Hunter's jaw, then met the man's steady gaze and gave an inward sigh. Looked as if he was wrong on that count, too.

"Can't you feebs get in there on your own?" he asked. The bureau didn't have the same mandate as the DEA, but still, they should have the resources to go in themselves.

"Let's just say I'd rather use my own resources first."

Caleb nodded. He'd figured it was something like that. Second-generation FBI, Hunter had a rep for playing outside the tangled strings of bureaucracy more often than not. His close rate was so high, though, that the higher-ups tended to ignore his unorthodox habits.

"You're looking at Black Oak as the supply center. Have you narrowed down any suspects?"

Caleb wasn't a fool. He knew where Hunter was going with this. But he wasn't biting. He'd pony up whatever info he had on the town that might help the case, but that was it. He wasn't going back to Black Oak.

Which Hunter damn well knew. One drunken college night, Caleb had opened up enough to share how much he hated his father, how glad he'd been to get the hell out of Black Oak. And how he'd vowed, once he'd left, to never return.

"Black Oak appears to be the supply center, yes. But that's not the big issue for me." For the first time since he'd strode into the bar and sat across from Caleb, Hunter's eyes slid away. Just for a second. That's all it took, though, to let Caleb know he wasn't going to like whatever came next.

No matter. Wasn't much about life these days he did like.

Still, he took a swig of the beer. Never hurt to be prepared.

"We've tracked the source. As far as we can tell, there's only one suspect."

Caleb waited silently. Most people, when faced with

six feet two inches of brooding intimidation blurted out secrets faster than a gumball machine spewed candy. But Hunter wasn't most people.

"A reliable source tipped me to the suspect."

Caleb dropped the chair back on all four legs, bracing himself.

"Tobias Black."

Caleb mentally reared back as if he'd taken a fist to the face. He managed to keep his actual reaction contained to a wince, though. So much for bracing himself.

"He's out of the game," Caleb said, throwing Hunter's own words back at him. He didn't know if it was true, though. Sure, his father might claim he'd quit the con, gone straight. But the only thing Tobias was better at than playing the game was lying. Still, while cons were one thing, drugs were an ugly place Tobias wouldn't go.

"He's been making noises lately." Hunter's dark gaze was steady as he watched Caleb.

"Noises don't equal manufacturing drugs."

Hunter just stared.

Fuck.

"It's not his style," Caleb said, none of his frustration coming through in his tone. "I'm not defending him—without a doubt, he's a crook, a con and a shill. The man's spent his life pulling swindle after scam. But he operates on his own. Drugs come with partners. Unreliable, unpredictable partners."

Which had been the crux of his family's explosion. Tobias had found himself a lady friend. A lonely widower, he'd become a cliché, falling hard for a nice rack and promises made between the sheets. She must have been damn good, because she'd blinded the king of cons into letting her into his game. Fifty-fifty split.

His little sister, Maya, had screamed betrayal, claiming her father cared more about his bimbo than his own kids, the memory of his late wife and the legacy they'd built together.

His younger brother, Gabriel, had been pissed over losing half the take.

Caleb had just seen it as a sign to get the hell out.

He ignored Hunter's arched brow. For the first time since sitting down, Caleb looked away. His gaze rested on the mirrored wall behind Hunter. In it, he could see the tattoo on his own biceps. The sharp, snarling teeth of the lone wolf was clearly visible beneath the black sleeve of his T-shirt.

A teenager's ode to the father he'd worshipped before the idol had fallen. An adult's acceptance of the simple fact of life—that he could depend on no one.

"What do you want me to do?" Caleb asked, swinging his eyes back to Hunter.

"Just nose around. You can get into town, get close to the right people, without arousing suspicion. Nobody there, other than your father, knows you're DEA, right?"

Caleb shrugged. "Most think I'm the lowlife I use as a cover. The rest probably figure I was shivved in prison years ago."

"That'll work."

Caleb sighed. He could walk away. It wasn't his gig and nobody was pulling his strings. But Hunter's accusation was a game changer. Whatever went down,

Caleb would be the one uncovering the truth. How or what he'd do with it, he had no clue.

"I'm not making any promises," Caleb said. "Dear ole dad isn't much for welcoming the prodigal back into the fold, you know."

"I have faith in your powers of persuasion."

Caleb smirked, tilting his beer bottle in thanks. "You're buying."

"One last question," Hunter said as Caleb pushed back from the table.

"Yeah?"

"Do you really do Christmas shopping?" For the first time that night, emotion showed on Hunter's face. Skepticism with a dash of amusement.

"Yeah. But now you can consider this little favor your gift, instead of the blow-up doll." Caleb stood, shrugging into his worn denim jacket. "She was a nice one, too. Vibrated and everything."

CHAPTER TWO

A LUNCH-LADEN TRAY held high over her head, Pandora nodded at Fifi's frantic signal to let her know she'd make her way into the store as soon as she could.

Rehiring Fifi, a young blonde as cute as her name, was the second smartest thing Pandora had done since she'd taken over the store. The first, of course, was to serve up the promise of hot sex.

She wound her way through the throng of customers packing the solarium attached to the back of the store. It was amazing how a few tables, some chairs and minimal investment had transformed what two months ago had been storage into Pandora's brainchild, the Moonspun Café.

All it'd taken was a list of her skills, a couple bottles of wine with Kathy and a huge hunk of Pandora's favorite seven-layer chocolate cake to nail down the details. She'd spent years off and on working in restaurants. She was a really good pastry chef, but sandwiches and salads had been an easy enough thing to add to the menu.

Between Great-Grammy's cookbooks, a list of foods reputed to be aphrodisiacs and the judicious start of a few rumors, and she'd launched the lunch-only venture last month.

And it was a hit. If this kept up, Pandora was thinking about starting a little mail-order business. Sexy
sweets, aphrodisiac-laced treats for lovers. A great
idea, if she did say so herself. And—*ha!*—one that
didn't require any special family talent.

She grinned and shifted the heavy tray off her shoulder.

"Here you go, the Hot-Cha-Cha Chicken on toasted
sourdough for two, a side of French-kissing fries and
ginseng-over-ice tea," she recited as she set the aphrodisiac-laced lunch order on the small iron table between a couple of octogenarians giving each other
googly eyes.

Pandora carefully kept her gaze above the table as
she smiled into the couple's wrinkled faces. Yesterday,
she'd bent down to pick up a dropped fork and saw
more than she'd bargained for. She'd never be able to
look librarian Loretta and the office-supply delivery
guy in the eye again after seeing Loretta fondle his
dewy decimals.

"This looks lovely, dear," said the elderly woman,
who's granddaughter had babysat Pandora back in the
day. The woman giggled and shot the age-freckled man
across from her a naughty look before adding, "You'll
bring us up a slice of the molten hot-chocolate cake,
won't you?"

"Wrap that cake up to go," the gentleman said, his
voice huge in his frail body. "We've got a little siesta
loving planned."

Pandora tried not to wince. She loved how well this
little venture was taking off, but holy cow! She sure

wished people wouldn't equate her making their sexy treats with wanting to hear the resulting deets.

Proving that wishes rarely came true, Mrs. Sellers leaned closer and whispered, "Since you started serving up these yummy lunches, I haven't had to fake it once. This stuff is better than Viagra. Now my sweet Merv, here, is a sex maniac."

Ack, there were so many kinds of wrong in that sentence, Pandora couldn't even wrap her mind around it. Trying to block the images the words inspired, she winced and shook her head so fast her hair got stuck in her eyelashes. "No. Oh, no, Mrs. Sellers. Don't thank me."

"Don't be modest, young lady. You've done so much for the sex drive of Black Oak as a whole. Not just us seniors, either. I heard Lola, my daughter's hairdresser who can't be much older than you, telling the gals at the salon how you've saved her marriage with your mead-and sexy-spiced chocolate-dipped strawberries."

What was she supposed to say to that? All she could come up with was a weak smile and a murmured thanks. She caught Fifi's wave again and held up one finger to let the girl know she was on her way.

"My favorites are those sweet-nothings ginger cookies, Pandora. I'd ask for your recipe, but I know you put a little something special in there. You have your gramma's magic touch, don't you?" Mrs. Sellers joked, poking a bony elbow into Pandora's thigh. "Your mom must have been so happy to have you come back to Black Oak. Are you running the store on your own now?"

"Mom's thrilled," Pandora said, the memory of

Cassiopeia's excitement at her daughter's plans to save the store filling her with joy. "But if you'll excuse me, I need to check in with Fifi. Don't forget to look over the fabulous specials for the holiday season. We're offering a Christmas discount in the store for our diners, if you wanted to do a little shopping."

With another smile for her favorite elderly couple, Pandora gratefully excused herself and hurried over to the wide, bead-draped doorway that separated Moonspun Dreams's retail side from the café.

"What's wrong?" Pandora asked.

Two months ago, whenever she'd asked that question it was because the store seemed to be spiraling into failure. She'd been freaked about vendors demanding payment, customers complaining about a lack of variety in the tarot card stock or, on one horrific occasion, a mouse so big it had scared the cats.

In the past five weeks, Moonspun Dreams had done a one-eighty. Now she had vendors begging her to take two-for-one discounts, customers complaining about waiting in too long a line and the health department stopping in for lunch.

And yet, her trepidation of that question hadn't lessened one iota. Funny how that worked.

"Nothing's wrong," Fifi said, her smile huge as she bounced on the balls of her feet like a kid about to sit on Santa's lap. "Sheriff Hottie's here again. Lucky girl, this is the third time he's been in this week. He's the best catch in Black Oak. And he's here to see you."

Pandora's smile was just a little stiff. It wasn't that she had anything against Sheriff Hottie, otherwise known as Jeff Kendall. He was a nice guy. A former class president, Jeff had an affable sort of charm that half the women in town were crazy about. She glanced over to where he was chatting with a shaggy-haired guy who kept coming in to moon over Fifi and winced.

She had no idea why he rubbed her wrong. Her mother would claim it was intuition or her gift for reading people. But Pandora knew she had neither.

Christmas carols crooned softly through the speakers, singing messages of hope as she crossed the room. It took a minute, since the space was filled with shoppers, quite a few with questions.

"Sheriff," she greeted as she stepped behind the counter. She offered him a friendly smile, then folded her hands together before he could offer to shake one. "What can I do for you today?"

He gave her an appreciative glance and a friendly smile that made it easy to see why the town called him Sheriff Hottie. Blue eyes sparkled and a manly dimple winked. Still, a part of her wished she could be back in the café, listening to Mrs. Sellers share the details of her last passionate excursion with Merv the sex maniac.

"Pandora, looks like business is booming nicely for a weekday," he observed, his eyes on her rather than the store. He was tall, easily six feet, and still carried the same nice build that'd made him a star quarterback in school. "Cassiopeia must be thrilled. Is she coming home soon?"

Having combined her yearly spiritual sabbatical with the psychics' conference, Cassiopeia was still in Sedona, Arizona. Pandora's mother was, hopefully, too busy balancing her chi to be worrying about the store.

"She's due home by Yule," Pandora answered. At

his puzzled glance, she amended it to, "The week before Christmas."

"Ah, gotcha. Your mom is really into that New Agey stuff, isn't she?"

Pandora just shrugged. She wanted to hide away from that friendly look. There was no innuendo, no rudeness, but she still felt dirty. Instead, she made a show of lifting Bonnie, cuddling her close so that the cat was a furry curtain between Pandora's body and the sheriff's gaze.

"My mother's interests are many-faceted. Right now, I'm sure if she were here, she'd be asking if you'd finished your holiday shopping, Sheriff. We're running a few specials in the café and have a stocking-stuffer sale on tumbled stones and crystals today. Maybe you'd like to check it out?"

"Maybe. But I'm thinking if I did all my shopping now, I wouldn't have an excuse to come back and visit you every day," he said, putting a heavy dose of flirt in his tone. Leaning one elbow on the counter, he gave her a smoldering look before he glanced at the shoppers milling around, many with wicker baskets filled with merchandise swinging on their arms.

"I really am blown away by how you've increased business here," he said. "That whole aphrodisiac angle is really drawing them in, isn't it? How'd you come up with that? Don't tell me it's from personal experience or I might have a heart attack."

His flirty grin was easy, the look in his eyes friendly and fun. Pandora still inwardly cringed.

"Actually," she corrected meticulously, her fingers defiantly combing through the soft, fluffy fur of the cat, "the recipes have been handed down from my great-grandmother. Do you remember her? She's the one with all the experience."

Pandora tried not to smirk when his smile dimmed a little. Nothing like offering up the image of a white-haired old lady to diffuse a guy's sexy talk.

"How about dinner Friday night?" he said. "I'll pick you up at seven and you can tell me all about your great-grandma and her recipes."

What a stubborn man. But she was just as stubborn. She knew she had no reason to refuse—that she was getting a weird vibe wasn't good enough—but still, Pandora shook her head.

"I'm sorry, but no," she told him. Then, seeing the disappointment in his gaze, she tried to soften her words with a smile.

"I really wish you'd change your mind," Sheriff Kendall said, reaching over Bonnie to give Pandora's cheek a teasing sort of pinch. She gasped, her fingers clenching the cat's fur. Whether it was in protest, or because the sheriff was just too close, Bonnie hissed and leaped from Pandora's arms.

"I'm sorry," she said again, stepping back so she and her cheek were out of reach. "I'm trying to focus on the store right now. I need to get us back on our feet before I start thinking about dating."

"Okay. I understand." He offered that friendly smile again and turned to go. Then he looked back. "Just so you know, though, I plan to keep coming back until I change your mind."

Crap.

She waited until he stepped over Paulie, who carpeted the welcome mat like a boneless blanket of fur, and watched him slide behind the wheel of the police cruiser he'd parked to blocking the door. Then she almost wilted as the tension she hadn't realized was tying her in knots seeped from her shoulders.

"No offense, boss, but you're crazy," Fifi declared, stepping next to Pandora and offering a sad shake of her head. "I'd do anything to date the sexy sheriff. I can't believe you turned him down."

What was she supposed to say? That her internal warning system was screaming out against the guy? That same system had hummed like a happy kitten over Sean.

So obviously, the system sucked.

She gave Fifi a tiny grimace and said, "I guess I might have been a little hasty turning him down."

"A little? More like a lot crazy. Dude's a serious heartthrob."

Pandora grinned as the blonde gave her heart a thump-thumping pat.

"Okay," she decided, squaring her shoulders against the sick feeling in her stomach. Just nerves about dipping back into the dating pond, she was sure. "I'll tell you what. The next time he asks, I'll say yes."

Fifi's cheer garnered a few stares and a lot of smiles, especially from the young man with shaggy brown hair who was watching her like an adoring puppy.

Well, there you have it, Pandora decided with a grin of her own. The town obviously approved.

Ten minutes later, Pandora was ringing up a customer and still worrying over whether Sean had ruined her for all men, when a sugary-sweet voice grated down her spine.

"My mother said there was a blown-glass piece in here she thought I'd like as a Christmas gift. She probably mixed up the store names again, though, poor dear. I don't see anything in here I need."

Crap. Pandora took a deep breath, gesturing with her chin for Fifi to close up the café for her. This would probably take a while. She'd gone to high school with Lilah Gomez, and eight years later the other woman still held the privilege of being Pandora's least favorite person—which, given the events of this last year, was really saying something.

Knowing the importance of not showing weakness to her sworn enemy, she cleared her face of all expression and turned to the brunette.

"Your mother has excellent taste. Too bad she didn't pass it, and the ability to dress appropriately, on to her only daughter," Pandora said sweetly. She made a show of looking the other woman up and down, taking in her red pleather tunic with its low-cut, white fur-trimmed neckline that showed off her impressively expensive breasts. She raised a brow at the shimmery black leggings and a pair of do-me heeled boots that would make any dominatrix proud. "What do you call this look? Holiday hussy?"

"I'm the customer here. Why don't you put on your cute-little-clerk hat and show me whatever overpriced joke my mother saw so I can reject it and go shop in a real store."

"From where I'm standing, which is right next to the cash register, in the handful of times you've been in

Moonspun Dreams you've never bought a single thing.
So you're not a customer. You're a loiterer."

Lilah responded with a haughty look. She'd never
bothered with her frenemy act before. Probably because
she knew that Pandora would see right through it. Instead, the brunette leaned both elbows on the counter
and bent forward to say under her breath, "You'd know
crime, now, wouldn't you? What was it you were busted
for? Something to do with drugs? Or was it lying?"

The only thing that persuaded Pandora to unclench
her teeth was the fact that she couldn't afford to get
them fixed if one broke. Instead, she turned on the
heel of her own unslutty boots and retrieved a blown-
glass peacock, each feather shimmering delicately in
the light.

Before she'd even set the piece on the counter, she
could see the covetous spark in Lilah's eyes. But instead of saying she liked it, the other woman turned
her nose to the air and gave a sniff.

"It's okay. Just the kind of thing I'd expect to find
in this dingy little store."

"The artist is one of my mother's clients," Pandora
said, surreptitiously scraping the sale sticker off the
price tag. She'd be damned if Lilah was getting thirty
percent off. "Her work is currently in the White House
and was recently featured in a George Clooney movie."

Drool formed in the corner of Lilah's heavily painted
mouth. Her hand was halfway to her purse before she
thought to ask, "How much is it?"

The desire to make a sale warred with the desire to
kick the bitchy woman out of the store. But responsibility always trumped personal satisfaction for Pandora.

Which was probably why women like Lilah, and Cassiopeia, Fifi and even old Mrs. Sellers, had a lot more fun that she did.

With one unvarnished fingernail, she pushed the price tag across the counter. Lilah's eyes rounded and her lips drooped.

"Will you hold it? My mother hinted that she'd get it for me as a Christmas gift."

"You want me to hold an overpriced joke?"

The woman's glare was vicious, but she jerked her chin in affirmation.

Hey, that was fun. Maybe all Cassiopeia's lectures about karma were true.

Before Pandora could decide whether to go for gracious or gloating, a loud roaring rumbled through the air.

She and Lilah both stared as a huge Harley slowed down, the helmeted rider turning his head to stare into the store. A shiver skittered between Pandora's shoulder blades. Another out-of-towner? Usually tourism went dry in Black Oak between Thanksgiving and Valentine's. It was probably someone visiting Custom Rides, the motorcycle shop that backed up to Moonspun.

"Company?" Fifi speculated, coming in from the café to stare, too.

"Must have heard about the yippee-skippy you're offering up," Mrs. Sellers predicted, heading out the door hand in hand with her tottering hunk of afternoon delight.

As one, Pandora sighed and Lilah sneered.

"That's disgusting," Lilah muttered.

"What is? The idea of two people enjoying each other's company?"

"You know they're sneaking off to have sex," the woman said, hissing the last word as if it were pure evil. The overblown brunette averted her eyes from the elderly couple as though she was worried that they wouldn't hold out until they toddled all the way to their love nest, instead giving in and doing the nasty right there in the doorway.

"And sex is bad… Why?" Pandora put on her most obnoxious, innocently sweet smile. "From what I heard, you were having it a couple nights ago. Wasn't it in the backseat of an old Nova parked behind Lander's Market?"

Fifi giggled, forcing Lilah to split her glare between the two women.

Before she could spill her ire, though, the chimes over the door sang. And in walked Pandora's worst nightmare. The sexiest man she'd ever seen, wearing black leather and a dangerous attitude. The kind of guy who could make her forget her own name, right along with her convictions, her vow of chastity and where she'd left her underpants.

Black hair swept back from a face worthy of a *GQ* cover. Sharp cheekbones, a chiseled, hair-roughened chin and vivid gold eyes topped broad shoulders and long, denim-clad legs that seemed to go on forever.

Pandora's hormones sighed in appreciation as desire flared, smoking hot, in her belly. She wanted to leap over the counter and slide that leather jacket off those wide shoulders and see up close and personal if his chest and arms lived up to the promise of the rest of his body.

"Oh, my," Fifi breathed.

"Hubba hubba," Lilah moaned.

"Go away," Pandora muttered.

The guy paused just inside the door, then knelt down to give Paulie's head a quick rub before straightening and looking around. His narrowed gaze seemed to take in everything in one quick glance. Then his eyes locked on Pandora's. Nerves battled with lust as she felt something deep inside click. A recognition. And that soul-deep terror that this was a man who spelled trouble in every way possible.

"LADIES," CALEB GREETED, barely aware of the two women on his side of the counter. His eyes were glued on the sweet little dish on the other side.

Her hair, a dark auburn so deep it looked like mahogany, tumbled over her shoulders in a silken slide, the tips waving over the sweet curve of her breasts. She wore a simple white shirt that draped gently over her curves instead of hugging them, and tiny silver earrings that made her look like a sweet-faced innocent. From the fresh-faced look, she didn't have any makeup on, either. Or maybe it just seemed that way because she was standing next to a gal who troweled it on like spackle.

"Well, hello there," Spackle Gal said. The brunette, dressed as if she moonlighted on the stroll, minced her way across the floor to lay a red-taloned hand on his arm. "It's a pleasure to have you here in Black Oak.

I'm the welcome wagon, and I'd be happy to show you a good time while you're visiting our little town."

His brow arched, Caleb glanced at her hand, then back at her face. It only took her a second to get a clue and move her fingers back where they belonged.

"I know the town just fine, thanks," he dismissed. His gaze went back to the sweetie behind the counter. "Apparently I don't know everyone in town as well as I'd like, though."

The brunette gave a little hiss. Caleb ignored her. Despite her clear message of a free-and-easy good time, he wasn't interested.

He'd only come in to check the place out. Not because he was interested in… He looked around, wondering what the hell they sold here. This store shared the alley with what was apparently his father's motorcycle shop. His dad had still been on the take when Caleb had lived in Black Oak, so his shop was new, and Caleb's familiarity with this side of town sketchy.

So this weird store was going to be his new home away from home. By hanging here he could scope things out. Get the lay of the land, keep low for a few days and see how much intel he could scout. Then he'd decide if he wanted to let Tobias know he was in town or not.

"Some people aren't as important to know as others," the brunette said, trying her luck again by nudging close enough to press one impressive breast against his arm. Caleb was grateful for the extra protection of his leather jacket. "Why don't you and I go to Mick's for a drink and I'll introduce you around."

Caleb wanted to sigh. God, he was tired. Undercover

standard operating procedure said take her offer. She was the perfect cover. A resident who probably liked her gossip, she could fill him in on all the townspeople. As blatantly sexual as she was, she might even have an in with the ecstasy crowd.

She'd obviously be happy to offer up any manner of information, favors and probably kinky acts, and walk away with a smile and no regrets the next morning. But he was tired of using himself, losing himself, like that.

And, dammit, he was supposed to be on vacation. A man shouldn't feel guilty about turning down cheap sex while he was on vacation.

"I'm good," he said, stepping away to make his rejection clear. From her glare, she got the message loud and clear. Color high on her cheeks, she shot an ugly look at the girls standing at the counter before heading for the door.

"You might want to slow down on testing your wares from the café, Pandora," the vamp warned over her shoulder as she teetered out of the store. "Not only is that aphrodisiac crap in danger of making you sound like a slut, but you're gaining weight."

Caleb's eyes cut to the women behind the counter, noting the shocked horror in the blonde's eyes and the sneer on the redhead's face. He grinned, liking her screw-you attitude.

"What's she so bitchy about?" he asked, keeping his smile friendly. Nothing connected with a mark—or suspect—faster than sympathy. Besides, facts were facts…the woman had been a bitch. He wandered the store ostensibly looking at merchandise while eyeing the back wall and its bead-covered doorway.

"That's her default personality," the redhead said. "Pandora, is it?"

He wondered why she was looking at him as if he was a wolf about to pounce. Sure, he'd been a troublemaker as a teen, but he'd been gone almost twelve years. Was his rep still that bad in Black Oak? He didn't recognize her. Younger than him, she was closer to his sister's age.

"Hello?" he said, giving her a verbal nudge as he picked up a clear rock shaped like a pyramid, pretending to inspect it. Her worried stare was starting to bug him.

"I'll go make sure everyone's out of the café since it's closed now," the blonde murmured.

"Yes, I'm Pandora," the other woman said, grabbing the arm of the blonde before she could move away. "I'm the, um, owner. Can I help you?"

"Owner? You don't sound so sure."

"I'm still getting used to the idea." Pandora's smile was as stiff and fake as the blow-up doll Caleb had shipped off to Hunter the previous day. "What can I do for you?"

God, so many things. Let him taste those lips to see if they were as soft and delicious as they looked. Slide that silky-looking hair over his naked body. Tell him about all her favorite sexual positions and give him a chance to teach her his.

"I'm just looking around. You've got a nice place here."

"Thanks. Was there anything specific you were shopping for?"

His grin said it all. A sweet pink flush colored her

cheeks, but he saw the flash of reciprocated interest in her eyes. Then, for some bizarre reason, she slammed that door shut with an impersonal arch of her brow.

What the hell? Unlike his brother, Gabriel, he didn't expect women to fall at his feet. And the hard-to-get game did have appeal sometimes. But to totally deny the attraction? What was up with that?

Focus, Black, he reminded himself. He'd come to town for a crappy reason and wanted to leave as fast as he could. So her denial was a good thing.

And maybe if he told himself that a few hundred more times, he'd believe it.

"So you have a café here, too?" he asked, poking through a basket of glossy rocks and trying to take his own advice to focus. Now that he was closer, he noted the noise and tasty scents coming through that beaded curtain. Was the back door to the alley through there?

Before he could poke his head through to see, a group of people strode out with a clatter of beads and a lot of laughter. They'd obviously been having a happy holiday lunch.

There, in the center of the group like a king surrounded by his royal court, was Tobias Black. His lion's mane of black hair had gone gray at the temples. His face sported a few more wrinkles, adding to its austere authority. Still tall and lean, he wore jeans and biker boots, a denim work shirt and a mellow smile.

Caleb froze. Control broke for a brief second as he closed his eyes against the crashing waves of memories as they pounded through his head—and his heart. Holidays and hugs, lectures and encouraging winks. Watching his dad pull a con, then pulling his first con while his dad watched. The trip to Baskin-Robbins afterward, where Tobias let Caleb treat to hot-fudge sundaes with his ill-gotten gains, cementing the lesson that winning was sweet, but the money had to be kept in circulation.

And then his last day of college. The day when Caleb had told dear ole dad that he was bucking family tradition and basically becoming the enemy. A cop. And when he'd threatened, in cocky righteousness, that if his dad didn't dump his new partner and go straight, Caleb was leaving the family. That'd been the point his dad had told him to get his ass out.

Good times.

Caleb took a deep breath, his eyes meeting the wide hazel gaze of the pretty redhead behind the counter. He frowned at the sympathy and concern on her face. In the past eight years, he'd faced down whacked-out drug addicts and homicidal drug lords for a living with a blank face. Why did this pretty little thing think there was anything to be sympathetic over? Something to mull over later. Right now he had to pay the piper.

Caleb slowly turned around, automatically shoving his hands into the front pockets of his jeans and rocking back on his heels. He'd known this moment would come, but now that it had, he wasn't ready. He'd walked away from his family and used that lack of emotional ties in building his career. But now he was back, face-to-face with his father.

And he had no idea how he felt about it.

Like a bull who'd suddenly hit a steel wall, Tobias slammed to a halt. His midnight-blue eyes went huge. But only for a second. Then he grinned. A charming grin that Caleb knew was hiding that shock he hadn't meant to show.

"Well, well," Tobias said, slowly walking forward. "What have we here? If it isn't the prodigal son."

CHAPTER THREE

OH, MY. MR. TALL, HOT and Dangerous was one of the wild and mysterious Black clan? Along with the rest of the gawpers standing around the store, Pandora stared, rapt, as the two men faced off.

"Wow," Fifi breathed.

Pandora nodded. Wow, indeed.

The Black clan was legend. History said a Black had founded the small town a hundred years back. But for all their standing in the town, people still passed rumors and innuendo in whispers, wondering where the Black fortune came from. Everything from inheriting from an eccentric relative to robbing banks to wise investments. All anyone knew for sure was that they were the wealthiest family in Black Oak, that Tobias's wife had died of leukemia before his youngest child could walk, and until five years ago when Tobias had opened a custom motorcycle shop, they hadn't appeared to work for a living.

"I'm surprised to see you here," Tobias was saying. Pandora frowned, though. The older man didn't look so much surprised as... What? She studied his body language, the way he rocked back on his heels, the set of his shoulders. If she had to guess, she'd say he looked satisfied.

"I didn't realize I had to check in with you as soon as I crossed the city limits," Caleb returned.

"Check in?" Tobias's hearty laugh filled the store, making half the customers smile in response. "Son, you know I don't make rules like that. But if I'd known you were gonna be in town for the holidays, I'd have had Mrs. Long get your room ready."

Caleb's only response was an arched brow.

Pandora tensed. They seemed amiable enough, but she still felt as if she was watching a boxing match. The two men circled each other without even moving. The gorgeously sexy biker looked even more dangerous than he had when he'd walked in. On the surface, he was relaxed, leaning against the wall. She could see the bored look on his narrow face and the general sense of *screw-you* surrounding him. But his feet gave him away. Instead of crossed at the ankle, or rocked back on the heels, his boots were planted as if he were ready to run.

This reunion was a family thing. Private. Especially if one of them decided to throw a punch.

"Maybe the two of you would like some privacy," she offered. The customers turned as one, a few shooting her guilty looks while the rest glared. Black Oak loved its gossip.

"No." Caleb shook his head before stepping forward to lay a warm, strong hand on Pandora's arm. The only thing that kept her from gasping and scurrying away was a desperate need to not add more fuel to the already out-of-control whisperfest brewing.

"We need to talk, son," Tobias insisted. His words

were quiet, they were friendly and they were offered with a smile. They were also hard as steel.

"Maybe later," Caleb dismissed them. "Right now Pandora's promised me lunch."

"What?" she yelped. Caleb's fingers tightened on her arm.

"Really?" Tobias said at the same time, drawing the word out and giving them both a toothy smile.

Rock, meet hard place. Pandora's eyes swept the store, noting the slew of avid townspeople staring, waiting to see what she did. A few even mouthed the words *stay here*. Even the cats were watching her, Bonnie with her head tilted in curiosity, Paulie peering at her through slitted eyes, as if she was disturbing his nap. Then her gaze met Caleb's.

His eyes didn't beg. His face was passive. He simply returned her stare, his eyes steady. She could only hold his look for a few seconds, the intensity of those gold eyes sending crazy swirls of sexual heat spiraling down through her belly.

"Um, yes. Lunch," she murmured, finally pulling her arm out from under his hand. Needing to move, she headed toward the café.

Caleb sauntered beside her, his long legs easily keeping up with her rushed steps.

Everyone in the store moved, too. Apparently, customers were positioning themselves for the best view into the café.

Tobias, however, followed them right through the beads.

"I'm so glad to see so many holiday shoppers," Pandora called back through the beaded doorway of the café. "I know Cassiopeia will be thrilled when I tell her who was in buying merchandise today."

That got them going. Customers scurried to shelves, displays and tables in search of something to keep the town woo-woo queen from cursing them. Or worse, not giving them a peek into their future the next time they asked.

"I'm sure Pandora won't mind if we have a little chat before lunch," Tobias said.

She shook her head no, and was about to offer to wait in the kitchen, when Caleb laid his hand on her arm again.

She froze. Her breath caught and her legs went weak at his touch. The guy wasn't even looking at her and she was about to melt into a puddle at his feet. While his only use for her was to avoid talking to his daddy.

Yep, he was bad news.

Needing to unfog her brain, and unlust her body, she stepped away.

"I'm just passing through," Caleb said, leaning casually against the wall. But the smirk he shot Pandora was amused, as if he knew exactly what kind of effect he had on her.

"How long until you passed through my front door?" Tobias challenged. "You were going to let me know you were in town, weren't you?"

Silence. The hottie had that intense, brooding rebellious thing down pat. Without him saying a word, Pandora knew he hadn't planned to see his father, would have preferred that dear ole dad didn't even know he was in town and was thoroughly pissed to be put in the position of defending himself.

The air in the café was heavy with tension. So out of her element she wanted to turn heel and run all the way back to San Francisco, Pandora shifted from one foot to the other, forcing herself to stay in place.

"Today's special is a hot and spicy double meatball sandwich and four-layer Foreplay Chocolate Cake for dessert," she blurted out in her perkiest waitress voice.

It wasn't until both men shot her identical looks of shocked amusement that she realized what she'd offered. Oh, hell. She wanted to smack her hand over her mouth in horror. Her lust for Caleb was bad enough, but for it to sneak out in front of his father?

"I mean, um, that's the menu. Not an offer, you know? I wouldn't do that. Hit on a customer, I mean. That'd be rude."

Holy crap, Pandora thought. It was like taking her foot out of her mouth and shoving her ass in instead.

Thankfully, Caleb was sticking with his brooding silence. Wincing, she glanced at Tobias, who still looked amused. With an actual reason this time.

"I'll let the two of you do lunch, then," the older man decided. He glanced through the beaded doorway. Pandora followed his gaze and cringed. How'd the crowd get even bigger?

She couldn't make Tobias go out there. They'd be on him like a pack of rabid dogs. And yes, she eyed the older man, noting the freakishly calm stance and lack of anger emanating off him, he could probably handle himself fine. Better than she could, that was for sure.

Still…

"Tobias, did you want to—"

Before she could finish the sentence, Caleb snapped

to attention, straightening from the wall like a stiff board. Nice to know he could get stiff that fast; she almost smirked. Then she saw the intense anger in his eyes and swallowed.

What? Did he think she was going to invite his dad to stay?

"It's a little crowded with shoppers in the store now," she finished slowly, choosing her words as if they would guide her through a live minefield. "So, um, would you like to go out the back and cut across the alley to your own shop?"

Tobias rocked back on his heels, mimicking his son's stance and considered the two of them. He glanced through the beads again and then arched a brow at Caleb.

Clueless, Pandora looked at the younger man, too, trying to figure out what the silent question was that had just been asked. But she couldn't read a thing on either man's face.

She wanted to scream. Even if it wasn't a talent, she'd at least had a decent grasp of reading body language—BS, that was. Before Sean. Now? She might as well be blind.

She eyed the two men and their stoic faces and apparently relaxed stance. They came across as totally mellow strangers. And the hair on the back of her neck was standing up due to all the antagonism flying through the room.

It was frustrating the hell out of her.

"Thanks, Pandora," Tobias accepted. Then he flashed her a charming smile. "And is there any chance

I could get a piece of that cake to go? I was too full after lunch, but it'd be a nice snack later."

Pandora bit her lip, not sure why she felt as if she needed to stick around and protect Caleb. The man obviously didn't need little ole her standing in front of him.

But still…

"I'd appreciate it," Tobias prodded.

Unable to do otherwise, Pandora nodded and hurried into the tiny kitchen at the far end of the sunroom. She cut a fat slab of cake and scooped it into a cardboard box, not bothering to lick the decadent ganache off her knuckle as she pressed the lid down and rushed back out.

Neither man had moved. From what she could tell, neither had said a word, either.

"Here you go," she said, staying by the kitchen and its door to the alley, instead of taking the cake over to Tobias. "I hope you enjoy it. It's my favorite recipe."

Tobias gave his son a nod, then strode toward Pandora. A goodbye? Or acknowledgment that Caleb had won this round? Pandora wasn't sure which.

Caleb, of course, just stood there. Did nothing rile the guy?

"I do appreciate your hospitality," Tobias said as he reached her. "For the cake, and for making my son feel welcome. I'm sure one bite of your delicious offerings and he'll be ready to stay in Black Oak and enjoy himself for a while."

"Um, you're welcome?" Pandora murmured. She wanted to point out that as delicious as chocolate was, it wasn't magic cake. He was asking for an awful lot from a lunch that she wasn't even sure Caleb would eat.

Without another word to her, or to his son, Tobias gave a jaunty wave and headed out the back door. Pandora plaited her fingers together, staring in the direction Tobias had gone until she heard the door close. She shifted her gaze to the café tables then, noting that half needed tidying.

Her gaze landed everywhere but on Caleb.

Murmurs rose from the store. She turned, grateful that something might demand her attention.

Then she winced. She could almost feel the barbs of fury shooting at her from the disappointed crowd. They'd obviously thought the show would move into the store, where they could get a better view. They'd probably positioned themselves to best greet, and grill, Tobias as he left the café. And she'd ruined it.

But she didn't hear the chimes over the front door ring at all, which meant they were still circling, waiting for fresh meat. Or in this case, a hunk named Caleb.

They could just keep waiting. And, hopefully, purchasing. After all, she was apparently giving away cake back here.

Speaking of…

"Would you like something to eat?" she asked, finally looking directly at Caleb.

Under his slash of black brows, his eyes were intense as he inspected her. His expression didn't change as his gaze traveled from her face, then skimmed down her body in a way that made her wish she was wearing one of those loose, New Agey dresses Fifi and Cassiopeia wore.

Or that she was naked.

Either one would be better than this feeling that there wasn't a chance in hell she could measure up to the sexual challenge Caleb presented.

A sexual challenge she wasn't even positive he was issuing. For all she knew, the guy gave that same hot but unreadable look to his mail lady when she asked him to sign for delivery.

Her body on fire, her mind a mess of tangled thoughts, she gave in to the desire to run.

"I'll be right back," she muttered as she hurried back to the small kitchen again. This time, instead of hacking through the cake and throwing it in a container, she carefully selected a plate, cut a precise slice and centered it on the cobalt glass plate. She retrieved a can of whipped cream and sprayed a sweet little rosette of white on top of the chocolate.

This was crazy. It wasn't as though the guy was going to ask her on a date. He was here to... What? Shop for Christmas gifts? Score an aphrodisiac-laced lunch?

Pandora groaned. Oh, wouldn't that be sweet? Insane, impossible and inconceivable—but so sweet to have sex with a man like Caleb Black. A man who, with just one look, could make her body go lax, her legs quiver and her nipples beg in pouty supplication.

But Caleb Black was the kind of guy who went for powerful women. A woman who could hold her own, who would demand he fulfill her every fantasy and in doing so, would show him things he hadn't even dreamed of yet.

In other words, totally not Pandora.

Except…she wanted him for herself.

She grabbed two forks, setting one neatly on the plate. With the other she stabbed a huge chunk from the cake still on the serving dish. Shoving it in her mouth, she closed her eyes and, with a sigh, let the chocolate work its way through her system. Calming, centering, soothing.

God, she loved chocolate.

More than sex, she insisted to herself. Which was a lie, of course, but with a little work she might start believing it. After all, chocolate's only threat was to her hips.

Swallowing hard as she imagined what kind of threat Caleb might pose to her body, she scooped up the plate and forced herself to return to the café.

"You look like that visit barely registered on your stress meter, but mine is off the charts. Nothing pulls me out of the dumps like chocolate, so I figured you might want some," she said with a sheepish smile as she set the cake on a nearby table. Glancing through the beads at the nosy crowd, she sighed, then sat opposite the plate and waited.

"Why's it empty in here?" he asked, his voice as surly as his scowl. But hey, words were words. Who was she to quibble over tone?

"The café closes at two. We still have shoppers in the store, but Fifi is helping them. People know we're closed. They won't come back here," she assured him. "It's not much, but at least it's a tiny semblance of privacy."

He gave her a look, those gold eyes dark. She could see the anger in them now, as clearly as she could see it in the set of his chin and his clenched fists. But now she could see hurt, too, in the way he hunched his shoulders, the droop of his lips.

"I guess this isn't a surprise visit for the holidays," she said with a tentative smile, wishing he'd smile again.

"Prodigal son, didn't Tobias say?"

"You call your father by his name?" Why was she so shocked? It wasn't as if he was the kind of guy to call his old man Daddy.

He shrugged, staring at the door to the alley. Finally, he came over and sat across from her. She didn't know if it was because she'd worn him down with her inane chatter or if he was emotionally exhausted from the confrontation. It definitely wasn't because he was suddenly in the mood to be friendly. Not the way he was glowering. The frown didn't detract from his mouth.

A deliciously sensual mouth, she noticed. She licked her own lips, wondering what he tasted like. How he kissed. Whether he was slow and sensual or if he liked it wild and intense.

"You interested in providing a little prodigal entertainment?"

"Hmm?"

She'd bet he was a wild kind of guy. One who'd take her mouth in a hard, mind-blowing kiss and leave her begging for a taste of his promised sexual nirvana.

"Yeah, you're interested."

Pandora ripped her gaze off his mouth to meet his eyes in horror. Was she that obvious? Was she so unskilled that she couldn't even hide her should-be-secret lusty thoughts?

What the hell was she doing? The man was off-limits. He was bad news, with a capital H heartbreak. And while she was intrigued enough to risk her heart, she still had the bruises from risking her reputation and ego.

"No, sorry. I'm not interested, I'm just curious."

"Curious?" His smile was pure temptation. Wicked and knowing. He didn't push, though. Instead, he cocked a brow at the slice of cake she'd set on the table between them, then pulled it toward him. He pressed his finger on a crumb and lifted it to his mouth.

Pandora swore her thighs melted. Heat, intense and needy, clawed through her good intentions.

PUZZLED, CALEB STUDIED the woman in front of him.

He'd got what he wanted out of this visit—to see the back room and access to the bike shop. Her interest would be easy to use to get back in, anytime he wanted.

But could he do it?

Seated at the table like a dainty lady about to serve some fancy-ass tea, Pandora looked as calm as a placid lake. Except for those occasional flashes of hunger he saw in her pretty eyes. With her smooth, dark red hair and porcelain complexion, she looked like the special china doll his sister had as a kid. If he remembered correctly, he'd broken that doll at one point or another.

Something to keep in mind.

He noted the lush fullness of her lips and the sweet curve of her breasts beneath the white silky fabric of her conservatively cut blouse. His body stirred in reluctant interest. Good girls weren't his thing, but his body wasn't paying much attention to that detail.

"Were you going to try the cake?" Pandora prodded, looking a little put out at his inspection. She sounded as if she wanted to say something—probably something rude—but good girls didn't do things like that.

He grinned. Yet another reason not to be good.

He had questions, so more to pacify her than because he wanted any, he swiped his finger over the frosted cake and sucked the sweet confection while holding her gaze.

Her eyes narrowed. He imagined she was trying to look stern, but came off as cute instead. Her store location was handy, she probably had an inside track to the town and townspeople, and she looked as if she was one of those crazy trust-until-proved-untrustworthy kind of people.

A much better cover than the loosey-goosey vamp who'd hit on him before. She was going to be easier to, well, manipulate.

"I remember this store now," he mused as he looked, noting the deep purple walls with garlands of flowers, stars, suns and moons painted along the ceiling. "I broke in here one night on a dare, hoping to see a rumored séance. It wasn't a restaurant then, though."

"Broke in? I always heard that you were wild, but I thought those rumors were exaggerated."

He just shrugged. It wasn't as though it was a secret that he'd been well on his way to a life of crime in his teen years. Hell, he considered it early training for his undercover assignments.

The frosting was good. Ready for more, he took the fork and scooped up a big bite.

"This room used to be set up for classes and readings," she explained, still frowning at him in a chiding sort of way. "My mother started using it for storage when the mayor changed the permit requirements to demand a twenty percent kickback."

Caleb snorted. He'd grown up the son of an infamous con artist and spent his adult years dealing with criminal dregs. But he was pretty sure politics were the biggest scam around.

"Gotta hand it to her. The mayor's big on clever ways to line the town coffers."

She gave him a narrow-eyed look at odds with his sweet, goody-goody image of her. "Isn't Mayor Parker your aunt?"

Realizing he was starving, he forked up more of the rich cake and grinned. "Yep."

"So this is like old home week. Will you be staying with your aunt instead of your father?"

"Nope. I'm at the Black Oak Inn. Room seventeen, if you're out wandering later," he said with a wink.

Her eyes rounded. She caught her breath as if grabbing back a response that scared her. The move made her cotton top slide temptingly over rounded breasts. He watched as her nipples beaded against the fabric. Suddenly starving, he wanted nothing more than to lean across the table and taste her.

Her reaction was gratifying. His own irritated him, though. She wasn't his type, and given the situation, she was off-limits. He just had to remember that.

"I'm sure I'll see her, though. Want me to talk her into dropping those fees for you?" he offered with another wink.

"I don't do readings."

That sounded bitter. His chewing slowed; he gave her a searching look.

She gave a tiny shrug and looked away.

Off-limits? A part of him wanted to push. To ask questions and get to know her better. The rest of him, the burned-out, disenchanted, cynical DEA-trained part of him, said that unless it pertained to the case, it didn't matter.

Since he wasn't sticking around longer than it took to clear his old man, the cynic got to call the shots.

"So what's the deal?" Caleb asked instead. "You seem to know Tobias pretty well, right?"

"I wouldn't say I know your father well," she mused, her eyes skimming toward the alley. "No more so than anyone else in town. I mean, he's the patriarch, isn't he? From what I understand, he's got more power than the mayor and the sheriff combined. People look up to him, turn to him for advice. I've been hearing accolades since the day I arrived."

"You're not a native of Black Oak?" Why had he thought she was?

"I am native," she said, drawing the words out. "I think I was even in a few classes with your sister, Maya. But I left for college and haven't been back much since."

"So why'd you get a job here? You're interested in this New Age stuff?"

She looked toward the dangling beaded doorway with shelves of crystal balls lining either side and rolled her eyes.

"Interested? I don't know about that. More like indoctrinated." At his arched brow, she shrugged and admitted, "Cassiopeia is my mother."

He might only have a vague recollection of the store, but he definitely remembered Cassiopeia. Third-generation woo-woo queen, all the guys in high school had had crushes on her. Bodacious, outrageous and eccentric, the outgoing redhead had a scary handle on that psychic stuff she sold to her customers.

"I remember your mom. She did readings at my senior carnival."

"Mine, too." Pandora didn't sound nearly as intrigued as he'd been. The son of a colorful character, Caleb could sympathize.

Talk about the apple falling so far from the tree it could make orange juice. Now that he knew what to look for, he could see the resemblance in the curve of her cheeks, the rounded eyes more hazel than her mother's emerald. And, of course, the red hair, again, more muted in Pandora's case. It was as if she'd stepped into a shadow instead of embracing the full wattage her mother liked to wave around.

Interesting.

Even more interesting was that Caleb was finding muted about the sexiest thing he'd ever encountered. He just couldn't figure out why since he'd always been a Technicolor kind of guy.

"You know what I heard while we were still in the store, then again while you were in the back getting cake?"

"You mean while you were hiding back here?" she corrected.

Caleb grinned, glad to see she had claws. It was always more fun to tangle with a wildcat than a pussycat.

"I heard people saying you serve up something besides food back here."

This time the color wasn't subtle. Nope, she blushed a hot, brilliant red. Her eyes flew to the store, then to the cake before meeting his gaze. A stubborn line furrowed between her brows.

"I have no idea what you're talking about," she dismissed.

"You're a horrible liar."

"A gentleman would take the hint and change the subject."

"Sweetie, I've never worried about being a gentleman."

"Obviously."

Grinning, Caleb decided it was time to change gears. He stood, and with a glance at the still-milling crowd in the store, decided to take his cue from his father and head out the back way.

"Walk me out?" he said, making the demand sound like a request.

"The back? The door's right there," she pointed out. But she got to her feet anyway.

Caleb didn't know why he was pushing it. He'd already declared her off-limits, and while he was a guy who was all about pushing boundaries, he never crossed lines he, himself, drew.

But right now, he didn't care.

"So is it true?" he asked, heading toward the door, counting on her being trapped by good manners into following.

"Is what true?"

"Do you really serve aphrodisiacs?"

She ground to a halt so fast, she teetered in her flat-heeled boots. "Don't believe everything you hear," she said dismissively.

"So, it's a lie?"

"It's more of an…exaggeration," she decided. "After all, who's to say whether aphrodisiacs are real or whether they're a figment of the imagination?"

"I have a really good imagination." He reached out and took her hand, lifting it to his mouth.

"What are you doing?" she asked with a gasp, tugging. But he didn't let go.

"You have chocolate," he told her, "just…here."

He swiped his tongue over her knuckle. Her eyes went heated, her breath shuddered and she leaned against the wall with the cutest little mewling noise.

In an instant, Caleb went from amused to rock-hard. An overwhelming urge to touch her, to taste her, washed over him.

Never a man to ignore his gut, he went with the feeling. Stepping forward, the rich taste of chocolate still on his lips, Caleb pressed her body between his and the chilly glass. One hand on either side of her head, he leaned closer.

"This is crazy," she breathed, twisting her hands together at her waist. But she didn't pull away. Instead, she lifted her chin.

That's all the encouragement he needed.

Holding her gaze captive, he brushed his lips over her soft, sweetly moist mouth. He slid his tongue along her lower lip, then gently nibbled at the cushioned flesh.

Passion throbbed, urging him to take it deeper, to go faster. But he resisted.

For the first time in forever, Caleb felt as if he'd come home. Even as the sexual heat zinged through his body like lightning, he relaxed. Need pounded through him, making him ache. But he was at peace.

It was that confusion more than any desire to stop that had him pulling back. He stared, waiting for Pandora to open her eyes. In them he saw confusion, hunger and a hint of fear.

The same as he was feeling.

"You might want to go easy on that cake," he suggested, brushing his knuckles over her cheek before forcing himself away. Stepping back from the warm, soft curves of her body was harder than it should have been. Way too freaking hard. Caleb frowned, not sure what the hell was going on here.

Hand on the doorknob, he looked back. She was still leaning against the wall, her breath ragged and her eyes huge.

"Like I said, I'm in room seventeen. Come on by if you want to do something about that interest. Or serve up something a little hotter than cake."

CHAPTER FOUR

"I'LL HAVE THE pasta special, the house salad with rasp-berry vinaigrette and the house white," Kathy ordered over the melodic jingle of crystal and silver.

"And you, madam? What would you like?"

"I'd like what's in room seventeen," Pandora mut-tered, staring blindly at the menu.

"Beg your pardon?"

"What's in room seventeen?" Kathy prodded with a nudge of her toe under the white linen-covered table.

Playing back what she'd said, Pandora scrunched her nose in a rueful grimace. God, she couldn't get Caleb Black out of her head. His intense gold eyes, his sexy swagger and oh, baby, those magic lips.

He'd tasted so good. So enticing. Like the most de-liciously decadent chocolate éclair. Rich and tempt-ing and mouthwateringly hedonistic. All she had to do was close her eyes and she could relive the sweet slide of his mouth over hers, her body heating instantly at the memory.

"Dory?"

Pandora blinked. Damn, she'd done it again. Spaced off into Caleb fantasyland. She'd been taking that trip over and over and over for the past two days. She'd just bet his body was a wild amusement park, too. One she was in desperate danger of knocking on the door of room seventeen to beg to ride.

"Pandora!"

Pandora winced and gave the waiter an apologetic smile and said, "Sorry, I'll have the same thing."

Not that she had any idea what Kathy had ordered.

Clearly clued in to big news by Pandora's dinginess, Kathy leaned forward on both elbows and demanded with her usual rapid-fire pace, "What's going on? You've got news, don't you? How's the store doing? Have you put your stamp on it? Do you love the café angle? Are people doing the deed on the tables thanks to that menu we came up with?"

Pandora's fingers tapped a rhythm on the table as she pondered.

"Well?" Kathy used one perfectly manicured finger to poke Pandora in the arm.

"I was waiting to see if you had more questions," she replied with a wicked grin.

"Cute. Now spill."

She'd called Kathy to meet her for lunch for just this reason, to spill the dirty deets about Caleb Black and his hot lips. Her friend was the only person she could tell, because not only was Kathy a great sounding board, she was sane. She'd be the voice of reason and keep Pandora from doing something insanely stupid, like chasing a man who was totally wrong for her. But she'd also keep Pandora from chickening out if her idea—and Caleb—were actually doable.

But now that the moment of truth was here, she couldn't quite share. Wasn't sure she was ready for this kind of risk. So she sidestepped.

"The store is actually doing well. There's a ton of business. The new café is bringing in lots of customers. They're shopping in the store, heck, even the online storefront is getting a lot more traffic. Sales are up forty percent over this time last year and I've banked almost enough to cover the quarterly tax payment."

Pressing her lips tight to stop the bragging, Pandora waited for a reaction. She was a little embarrassed at how proud she was of the store. Even more embarrassed at how much she wanted people, any people—but especially people in Black Oak—to know she was kicking butt. To know that she wasn't a failure.

"Wow," Kathy said with a huge grin, clapping her hands together in delight. "I told you it would work. You're totally rocking the businesswoman gig. I'm excited for you."

"I wouldn't say rocking it," Pandora said, blushing a little. "But it is going so much better than I'd expected. I thought I was going to have to work a lot harder to convince people that oysters, strawberries and asparagus would make their love lives more exciting. But I barely had to advertise. Just opened the café, showed the menu and once word got out, it's been packed."

"Beats little blue pills, right?"

Pandora laughed, leaning back in her chair and letting the soothing elegance of the restaurant wash over her.

"Oh, yeah, I have it on good authority that I'm way ahead of the little blue pill," she agreed with a grin. "Do you know how much I now know about sexual aids for the elderly? I mean, yes, the customers are all ages, but it's the elderly who want to share."

Pandora paused while the waiter set a basket of sourdough bread and a dish of roasted garlic and olive tapenade on the table. As soon as he left, she continued.

"They are so grateful and excited about the aphrodisiacs—and to give them credit, about a place to get killer desserts—that they seem to have a need to fill me in on their newfound vigor, enthusiasm, length.... It's TMI run amok."

Kathy choked on her wine. "Length?"

Pandora's brow quirked, then as she realized what Kathy must be thinking, she giggled. "Eww, no. I meant how long their little trysts are lasting now. Apparently chocolate cake is accredited with an extra twenty minutes of good lovin'."

"And they never discovered the power of chocolate before?"

"Not naked."

This time it was Kathy who wrinkled her nose.

"It sounds like you've had plenty of entertainment. Leave it to Black Oak to stay lively."

"Yep, the town is chock-full of characters." Pandora hesitated, then took another fortifying sip of wine. "Including Tobias Black's kids. Do you remember them?"

"Ooooh, baby," Kathy said with a low-throated growl. "I had one memorable night with Gabriel right after graduation, remember? I still consider that my introduction to real pleasure, if you know what I mean."

Pandora winced. Maybe she really did have a sex-confessional sign floating over her head. Before Kathy could share details, she changed the subject. "Did you know the rest of his family?"

"Not so much. Maya is a little younger than we are,

Caleb a few years older than Gabriel. Their mom died when they were really little and I think their aunt tried to get custody but Tobias wouldn't let them go. I remember my mom saying he might not have done them any favors since the boys ran pretty wild. He used to travel a lot, and sometimes he took the kids, but mostly they stayed home on their own." She frowned, sopping up oil with her bread before picking it apart in tiny little bites. "They had a few minor brushes with the law, teenage things, but nothing major. I remember they were scary smart in school, though. Like they didn't even have to study to ruin the curve, you know?"

Mulling this over, Pandora nodded.

"Why? Are you selling bed-y-bye snacks to old man Black? Now, *that's* a guy who's aged well. Talk about a hottie. I'd think he'd have little need for a chocolate-coated pick-me-up."

Mr. Black? A hottie? Pandora wasn't sure what to say to that. It wasn't that she didn't agree with Kathy, because Tobias Black was definitely a good-looking man. But it was kinda creepy thinking about him that way when she was nursing a serious case of the hots for his son.

"If he's as good a kisser as his son, I'm sure he doesn't," Pandora agreed, nibbling at her own piece of bread and nervously waiting for the reaction. Once upon a time, she'd have relied on her own ability to read a person, to gauge their body language, and had trusted her own judgment. But now? Now all she was sure of was that she couldn't be trusted.

The question was, did that mean she shouldn't trust her lust for Caleb? Or her fear of him?

Kathy gave a gratifying gasp, tossed what was left of her bread on her plate and leaned forward to grasp Pandora's arm. "Spill. All the details. Which brother, how was it, where'd you do it and were you naked?"

Pandora giggled.

"Caleb. It was amazing. In the café, and oh, my God, of course not."

"But you wanted to be?"

"Absolutely," she admitted with a sigh. Her smile softened as she remembered his lips again. The taste of him, male, hot and just a little chocolaty. Their bodies hadn't even touched, yet she'd been more turned on than the last time she'd had full-on, two-naked-bodies and real-live-orgasm sex.

More turned on than she'd ever been in her life, actually.

"In the café?" Kathy said, a naughty look dancing in her green eyes. "Had you shared one of those sexy treats?"

Pandora opened her mouth to say no, then closed it.

She hadn't put much thought into it, but he'd had a few big bites of the Foreplay cake. So had she, for that matter. But their lust had been the real deal. At least, hers had.

Doubt, always lurking somewhere but now painfully close to the surface thanks to Sean, reared its ugly head.

"A couple bites is all," she admitted with a frown. "But a lot of the power of an aphrodisiac is in the mind, isn't it? My grammy always said that most magics require belief to work. The power of suggestion and all that."

"Kinda like a low-cut dress, huh?"

Pandora grinned, acknowledging Kathy's point with a wave of her fork. "A little."

Then her smile fell away. "Do you think that's why he kissed me? Of course it is," she answered herself. "I mean, he just got to town, he's so gorgeous he probably has women throwing themselves at him. Why else would he kiss a perfect stranger?"

Why had she thought he'd found her special? That was crazy. She wasn't the type to inspire uncontrollable lust. Heck, she rarely inspired a second look.

Seeing where her mind was going, Kathy shook her head and gave Pandora's forearm a chiding tap. "Stop that. You're counting yourself out before you even consider the situation."

"What's to consider?"

"The details, of course. Start at the beginning."

Pandora arched one brow. "When the dinosaurs roamed? Or back further than that?"

"Smart-ass. When did you first meet Caleb Black?"

Pandora picked at her slice of bread again, wishing she'd never brought the subject up. For just a while there she'd been riding high on the idea that a man so sexy he made her toes curl had been attracted enough for a kiss at first sight. But now? Now she figured she should raise the prices in the café, since her aphrodisiacs were that strong.

"Deets," Kathy prodded. "Has he been in town long? When was the kiss?"

"Two days ago," she finally confessed. "He came into the store. There was this big confrontation between him and his dad, then I gave him a piece of cake and he kissed me."

Just remembering gave her shivers. It'd been so incredible. For a guy who came across as a total hard-ass, his lips had been so, so soft.

She took a shaky breath and brushed the bread crumbs off her fingers.

Maybe the why didn't matter. She'd had an incredible kiss. Wasn't that what counted?

"Wow, talk about a lot going on. I'll want the details of all the rest later. But for now, how was the kiss?" Kathy asked, her eyes huge. "Was it amazing?"

"It was…special," she decided with a soft smile.

"Uh-oh."

"What uh-oh?" Pandora saw the concerned look in Kathy's eyes and shook her head. "No. No uh-oh. I'm not getting romantic ideas. That'd be crazy, considering he only kissed me because of the cake. I'm just saying, it was a hot kiss that didn't follow the standard moves, you know?"

"Standard moves?"

"Yeah. You know how usually the first kiss with a guy is more about the anticipation and, well, introduction to his style?"

Kathy nodded.

"There was no anticipation because, I mean, who the hell kisses a complete stranger in a café while sneaking out the back door?" Kathy's brows creased, but before she could ask, Pandora continued, "And he wasn't so much introducing his style as he was…"

"Was…what?"

"Making me melt?" Pandora admitted with a helpless little laugh. "Honestly, I have no idea why he kissed me. I just know that it was amazing."

"Once again, uh-oh," Kathy worried, apprehension clear in her eyes.

"What?"

"Be careful. Those Black men are heartbreakers. They went through girls like crazy. They always left them smiling, sure. But they never stuck around. Still, you don't need that," Kathy warned.

"I know he's off-limits," Pandora said with a bad-tempered shrug. "I didn't say I was crazy enough to think one flirty little kiss—especially one that didn't include tongue—means I'm in for some hot and wild bad-boy sex."

"He's not off-limits. He's just trouble. But if all you're thinking about is getting naked and doing the horizontal tango, then maybe you should. Just as long as you're clear from the start that it's just sex. Nothing more."

Caleb Black. Naked. Oh, man, she'd bet he was deliciously built. Those wide shoulders would have the kind of muscles she could cling to as he moved in her, his long torso and slender hips arched over her straining body. She knew he had a sweet little hiney, but it'd look even better bare than it had covered in denim. She'd bet it was firm, so hard she'd barely make a dent if her fingers gripped it. Heat washed over Pandora so fast she had to take a sip of her wine before she combusted.

"That is all you're thinking about, isn't it?" Kathy prodded.

"Well, now I'm thinking about Caleb naked and

can't remember your question," Pandora said with a pout.

"You're only looking for sex, right? Not a relationship? Not a wild time that might turn into something special once he realizes how great you are?"

"No," she protested vehemently. This was a stupid conversation. All she'd wanted was to share her little bit of sexy news and suddenly she was defending a fling with a guy who probably kissed every woman he met. That didn't mean he had any interest in actually getting naked and slippery. "I'm not going to do anything stupid. I'd have to be crazy to fall for a guy like Caleb Black. I'm not his type and that kiss was probably the last contact we'll ever have."

Kathy leaned back in the booth and gave her a long, searching look. After a few seconds, Pandora squirmed. She didn't like people looking that close, or that deep.

"Okay, I've changed my mind. I think you should go for it."

"Go for what? It wasn't like an invitation to a relationship. It was more like a hit-and-run."

"Maybe. But maybe not. I'm just saying if he hits again, you should take him up on a little ride. I'll bet he's the kind of guy who'll make you see stars."

Stars. Pandora wasn't a virginal prude. She liked sex. Especially if it was good sex. She read the how-to articles in women's magazines and erotic books, she knew her body and wasn't shy about giving directions when necessary.

But, typically, the guys she'd been with weren't big on directions.

Which was probably why she'd never seen stars. With Sean, she'd seen a flicker or two but never full-oh-my-God stars.

"So?" Kathy prodded.

"So what?"

"So, are you going to shoot for the stars? Or are you going to take the route of avoidance?"

Avoidance. All the way.

After all, the last time she'd given in to a sexy fling, she'd paid. Big-time. And Sean hadn't been anywhere near as hot, gorgeous or tempting as Caleb. Getting involved with him was crazy.

The last thing she needed was to get herself all upside down over a guy. Even a just-sex-and-nothing-more kind of guy. A more confident woman might be able to handle a sweet fling with someone like that, but her? She wasn't that kind of woman.

For once, though, she wanted to be. She wanted to have a purely sexual fling based on nothing more than physical satisfaction and excitement. She wanted to be exciting and dynamic. Fun and maybe a little wild. No expectations of anything long-term or emotional.

And maybe, just maybe, to relax knowing that because she didn't expect anything, her inability to read him couldn't be termed a failure.

"He's not going to ask me out," she said again.

"So why don't you ask him out?"

Why didn't she jump up on the table and strip naked while singing Katy Perry's "Hot N Cold"? "I can't do that," she excused.

Kathy just gave her The Look.

Pandora pressed a hand to her stomach, feeling as if she was about to jump off a very high cliff.

It was scary.

But it was also exciting as hell.

"I'm not promising anything. But—and it's a teensy-tiny but—but…if I do, and if he says yes, then our next kiss *will* involve tongues," she vowed.

CALEB LEANED HIS LEATHER-CLAD shoulder against the black iron lamppost and stared across the street at the warm welcome of Moonspun Dreams.

He'd promised Hunter he'd give it two weeks. So in between watching the store, he'd spent the past four days nosing around. He'd hit what passed for the party scene in Black Oak. Bounced through a few bars, made himself known to the major partiers and netted a couple easy introductions to the town's lower-level drug dealers. The first step was to get the lay of the land, to gauge how challenging the bust would be and to establish his identity.

The ecstasy was definitely available and at discounts usually only seen in Black Friday sales ads. Marketing 101, make the product cheap and plentiful until you'd hooked enough suckers, then bleed them dry. As he would on any DEA job, he'd scored a little from each dealer, sending it all to Hunter for analysis. But experience and instinct told him it was all coming from the same source. A source nobody could—or would—pinpoint.

So far this visit was a bust. He hadn't found out much for Hunter. He hadn't cleared his father. Of course, he'd done his damnedest to avoid seeing his father at all after that first surprise visit, but that was neither here nor there.

And all he could think about was that one small kiss from the intriguingly reticent Pandora.

Unlike his usual M.O. in breaking a drug ring, this time he had no cover. Around here, everyone and their granny knew who he was. Many had pinched his cheeks at the same time they'd bemoaned his probable criminal career. That all worked in his favor, his lousy rep ensuring that nobody questioned his activities.

Still, that was then. He'd have liked to come home and be appreciated for who he really was now. An upright citizen who'd made a life outside of crime.

Except, he realized with a tired sigh, that he really didn't have any life outside of crime. Which was why he'd quit. To relax, to get a hobby and to figure out what he wanted from life.

Which brought his thoughts back, yet again, to Pandora. He couldn't figure out why the woman fascinated him, but she did. She was quiet, when he usually went for the flamboyant. She seemed sweet, which he was pretty sure he was allergic to. And she was friendly with his father, which meant she had questionable taste.

As he pondered, and yes, stared at Moonspun's window hoping to catch a glimpse of the sexy Ms. Easton, something on the corner across the street caught his eye. Two guys in black hoodies, both hunched over as if they were trying to blend in with the brick siding of Pandora's building. Caleb shook his head in disgust. He didn't need years of DEA experience to recognize a drug deal going down. Hell, the little old lady walking her Pomeranian was shooting the two guys the same disgusted look. When one of the guys made a hulking gesture toward her, obviously trying to intimidate, she flipped him the bird and kept mincing along in her fluffy pink knitted hat. Caleb could see the goon growl from across the street. He made as if to go after her, when his buddy grabbed his arm, saying something and showing him a bag of what Caleb assumed were the drugs in question.

Hulk flexed a little, then followed the Baggie into the alley. Caleb considered trailing them. He had no jurisdiction. Hell, he was on a pseudovacation with his resignation sitting on his boss's desk. It was the *pseudo* part of that equation that made him hesitate, not the vacation or the resignation.

But, really, how far did fake authority go? Favors for buddies and an unexplained need to vindicate his father didn't give him the jurisdiction to bust a deal going down.

Then again, when had he ever worried about rules?

Before he could step off the curb, though, Hulk slunk out of the alley. His hoodie pulled low so his face was shadowed, he loped down the street.

No point following the doper. Caleb wanted the guy hooked into whoever was running the game. He waited for him to come out.

But the alley opening stayed empty.

Five minutes later, Caleb was mentally cussing and ready to hit something. There were only two businesses accessible through that alley. Moonspun Dreams and his dad's bike shop.

Dammit.

Before he could decide how he wanted to handle it,

a car pulled up next to him. Caleb's sigh was infinitesimal as he cut his gaze to the sheriff's cruiser. His eyes were the only thing he moved, though.

Because he knew damn well the lack of reaction would piss Jeff off.

"I heard you were back in town," Jeff Kendall, the bane of Caleb's high school years, said as he unfolded himself from his car, leaning his forearms on the open door and offering an assessing look.

"Looks like you heard right."

"C'mon, Black. Just because we didn't get along before doesn't mean you should be holding a grudge," Kendall said with his good-ole-boy smile. The one he'd perfected in grade school, usually used in tandem with tattling to the teacher about the bad Black kids.

It still made Caleb want to punch him.

Hunter had broached the possibility of bringing in local law enforcement, but Caleb had nixed the idea. If the locals knew about the drugs and hadn't shut them down, they might be dirty. And that'd been before he knew who he'd be dealing with. When he'd heard that this guy was in charge of the law in town, Caleb had sneered. No wonder they had problems.

"Look, I'm just offering a welcome home, okay. I hear you've seen your share of trouble after leaving town. I'm not here to add to it. But if you don't mind a friendly warning, keep it clean while you're enjoying Christmas with your dad."

Caleb didn't even blink. After all, that was his cover. Prodigal loser back for the holidays, nothing to his name except a bad attitude and a crappy reputation. And, of course, a whole lot of family baggage.

All in all, it was pretty damn close to the truth.

His silent stare seemed to bug Kendall, though. The guy shifted from foot to foot, then frowned.

"Are you standing here for a reason?" the sheriff prodded.

"Just biding my time."

Kendall glanced around, his gaze lighting on Moonspun Dreams, then flashing back to Caleb. "Looking for a little help in the sack, are you?"

Caleb didn't move. Didn't bat an eyelash. But his entire being snapped to attention.

"Thanks to Pandora and her little concoctions," the sheriff continued, "Black Oak is seeing more sex than a teenager with his daddy's credit card and a link to online porn."

"Geez, Kendall. Can't you score your own credit card yet?"

The sheriff glared, then jerked his head toward the store again. "You must be in the market for a little bedroom boost. There's nothing else in there for you."

It took a second before that sunk in. Caleb's grin was just this side of a smirk as he raised his brows to the other man. "You warning me off?"

"I'm just saying you need to watch your step." Kendall rested one hand on the gun at his hip and tilted his head. "This isn't your town. It's mine. Crime is low and trouble is rare. I'm not going to like it if you sweep in here, stir up a bunch of problems, then make me kick you out."

Low crime and rare trouble? Was the guy really that bad at his job? Caleb's eyes slashed to the corner where the drug deal had gone down. Good thing Hunter had sent him here, since Kendall clearly had no clue what was going on.

"Do you watch John Wayne movies on your nights off and practice that shit in front of the mirror?" was all he said, though.

Kendall's red face tightened, right along with his fist. "I'm a sworn officer of the law. That makes me in charge of this town, Black. So watch your ass."

The guy's delusional self-importance amused Caleb enough that he could easily ignore the jabs.

Besides, he was pretty sure he'd just seen the first break in this case. And he'd much rather follow that up than exchange insults with this dipwad.

"Tell you what. You've piqued my interest," Caleb said, straightening for the first time and stepping toward the curb. "I'll head on over and see if the lady's interested in fielding a hit or two."

"I warned you, Black—"

Caleb just grinned and offered a jaunty salute before crossing the street.

The only thing better than having an excuse to flirt with Pandora handed to him on a silver platter was knowing how much it pissed Jeff the jerk off.

He was still grinning when he walked through the heavy brass door of Moonspun Dreams. Not seeing Pandora among the dozen or so people milling about the store, he made his way toward the back.

"The café is closed," the airy blonde said, tearing herself away from a shaggy-haired guy by the counter.

"I'm here to see Pandora."

"Oh." Her look was speculative, but she just shrugged and went back to helping her client.

Caleb swept the beads aside and stepped through the door.

Then he almost tripped over his own size thirteens.

And grinned at the sight before him.

Holiday music playing loud enough to inspire a little swing of the hips as she arranged a bunch of green Christmas stuff, glittery bows and… Caleb squinted, were those blown-glass suns and moons…? Pandora stood at the top of a tall ladder before the wall by the door to the kitchen.

Her arms stretched high, her purple sweater pulled away from her jeans, showing off the pale silkiness of the small of her back. His gaze traced the tight fit of the denim, noting the hint, maybe, of a tattoo on her left hip.

Nah. She wasn't the tattoo type. She was the good-girl type.

Wasn't she?

Damned if he wasn't tempted to find out.

Whichever she was, she was one sweet sight.

Caleb's grin turned contemplative as he studied the curve of her butt, noting how perfectly those hips would fit in his hands.

A man who rarely tempered his impulses outside of work, Caleb figured why not find out. He glanced around, noting that there weren't any customers, or drug dealers, lurking about. Striding forward, he stepped behind the counter and planted a hand on either side of the ladder.

Just in time for Pandora's descent.

One step down, and her butt was level with his face. Right there within nibbling distance. Another step and he could push aside that nubby purple sweater and slide his lips along the small of her back. One more and, oh, yeah, baby…

Pandora gasped, her head swiveling to give him a wide-eyed look of shock.

"What the…?"

"Hi," he said, his voice low with more desire than he should be feeling for a woman he hadn't even groped yet.

A woman who was staring at him as if he was a combination of the Grinch and the Ghost of Christmas Future. The one who pushed poor Scrooge Mc-Duck into his grave. In other words, she looked just as thrilled as dipwad Kendall had.

He shouldn't tease her. She was obviously on the shy and quiet side. Caleb didn't bother to move, though.

"What are you…? I mean, why…?" She stopped, closed her eyes and took a deep breath, then opened those hazel eyes again and offered a stiff smile. "What are you doing?"

"Making sure you don't fall off the ladder."

She looked down at the five inches between her feet and the ground, then met his gaze again with an arched brow. She had a little more makeup on today than she had earlier in the week. Something was smudged around her eyes, darkening those lush lashes. Her lips, though, those soft, soft lips, were temptingly bare.

"Aren't you the hero."

Caleb barked out a laugh. So much for shy and quiet. He'd expected her to get a little huffy. But no, she was a lot more fun than that.

And then she blew his mind. She slowly turned on

the ladder, her hip brushing against his chest as she did. Awareness spiked through his body, hot and needy.

She licked her lips, the sensual move at odds with the nerves shimmering in her golden-green eyes. And she stepped down. They were so close, the tips of her breasts skimmed, just barely, a path down his chest, leaving behind a fiery trail.

Caleb's smile slowly faded.

He'd pegged Pandora as a sweet, small-town girl, maybe a bit naive but with an open, curious mind. He'd figured on having a little fun flirting while he gathered info.

He definitely hadn't counted on a hard-on within the first three minutes of seeing her again.

Had he underestimated the sweet Pandora?

"Are you looking for a hero?" he asked, mentally rolling his eyes. At the question, because wasn't that what all women were looking for? A mythical guy to sweep them away and make all their dreams come true? And at the idea of *him* being hero material.

"Nah, I'd rather take care of things myself," she said with a smile and a tiny shrug. Her shoulder brushed against his wrist. "The term *hero* always makes me think of perfection. Since I can't live up to it, why would I want to have to deal with it?"

"So… What? You're looking for an antihero?" he joked, his gaze wandering over the soft, round curve of her face, noting the tiniest of dimples just there, to the left of her mouth.

"More like I'm not looking for anything," she said.

Yeah, right.

He looked closer, noting the stubborn set of her chin

and the hint of anger in her eyes. Something, or someone, had burned her. Which meant she might be serious. A not-anything relationship, short and sweet, was right up his alley.

Besides, she had info he needed.

"You might not be looking for a hero, but from what I hear, you're exactly what I'm looking for," he told her.

"And what do you hear?" she asked, leaning back against the ladder, apparently not bothered at all that he was still holding her there, trapped by his arms. He didn't know if he liked that. He was used to making women nervous.

So he leaned in a little closer. Close enough that the scent of her perfume wrapped around him like a sensual fog. Close enough to see her heart beating a fast tattoo against the silky flesh at the base of her throat. Close enough to feel the tempting heat of her body.

His voice husky with need, his grin just a little strained, he said, "Rumor has it you're the lady to see if I'm looking for some really hot sex."

CHAPTER FIVE

PANDORA'S MOUTH DROPPED, and with it all her bravado. Color washed, hot and wicked, over her cheeks as she blinked fast to try to clear her desire-blurred vision.

She stared at him, desperately trying to read him. Was this for real? Was he asking her for sex? Without even a bite of Foreplay cake or a nibble of an Orgasmic Oatmeal cookie? Did she say yes? Or ask him to wait until after her shift? The back room was empty, but still…

God, was she crazy? She gave herself a mental smack upside the head and tried to pull herself together. *Control, girl. Grab some control.*

But all she could think of was what he'd taste like naked and whether his chest was as tanned as his face under that tight black T-shirt.

Caleb's laughter washed over her, breaking the shocked spell. As soon as it did, color slid from her cheeks, leaving behind icy-cold humiliation.

"I guess that's what I get for listening to rumors," he said, still chortling. "Crazy, huh? That you'd be selling sex in here."

She frowned, his easy dismissal taking the edge off her embarrassment. What? He didn't think she could sell sex? He didn't think she was hot enough, wild enough, savvy enough? Was she so dismissible that he didn't think of sex after kissing her? Even now, when he had her trapped between his body and a ladder?

What the hell?

She'd put makeup on. She'd bought perfume, something sexy and inviting. She'd worn her tightest freaking jeans. And he dismissed her? Shoulders hunching, Pandora felt herself withdrawing. Pulling inside, where she could pretend it didn't hurt that, yet again, she didn't measure up. Or in this case, was so easily dismissible.

Here she'd spent the past three days in a state of horny anticipation, acting like a teenage girl wishing and wondering when her crush would reenter her sphere of existence. And what happened when he did?

He laughed at the idea of her and sex.

Before she could duck under his arm and scurry off, back to the obscurity of the kitchen or storage room, she caught sight of Bonnie the cat staring at her from the window seat with her pretty black-and-white head tilted to one side as if she was waiting for Pandora to find her spine.

The spine Sean had damaged with his lies, betrayal and oh-too-believable charm.

Then she thought of her vow to Kathy. Sure, it'd mostly been bravado, but still, she wanted to taste him. To feel his tongue on hers. To experience, at least one more time, hot and sexy Caleb kisses. She pressed her lips together, remembering. Then she squared her shoulders and gave him an arch look.

"Actually, most of Black Oak is thanking me daily

for the effect I've had on their sex lives," she told him, lifting her chin.

His laughter trailed off, his smile slowly fading as a weird look came into his eyes. A chilly sort of calculation that made Pandora, for the first time since he'd swaggered into her store four days ago, want to pull away from him.

He looked dangerous. And just a little scary.

"You don't say? Half the town, hmm? And why's that?"

"Aphrodisiacs, of course."

His gaze didn't change.

She shivered, this time letting herself duck under his arm and move away from the ladder. She needed some distance so she could reengage her brain. She made a show of petting Paulie, who was draped over a chair like a black, silky blanket. With a couple of feet between them, she watched Caleb turn, his leather-clad arms crossed over his chest as he leaned casually against the ladder.

"Aphrodisiacs?" he asked, his words as drawn out as his frown. "Like drugs?"

"What?" She yelped so loudly the mellowest cat in the world gave her a kitty frown before leaping in disapproval to the floor. Seriously shocked, Pandora gaped for a second before shaking her head. "No. Of course not. We're holistic here at Moonspun Dreams. The store, and my family, believes in herbal remedies. We even sell charts on acupressure pain relief instead of aspirin."

He kept staring as if he was measuring each word carefully. He didn't look happy, though. Pandora frowned. What? Was he looking for some kind of drug? She took in his long, shaggy hair, the hard look on his face and the black hoop piercing his ear. Her gaze skimmed over his beat-up leather jacket and the faded black T-shirt, down to the frayed hem of his jeans and his scuffed biker boots.

Sexy as hell? Check.

Bad boy personified? Double check.

A drug user?

She'd heard myriad rumors about those bad Black boys. They were wild and untamed, they were trouble through and through. But she'd never heard even a whisper about drugs.

Her eyes skimmed that deliciously broad chest again, his muscles defined beneath the soft-looking fabric of his shirt. She looked into his vivid gold eyes, noting that they were shuttered but clear.

He looked as if he could and would beat anyone up, was hell on wheels and was way out of her league. But he didn't look like a druggie.

Of course, she had lousy man skills and was body-language illiterate, so what did she know? What she couldn't afford, though, was to be mixed up with a guy who played fast and loose with the law. Never again.

Suddenly as irritated with herself for wanting to cry as much as she was with Caleb for putting himself on the off-limits list, she scowled.

"If you're interested in drugs, you need to look somewhere else," she said in a chilly tone, wrapping her arms around herself to ward off the disappointment. She wished she hadn't scared away the comfort of the cat.

Caleb didn't say a word. He just arched a brow and continued to study her with those intense eyes of his. After a few seconds, she wanted to scream at him to say something. Anything. Or better yet, to leave. She couldn't pout properly with him there, staring.

"I didn't say I was interested in drugs," he finally said, stepping closer, invading her thinking space yet again.

"You—"

"No," he interrupted. "I said I'd heard you were the lady to talk to about hotting up my sex life."

Pandora bit her lip, mentally replaying their discussion. Had she jumped to conclusions? Was she so awkward at this flirtation thing that she'd misinterpreted a gorgeous man hitting on her?

Caleb reached out, rubbing the pad of his thumb over her bottom lip. Pandora barely held back her whimper as her entire body melted into a puddle of goo.

"I hate to see you damage such a pretty mouth," he murmured.

Nope. No misinterpreting that move. She didn't need a dictionary to define his meaning. Nerves simmered low in her belly. She wanted nothing more than to reciprocate the move. But as she'd told Caleb, and despite her teasing with Kathy, she wasn't in the market for a relationship.

Then again, Caleb Black wasn't a relationship kind of guy.

He was, however, a hot, sexy, have-a-wild-time and give-thanks-afterward kind of guy.

She didn't know if it was the freedom she felt in

accepting that her only goal in being with him was to enjoy the ride.

Or maybe it was the sphere of calcite she'd taken to carrying in her pocket, hoping it'd help with her self-esteem.

Whatever it was, it was giving her a sense of purpose, a sense of self-confidence, that she welcomed with open arms.

She was so ready to give herself the best Christmas present ever. A guilt-free pleasurefest that she'd enjoy in decadent delight for as long as it lasted.

As far as gifts went, it beat the hell out of a new pair of slippers.

So when he rubbed her lip a second time, Pandora forced herself to dive out of the safety zone. She took a deep breath, then touched, just barely, the tip of her tongue to his thumb.

His eyes narrowed like golden lasers, then he grinned. A slow, wicked curve of his lips that set off warning bells in Pandora's head.

She was playing with fire.

After one last brush of his thumb across her over-sensitized lip, his fingers caressed a gentle trail over her cheek, along her jaw, then down her throat. It was like being touched by a cloud, his fingers were so soft, so barely there.

Pandora stopped herself from whimpering.

"Is that why you came in here?" she asked breathlessly as his fingers worked their magic along her throat. A slide up, then down, sending tingles through her body. "Because you wanted to ask about aphrodisiacs?"

"Yes," he said, stepping closer. So close she could feel the heat of his body wrapping around her like a warm blanket of lust. "And no."

"Which?"

"Both."

His hand curved behind her neck, fingers tangling in her hair as he pulled her closer. Her head rested in his huge palm as she stared up into his eyes. He looked amused, but his dilated pupils and the tension in his jaw told her he was just as turned on as she was.

At least, that's how she was reading him.

Nerves, huge and frantic, scrambled in her stomach. But she had to know. Finding out how he would respond to her was worth the risk of rejection.

Pandora took that last step, closing the distance between them. Pretending her fingers weren't trembling, she pressed her hands against the cool leather covering Caleb's biceps. Even through the thick fabric, she could feel his muscles bunch tight.

"I wish you weren't wearing this jacket," she said, her words so low even she could barely hear them. But he heard. He gave her a long look that made her nipples harden, shrugged off the leather and tossed it on the counter.

Paulie instantly padded over and curled himself into a puddle on the discarded jacket, his black fur blending perfectly with the leather. Caleb grinned before turning his gaze back to Pandora. "Anything else?"

The mouthwatering sight of his arms, the muscles round and hard beneath the long sleeves of his T-shirt, made her want to wish he'd take that off, too.

But it was his amused reaction to her pet that sent her over the edge.

"I want a kiss," she told him. "A real one."

"I only do real," he countered, curving his hands over her hips and pulling her close. Close enough to feel that his arms weren't the only impressive muscles Caleb was sporting.

She wanted him to keep going. To take control, to kiss her crazy. But he didn't. It was as though he'd looked deep into her soul and saw how scared she was of taking center stage and being in charge, and was forcing her to face that fear if she wanted a taste of him.

Her head was spinning so fast, she needed to steady herself, and desperately wanted something to hold on to. Pandora gripped those deliciously hard arms and let her body melt into his.

She stood on tiptoe, her thighs brushing that hard length of his. Her nipples pebbled against his chest as she breathed in his scent. Excitement and anticipation fought for control of her emotions and she sucked in a breath. Then she did it.

She kissed Caleb.

And when her lips pressed against the firm fullness of his, it was suddenly the easiest hard thing she'd ever done in her life.

She wanted to close her eyes and sink into the pleasure. To hide, deep in the intense delight of his mouth on hers. But his gaze held hers captive.

Needing more, she gave in to the desire and slipped her tongue out to trace his lips. As if that's all he'd been waiting for, he suddenly turned voracious. His mouth took control. His tongue swept over hers, dancing at a wild pace that made her whimper and give over fully to the power of his kiss.

His fingers shifted from her hips to press, palms flat, against her butt. She almost purred with pleasure when she felt his rigid length—and holy cow, was he long!—pressing hard against her stomach.

Just as quickly as he'd gone wild, Caleb shifted into low gear. The wild, untamed intensity left his kiss and cool control took its place.

His mouth softened, his lips brushing gently over hers. His fingers unclenched, smoothing their way up to the small of her back as he pulled away, not completely, but enough that she couldn't revel in the power of his erection anymore.

Then, another brush of his lips, and he stepped away.

Oh, God. He was incredible. Eyes fluttering open, her knees wobbled as she settled her feet flat on the floor again.

Not caring if he saw how overwhelmed she was, Pandora closed her eyes and heaved a deep sigh. Then, meeting his gaze again, she bit her lip before forcing herself to step up to the plate.

All she wanted to do was strip that soft T-shirt off him so she could plaster herself against his hard chest before licking her way down his belly. His taste filled her senses, his scent wrapped around her and her butt still tingled from the pressure of his fingers.

He was like her every sexual fantasy come true.

But she'd been in trouble once already, with a guy who didn't even make the fantasy list. So she'd be an idiot not to make sure Caleb wasn't more trouble than she was willing to answer for.

"Can I ask you something?" she said softly. Needing every intuitive, people-reading skill she'd ever learned, and any that might be floating through her genes, she forced herself to relax and open her third eye. She scrunched her forehead, not feeling anything special there, and settled for just relaxing. "And will you promise me you'll be honest?"

Her eyes locked with Caleb's. His gaze was intense, as if he was trying to read her mind before he committed. His shoulders were back, in honesty? Or braced for a hit?

She waited for him to tell her that she didn't have the right to ask for such a promise. She knew she didn't. Just because they were having a mind-blowingly sexual affair in her imagination didn't mean that in reality he owed her a damn thing.

But she couldn't risk her heart, her reputation or her fragile self-esteem on a man who broke the law. And even though she didn't trust her intuitive skills enough to believe she'd know if he lied, she needed to ask the question anyhow.

Finally, just as she was about to start fidgeting again, he nodded. Then he qualified his nod with, "You can ask whatever you want."

Good enough.

"Do you, um, are you into…" She bit her lip, wishing her cheeks weren't burning, then blurted out, "Do you do drugs?"

CALEB HAD BEEN ASKED that question plenty of times. And he'd always answered yes. More often, he didn't even have to answer; his image spoke for itself.

But this time…? He stared at Pandora, her hazel eyes wide but wary. He could still taste her, sweet and tempting. He was here in Black Oak for a reason. He had a crime to solve. And he'd never, ever, broken cover before. Not for anything, and especially not for a woman.

But with those pretty eyes staring at him, he saw only one option available.

Tell the truth.

"No," he answered. "I'm clean."

He watched her face, waiting to see the doubt. He told himself it didn't matter if she didn't believe him. After all, he'd spent six years crafting his image as a badass with drug connections. An image that had held up to South American drug lords, to the FBI and to L.A. street-gang leaders. An image that was based on the reputation he'd had growing up here in Black Oak.

Her sigh was so deep, the tips of her breasts singed his chest. Talk about a sweet reward for copping to the truth.

A part of him wanted to pull her close, just to wrap his arms around her and revel in the closeness. There was a sense of peace in Pandora, like a calm lake of serenity, that he craved desperately. At the same time, she made him want to strip her naked and lick her body from head to toe, seeing how many times he could make her come before he got to her feet.

Baffled by the conflicting emotions, both in direct opposition to his training and his own reticent nature, Caleb took a step back. He immediately missed the warmth of her body, the heat of her breasts against him. But he needed room to think. And to make sure he didn't screw up. His life might not be on the line this time, but his father's reputation was.

For what that was worth.

Caleb's mind raced, wondering whether he'd just made a major mistake. Time to do damage control.

"Not that I believe in aphrodisiacs, either," he told Pandora, needing to get them back on track.

And he might as well keep up this honest trend and see where it went. It was like following an unfamiliar road. There might be a treasure at the end. A very delicious, very sexy treasure. More likely, though, he'd slide right off some damn cliff.

She just laughed, though.

"Believing in aphrodisiacs is like believing in evolution. Some buy into the idea, some don't."

"Sure, but the theory of evolution has been around for, well, ever. Sex food, though? Isn't that a by-product of the seventies?"

Amusement flared in her eyes as Pandora gave a shake of her head that indicated that he was a sad, misinformed man.

"Their history can be traced back centuries," she pointed out. "My great-great-great-grandmother was a wisewoman who created aphrodisiacs for royalty. Those were the kind of people who beheaded fakers, you know."

Caleb remembered Pandora's mother. Flowing dresses, fuzzy headpieces and huge jewelry glinting through mounds of long red hair. Her granny was a little fuzzier. He wasn't sure what the woman had looked like. His only impression was granola.

But Pandora looked… Well, normal. Not that that

was saying much coming from a guy who spent most of his life around women who thought a G-string was ample coverage. Her hair fell in a smooth curtain, warm and sedate. She wore makeup, but nothing like the showgirl look he remembered her mother sporting. She wore a crystal on a chain around her neck, but her jeans and thick purple sweater seemed ordinary enough.

He looked around the café, noting the display of candles, pretty statues and chunks of rocks on the bistro tables. Circling the perimeter were bookcases, decks of cards and yes, a few crystal orbs and glittering things. He didn't know what most of the stuff was, but it didn't look that weird to him.

It looked pretty. Inviting, interesting and unthreatening. Word on the street, and his own impressions, said that was Pandora's doing. From what he'd heard, the store had been sinking to its death before she'd come along. Which just proved that she was a smart businesswoman. Not that she was weird.

And yet, she believed in aphrodisiacs? Really?

"This is all an act, though, isn't it?" he asked with a tilt of his head to indicate the most obvious New Agey thing he saw, a statue of a half-naked woman riding on the back of a flying dragon. "You're not telling me you really buy into all that…" Crap? "…stuff? Psychics and aphrodisiacs and woo-woo? Isn't it just a part of the show? Something to help sell a few candles and rocks?"

"Woo-woo?" she echoed, sounding as if the magical effects of his kiss had pretty well worn off. "Did you know the art of divination dates back to Greeks and Romans? Tarot cards to the Renaissance? Cleopatra used aphrodisiacs. This isn't a New Agey sales scam to buy into or not. And while these methodologies might have cultural stigmas, it's wrong to dismiss them as being part of a show."

Caleb mentally grimaced. He was usually better at gauging his quarry before he opened his mouth. But Pandora had a way of short-circuiting his brain.

"I'm not saying it's all bullshit. But you have to admit there're a lot of scams associated with this type of thing. And you don't come across as naive," he prevaricated. "I mean, your granny danced naked around the old oak at the base of the mountain, and your mom… Didn't your mom tell the future for dogs and cats?"

Her lips twitched, but she didn't let him off the hook. "My grandmother only danced naked on the full moon, and that was for religious reasons. And as for my mom… What? You don't think cats and dogs have futures?"

"Do you?"

"I do." She nodded, her hazel eyes wide and sincere. Caleb sighed, disappointment pouring through him as he revised his seduction plan. Then Pandora grinned. "But I doubt their thoughts and feelings can be scryed in their water dishes."

So used to being tense, he barely noticed himself relaxing under her smile. He did pay attention to the stirring interest his body felt, though, when he shifted a little closer so he could smell her sweet perfume again. It was a warm scent, making him think of a dark, mystical forest.

"So? What's the real deal? Are you a believer? Or are you just here to make a living?"

She narrowed her eyes, obviously sorting through his words. He liked watching her think. He'd just bet she had mental lists and a brain like one of those supercharged computers that'd calculate, analyze and summarize in seconds flat.

He gave in to temptation and reached out to rub a lock of her rich, thick hair between his fingers. It was as silky as it looked. He'd bet it'd feel even better sliding over his thighs.

"There's bullshit out there, sure," she acknowledged with the tiniest of nods. "There's a group, the Psychic Scenery tour bus, that stops here twice a year. These people travel all over the West Coast, visiting metaphysical stores and psychics, readers and healers. You could say they are the experts on the subject. Believe me, they've seen it all. And they never visit anyone or anywhere more than once if they deem it bullshit."

"How many times have they visited Moonspun Dreams?" he asked, both amused and impressed at how strongly she defended her store and her beliefs.

"Every spring and autumn for the last ten years," she said with just a hint of triumph in her smile. "Our store is one of the highlights of their tour, a selling point they use in their brochure."

"Because of the aphrodisiacs?" Tension he'd thought was gone returned to poke steely fingers in Caleb's back at the idea of hordes of people swarming into town looking for a sex fix. It was the perfect cover for moving drugs, and it pissed him off that Pandora was ruining his comfortable assurance that she was innocent.

"Oh, no," she told him. "I just opened the café two months ago, after the last tour. But I'm sure the regulars at Psychic Scenery are going to be over-the-moon excited when they visit in April."

"Okay, so you're popular with these people and they're going to go crazy over your cookies when they visit. What does that have to do with whether or not you believe in all this?" he prodded.

He had no idea why he cared so much. Maybe it was the result of growing up the son of a clever con man. It'd taught him that people could sell a whole lot of things with a big fat smile on their face, even as they handed over a shopping bag filled with nothing but hot air.

That wasn't criminal. Not like selling drugs. But it'd sure as hell ruin the sweet image he had of Pandora to find out she was happily invested in selling lies.

"What that does is prove that we're time tested and cynic approved," she said. "I think there's a whole lot of stuff out there that we can't explain. I think some people tap into it more easily than others. And I think that believing has a power of its own."

"Isn't that the same thing as gullibility?" Caleb asked.

"Do you think that all this—" she waved her hand to indicate the store filled with the promise of magic "—is based on the power of suggestion?"

Caleb's brow shot up. She didn't sound offended. More like… Satisfied. Wasn't that interesting? Pandora was more intriguing by the second.

"Isn't most everything based on the power of suggestion?" he mused. "For instance, if I suggested that I'd like to kiss you again, you'd think about it, wouldn't you?"

Color washed from her cheeks, pouring down her slender throat and tinting the mouthwateringly showcased curves of her breasts with a pale pink glow. He wanted to touch and see if her skin was as warm as it looked.

"The brain is the most powerful erogenous zone," he told her, his tone low. "Half of seduction takes place in the mind, first. Before I ever touch you, I could have you crazy with wanting me."

She bit her lip, her eyes huge as they darted from him to the store filled with customers just a few beads away.

Caleb gave her a smug wink as he leaned against a table, his feet crossed at the ankles and hands tucked in the front pockets of his jeans.

He was having fun. It'd been so long, he hadn't realized how good it could feel. At least for him. He wasn't so sure Pandora was the teasing type.

"And one meal of my aphrodisiacs could make you so turned on, you'd almost forget your own name," Pandora countered with a wicked smile at odds with the nerves dancing in her eyes. "You'd have the most delicious meal and the most memorable dessert you've ever dreamed of."

Even though his expression was as smooth as glass, Caleb was mentally reeling. What the hell? He blew out a breath, wanting to tug at the collar of his T-shirt.

Yeah, she was pretty damn good at the teasing. Had she just propositioned him?

"What do you say?" Pandora prompted, her smile a soft curve of those luscious lips as she leaned against the counter so her hip bumped against his.

"You realize I'm attracted to you, regardless of what you serve for dinner," he said, trying to figure out what she thought a plate of oysters was going to do when he'd happily take her right then and there on the bistro table, in full view of her cats and anyone who walked by.

"Attraction is a necessary ingredient for an aphrodisiac to work," she explained quietly. "Unlike pharmaceuticals that change a person's will, aphrodisiacs are a natural enhancement. They make so-so sex fabulous. And great sex? Mind-blowing."

This time Caleb did run his finger around the collar of his shirt, needing to release a little of the heat. It was either that or grab her in front of her customers.

As if they knew he was about to pounce, a giggling pair of women walked through the beaded doorway. They both carried overflowing wicker shopping baskets. Looked as if Pandora was about to score.

In more ways than one.

"Fifi asked me to get more cookies," a guy said, sticking his shaggy head through the beaded curtain. "You have a few customers out here asking for them. You know the ones, the sexy cookies."

Pandora's gaze cut from him to Caleb, then back again. She looked torn, and just a little mischievous. He was afraid she'd drag the kid into this discussion to support her point.

"C'mon back, Russ," she said, her smile widening.

Time for him to get the hell out of there. Caleb grabbed his jacket, then leaned in close to whisper in Pandora's ear.

"Prove it to me."

CHAPTER SIX

THIS WAS THE PROBLEM with wanting something as desperately as she wanted Caleb, Pandora mused. Once you got it, you had to figure out how the hell you were going to handle it.

"So what's the plan?" Kathy asked from her perch in a chair by the glistening lights of the three-foot-high Christmas tree with its shimmering golden balls and little red bows. "Are you ready for tonight?"

Ready? Biting her lip, Pandora scanned the plethora of food spread over the counter of the tiny cottage she was renting. Walking distance from the store, she'd chosen it for its location. Asparagus and oysters, celery and ginseng and chocolate. A roast was marinating in red wine and mushroom caps were waiting to be stuffed. All the fixings for an aphrodisiac-rich dinner for two.

Completing the theme, she'd brought home a dozen red candles for passion and had frankincense incense waiting to light.

"Maybe I shouldn't have him here," she worried. "I mean, it's like saying, 'Hey, eat up fast. I'm horny and wanna do it.'"

"Well, it's not like you could have him to dinner in the café. After all, you have a point to prove. And since it's one of those naked kind of points, it's better done in private, don't you think?"

"Naked…" Pandora pressed her palm against her belly, trying to quiet the butterflies flinging themselves against the walls of her stomach as they attempted to escape. "What the hell was I thinking?"

"That Caleb Black would look mighty fine naked," Kathy said with a wicked grin. Then her smile faded and she gave Pandora a searching look. "Are you sure you want to do this? You don't have to go through with the evening if you don't feel comfortable, you know. You can call it off, or just call it quits after dinner."

A part of Pandora grabbed on to that exit option like a lifeline. It was one thing to challenge Caleb face-to-face, when she was in the throes of sexual overload. But the idea of following through, here and now, once she'd had plenty of time to worry? That was something else entirely.

"I don't want to call the evening off," she decided. "I want this. I really do."

Sorta. She wanted the fantasy of having mind-blowing sex with Caleb. The man was obviously a sexual god. He was gorgeous. He was mouthwateringly sexy. He had that bad-boy, done-it-all and gone-back-for-seconds vibe going on.

And her? The naughtiest thing on her sexual résumé was wearing a see-through Santa nightie with black stiletto do-me boots.

"If you want him, and he wants you, then you'd be crazy to let nerves stop you. I mean, how many chances does a girl have for incredible sex?" Kathy challenged.

"Easy for you to say. You've already done one of the Black brothers," Pandora retorted.

"Yes, I did," Kathy said with a wicked smile, running her hand through the smooth curve of her hair. "Which is why I feel qualified to say do it, do it, do it."

Pandora laughed. Living close to Kathy was her favorite benefit to being back in Black Oak. A girl needed her best friend when she was gathering up the nerve to get naked with a guy.

"Okay, let's just say the night is great," Pandora suggested, pacing over to the tree to rearrange the bows and balls on the crisp evergreen boughs. Can't have the two gold balls next to each other, after all. It might ruin the ambience. "Say the sex is incredible. The best in my life. Maybe even one of his top ten. Multiple-orgasm, headboard-banging, seeing-stars incredible. Say it's all that. What do I do then?"

After a long pause, Kathy got to her feet and headed for the tiny kitchen.

"What are you doing?" Pandora called after her.

"Getting a glass of ice water."

"Seriously!"

"Seriously?" Kathy filled a cup with water from the pitcher in the fridge and gulped it down. "Seriously, then you'll probably collapse in an exhausted, albeit very satisfied, heap."

"But…" Pandora dropped onto the overstuffed chair, picking at the deep blue fabric with her fingernails. "But what if it's so great I want more? How did you have the greatest sex of your life, then walk away?"

"It's all about expectations," Kathy said, setting her water aside and coming over to sit across from Pandora. She leaned forward, her pretty face serious. "You know going in that it's special, that it's just that once, and you ring every drop of pleasure from it possible. Like seeing Baryshnikov dance, or visiting Stonehenge or meeting Johnny Depp at Comic-Con last year. They were all amazing experiences, but you don't expect to do them repeatedly, right?"

"What are the chances that sex with Caleb Black will be as good as Baryshnikov, Stonehenge and the amazing Johnny Depp all rolled into one experience?"

"I think the chances are pretty damn good."

Pandora sank her head into the chair's pillowed back and sighed. She thought so, too.

"Look, you deserve this. Every woman deserves this. One night of absolute pleasure, with no strings or worries or stress. Just wild and mindless sex, with no rules or expectations."

"You think?"

"Don't you?"

Pandora looked at the array of food covering the two short countertops. Her grandmother's recipe book was there, too. Filled with recipes that had, so far, increased Moonspun Dreams's coffers beyond her wildest dreams.

Despite her run-don't-walk departure from all things associated with Black Oak and her mother, Pandora had been raised to believe certain things. And many of those tenets she still subscribed to whole-heartedly. Karma and the golden rule. Respecting nature and conserving resources. Prayer and faith. And as she'd told Caleb, she believed in what she did. In what the store offered.

Sure, she'd launched this aphrodisiac sideline as a

desperate attempt to dig the store out of a financial pit. But obviously the aphrodisiacs worked. She saw proof five days a week between the hours of eleven and two, after all. All they required was a spark.

And even she had to admit, she'd definitely inspired a few sparks in Caleb.

"The bottom line is, do you want to do this?" Kathy prodded. "Or don't you?"

A thousand arguments still running through her head, Pandora sighed. Yes, she wanted it. It being this night with Caleb. And more important, a chance to step out of the shadows and have a little excitement in her life. The kind she'd enjoy, not the kind that made her cringe.

Pandora bit her lip again, then squared her shoulders and headed for the kitchen to wash her hands.

"What are you doing?" Kathy asked.

"Getting dinner started." She shot her friend a look of combined terror and excitement. "Who am I to deny myself the absolute pleasure I deserve?"

THREE HOURS LATER and that statement had become Pandora's mantra.

"I deserve absolute pleasure," she muttered to herself as she pulled a floaty black dress knitted of the softest cashmere over her shoulders and slipped the tiny mother-of-pearl buttons closed from cleavage to knee. The fabric molded gently over her breasts, showing just a hint of her red lace bra, and ended a few inches shy of her ankles, where she'd chosen to go barefoot except for a glistening ruby toe ring and gold anklet.

Not quite a see-through Santa nightie, she mused

as she stared at her reflection, but it'd do. She fluffed her hair around her shoulders, added a smidge more mascara and took a deep breath.

"I do. I deserve absolute pleasure." The reminder had turned into an affirmation about an hour ago, but like most law-of-attraction-type things, she knew it was basically useless without real belief behind the words.

So she'd fake it. A quick glance at the clock told her that Caleb was due in five minutes. Which meant that as appealing as hiding under the bed was, she'd better get the appetizers ready.

Pandora hurried from the room, checking to see that the fire was burning bright in the fireplace and that all the red candles—for passion—were lit around the room. The cottage smelled delicious. The subtle waft of incense, the appealing scent of smoky apple wood. And the food.

That was the only thing she had complete confidence in tonight. Her food rocked. The roast was done and resting, tender and juicy in a gravy of rosemary, celery seed and just a pinch of ginseng. There wasn't really any aphrodisiac ingredients in the fresh rolls, but Pandora had filled in the menu with things that played to the theory that the way to a man's heart was through his stomach. If the rolls could open that door, she figured the aphrodisiacs should reroute things southward.

"Absolute pleasure," she murmured as she checked the chocolate-espresso mousse with whipped caramel crème in the fridge, then the wine that was breathing on the counter. Figuring it'd make her look less anxious, and might just help her chill out, she poured herself a glass.

"Yep, all ready for that pleasure. Absolutely."

The doorbell rang.

Pandora started, slopping wine all over her hand.

Right that second, if the cottage had a back door, she would have taken absolute pleasure in sneaking out through it.

Deep breath and a quick rinse of her fingers under the tap, she then wiped nervously down her dress before almost tripping over her own bare feet on the way to the door.

Another deep breath and she pulled it open.

"Hi," Caleb said.

Hubba da hubbada, her brain stuttered. Holy hunks, the man was pure eye candy. The moon at his back, his face was thrown into shadows. His black hair slicked down so it flowed like silk over his collar, he wore slacks, boots and a dark dress shirt. He smelled incredible. Male but with a hint of musk.

His smile was just this side of wicked as he gave her an appreciative look, those warm gold eyes tracing her curves, from collar to breast, down her waist and over her hips until he reached her naked toes.

One look from him and she was ready to strip the rest of herself bare and see how many kinds of pleasure they could offer each other. Whether it was because he looked sexy enough to slurp with a spoon, because she was wearing her do-me undies, or if it was the day spent creating a meal meant for seduction, all Pandora could think about was how long she'd have to wait for dessert.

"Pandora?" he prompted, his smile tipping into a

grin as he leaned his shoulder against the door frame. "You gonna let me in?"

Doh. They couldn't do dessert until he was inside, could they?

"I'm sorry. It's just… Wow." She stepped aside for him to enter. "You look fabulous."

Realizing how that'd probably sounded, color warmed Pandora's cheeks. "Not that you didn't look great before," she said. She winced, then tried again. "I mean, I wouldn't have thought you'd have dress clothes tucked away in your motorcycle saddlebags."

"Always pays to be prepared," he said as he dried his feet on the mat before entering the cottage. She shut the door behind him, its click echoing the beat of her heart in her chest.

"Do you have to dress up often?" she asked, suddenly realizing that she had no idea what Caleb did for a living. Gossip had run wild since his return to town last week, speculating on everything from career criminal to mechanic to construction. One person had thought he might even be a lawyer.

"It's the holidays," he said absently, looking around. "I figured I'd get roped into some Christmas fluff or other."

He gave her a slow smile, making her tummy slide down to her toes. "But this is a much better option."

Heat poured through Pandora's body like molten lava, hungry and intense.

She had to say something before she wrapped herself around his body and begged him to let her lick him from head to toe.

"So what do you do for a living?" she blurted out.

His smile changed. It was a tiny change, one she doubted most people would notice. It got a little hard, like his eyes. "I'm in the middle of changing jobs right now," he said.

Trying to study his body language without being obvious, Pandora bit her lip. Other than the slightly scary look in his eyes, he seemed totally relaxed. Did that mean he was out of a job, or just looking for something else before he left? And did it matter? It wasn't as if she needed to see his résumé. This was a one-night, prove-the-aphrodisiacs-work and have-great-sex fling.

So change the subject.

"Are you going to the big party tomorrow night at your father's motorcycle shop?" she asked.

His smile fell away, his shoulders tensed up. His body language had gone from friendly to unfathomable in less than a heartbeat. Her fault. She knew there were issues with him and his father. So she should have known that bringing him up wouldn't be a great conversation starter.

Wasn't she the hostess with the mostest.

"No."

Awkward.

Crazy with curiosity but not wanting to ruin the evening by asking more uncomfortable questions, Pandora was grateful when the oven timer went off.

"Please, make yourself comfortable," she invited as she hurried toward the safety of the food.

"I thought you'd be staying at Cassiopeia's place," Caleb said as he followed her into the kitchen.

Payback? She gave him an arch look over her shoulder, trying not to grin. Gotta love a guy who knew how to get revenge without drawing blood.

"Oh, no," she said, laughing a little at the idea of staying in her mother's. It would be like staying on a movie set. Nobody who knew Cassiopeia ever had to ask if she believed in the woo-woo. She lived it, right down to the celestial designs on her carpet.

Pandora pulled the roasted asparagus from the oven and set it on the stove top, then turned back to Caleb.

"No. My mother's house is too crowded for me. She collects as much stuff there as she does in the store, plus there are always people in and out when she's home. Even now, with me just stopping by to collect her mail and water the plants, they pop in hoping for a reading or chat. I think it drives her nearest neighbor, the mayor, a little crazy."

Caleb flashed a quick grin as he handed her a bottle of wine. She glanced at the label and raised her brows. Pricey.

"I forgot my aunt had moved."

"Haven't you been to see her yet? I hear she throws a huge holiday open house. Is that next weekend? Someone was saying that your dad never goes, but you probably will, right?" Busy setting the mushroom caps and oysters Rockefeller on a serving plate, it took her a few seconds to pick up on the sudden tension in Caleb.

She'd done it again.

"I'm sorry. I don't mean to make you uncomfortable by bringing up your father." She met his eyes. He didn't look uncomfortable anymore, though. More like…intrigued.

"Don't worry about it. If I had a problem talking about Tobias, I'd say so."

"Okay," she said slowly. Except that he didn't talk about his father. Or his family at all. Despite the tension and hurt she saw in his face, she had to know more. Was desperate to understand more about Caleb Black. So she quirked a brow and continued, "Although I haven't seen her since I moved back, or since she became mayor for that matter, I do remember your aunt. I'm not sure she's a fan of my mother's, though. Mom said the week after she moved in, Her Honor raised the fence height in her backyard and instructed the gardener to plant a hedge between the houses."

Caleb snickered.

"Aunt Cynthia is a hard-ass all right," he agreed. "It must drive her insane having a free spirit like your mom next door. Probably afraid people will think she and Cassiopeia are having wild parties in the hot tub after dark."

Pandora laughed, her nerves over the evening starting to fade as he pulled out a chair and got comfortable. She held up the bottle of wine in question, and when he nodded, got him a glass from the counter.

"I guess you've worked really hard to distance yourself from your dad," she said as she poured.

"It wasn't hard. I just had to move out of Black Oak and his sphere of influence."

"Smart," she complimented. Then, honesty forced her to admit, "Tobias comes into the store and the café pretty regularly. Having a parent with an, um, forceful personality myself, I can understand how it'd be challenging to live with such a strong person. But I have to admit, I do like him."

She didn't add the bit of gossip she'd heard earlier that day, that Tobias had hooked up with that nasty piece of work, Lilah Gomez. Telling a man his dad was dating someone younger than him was hardly dinner-time conversation.

"Most people like Tobias," Caleb said with a shrug. "He's got a way with the charm."

"Like father like son?" She smiled, handing him the glass of wine.

"You're kidding, right?" Caleb shook his head, obviously not seeing himself as a charmer. "I was a disappointment on that score. Maya's got a way about her, that's for sure. But Gabriel got the bulk of the charm. Me, I got the short end of that particular stick."

Pandora wanted to tell him just how appealing rough edges could be, but took a sip of her wine instead. Then she gathered her nerve and lifted the platter filled with the promise of sexual nirvana.

"Speaking of sticks and their length," she said with her naughtiest smile, "I have your proof here. If you'd care to give it a try?"

Caleb swore he felt the energy in the room shift. Friendly good humor changed to a sexual thrum in the blink of Pandora's hazel eyes.

Not that he minded, but there had been something nice in that friendliness. He didn't think he'd ever been friends with a woman. Coworker, acquaintance, lover. That was about it.

But, hey. He'd be an idiot to complain about step-ping over to the sexy side. And a bigger idiot to regret having her take away something he hadn't even realized he might want to enjoy a little longer.

"Proof, huh?" he challenged as he took an appetizer from the tray and inspected it. "Looks like any other stuffed mushroom. How's this proof?"

"Mushrooms and sausage together are a strong aphrodisiac," she assured him before she bit into one herself.

Caleb had his doubts, but he had just enough of his father's fabled charm to know better than to call his hostess a liar. Especially when she looked so sexy sitting across from him.

So he took a mushroom.

By the end of the meal, Caleb realized two things.

One, he'd never spent this long with a hard-on, and not done anything about it, in his life.

And two, he'd never talked—just talked—to a woman before like this. By unspoken agreement, they'd avoided the biggies like family and career. Instead, they'd shared their favorite Christmas memories, discovered they had the same taste in music and movies, and debated the merits of paperbacks versus ebooks.

It was like an actual date. Caleb had always wondered if that getting-to-know-a-person-on-a-date thing was real or just a myth. But this was, other than the painful pressure against the zipper of his slacks, totally awesome.

"Dessert?" she offered, noting he'd cleaned his plate for the third time. She'd been a little more delicate in her eating, only having one helping.

Despite his gluttony, Caleb glanced at the rich, chocolaty mounds of fluff with the caramel topping and sprinkling of nuts and his mouth watered.

"Sure," he agreed. Then he realized he'd better clear some stuff up before they got into anything else that made his mouth water.

"But here's the thing," he said once she'd served them both and sat back down at the table. Then she started fiddling with the button, just there at the very center of her cleavage, and he forgot what he'd wanted to say.

Instead, he focused on the silky smoothness of her pale skin. Unlike most redheads, she was freckle free. At least, she was as far as he could see. Instead, her skin was almost translucent. Delicate.

"Caleb?" she said.

He dragged his eyes away from the contrast of the rich black fabric against the tempting swell of her breasts.

"Huh?" he asked, meeting her amused gaze. His lips quirked, knowing he deserved that look.

"The thing?" she prompted.

"The thing…" He frowned, thinking back. "Yeah, here's the thing. This meal was delicious."

Her smile was slow and sweet, those full lips curving in delight as she reached across the tiny table and rubbed her hand over his. Caleb's dick reacted as if she'd licked it.

"Thanks," she said softly. "I'm so glad you enjoyed it."

"I did. And I'm sure I'm going to enjoy this dessert just as much," he assured her, gesturing with the spoon he'd picked up. "But as great as it all was, I'm not getting how you think this proves that aphrodisiacs work."

Pandora gave a slow nod, as if she was agreeing, or at least considering his words. Then instead of picking up her spoon, she swiped her finger through the caramel-drizzled whipped cream.

Caleb tensed.

She lifted her cream-covered finger to her mouth, then rubbed it over her lip, licking the sweet confection away with a slow swipe of her tongue.

Caleb's eyes narrowed. He tried to swallow, but his throat wasn't working right.

Some cream still on her finger, Pandora sucked it into her mouth, her lips closing around the tip just enough so he could still see the pink swirl of her tongue as she licked it away.

Son of a bitch.

He swore he could smell the smoke as his brain short-circuited.

When she reached back into that crystal bowl and scooped up more dessert, this time cream and chocolate both, Caleb held his breath.

But instead of repeating the tasting show, she leaned forward to reach across the table. The move made her dress, unbuttoned so temptingly, shift to show more of the red lacy fabric of her bra. Before he could groan at the sight, though, she offered that fingerful of temptation to him.

"Taste?" she said, her words low and husky.

As hard as it was not to stare at the bounty bound in red lace, his gaze locked on hers. Her eyes were slumberous. Still sweet, he didn't think anything could change that. But sexier. There was a knowledge in them that said she knew exactly what she was doing to him. And that she planned to do a hell of a lot more.

Holding her gaze, he wrapped his fingers around her wrist, bringing her hand to his mouth. The chocolate was rich, with a hint of coffee. Her finger tasted even better. He sucked the sweet confection off her flesh, then ran his tongue along the length of her palm, scraping his teeth against the mound at the base of her thumb.

Pandora gave a little mewl of pleasure.

Caleb grinned.

"So…" she said after clearing her throat.

"So?"

"So that's the thing."

Caleb frowned.

"You said you wanted me. And I obviously am attracted to you," she told him, gently extricating her fingers from his hand.

"Yeah?"

"But let's face it. I'm not your type. I'm what's usually termed a good girl."

"How good are you?"

"Really, *really* good," she promised. "But you don't do good girls. You're a quick and painless, love 'em and leave 'em kind of guy. You keep life, and sex, commitment-free and just a little distant."

Caleb frowned, not sure he liked how well she read him.

"So?"

"So that's my proof," she said.

Before he could point out that it really wasn't proof,

she held out her hand. He took it, getting to his feet. She didn't move back, though. So his body brushed against her smaller, more delicate figure.

"Your proof is that we're not each other's type?"

"That," she agreed, turning to lead the way out of the kitchen. Then she looked over her shoulder and said, "And the fact that you're not the kind of guy to sleep with a good girl."

He couldn't deny that truth. In the two days since she'd challenged him and tonight, he'd made some inroads, buddying up with one of the drug dealers unhappy with his slow move up the food chain. He'd come to dinner with the idea of finding out more about her little aphrodisiac sideline. He'd planned to subtly grill her about what she might have seen in the alley between her building and Tobias's.

Despite the excuse for their date, he'd had no intention, none at all, of getting naked with her. But he still wasn't giving credence to some crazy food combination. Nope, the credit for that was all Pandora's.

Before he could tell her that, she stopped in the middle of the living room and turned to face him. She was so close, he could see the beat of her heart against her throat.

He could see the nerves in her eyes, there just beneath the desire. The nerves didn't bother him, though. They were a lot more exciting than acceptance or complacency.

"We spent the last hour and a half talking," she told him. "There was no flirting. No innuendo or teasing or sexual promises, right?"

Caleb frowned as the truth of her words hit him.

He'd spent the entire meal horny as hell. Hornier than he'd been with any other woman in his life.

But again, that was due to Pandora. Not the food.

"What's your point?"

And then those delicate fingers skipped down the row of pearly buttons, unfastening her dress as they went. Caleb had faced strung-out drug dealers shoving guns in his gut and kept his cool. But the minute that dress cleared her belly button, he swore the room did a slow spin.

Damn, she was incredible.

She walked toward him, the black dress hanging loose from her shoulders to her belly.

When she reached him, Caleb's hand automatically gripped her hips. She smiled, then leaned even closer so her body pressed tight against his. She reached between them and slid her palm over the hard length of his erection, making his dick jump desperately against the constraining fabric of his slacks.

He groaned in delight.

"And that's the proof that the aphrodisiacs work," Pandora told him just before she pressed her mouth to his.

CHAPTER SEVEN

WHEN NERVES MADE HER want to turn around and run, Pandora reminded herself that the best things in life were worth fighting for. Even if that meant fighting her own fears.

When her fingers trembled, she just dug them tighter into the deliciously muscled expanse of Caleb's shoulders. He felt so good. Strong and solid and real.

She wasn't going to chicken out, dammit. This was her one and only opportunity for awesome, aphrodisiac-inspired sexual bliss. The experience of a lifetime with a man reputed to be incredible.

So when her knees wobbled, she leaned forward, resting her hips against his for support.

Yeah, baby. There it was.

A whole lot of long, hard, throbbing nirvana.

He wanted her, just as much as she wanted him. Proof was right there, pressing insistently against her belly.

Hello, baby, her body sighed.

"More," she demanded against Caleb's lips.

He gave her the more she asked for, then even more than she'd dreamed. He made her feel like the only woman in his world.

Caleb's mouth slid over hers, taking the kiss from

soft, wet heat to intense, raging passion with a slip of his tongue. His hands settled on the curve of her waist, pulling her tighter against that promising ridge pressing against his zipper.

Pandora melted.

She twined her arms around the back of his neck, holding tight as their tongues danced a wild tango. Anticipation coiled tighter in her belly when his fingers slipped up her side, from her waist to the curve of her breast. Her nipples ached with the need to feel his fingers, to know how he'd touch her.

Would he be gentle and sweet? Or wild and demanding?

Wanting desperately to know, she eased back. Not her mouth. Oh, no, she wasn't giving up one second of this delicious kiss. And her hips were fused, as if of their own volition, to his. Although she was pretty sure she could ease back a few inches and still feel the thick heat of his erection pressing in temptation against her stomach.

Instead, she eased her shoulders back. Just a little.

And purred in delight when he proved to be as clever as he was gorgeous, taking the invitation and curving his fingers over the heavy, aching weight of her breast. Her nipple beaded tighter against the erotically scratchy lace of her bra as he circled his hand in a slow, tempting spiral.

Had she ever been this turned on? Heat swirled through her body like a whirlwind. Building, twisting, teasing. Higher and higher, tighter and tighter.

He squeezed. She gasped, moaning and leaning into his hand.

"More," she demanded again.

His hand didn't leave her breast, but the other moved higher up her back. She felt a tiny snap as the hooks gave way. The straps of her bra sagged, slipping down her shoulders.

Before she could decide if this was good or bad, his fingers skimmed under the fabric and flicked her nipple. Like an electric shock, the sensation shot through her body with a zinging awareness. Pandora whimpered, shifting left, then right, as her favorite sexy panties dampened with evidence of her need.

"I like how you follow directions," she said against his lips, her laugh only a little bit nervous.

"Let's see how you do," he returned, leaning back so he could see the bounty he'd released. "Take it off."

"I beg your—"

"Off," he demanded. To emphasize his command, he took those amazing hands off her and stepped backward. Pandora wanted to whimper. She wasn't sure if it was over the loss of his magic fingers, the denial of his body. Or if it was pure embarrassment of having him this focused on her body. It wasn't bad, but it wasn't centerfold quality, either.

Blushing, Pandora twitched the sides of her dress inward. She didn't pull it closed. She didn't want to send a message that playtime was over. But, still, she wasn't sure she wanted to play peekaboo like this.

"C'mon, Pandora. I want to see." His words were husky. His vivid gold eyes were intense and just a little needy.

"Wouldn't you rather taste?" she asked with her most wicked sexy look.

"I'm the kind of guy who likes to cover all the bases," he said with a grin. He sounded relaxed, but she could see the heat in his eyes, the tightness of his body. The oh-my-God huge ridge pressing against his zipper. "So let's start with the visual, then we'll move on to the other senses."

She wanted this, she reminded herself. Wanted to be front and center of attention. And even more, she wanted Caleb. Wanted a night of mindless, wild sexual exploration.

Which meant she had to step up to the plate and play the game. With that reminder ricocheting around her head, Pandora lifted her chin, then took a step backward.

She released the edges of her dress, rounding her shoulders for just a second so her bra straps slipped down under the sleeves, catching on her upper arms. Caleb's eyes were like lasers, sharp and intense as he stared.

She skimmed her fingers up her bare abdomen and cupped her lace-covered breasts. His stare intensified. Pandora's fingers folded over the top of the cups of her bra in preparation for tugging it down. But she couldn't do it.

It was as if her shyness was in battle with the power of Caleb's sexual magnetism, amplified by the aphrodisiacs. She wanted this, like crazy. But it scared her.

Slowly, her eyes still locked on his, she turned. Back to him, her head angled so she could still see him, she pulled the bra straps off her arms, under the fabric of her dress, then let the bra dangle at her side.

"Toss it aside," he ordered.

She tossed it toward the couch, the red lace catching the edge of one magenta pillow and hanging there like a flag of surrender.

"Turn around," he commanded. His voice was husky, his body tense. He looked like the bad boy that rumor claimed him to be. He didn't scare her, though. Instead, his demeanor made her feel…amazing. Sexy and strong.

All because he looked at her as if she was the hottest thing he'd ever seen. The answer to all his sexual fantasies, even.

Holding on to that thought, Pandora turned.

As she faced him again, Caleb kept his eyes on hers for three beats, then dropped his gaze. He arched a brow at her hands clutching the filmy fabric of her dress closed, so she let it go and dropped her arms to her sides. As her breath shuddered in and out, the fabric shifted, sliding over her rigid nipples, adding a whole new layer to the torturous delight going through her body.

He stepped closer. He reached up, his fingers tracing her areola, visible through the veil of black fabric. Her nipples beaded tighter. Heat circled low in her belly, making Pandora press her thighs together to intensify the wet delight.

His gaze shifted, meeting hers.

His eyes were molten gold. Slumberous and sexy.

"Nice," was all he said, though.

Before she could ask him what that was supposed to mean, he leaned forward and took the opposite nipple into his mouth, sucking on it through the fabric. The wet heat of his lips, combined with the subtle abrasion of the material, made her gasp in delight.

Desire melted her body. Her knees felt soggy, so she grabbed on to him to keep her balance.

"You like?" he asked, his teeth scraping over the aching tip before he sucked again.

"I really, really like," she hoarsely agreed.

Her fingers scraped a gentle trail over the wide breadth of his shoulders, then down until she reached those freaking rock-hard biceps. She gave a low growl deep in her throat as she tried to wrap her hands around his arms. Too big, too large, too wide. She hoped that meant other things were big and wide, too.

He swept his hand up the opening of the fabric, his palm hard and warm as it skimmed her body, leaving a trail of tingling awareness behind. He cupped her breast, his long fingers squeezing in rhythm as he sucked.

Her body went into heavenly spasms. Wet heat pooled between her legs, emphasizing the aching pressure building there. So needy she wanted to beg, Pandora wrapped one calf around his leg, pressing tight to try to relieve the ache.

He growled his approval. Then he grabbed her butt with both hands and lifted, making Pandora squeak in shock. Not lifting his mouth from her breast, he swung her around so her back was against the wall, anchored between it and the hardness of his body.

"Oh, yeah," she murmured, letting her head fall back with a thud. It was definitely easier to focus on the pleasure if she didn't have to worry about not falling on her ass.

Finished playing through the fabric, Caleb pushed open her dress and gave a low, husky growl at the sight of her bare breasts. Pandora knew her chest was flushed almost as pink as her nipples, but she didn't care. She loved his reaction. Loved the appreciative heat in his eyes and the way his fingers tightened on her waist as he stared.

"Kiss me," she whispered.

Caleb's eyes met hers and she swallowed the sudden lump in her throat. His gaze was hungry, but there was an appreciation, a sort of soft wonder, in his eyes that made her feel as if she was the most incredible woman in the world.

Then his mouth met hers and she forgot to think at all. His tongue caressed, then slipped gently between her lips. He tasted delicious. Hot and mysterious, with just a hint of chocolate. As he kissed her, his hands slid up to gently cup her cheeks, tilting her head to the side just a little so his mouth could better access hers.

Pandora swore she was melting. Not just sexually, although one more rub of his thigh against hers and she'd explode. But emotionally. The kiss was pure romance. Sweetly sensual, sexually charged and oh, so perfect.

Then he changed the angle. His mouth devoured. His hands skimmed over her shoulders, taking her dress down her arms. He gripped her hips for just a second, pulling her body away from the wall so the fabric could fall free to the floor.

Leaving her naked, except for her tiny little black panties.

She shivered as his fingers, just the tips, trailed a

path along her spine. Up to her shoulder blades, where with the gentlest of pressure, he pressed her bare breasts tighter against his chest. Down to the small of her back, right above her butt, where his fingers curved down beneath the strip of elastic and gripped her buns. His fingers grazed her thigh, leaving heated trails of pleasure.

The move brought Pandora closer, so she locked her calf around the back of his knee and hugged tight, trying to relieve some of the pressure building between her thighs, swirling and tightening. Her breath came in gasps now as his fingers slipped around her hip, tracing the elastic of her panties. First at her belly, then around her thigh.

She shifted her knee, pulling back just a little. Inviting his fingers. Hoping he'd take the hint and touch her. She needed him to touch her, to drive her those last crazy steps over the edge.

But he just kept tracing the elastic. Caressing in soft, teasing moves.

He wasn't trying to drive her to passion, he was just driving her insane.

"More, dammit," she said against his mouth.

Then she felt his kiss shift as he grinned. Before she could decide if she was amused or irritated that he'd made her beg, his fingers slipped beneath the silk of her panties and found her.

They traced her swollen folds, teasing, stroking, enticing. Pandora swirled her hips, matching her rhythm to the dance of his fingers.

His mouth left hers to trail kisses, tiny sweet kisses,

over her jaw and down the smooth flesh of her throat, laid bare as she tilted her head back against the wall.

His head dipped lower.

Her heart pounded harder.

His fingers slipped, first one, then two, then three, into the hot slick heat of her welcoming flesh.

Her breath came in pants.

His fingers thrust. In, then out. In, then out.

His lips closed over the rigid, pouting tip of her breast, sipping and laving the aching bud in time with his dancing fingers.

Pandora's head spun. Heat coiled, tight and low. Her hips twisted, shifted, undulating in time with the thrust of his fingers. Need screamed through her, demanding release.

Then he flicked his thumb over her slick folds.

And she exploded.

She cried out in delight as the climax pounded through her, taking her over once, then twice. Her body rang with pleasure. The lights of the Christmas tree flashed before her eyes, echoing the fireworks exploding in her mind.

It wasn't until she floated back to earth a couple of minutes—or years—later, that she realized he'd wrapped his arms around her in a soothing, rocking sort of hug.

Pandora's heart dissolved into a gooey mess.

"See," she murmured against the hard comfort of his shoulder, curving in tighter as he hugged her close. "Told you it'd be great."

"Great?"

"Incredible? Amazing? Mind-blowingly awesome?" she returned, leaning back to smile up at him.

He returned her smile, brushing a damp tendril of hair off her face with gentle fingers.

"Sweetheart, don't get me wrong. This was, and will continue to be, incredible. But in the spirit of honesty, I need to tell you something."

Oh, God. Tell her what? Was she doing it wrong? Passion fleeing Pandora's head like fog in the morning sun, she pulled back to stare in horror. "What?"

Other than his arched brow, his gorgeous face was unreadable.

"You're hot," he assured her. "And this intensity, the chemistry between us, is amazing."

Horror was replaced by confusion. "So…what's wrong?"

"Wrong? Babe, this is way too good to be wrong. No, nothing's wrong. I'm just saying that you had a point here and I don't think you're going to prove it."

"A point?" She'd had a point? Something beyond an orgasm or three?

"You said you were gonna prove that your aphrodisiacs work, remember?" he said with a grin. "I'm still wondering what you're gonna offer up as proof."

Oh. That.

Relief washed over her in a wave, making her want to drop to the couch and sigh in thanks.

"Proof?" she said, her words husky against the soft dusting of hair on his chest. "The proof will be you panting, exploding with an orgasm."

He groaned, his fingers combing through her hair.

She could feel his laughter, though, as his chest vibrated against her mouth.

Her lips still exploring his chest, Pandora forced her eyes open to give him an arch look of inquiry.

"Sweetheart, you're hot. I'm wild for you. So the orgasm, that's a given."

She liked that. Wild for her. Pandora shivered in delight, thrilled beyond delight that a guy like Caleb wanted her this much.

"It *is* a given," she agreed. "It definitely is. But you'll be coming before you get your boots off."

His laughter wasn't so silent now.

"That hasn't happened since I was fifteen."

"Kiss that memory goodbye, then," she instructed. "Because thanks to me, and my aphrodisiacs, you'll never be able to say that again."

She didn't know where the words came from. But once they were out, she wasn't scared. Instead, she was empowered. Inspired. Excited.

It was like someone had just broken her from a prison she hadn't realized she'd spent her life in.

And now she was free. Free to enjoy, free to explore. And most of all, free to use Caleb's body for every single kinky sexual fantasy she'd ever had.

CALEB LAUGHED AS PANDORA twirled one finger in the air to indicate they should switch places. She thought she was going to take control of the fun. Not likely. He never, ever gave up control.

But neither did he deny a lady her pleasure.

So in the name of humoring her, he released her leg to let the silky-smooth length of it slide down his thigh.

Then, his hands wrapped around her waist, he lifted her and twirled, so they'd changed positions.

"Now what?" he challenged, grinning.

She looked so earnest.

Her hair was a silky cloud around her face, rumpled and glowing in the light of the fire. Hazel eyes, still hazy with pleasure, studied him as though she was figuring out a puzzle. Good luck with that, he thought.

"It's time," she intoned with a smile.

"Go for it," he invited, trying not to laugh.

It wasn't that he didn't think she was gorgeous. Sweet and pretty and so damn sexy. She was all that. But she was hardly a practiced seductress. So he figured this was going to be a hot and sexy time, but he wasn't too worried about control.

Or the state of his boots.

"See, here's the thing, though," she said slowly, her words as soft as the fingers she was tracing down his chest.

"Which thing is that?"

She gave him a chiding look, then shrugged a little, making her breasts bounce and his mouth water.

"The thing is, I'm new to seduction."

Caleb laughed, then grabbed her hands and lifted them to his lips, pressing kisses on her knuckles. "Sweetie, you don't have to do anything you don't want to."

"Oh, but there is so much I do want to do. I'm just letting you know, ahead of time, in case I drive you too crazy, too fast," she said, her smile turning wicked.

His laughter turned a little hoarse as she pulled her hands away and planted them directly on his belt

buckle. Talk about getting right to business. Not that
he objected, but he'd been kinda looking forward to a
little bit of what he'd imagined would be shyly sweet
exploration.

She didn't tug his buckle open, though. Instead, she
slipped her fingers inside his jeans and caught hold
of his shirt, pulling it free. Her palms flat against his
belly, she slid them upward, taking his shirt with them.
Following her cue, he lifted his arms, then finished it
off himself, tossing it toward the same couch currently
holding her bra.

One for one, they were on a roll.

"Mmm," she hummed, staring at his chest as if she
was mesmerized. Caleb was already sporting a pretty
nice erection, but that look on her face, pure appreciative awareness, made his dick throb.

Her palms still flat, she smoothed them over his
shoulders, her fingers warm and teasing as they
skimmed his skin. Her nails scraped a hot trail of fire
down his arms, pausing to curve over biceps that,
yes, he knew it was stupid, but he flexed a little. Her
soft sigh of appreciation didn't make him feel stupid,
though. It made him feel like a freaking superhero.

Her eyes flicked to his, then back to his chest. But
he saw a wicked light in their depths. Like she was up
to something. Not wanting to ruin her fun and tell her
there wasn't anything he hadn't seen or done, he relaxed and waited.

Then she pressed her mouth, hot and wet, against
his nipple. And he damn near exploded.

What the hell? Her hands were skimming, caressing their way over his chest, but it was her mouth that

was driving him crazy. Her tongue slipped out, tasting, testing. Tempting. Since she hadn't made a rule against it, Caleb grabbed on to the silky warmth of her waist before sliding one hand up to cup the weight of her breast. Fair was fair, after all.

Apparently she wasn't interested in fair, though.

Pandora shifted, trailing those hot, openmouthed kisses down his chest.

Caleb was going insane. That was the only justification he could find for his inability to hold on to any semblance of control.

For a man who prided himself in his skill, both with women, and over his body, he didn't know what to do here. How to react. It was as if Pandora had woven a magical spell over him. Like she was an addiction, one he couldn't resist.

Her lips, wet and silky, trailed lower down his belly, the rasp of his zipper filling the room as her teeth tugged it down.

Caleb groaned, his fingers clenched in her soft hair. He realized he didn't give a damn.

She could keep the power.

Just as long as she continued driving him crazy.

Then her lips pressed against the tip of his dick.

Caleb growled a combination of shock and pleasure. Taking that as a go-ahead, she tugged his shorts and pants down below his knees, then her fingers trailed a teasing path back up his thighs.

She pulled back, just a little, and looked up at him. With those deceptively innocent hazel eyes locked on his, she leaned forward and wrapped her lips around the throbbing head.

He almost yelped in surprise. Then he closed his eyes, enjoying the delight of her mouth.

She was so good at this. She licked and nibbled him like a freaking lollipop.

Intense pleasure pounded through him, demanding release. Her mouth felt like heaven, the kind that only bad boys got into. Her tongue swirled, then she sucked. Hard.

He damn near exploded.

"No," he shouted instead.

"No," he repeated, gentling it this time and soothing his hands over the tangle his fingers had made in her hair. "Not like this. The first time I come, I want it to be inside you."

Her brow arched and she leaned forward again, but he gripped her hair. "Not inside your mouth, either."

Her smile was a work of art. And not just because she offered it up from her knees in front of his bare, throbbing erection. He reached out and pulled her to her feet, needing to kiss her almost as much as he needed to come.

"More," he said, borrowing her earlier demand.

"Definitely more," she gasped, wrapping her arms around his neck and kissing him back. Before he could get too serious about it, though, she pulled away.

"Hey!"

"I don't think we want these in the way," she teased, shimmying out of her panties. She hurried over to her purse and grabbed something, showing off the condom with a grin before sauntering back.

Not trusting his body to behave if she touched him again, he held up one hand to indicate she stay where she was. Then he took the condom and slipped it on, reveling in the view as he protected them.

"You're beautiful," he told her, pulling her toward him. "I want you so much."

"How much, exactly?" she teased.

"This much."

Done talking, he grabbed her tight and took her mouth in a deep, devouring kiss. Her moan of delight was all he needed to know she was ready. He grasped her hips, his hands curving into her butt and lifting. Her arms tight around his shoulders, she wrapped her legs around his hips.

In one quick, delightful thrust, Caleb was inside her. She was tight, hot and wet. Delicious. His hands gripping her hips, he thrust, his hips setting a fast rhythm.

"More," she breathed against his throat as she undulated in a tempting dance, pulling him in deeper.

Deeper and deeper. Harder and faster.

Her moans became whimpers. Her breath heated his neck as she dug her fingernails into his shoulders, gripping him so tight her heels dug into the small of his back.

He couldn't think.

All he could do was feel the incredible sensations building. Tightening. Need pounded at him. Her mewling pants were driving him higher.

Then she came. Her gasp was followed by the soft chanting of his name. Over and over and over, she called out to him.

He couldn't restrain himself any longer. As her body spasmed and contracted around him, he exploded in delight.

His mind spinning, aftershocks of the sexual blast still zinging through his body, Caleb let his head fall back against the wall. He unclenched his fingers from the soft cushion of Pandora's butt to let her slide her legs back to the floor. She puddled against him like a purring kitten, nuzzling her head under his chin and giving a moaning sort of sigh that made him feel like king of the sex gods.

"Bed?" he groaned against the warm, smoothness of her throat.

"That door over there," she murmured, her words more a husky purr than anything. Caleb forced his eyes open, looking around for *over there*. There were two doors, one cracked open enough that he could see was a bathroom. Handy. The other was closed. There was a bed waiting on the other side of that door.

The trick was to get to it.

He had a whole lot of warm, wonderful woman wrapped in his arms.

His slacks were around his ankles. Pure class, he thought as he rolled his eyes. His boots were still laced tight, so he couldn't kick his pants off and romantically sweep Pandora into his arms.

Romantically. Holy crap. A hard-core realist, Caleb knew the effects drugs could have on the body. But asparagus and oysters? That all-natural aphrodisiac thing was pure bullshit.

At least, he'd thought it was until now, as he stood with his head still reeling, his jeans jammed down around his socks like a pimply faced adolescent getting it for the first time behind the school gym.

Now? Now he was thinking up ways to be romantic.

Again…holy crap.

Pandora gave a sighing little wiggle, her curves pressing tighter against him, the deliciously pebbled hardness of her nipples scraping against his chest and her flowery-scented hair rubbing under his chin.

A part of him—he swore it was Hunter's voice—was kicking in to lecture mode. He shouldn't be doing this. The plan was to use her store's proximity to keep an eye on his father. Not to use her, in any way, shape or form.

But was it using? his body argued. He was seriously interested in her. She was gorgeous and sexy and fun. And this didn't have to get in the way of his investigation, so what did it matter?

Who gave a damn how he'd got here.

Caleb vowed in that second, as he brushed a soft kiss against the top of her head, that he was going to enjoy the hell out of this night. Whatever was driving it, he was the one having the fabulous ride.

Well, he and Pandora.

And it was time to make sure she got a ride she'd never forget, either.

"Round two," he promised. "This time, I'll show you what I can do with my boots off."

CHAPTER EIGHT

"WELL?" KATHY PRODDED in a frantic admonition, leaning across the sales counter so far her butt was almost up in the air. "I can't believe you didn't call me last night to tell me about your dinner. I'm your best friend. Your confidante. Your coconspirator of all things naughty. And I have to drag myself out of bed on a cold Saturday morning and brave the crazy shoppers to nag you into filling in the deets?"

A little freaked at the idea of verbalizing all the images that'd been playing in Technicolor through her head all day, Pandora rolled her eyes. She was trying her best to ignore Kathy's chipper curiosity. Especially since the store *was* filled with holiday shoppers, all with varying degrees of gossip expertise.

Trying to act professional, she struggled to wrap gold foil paper around an octagon-shaped box while the customer tapped her foot impatiently in time with "Jingle Bells" playing through the store's speakers.

"Whose idea was it to offer free gift wrapping?" she muttered as the tape stuck to the wrong part of the foil paper, pulling the glittery gold off when she tried to move it. Wrinkling her nose, she glared at the package, then glanced at the eagle-eyed customer who'd now taken to finger tapping to show her displeasure.

Oops.

"That'd be the same person whose idea it was to try out her hot and horny holiday meal last night and isn't sharing how it went," Kathy said, her voice escalating from whisper to hiss loud enough to garner shopper attention.

Her face on fire, Pandora gave a hiss of her own.

"Shh. I'll share. Later," she promised as she gave in to the finger-tapping pressure and started the wrapping all over. "Now, help me with this ribbon, okay?"

"No." Kathy straightened, keeping her hold-the-ribbon fingers hostage and giving Pandora a stubborn look.

"Pandora, the gossip grapevine is running amok," Laurie, a waitress from the nearby diner, said as she approached the counter with a basketful of holiday shopping. "Lacy Garner claimed Caleb Black was in here flirting up a storm the other day. But Jolene Giamenti was telling everyone and their neighbor that Sheriff Kendall was interested in you. Now I'm dying of curiosity—which of those fine-looking gentlemen are you interested in?"

Pandora's lips curved as she wondered how to answer that. She'd never had two eligible men interested in her, and definitely never had the town gossiping over which one she'd choose. Her ego, starting to show its fragile face again, glowed a little at the idea.

"Which one?" repeated the finger-tapping Mrs. Vincent, giving a nod of approval for the wrapping and indicating that Pandora hurry up with a little wiggle of her fingers. "As if there could be a question. A sweet girl like Pandora is going to date our fine sheriff. Why would she have any interest in a hoodlum like Caleb Black? Of course, all three Black kids were wild. But Caleb, being the oldest, seemed to make a point of being the best troublemaker, too. Why would Pandora date someone like that?"

Why? For fourteen orgasms in one night, maybe? Or the soft sweetness of the kiss he'd brushed over her forehead before he'd left in the wee hours of the morning? Maybe because Caleb had a sense of humor almost as fine as his gorgeous body. Or that he was fun and entertaining and made her feel amazingly sexy and clever.

Pandora shifted from one foot to the other. The movement brushed her thighs together and instantly shot tingling little reminders of her wild night through her body. She shivered. She didn't regret for one second the evening that had led to such pleasure. But still, she needed to keep her professional persona intact. It didn't matter that this was her own sex life and as such, nobody else's nosy business. Just as it hadn't mattered that she was innocent in the debacle with Sean. She'd learned the hard way how easy it was for public opinion to destroy a career.

"Are you going to share, or aren't you?" Kathy prodded, snatching the package and tying the bow herself with a quick, sassy flick of her fingers. "I have a lot to do today. My mother wants to go shopping for matching Christmas sweaters, then I have to take the dog to the photographer to reshoot the holiday card."

"You know if you had cats, those cards would come out a lot better," Pandora pointed out, taking the package back, bagging it and handing it to Mrs. Vincent with a smile. "Cats are great at lying still."

She, Kathy and the two customers all looked toward Bonnie and Paulie, who were curled up together in the window, a picture of furry contentment on the alpaca throw displayed there.

"So what's going on?" Mrs. Vincent prodded, taking her bag but not leaving like a polite customer who minded her own business should. "Are you associating with that riffraff, Caleb Black? I hear he's been a huge stress to his daddy. Not that Tobias Black is a pillar of all that is good and right in the world, what with dating girls his daughter's age, those motorcycle types in and out of his shop and the constant traffic of questionable personalities. But he deserves better than a do-nothing son like that boy."

"Caleb isn't a do-nothing, Mrs. Vincent," Pandora defended, seeing the trap an instant too late.

"Guess that answers our question, then, doesn't it," Mrs. Vincent said with a wicked smile on her benign old-lady face. She and Mrs. Sellers hooked arms and sashayed out of the store, whispering and tossing dire looks back over their shoulders.

Another customer, one who Pandora didn't know personally, gave a judgmental sort of tut-tut, then went back to her shopping.

Panic gripped a tight fist in Pandora's stomach. What had she done? She should have kept things with Caleb quiet. The mess with Sean had been horrible, but the whispers and snide innuendo from everyone who knew them, everyone she'd worked with, that'd almost been worse.

"Pandora, I love what you've done here," a pretty blonde interrupted as she carried a large statue of Eros, the god of love to the counter. She patted his naked ceramic butt before pointing to the tower of boxed aphrodisiac pepper cookies, the day's special. "Can you throw in a box of extraspicy cookies, too? I think they'll be a perfect gift for my Jazzercise instructor."

"She likes cookies?" Kathy asked, apparently not in such a hurry that she didn't have time to be social. She leaned forward on the counter, trying to peek up Eros's flowing strip of fabric to see how he was hanging.

"Sure. But mostly it's because she's got this new boyfriend and wants to make sure this relationship has a chance," the woman said, adding an astrology book, two CDs and a woven celestial shawl to the counter. "I guess she was dating this guy last month who was all about a little chemical enhancement, if you know what I mean. He claimed it'd boost their sex lives and make her look and feel gorgeous."

Starting to ring up the fabulous sale, Pandora exchanged a confused look with Kathy. Before she could ask, though, the woman continued. "She wasn't having anything to do with that fake stuff, though. But now she's paranoid that her new guy thinks she's ugly and that she sucks in bed. So I figured some cookie encouragement, along with a spa gift certificate, might help boost her confidence a little."

"Cookie courage," Pandora intoned with a wise nod.

The three of them joked their way through the rest of the transaction, but as soon as the door bells rang behind the blonde, Pandora frowned at Kathy.

"What do you think she's talking about? Chemical

enhancements? Like…" She trailed off, then shrugged. "What do you think she meant?"

Kathy gave her a long, knowing look that clearly said she realized this was a pathetic topic change and she was allowing it for now. But there would be a price to pay. Pandora figured she'd better bring chocolate.

"Well, chemical usually means drugs," Kathy pointed out finally. Pandora nodded. "But the looking-good part? Maybe that means hallucinogens or something? Who knows?"

The two women shared a puzzled look.

"Pandora, did you want to open the café early today?" Fifi asked as she hurried from the back where she'd been prepping the cash register for lunch.

"We don't start serving until eleven," Pandora said, glancing at the clock shaped like a cat wearing a wizard hat. Most of the food was already prepped and ready in the kitchen, but she still needed to put the finishing touches on the asparagus salad and whip a fresh bowl of cream. "That's an hour away."

"I know, but I've had three people ask if we'd consider it. They need to be other places but really want your saffron chicken special."

"It'd be cool to bump up our income with an extra hour of lunch," Pandora mused, glancing at the beaded doorway leading to the café. "But I don't think we can. The store is too busy, I can't afford for one of us off the floor that much longer."

"Maybe we should hire holiday help?" Fifi said, her voice lifting in excitement. "I mean, even if it's only for the holidays. Things are so busy now, we could use another set of hands. I have a friend who'd be great.

Russ. You've met him, right? He could come in during café hours. Maybe just until the new year when things slow down again?"

Hire help? Pandora bit her lip. What did she know about choosing employees? Fifi had worked at the store off and on for years, so it hadn't been as if Pandora had hired her so much as rehired her. But someone totally new? With her lousy judgment in people? She shuddered.

"You remember Russ? Kinda geeky guy who's been hanging around the store the last few weeks. He's a nice guy. Sweet and great at math," Fifi prodded. "Want me to give him a call?"

Pandora took a deep breath, looking around again. Her stomach was churning and she wanted to go hide in the office, make a list of pros and cons and debate the idea for a few hours.

But Fifi and Kathy were giving her expectant looks, and she had a store to run.

"Sure," she decided. Then realizing that she needed to be a businesswoman, not a wimp, she added, "I'll talk to him and see if I think he'd fit in well here at Moonspun Dreams."

"Oh, I think he will. He's fascinated by all things mystical and really wants to learn," Fifi said with an excited clap of her hands. "And he knows a lot of people. So I'm sure he'll be talking up the store and how great you're doing here, too."

Great, Pandora thought. Someone else talking about her. Just what she needed.

CALEB STRETCHED OUT on his hotel bed, staring in satisfaction at his stockinged feet. When the hell was the last time he'd taken a nap, let alone lounged around without his boots on?

Always being properly shod was a necessary component of always being ready to run. And he'd spent the past eight years, hell, his entire life, actually, ready to hit the road at a moment's notice.

A job gone wrong. A drugged-out dealer breaking in to kill him. A fight with one of his siblings. One of his dad's cons turning sour. All required footwear.

Wasn't it just a little ironic that the first taste he'd had of the ultimate deliciousness that was Pandora, he'd had his boots on? Or maybe it was some kind of cosmic payback for all his years of running.

He was still grinning a sappy, dork-ass grin when his cell rang.

"Black," he answered.

"Report?"

"Happy holidays, Hunter. How's the shopping coming along? Do you feebies do the secret Santa thing? Or do you buy for the entire task force? If so, don't forget my favorite color is grey."

"Not black?"

"Too obvious."

"Something you never are."

"Exactly."

"Are we finished?"

Caleb considered the white cotton of his stocking-clad toes for a few seconds, then nodded.

"Yep, sure. We're finished. What's up?"

"I'm calling for your status report."

"Is this how you handle your minions? Formal report requests? This businesslike tone that says, 'Dude, I'm in charge!'?"

"Is this how you talk to your superiors? With total disregard for authority? Your smart-ass mouth running on fast-forward?"

Caleb wiggled his toes, then nodded. "Yep. Guess that's why they aren't crying too hard over me retiring, huh?"

"I have trouble believing you actually think you can retire," Hunter said, now sounding more like Caleb's old roommate and beer buddy than an uptight FBI agent. "You're an adrenaline junky. You might be sick of the streets, but you're not going to be able to give up the job. Not totally."

Caleb's toes weren't looking so appealing anymore. Tension, as familiar as his own face, shot through his shoulders as he swung his feet to the floor.

"I could get used to not having people shoot at me. I'm thinking I'd like a life spent not dealing with strung-out hookers and South American drug lords with their zombie army of addicts."

"You'd just let them all go free?"

"I'm not the only guy out there, Hunter. There're plenty of DEA agents who can bring them down."

"As good as you?"

"Of course not."

Neither of them were kidding, Caleb knew. Hunter, because he didn't know how. And himself, because, well, he *was* damn good. But that didn't mean he wasn't finished.

"What'd you call for?" he asked, not willing to keep circling the same useless point he'd already discussed with his boss four times since he'd hit Black Oak for his fake vacation.

"Just what I said. I'm calling for your report."

"No, you're not. You're not a micromanager. If I had something to report, I'd have called you myself. And you know that. So what's the deal?"

The other man's hesitation was a physical thing. If he'd been in the room, Caleb knew he'd see the calculation in his old friend's eyes as he decided the best way to handle the situation. Good ole Hunter, always strategizing.

"Your father has some odd activity going on. A lot of major part orders, hiring a couple guys with dealing records, parties in the shop after hours."

Stonefaced, Caleb analyzed that info as objectively as possible. Then he shrugged. "It's the holidays—from what I've heard, he has a lot of big holiday orders. He probably needs mechanics to meet them, and isn't that picky about their backgrounds."

"He's dating some hottie in town. She was in your sister's graduating class."

Wincing, Caleb hunched his shoulders. Just when he thought his father couldn't embarrass him anymore…

"So my old man is snacking on a Twinkie. So what?"

"You know sex is one of the prime motivators. Have you checked this woman out?"

"I'm not checking out my father's old lady."

In the first place, the idea was gross. In the second, it would up the chances that he'd actually have to speak with his father. In the week he'd been in town, he'd managed to duck the guy's calls and avoid actually being in the same breathing space. He was calling it deep undercover. So deep, he wasn't even coming into contact with the suspect.

"She's the stepdaughter of a known South American dealer. She's reputed to be estranged from her family, but the connection can't be ignored."

"Lilah Gomez?"

God, this was like some twisted soap opera. Striding over to the window, Caleb shoved his hand through his hair. This day had started out so nice. Incredible sex, a woman who filled his head with crazy thoughts of tomorrow and, dammit, relaxing in his stocking feet.

"You know her?"

He wasn't about to admit that after that first day when he hadn't recognized her, she'd gone on to hit on him three more times since he'd come to town. He grimaced. Especially since that he didn't know if her thing with his father was new or not.

"She and my sister were tight growing up. They hung out, had sleepovers, that kind of thing. Then Lilah went over to the wild side, and she and Maya went their separate ways."

Caleb waited, but Hunter didn't say anything about Lilah's current sleepover choices. And that, friends, was why he was still Caleb's best buddy.

"Look, I'm sorry," Hunter said instead.

Staring out the window at the frosty cold coating the bare tree branches, Caleb grunted.

"I'd hoped you'd find someone else. Another suspect or connection."

"Even if my old man's acting like a hound dog, there's still nothing to tie him to this," Caleb argued.

"There's nothing to point the finger in any other direction," Hunter rebutted. "Is there?"

Caleb sighed. "The case is moving slow. I've been connecting my way up the food chain. I'm cozying up to one of the midlevel dealers. He knows names, clearly has the inside track. But he's not sharing. Yet."

"Any hint about who's on top?"

Caleb grimaced. "These guys are cocky, sure they are untouchable. So it's someone with pull. Someone who can influence the law."

He waited, but again, Hunter didn't take the obvious opening. Gotta love the guy.

"I saw one of the couriers last night from a distance. He's familiar. As soon as I figure out where I've seen him before, I'll have the break we need."

"You've seen him on another case?"

Caleb thought back to the brown shaggy hair, all he'd been able to identify from two blocks away. "No, he's local. I'll do the rounds again, figure it out."

"Good job," Hunter said. "In the meantime, I have a remote, wildly impossible thread that if tugged could disintegrate instantly."

"Sounds promising."

He could handle delicate. Hell, if it meant keeping his old man out of jail, he could handle delicate while juggling porcelain and wearing roller skates.

"Intel shows that a new citizen to Black Oak has some connections. A relationship with a pharmacist busted for a prescription scam. She was implicated but skated."

"So why are you grudging after my old man? Why aren't you pounding on her door instead?"

"In the first place, it's not a grudge. Your old man has a record longer than I am tall."

"A record of suspicions. No convictions."

"Minor detail."

"Major legality."

"Whatever," Hunter dismissed. "And in the second place, while there is enough here to warrant a first glance, it's pretty much a waste of a second look. Other than this one relationship, the woman has a spotless rep. No record, no connections, no history to support drug suspicions."

"Once is all it takes." Especially if that once was the hook he needed to prove his old man's innocence. Just because he had issues with his upbringing, a lack of respect for his father's choices and a whole lot of pent-up anger toward the past, that didn't mean he wanted the old man in jail.

"Look, give me the name and I'll look into it," he told Hunter.

Even though the sigh was silent, Caleb knew his friend heaved one. Patience with avoidance had never been the guy's strong suit.

"Fine. Check on a Pandora Easton. I'll email you the deets of her record."

Sucker punched, stars swirled in front of his eyes as he tried to catch his breath. Caleb had been in bed with a pole dancer once, both of them buck naked and sweaty, when she'd pulled a gun on him. To this day, he had no idea where it'd come from.

That's about how he felt at this moment.

"Pandora…"

"Easton," Hunter confirmed. "Twenty-seven, resident of Black Oak and employed at a store there. Her mother, Cassiopeia Easton, has a file. I'll send that, too."

A part of Caleb's brain heard and filed away the details of Hunter's words. The rest of it was in shock.

Pandora? The sweetest woman he'd ever met? The one who'd shown him heaven by the lights of her Christmas tree, blown his control all to hell while giving him the best orgasm of his life? With his damn boots on?

Suddenly, busting his father for running a drug ring held a sort of appeal.

He'd spent hours in that store. Days watching it. He hadn't suspected her for one second. Now this? Unless he'd seriously lost his edge, this was all bullshit. Or was it?

"I've gotta go," he said, cutting off whatever Hunter was saying. He flicked the cell phone closed, shoved it in his pocket and grabbed his jacket. It wasn't until he had the door to his hotel room open he remembered that he didn't have any damn boots on.

There was irony in there somewhere.

Five minutes later, he was on his way. To do what, he wasn't sure. Something with Pandora. He wasn't sure if that something was along the lines of the naked, intense pleasure that he'd been contemplating an hour ago, or if it was because he didn't like being lied to. Zipping his jacket, the leather minimal defense against the cold, Caleb stepped out of the hotel lobby and onto the wide porch steps and almost ran into the body coming up the stairs.

"Excuse me," he muttered, sidestepping and patting his pockets for his bike keys.

"I was coming in to look for you."

Could this damn day get any worse?

Caleb glanced at the keys in his hand, briefly wishing they were his gun. He shoved the keys back in his pocket, eyeing the railing and the drop. Whether it was to jump or to toss someone over, he wasn't sure.

"Dad," he returned, his tone resigned. He kept one eye on the railing, though. Just in case.

He'd been unprepared that first day when he'd seen his father. Since then, he'd spent every minute prepared for this second encounter. Now, he could study the old man with objective eyes. Or at least without the resentment and irritation he'd been sporting.

Tobias Black stood straight and tall, like his sons. His black hair was showing a little gray in the sideburns, but was still as thick and unruly as ever. As a kid, Caleb had seen his father in everything from a three-piece suit with an ascot, to a repairman's coveralls, to surgical scrubs. A chameleon, Tobias had obviously taken to this new role as custom-bike shop owner like a fish to water. Biker boots, similar to Caleb's own, jeans and a leather jacket made up his work uniform.

"I've been waiting for you to come by the house. Or the shop. Either one," Tobias said, shifting to the left and blocking the stairs leading to escape. Caleb smirked, knowing he could take the railing at any time he wanted.

"I've been busy."

"Doing?"

Leaning against one of the porch columns, his arms crossed over his chest, Caleb's smirk widened.

"Tell me, son, why'd you come home? Clearly not to see family, so what's up?"

"I stopped by to see Aunt Cynthia yesterday."

"How is that old bat?"

"She had a lot of great things to say about you."

Tobias's smirk was an exact replica of his son's.

"I'll just bet she did. The woman is still trying to run me out of town. You'd think she'd give up after all this time, but no. That's why she ran for mayor, you know. To make my life hell."

If anyone else had said that, Caleb would have rolled his eyes and called them on their whiny persecution complex. But in this case, he knew Tobias was right. Cynthia Parker had made it her mission to make her late sister's husband's life hell whenever possible. His kids, she tolerated. But Tobias? Not even a little bit.

"I gotta say, even for a harpy, I had higher expectations of her, though," Tobias continued. "She's too busy glad-handing rich donors and getting her picture taken to take care of business, I guess."

Caleb knew the game. If he asked what business, he'd be agreeing to play. Con 101, get the mark to agree. To anything, even if it was only to agree to talk about the weather. And for a master like Tobias, all he needed was that agreement, and he'd win. Always.

So Caleb waited.

Tobias clearly knew what his oldest son was doing.

"I don't suppose you're interested in coming by the bike shop this evening? Big holiday bash, all the vendors, customers, hell, even a few strangers. Probably a few of your old school pals. Good times, food provided by that little sweetheart at Moonspun, booze from Mick's bar."

Caleb saw the trap. Hell, it had a big neon sign flashing a warning at him. But he couldn't stop himself.

"You're tight with Pandora, are you?" he asked.

"Tight? What're you implying? The girl's young enough to be my daughter."

"So's Lilah Gomez."

Tobias's grin widened. Nope, this was his game and he was setting the traps, not stepping in them.

"Girl's gonna be at the party," he said.

"Lilah?" Caleb returned, even though he knew who his father meant.

"Pandora. I heard you had dinner with her the other night. Hope you're not taking on more than you can handle there."

Caleb's stare was bland. He hadn't discussed his sex life with his father since he was twelve and the old man had shown him the hall closet where the supply of condoms was kept. He was hardly going to start now.

"There's a lot of interesting…stuff coming out of that store," Tobias continued. His blue eyes were intense, the same look Caleb often saw when he looked in the mirror.

"Define *interesting*," Caleb invited. He knew Tobias wouldn't—after all, why waste bait? But he wanted to see where his father was taking this.

"Come by tonight," Tobias invited with a nod. Apparently Caleb had done something right—who the hell knew what—in the old man's eyes. "You might learn a few things."

With that and a jaunty salute, Tobias turned on his heel and sauntered down the stairs.

CHAPTER NINE

BY SEVEN-THIRTY IN THE evening, Pandora was closing up the store and about ready to scream.

She'd thought she was having a little fun with the most incredible sex of her life. But according to popular thought in the store today, she was actually making a social statement that was quite possibly going to cast her as a pariah in town and ruin her reputation. Having played that role recently, she knew she pretty much hated it.

And, apparently the cherry on top of public opinion was that by choosing Caleb over Sheriff Hottie, she was rejecting all that was good and right in the world for the lure of the bad.

It was enough to make a girl's head explode right off her shoulders. But she knew from experience that obsessing didn't help, so she forced herself to start her closing routine.

It was just as well that Caleb hadn't come by. Or called. Or expressed any interest in a repeat performance. If one night together had the potential to ruin everything she'd built here, what would two nights do? Ruin it twice as much?

And how pathetic was she to stop and consider whether twice as ruined wasn't worth it. Because, dammit, the sex had been incredible. Mind-boggling. So awesome that she got damp just thinking about it.

And she knew he'd been just as blown away.

"Why the hell hasn't he called, then?" she muttered as she wheeled the dolly with its precariously balanced crate into the showroom.

She stopped just short of Paulie, who was splayed over the floor like a cat-skin rug, and wheeled the dolly to the right instead.

"I'm crazy for being upset. I should be grateful he isn't coming around, right? This way I don't have to worry about trying to resist him."

This time she directed her comment to Bonnie, who was sitting on one of the display counters next to a three-foot-high cluster of amethyst, her head tilted to the side as if contemplating Pandora's whining.

Bonnie meowed her support. But Paulie just rolled onto his side, shot one leg into the air and started licking himself. There was nothing like the male perspective.

"Sure, I guess he could take that route," she agreed with the cat as she started wiggling the five-foot-tall statue of Eros from the box, careful not to nick his wings. "But lovin' is never as fun by oneself."

Pandora's lower lip jutted out, but before she could get a real pout on, there was a tap at the door.

She and the cats all turned their heads. Her heart leaped, giddy excitement filling her tummy. Dread filtered in, too. She'd had no idea she was making a public statement last night. But now she was fully informed. Upset, confused and a little intimidated…but still fully informed.

Oh, joy.

Giving Eros's butt a quick pat in the hopes he'd help her choose well, she unwrapped herself from the statue and hurried across the store to unlock the door.

"Caleb," she greeted, her smile a little shaky at the corners. She wiped her hands on the heavy velvet of her skirt and gave her voile blouse a quick tug to make sure the lace was straight at the bodice.

Should she ask him in? Or ask him to leave? Her stomach churned as she tried to decide. Did she go with her instincts and intuition, which said that despite the town's opinion, he was a good man? Or did she accept that her intuition sucked and listen to public opinion?

Thankfully, Caleb took the decision out of her hands by walking right in.

"Hey," he greeted. He didn't kiss her, though. Instead, he gave her a long, searching look, then, hands still shoved in his pockets instead of groping her the way they should be, he stepped into the store.

"What's up?" she asked. She bit her lip. Had he heard the rumors about the two of them? Was he regretting it now, too? "You look a little stressed."

"Nah. I just had a full day, that's all."

Full of what? He wasn't working, was avoiding his family as if they were carriers of the seventh plague and didn't seem like a holiday-partying kind of guy.

Maybe he'd been looking for a job. Or a place to live. Something that'd keep him in Black Oak past the first of the year? Maybe he'd spent the day in bed, recovering in exhaustion from his wild night with her.

And maybe she'd been inhaling too many oyster fumes. Pandora gave herself a quick mental forehead smack, followed by an even quicker get-a-freaking-clue-he's-not-for-you lecture.

"I'm replenishing stock," she told him, returning to unpacking the statue so she could resist the desperate urge to squeeze his ass. Keep it light, keep it polite. Ass grabbing was definitely off-limits. "It was a busy day. The busiest this year, actually."

"That's great that you're rocking the sales," he said. "Have you pinpointed what's making the big difference? Besides your charming personality, of course."

The last was said with a wicked smile and a wink.

"I'm guessing it's either that, or the aphrodisiacs," Pandora said with a smile, unable to maintain her distance when he gave her that look. "I'm not actually sure. I haven't quite figured out how to run the bookkeeping program yet, but I think there's some kind of income-comparison report I can run. As soon as I do, I'll know what to focus more time on."

His eyes narrowed, an odd look crossing his face before he stepped farther into the room. "I'm handy with computers. How about I run the report for you while you unpack?"

"You don't have to do that," she protested, her words a little breathless. "I'm sure you have other things to do."

"Just the party at the motorcycle shop," he dismissed. "And I was hoping you'd go with me, so I'm just chilling until you're through here anyway."

Pandora pressed her lips together. Wasn't that tantamount to publicly stating her intention to take the bad-boy path?

"The party?" she hedged. "I didn't think you were going."

In that second, Pandora wished like never before that her mom were here. As conflicted as she felt, she needed Cassiopeia's clear-sighted vision and maybe a session with the tarot cards to sort through all of this.

Instead, she was stuck with herself. And her own lousy intuition. Tiny pinpricks of panic shivered up and down Pandora's spine as she tried to decide what to do. Her intuition was telling her to go for it with Caleb. Of course, her body's desperate need to taste him at least one more time was probably overriding any teensy bit of actual gift she had.

Obviously catching a whiff of her internal struggle, Caleb waved one hand as if brushing away the invitation.

"Look, I don't blame you if you don't want to go. It's not my idea of a good time," Caleb said with a shrug, moving behind the counter to where she'd left the laptop open. "What program do you use for bookkeeping?"

If they stayed here, she could enjoy his company and not have to face crowds. Or decisions. Oh, God, Pandora thought with a mental eye roll. She was such a wimp.

"You really don't have to do that," she said, feeling guilty over the relief. "I can come in early tomorrow and finish up the stock. We can go to the party now. Or, you know, go do something else."

Subtle, Pandora, she told herself with a mental snicker. Why didn't she ask him to drop his pants and do her instead?

"Nah," he said. "This won't take long and I'd like to help."

Her heart melted a little. So did her knees, so Pandora leaned against the dolly and cleared her throat, not wanting to sound all choked up when she said, "I appreciate it. I feel like I'm…"

She trailed off, scrunching her nose and scraping at the chipped paint on the dolly.

"Feel like…?"

Flustered and wishing she'd kept her mouth shut, Pandora met his gaze with a shrug.

"Pandora?"

"I feel like I've finally found my thing, you know? My niche. I'm having fun getting to know the customers and matching them to the right motivation." She blushed again, giving him an abashed look. "That's how I think of it. Motivation. What products will get them excited, give them the boost or direction they need. Even the aphrodisiacs in the café are all about motivation."

Pushing the dolly toward the back room, Pandora caught his doubtful look.

"They are," she insisted. "The aphrodisiacs aren't like popping a little blue sex pill and getting it up for anyone or anything. They're about amplifying a connection that's already there. About giving a couple the impetus, the energy, to lose their inhibitions and explore everything that's between them."

Caleb leaned against the counter, his fingers tapping the edge of the laptop as he smiled.

"You love it."

Centering her statue, Pandora rubbed Eros's bare shoulder and nodded. "I really do."

"Then let me help you out. I'll just take a peek at your program, see what info I can pull together for you."

Could anyone be sweeter? To hell with the town and the gossip. She was going to listen to her heart. It might not be a special gift like intuition or a honed skill like reading body language. But it was hers and she was going to trust it.

"I APPRECIATE YOU LOOKING at my books," Pandora said, her smile both sweet and sexy at the same time. She crossed the floor, pausing to pet one of the cats, who was sprawled inside a large copper bowl. "I figure I'll take a business class or something after the first of the year. But in the meantime, I really am grateful for the reassurance that the store is really doing well."

Caleb felt like the world's biggest dick. And not in a good way. He spent most of his life lying to people. Using them for information. He'd learned the art of taking advantage of people at his father's knee.

And now?

Now he was standing in front of a woman who made him feel things, believe in things that he'd always scoffed at as feel-good lies before. And he was bullshitting her, poking into her business while pretending to help her out. He was digging into her books trying to find the dirt to convict her of an ugly crime.

No, he corrected himself. He was assuring himself that there was no dirt, so she didn't get unfairly accused.

Big difference, he thought with a mental eye roll.

She reached the counter and hesitated, her smile dimming as she studied his face. A tiny crease marred her forehead and she took a little step back, as if to get a better view of him.

"Seriously. What's the matter? You're really tense and, well, off feeling," she said, studying him through suddenly narrowed eyes.

Caleb was impressed. He'd spent the past eight years working with career cops whose lives depended on their ability to read people. And most of them didn't come close to her aptitude.

"What's wrong?" she asked again, her voice rising to a squeak as she wrung her fingers together. "Is the store losing money and I didn't realize it?"

"No. I mean, I don't know, I haven't started poking into your books yet," he told her. Giving a quick flick of the mouse pad, he gestured. "I need your password to get into the program."

"Ooooh." She reached around, angling the laptop and tapping a few keys, then trailed her hand over the back of his. He felt tingles, freaking tingles, from his fingers to the tip of his dick. It was as if she had some special power or something.

"Have at it," she told him, offering another warm smile before turning back to her naked-angel statue and boxes of stuff. "There are cookies there in that box, too. Help yourself."

He glanced at the box of Decadently Orgasmic Double-Chocolate Delights. Homemade horny treats. Curious, he flipped the lid and tasted one.

Delicious.

As Pandora restocked, tidied and replenished the bookcases and swept the floor, she kept up a steady stream of chatter. Caleb was alternately intrigued, amused and filled with an alien sense of comfort.

All the while, he invaded her privacy in horrible and disgusting ways, poking into all her files, opening her emails and reading her OneNote journal of store plans. He scrolled through the photo album, he checked her recycle bin and he surreptitiously jotted down names and numbers. He also ate her entire box of cookies.

The only loose end he was seeing was Fifi, though. But as far as he knew, she'd been employed at Moonspun off and on for years. He'd dig deeper into her history later, but from what he'd seen in the reports Hunter sent, she had a few financial issues and had been caught with the wrong crowd from time to time. However, she had no record and no real criminal ties.

Done with the laptop, he closed the lid. And gave thanks that Pandora was one of those organized, ethical people who kept their work and private computers completely separate. Because her work computer was clean, and he hadn't had the opportunity—i.e., had to force himself—to look through her private files. Poking into her private emails and photos would feel really grimy. As opposed to just slightly nauseating.

"So how's it looking?" she asked as she came out of the storeroom.

It?

His conscience? That was looking like shit.

But he figured she wasn't interested in that. And if he played his cards right, she never had to know that he was so far beneath her in terms of moral values that he should be eating worms.

"The store's doing great. I'm impressed at how low you keep your overhead," he commented, bringing up the only area left that might offer an opening for drug sales through her store. Unrealistic, of course, but once he'd crossed it off the list, he could tell Hunter this was definitely a closed door.

"Overhead?"

"Yeah. You don't have a big employee list. Just you and Fifi, right?"

"Well, yeah. Until tomorrow."

"Beg pardon?"

"Fifi thought we were going a little crazy with how busy it's been. Without knowing exactly how solid we were financially, I wasn't sure about hiring, but she convinced me that her friend Russ would be willing to work just the lunch shift while the café is open, and that he was cool with the fact that the job will end after Christmas." She gave a little shoulder wiggle and added, "Isn't that lucky?"

Caleb sighed. Of course she'd hired someone. She, and Fifi, who had a maxed-out VISA card and rent issues.

"Yep. That's lucky, all right." Bad luck, though. While he hadn't found anything to point fingers, he couldn't in good conscience cross the store off, either. Not until he'd checked out everyone.

"I guess I need to figure out how to add him to the payroll program, don't I?" she asked, biting her lip and giving Caleb the cutest eyelash-batting look that just screamed pretty please.

178 SEX, LIES AND MISTLETOE

"I can do that," he offered, feeling like ten times the jerk because she looked so grateful.

"His application is back in the storeroom," she said, hurrying around the counter and stepping over the blanket of black furry cat lying in the doorway.

Since he couldn't have manufactured a better excuse to poke around in her storeroom, no pun intended, Caleb sighed and followed her. The cat lifted his fluffy black head and gave Caleb a long, narrowed look that made him want to hunch his shoulders and apologize.

God, it was time to get out of this business. Now a cat was calling him out on his bullshit.

"This is a storeroom?" Caleb asked, his eyes wide as he stepped into the tiny room. It was maybe eight-by-eight, with shelves lining three walls, boxes stacked in what he assumed were organized piles and a desk shoved in the back.

With a little squeak, Pandora turned to face him. Hand pressed to her chest, she laughed at herself. "I didn't realize you'd followed me."

He knew he shouldn't be here. He knew it was every kind of wrong to pursue her when she was under investigation. But, dammit, he'd already had a taste and now he was addicted. She was delicious. And he wanted more.

Caleb tried to justify it. He told himself he wasn't officially on the job. He argued that he'd already investigated her enough to know she was clean.

It was all bullshit.

But it was still good enough for him.

"The view wasn't as nice without you out there."

He loved how the color warmed her cheeks, bring-

ing out the red highlights in her hair and making her
eyes sparkle even brighter.

"I like it in here," he commented, stepping into the
tight space and crowding her against the desk.

"Cassiopeia used this as an office," she said, gesturing over her shoulder to indicate the desk and file
cabinet. She sounded a little breathless, though. Good.
He liked the idea of taking her breath away. "She, um,
she stored most of the stock in the back room. But, you
know, I turned it into the café."

Her eyes were huge, so huge he could see the brown
rim around the green irises. Her lashes, thick and black,
swept down to hide her eyes. But he'd seen the desire
in those hazel depths. Which was all the permission
he needed.

Caleb took that last step. The one that brought
his body within inches of hers. Hot, welcoming and
so freaking soft she made his head spin, her curves
melded into the hard planes of his chest.

Pandora tilted her head back so her hair swept over
his wrists. Her hands slipped over his shoulders and
she gave him a saucy wink.

"So you like tight spaces, do you?"

And just like that, his brain short-circuited. Caleb
knew he was on the job here—even if he wasn't exactly
'on the job.' He knew there was a specific purpose to
his being in this office, which was to find proof that
would eliminate Pandora from suspicion so he could go
back to happily enjoying the delights of her company
without guilt. He should be looking for the job application so he could eliminate the new guy as a suspect.

But all he could see was Pandora, her hazel eyes

laughing up at him. Her smile, so wide and amused. Her. Just her.

When had she gained so much power over him?

He had to get the hell out of here. Years of living on the edge of his nerves had honed his awareness razor-sharp. He knew when he was in trouble. He knew when he was in danger. And he knew when things had the potential to get freaking scary.

This situation? It was all three.

"Are you hungry?" Pandora asked, running her tongue over the fullness of her lower lip. "Did you want another…cookie?"

He didn't think she meant those delicious chocolate treats he'd eaten earlier. But he didn't care any longer. All he wanted was her. She was worth whatever problems he had to face—on the case, or with his conscience.

"I'm starving," he said. Then he gave in to the desperate need and skimmed his fingers down to gather the material of her skirt. Inch by inch, he pulled it higher, baring the deliciously soft skin of her thighs. "Another round with my boots on?"

"It's going to have to be, since I don't think you're going to have time to take them off," she mused, trailing her hands down to his belt buckle and having her way with it.

Her mouth met his with fervor, her tongue challenging his. She had his jeans unzipped and his dick free before he could do more than groan.

Suddenly desperate, he grasped her waist and lifted her onto the desk. His fingers found her wet, hot core, stroking her through the soft fabric of her panties. Impatient, needing more, he ripped the material away.

Her response was half laugh, half moan. And all delight.

Not sure he could stand much more of her fingers' wicked dance over his straining erection, he grabbed a condom from his pocket and sheathed himself.

His fingers returned to her soft folds, but she wasn't having any of that foreplay crap. Pandora grasped his hips, slid forward on the desk and rotated her hips so her wet heat stroked him.

Losing his mind, Caleb plunged.

It felt incredible. Her body, the power of the passion between them, the need.

Desperate for release, his eyes locked on Pandora's as he pounded into her. She didn't look away. Even as her eyes fogged, as she panted and started keening excited cries of her orgasm, she kept her gaze on his.

It was the most incredible experience of his life. Passionate, raw and emotional.

Terrified and exhilarated at the same time, he gave himself over to the pleasure of her body. His orgasm slammed him hard, exploding out of control. He shouted his pleasure, then, his face buried in the sweet scent of her shoulder, he tried to catch his breath. And restart his brain.

Because while he might not have a clue what he was going to do about the case, he did know one thing for damn sure.

He was in trouble.

And he liked it.

Ten minutes later, Caleb still couldn't think straight.

He'd barely had the presence of mind to slip that job application in his pocket while she wasn't looking. He could check into the new employee later, then slip it behind the desk tomorrow. She'd never know.

"Thanks for the, um, help with my books," Pandora said with a laugh as she gathered her purse, keys and coat in preparation for closing up shop for the night.

He held her long suede coat so she could slide her arms into the sleeves.

"Ready to party?" he said, lifting the silky swing of her hair aside so he could brush a kiss over the back of her neck. God, he couldn't get enough of her. She was like a drug, addicting and delicious. And as far as he could tell, without any debilitating side effects.

"I have to say I feel a little weird going to a party with no undies," she said with a naughty glance over her shoulder. "Even weirder when it's your dad's party."

He wanted to tell her they'd skip it. He'd much rather go back to her place. Or to his hotel room with that big claw-foot tub. He wasn't a foofy bath kind of guy, but he could totally imagine Pandora lounging there, surrounded by steam and frothy bubbles.

But he had a job to do. He'd identified most of the dealers in town by now, so he needed to see if any showed up. And find out who they were hanging out with if they were there.

"We'll just stop in. Thirty minutes, tops," he said. That's all he'd need to gauge the players and gather a few names. "And if we're there too long, all you have to do is whisper in my ear a reminder of your lack of panties, and we'll be out the door in an instant."

Pandora's laugh was low and husky, making him

wish like hell that he could toss this whole mess aside and just focus on getting on with his damn life.

As soon as this case was solved, he was through. He had no clue what he'd be doing. He didn't even know where he'd be doing it, although Black Oak offered some serious temptation. Not quite enough to allay the issues it presented, though.

"You sure you don't want to just skip the party and get right to the lack of panties," Pandora said, only sounding as if she was half teasing as she gathered her purse and gave the cats each a cuddle.

"I want to," he said in an embarrassingly fervent tone. Caleb coughed, trying to clear the dorkiness from his throat. "It sounds crazy, but I feel like I have to stop in. I can't figure out what I'm doing until I figure out where things are at with my father. Not just for tonight, but in the big picture, you know."

Pandora paused in the act of pulling catnip-filled toys out a little mesh bag and tossing them around the room for Paulie and Bonnie to entertain themselves through the night. "Big picture?"

"Yeah." Caleb felt like an ass, but still something forced him to say, "I figure it's time we made our peace. Or at least found some neutral ground. See if we can both handle being in the same town for a length of time."

An earless furry bunny dangling from one hand, Pandora pressed the other to her lips for just a second, as if she was trying to hold back a slew of questions. There was just as much worry and hesitation in her eyes as there was curiosity and delight. He wasn't quite sure what to make of that.

"By length of time, do you mean the week left until Christmas?" she asked hesitantly.

While she waited, her eyes all huge and sexy, Bonnie, the black-and-white cat, padded across the floor and started batting the bunny with her paw. When Pandora didn't respond to the command to play, the cat batted harder, sending the toy flying from Pandora's fingers across the room. Both cats bounded after the furry treat.

"I'm..." He trailed off. How did he answer? He didn't want to get her hopes up. He wasn't the kind of guy who made promises. Not even ones he was pretty sure he could keep.

"Don't," she said, interrupting his mental struggle. She crossed over and took his hands. "Please, I didn't mean to make you uncomfortable. I should warn you, though, that the town grapevine is working overtime and you're the main topic. So if you stay, that's only going to get worse."

It wasn't the town he needed to worry about, he realized as he looked into those heavily fringed eyes. It was Pandora. She was more dangerous than an arsenal of AK-47s. At least, she was to his once happily frozen heart.

"Sweetheart, I honestly don't know where I'm going to be, or where I want to be, in two weeks. But I do know I'm exactly where I want to be right this minute."

Pandora's eyes were huge and vulnerable. He'd like to think it was because of his heartfelt declaration. But there was something else there, lurking. Something that made his gut clench. Because beneath the nerves and sweetness there was a fear. Like she was afraid of him sticking for too long. Afraid of what he'd find out.

"Pandora?" he prodded. "Is there something you want to tell me?"

He didn't know if he was hoping more that she would, or that she wouldn't.

"You're exactly where I want you to be, too," she finally murmured. Whether that was true or not, he didn't know. But he was positive it wasn't what she'd been thinking about.

But before he could push, she rose on tiptoe, and, even as nerves simmered in her eyes, brushed a soft kiss over his lips.

It was as if she'd flipped a switch that only she knew existed. His body went on instant hard-on alert, and his mind absolutely shut down. All he wanted was her. All he could taste, could think of, cared about, was her.

More and more of her.

He slanted his mouth to the side, taking their kiss deeper with one swift slide of his tongue.

His fingers still entwined with hers, Caleb let his hands drop, then wrapped both their arms around her waist to pull her tighter, effectively trapping her soft curves against the hard, craving planes of his body.

Why the hell was she wearing this bulky coat? All he wanted, now and for as long as it lasted, was to get her naked.

Lost in the pleasure of her mouth, Caleb didn't hear the key in the door until a loud clatter of the chimes hit a discordant note. Pulling her lips from his, Pandora jumped, blinking the sexual glow out of her eyes as she looked over his shoulder toward whoever had come in.

Her jaw dropped and her face turned bright red even as embarrassment filled her eyes.

"Hello, Mother."

CHAPTER TEN

"WELL, DARLING?" CASSIOPEIA said as she settled comfortably on Pandora's couch and sipped chamomile tea. "It looks like you have a lot to share. When did you get involved with the likes of Caleb Black? And more important, why didn't you ever mention him in your emails? I'd have stayed away a few extra days if I'd known you had that kind of entertainment on tap."

That entertainment, as Cassiopeia called him, had barely stuck around long enough for introductions before he'd hightailed it out of the store for his father's party.

Now, twenty minutes after Cassiopeia's shocking arrival, she was soothing her travel woes with tea while Pandora resisted the urge to pace.

"I've got so much to tell you. I shared the basics in our emails, but things are really going great at the store," she said, even as a part of her wondered if she hurried her mother along, could she catch Caleb at the party. The other part of her, the one that bwawked like a chicken, was glad her mother's arrival had given her an excuse to keep their relationship quiet for a little longer. Sort of. Nothing was ever hidden from Cassiopeia.

As if reading her mind, her mother gestured with her teacup.

"I'd rather talk about the man," Cassiopeia said with a smile too wicked for someone's mother.

"I'd rather not," Pandora decided. Not while she was so mixed up over the issue. "Let's focus on the store instead, okay? Before we left, I printed out the financial statements. Do you want to see them? I saved the store, Mom."

She felt a little giddy saying that. As if she was tempting fate. But she was so excited she had to share. And hoped, like crazy, that her mom would be proud.

"I mean, it's obviously too early to tell for sure, but I'm betting the café and the aphrodisiacs stay solid, long-term."

"Most likely," Cassiopeia agreed with a shrug that seemed more disinterested than dismissive.

"Don't you care?" Pandora frowned, trying to read her mother. Calm and centered, as always. A little worn-out, which wasn't surprising since it was a long trip from Sedona. But shouldn't there be some relief? Some joy at the prospect of keeping the store a success? Some pride in her only child?

"Darling, of course I care. The café is a brilliant idea and you've done a wonderful job. I knew if left to your own devices, you'd come up with something."

Her mother's smile widened, a self-satisfied look just this side of gloating in her eyes.

"You left to force my hand?" Pandora realized, almost breathless from the shock.

"Well, the store *was* in trouble, of course. And I was having a heck of a time figuring out how to keep things afloat and still meet my commitment in Sedona. But I imagine I could have probably muddled through,

canceled the appearance and crossed my fingers until
the spring bus tour if I'd had to." Cassiopeia waved a
heavily bejeweled hand as if her manipulation didn't
matter. "But the point is, I didn't have to. Thanks to
your return to Black Oak, and your clever café idea,
we're in wonderful shape for the first time in years."

"That was a huge risk to take if you didn't have to,"
Pandora pointed out, trying to calm her sudden jitters.
"I could have ruined the store. What if I'd failed?"

"Then you'd fail," Cassiopeia said with a shrug.

"You'd risk the family legacy to teach me a lesson?"

"The family legacy is talent, dear. It's intuition. It's
not a building and a bunch of candles and crystals."

Pandora choked down the urge to scream. She knew
what the hell to do with the shop, dammit. But she
didn't have any talent. So where did that leave her?
She'd thought she'd finally contributed to the family
name. That she'd done something worthy of the women
who'd come before her.

"Darling, you make it so hard on yourself. Instead
of embracing hope, which will help you realize your
gift, you spend all your time chasing the Furies, trying to corral misery before it causes hurt," Cassiopeia
said, launching into one of her favorite stories. In the
Easton family, they didn't believe in choosing a name
until they'd discovered the newborn's personality. Pandora had been Baby Girl for eight months until the
gods, fate and the tarot cards had revealed her destiny
to Cassiopeia. "You need to quit worrying about those
miseries, darling. Instead, focus on joy. That's the only
way you'll find the right path."

With that, Cassiopeia rose and glided to the kitchen

to set her teacup in the sink, returned to kiss the top of her silently fuming daughter's head and left.

An hour later, frustrated tears still trickled down Pandora's cheeks. She didn't even answer when someone knocked tentatively on her door. Eleven o'clock on a Sunday night, it could only be one person. And she was too worked up to deal with her mother twice in one day.

The knock sounded again, a little louder this time.

Who the hell needed to chase misery when it was always right there, tapping her on the shoulder and reminding her that she didn't measure up. That she was a waste of her family name. Ungifted and unworthy.

The urge to run away—again—made her body quiver. But unlike her escape when she'd been eighteen, this time she didn't have anywhere to go. Nor did she still have that cocky faith that she could prove to her mother, her grandmother and everyone else in Black Oak that she could be a success without the family gift.

Pounding replaced the tentative knock.

"Fine," she huffed, jumping to her feet.

Her mother wouldn't give up. She had probably headed home to gather some crystals and cards, determined to help her daughter find that damned path she always harped on.

"What?" Pandora snapped as she threw open the door.

The bitter cold from the icy rain swept over her bare toes as she stared.

"Oh."

It wasn't Cassiopeia on her doorstep.

It was a delicious-looking chocolate éclair with what

looked like a tub of ice cream and, if she wasn't mistaken, hot-fudge sauce.

Her eyes met Caleb's golden gaze.

"I thought you could use a sugar rush," he said, lifting the dessert a little higher. "It comes with, or without, a second spoon."

She hesitated. Attention was a good thing, but attention while she was having a tantrum? Hardly something she wanted Caleb to remember her for.

"I'm not very good company right now," she demurred, rubbing her hands over the velvet of her skirt and wishing she were wearing sweatpants and a baggy T-shirt. Something innocuous to hide behind. Although, if she was going to do some wishing, she should put all her falling stars and birthday candles toward having washed her tear-stained face instead of answering the door looking like a sad raccoon.

"I'm not looking for entertainment," Caleb said, shrugging before leaning one broad shoulder against the door frame. Catching the arch look she shot him, he grinned. "I'm not looking for that, either."

"Oh, really?"

"Well, I wouldn't say no if you decided to strip naked and paint my name across your body in this fudge sauce before inviting me to lick it off." He waited for Pandora's laugh before continuing, "But that's not what this is about. I'm just here as…as…"

Pandora swallowed hard to get past the lump of emotions suddenly clogging her throat. "As?"

"As a friend."

The only thing that kept the tears from leaking down her face was fear of adding another layer to the raccoon effect. Instead, Pandora sniffed surreptitiously and stepped aside to let him in.

"How'd you know I needed a friend tonight?" she asked as Caleb crossed the room. "Better yet, how'd you know my mother wasn't still here?"

"She stopped by the party." He gave her a quick look, something shuttered in his eyes making her wonder if he'd had his own parental confrontation. "She looked a little stressed herself, so I figured I'd check on you."

So Cassiopeia had decided to skip the crystals and cards and had sent in a sexy ego boost instead. Too dejected to even fake being a good hostess, Pandora dumped two bowls on the table. Caleb, jacket gone and his shirtsleeves rolled up, scooped big fat mounds of vanilla-bean ice cream into them.

Her frustration and hurt feelings shifted, sliding into second place behind her sudden urge to lick hot fudge off his knuckle. Her body warmed, excitement stirring at the sight of Caleb's hands. So strong. So big. So wonderfully good at sending her into a fog of desire where she could forget everything except him and the pleasure he brought.

"What?" he said, noting her stare.

"Just realizing something," she said, color warming her cheeks.

"Again... What?"

"You have magic hands," Pandora admitted despite her embarrassment. "I knew they felt incredible. I've had plenty of proof of their copious talents. But I didn't realize until just now that they are magic."

Caleb's grin was huge as he plopped sloppy globs of

whipped cream on top of the fudge-covered ice cream. "Magic, huh?"

"Yep." Pandora pulled one of the bowls toward her, grabbing a spoon with the other hand.

She suddenly felt a million times better.

"Tell me more," he invited, stashing what was left of dessert in the freezer. He joined her at the table, but didn't sit.

"More, hmm?" she said, giving him a slow, teasing smile as she licked hot fudge off her spoon. The rich, bittersweet flavor slid down her throat. "How about we make it a show-and-tell kind of thing?"

His wicked smile didn't change, but his eyes did. They sharpened and heated at the same time. He reached out a hand, pulling her to her feet. Then he scooped up his bowl, handing her the other one, and led the way out of the kitchen.

"We're eating in bed?" she teased as excitement spun and swirled like a snowflake inside her, buffeting through her system and making her breathless with need.

"Too messy," he deemed, continuing through the living room, one hand wrapped around hers to keep her close. He stopped at the bathroom and glanced in, gave a decisive nod, then turned to her with an arched brow. "Do you have a blanket you don't mind getting sticky?"

"Sticky?"

"Babe, even if I paint as carefully as I can, my magic hands might drip a little bit before I can lick this hot fudge off your naked body."

"That's going to make a mess," she said, not really caring.

"That's what bubble bath is for," he assured her. "I assume you have bubbles."

Bubbles?

Ten minutes ago she'd been wallowing in misery, sure her life sucked hard. And now? Now she had Caleb, with his tub of vanilla ice cream, his gorgeous smile and an intuitive understanding of her that nobody, not even her best friend, had ever had.

He made her feel so many things. Sexual and passionate. Exciting and fun. Brave and strong and interesting.

But most of all, he made her feel safe. Like it was okay to stand in the middle of the room and make a fool of herself. Like he accepted and appreciated her. All of her.

And now he wanted to feed her dessert, then take a bubble bath with her. Yes, it was sexual. But she knew it was more than that. She could see it in his body language. In the set of his shoulders and the concern on his face.

He was doing it to make her feel better.

"I do have bubbles," she said, trying not to giggle at the image of the ultramasculine Caleb Black surrounded by frothy floral-scented bubbles.

And from the terrified nerves jumping through her system at her realization. She was in love with him.

That wasn't the plan. It was crazy. It was a huge mistake. And she didn't care. She wasn't going to let herself. Not right now. It might not be her path, but it was a wonderful place to be. And just for now, she was going to give herself the gift of enjoying it.

"And I'll be happy to share my bubbles with you,"

she assured him as she grabbed a blanket off the couch and laid it in front of the Christmas tree. "Right after we find out who can get whom stickier."

"YOU SMELL LIKE FLOWERS," Fifi observed as Pandora swept into the store the next day. "Is that a new perfume?"

"Bubble bath," she told the blonde, winking. "I'm going to get started on the cookies and desserts for today's lunch crowd, okay? Can you handle the store yourself?"

"Russ is in soon, I'll be fine," Fifi assured her.

Pandora winced. She'd forgotten Russ was starting today. Adding that to her to-do list, she headed back to the café and its tiny kitchen. As she went, though, she heard the whispers start.

Like a wave, the words flowed toward her, softly at first, then crashing in a big splash. *Caleb Black. Dumped the poor sweet sheriff. What could she be thinking? Poor mother, had to come home to fix it.*

Pandora's feet froze on the threshold of the café. A part of her wanted to turn around and face the gossips. To insist they say it to her face so she could refute their words. The rest of her wanted to run into the back room as fast as she could, tugging her hair as she went to relieve the pressure on her brain.

She wasn't going to think about it, she decided as she forced her feet to move. She couldn't. Her mother had told her to choose a path and this was the one she was on. She was in love with Caleb Black. And if that meant dealing with gossip, then she'd deal.

Washing her hands, she let the water trickle over her

skin, warming her and easing the tension. Eyes closed, she took some deep breaths and tried to center herself.

Out the kitchen window, a movement caught her eye. Three scruffy-looking guys were arguing in the alley. She frowned, realizing one of them was Russ. What was he doing back there?

Then one of them took a swing at another. She gasped, stepping back and cringing. Before she could go get the phone to call Tobias for help, a fourth guy waded in.

Pandora's heart calmed. Sheriff Kendall. He'd deal with it. Remembering her mother's warning about chasing miseries, she turned away. She didn't want to see, hear or experience anything else that stirred up tension, so she ignored the rest of the drama and got to work. She had cookies to bake, sandwiches to prep and éclairs to pipe.

An hour later, she was still in her Zen mood as she arranged half the cookies on a large silver platter and the others in to-go boxes.

"Darling, this is wonderful," her mother drawled as she swept into the tiny kitchen, mingling the scent of peanut butter and chocolate with the aroma of Chanel and the nag champa incense she always burned at home. "I love the ambience. And these tables are so adorable. It's so clever, the way you've used the red soy candles in the dish of rose quartz. Love and lust, with just enough liking to keep things from getting sticky, hmm?"

Her Zen shot all to hell, Pandora just shrugged. She knew she was pouting like a brat, but she didn't want to face her mother yet. She'd been happily distracted by Caleb. Incredible sex and the realization that she was falling in love was enough for any girl to handle for one morning, wasn't it?

"Darling, don't be in a snit. You came home for a reason, didn't you?" As soon as Pandora opened her mouth to say that yes, she'd come home because she needed a job, Cassiopeia waved her hand. "And it had nothing to do with that drama you'd fallen into. That was just an excuse. A crossroads, if you'd like. It was time for you to face your destiny, and fate obviously felt you needed a nudge to get you to do so."

"Right. Being under police suspicion, used by the man I was sleeping with and then fired from my job were all the work of fate," Pandora snipped.

"Of course not. Those were all the result of your choices, dear. Not bad or good choices, mind you. Simply ones you made without stopping to listen to your intuition. Fate just used them to move you along."

"Mom, stop," Pandora barked, perilously close to tears again. Was anyone on earth as frustrating as her mother? "I obviously have no intuition. So will you please let it go? I'm never going to be what you'd like. I wish you'd just accept that I'm a failure as an Easton so we can both relax."

Stepping back so fast her rust-and-hunter-green caftan caught on the corner of the counter, Cassiopeia gave a shocked gasp and slapped her hand over her heart. Even though her shoulders were tense with anger and her stomach was tight with stress, Pandora almost giggled. Nobody did the drama show quite like her momma.

"A failure? That's ridiculous," Cassiopeia snapped.

She lifted her chin so her red curls swept over her shoulders, and crossed her arms over her chest in the same gesture Pandora herself used when she was upset. "Let's not confuse things here, young lady. You're not angry with me."

"No? Care to bet on that?"

"You're angry with yourself. And with good reason. You can't blame me for your choices, Pandora. Or for your inability to step up and accept responsibility for making them."

Pandora felt as if she'd just been punched in the gut and couldn't find her own breath. Yes, she'd made a mistake. But the mistake was that she'd trusted the wrong person. That she'd fallen in love with the idea of love, and overlooked the warning signs. Blinking tears away, she wanted to yell that she wasn't irresponsible. But her throat was too tight to get the words out.

"Until you trust yourself, you'll never see what's right in front of you," Cassiopeia said with a regal toss of her curls. "You're too busy being scared, running and doubting. And, sadly, placing blame instead of having faith in yourself."

"You have no idea what it's like," Pandora snapped. Fury was red, hazing her vision and letting truths fly that she'd spent most of her life hiding from. "I grew up in the shadow of your reputation."

"And you have a problem with my reputation?" Behind the haughtily raised brows and arch tone, Pandora heard a hint of hurt. But the words were already tumbling off her tongue and she couldn't quite figure out how to grab them back.

"I couldn't live up to your reputation, Mother. Nobody could. Especially not with everyone in town poking and judging me, and you always prodding me to find something that we both know damn well doesn't exist."

Cassiopeia sagged. As though someone had let the air out of her, her shoulders, face and chin drooped. She gave a huge sigh, then shook her head as if defeated.

"I can't do this again, Pandora. You refuse to hear me. You snub my guidance while hiding behind your insecurities." She swept a hand through her hair, leaving the curls a messy tangle around a face that suddenly looked older than her years. "Perhaps it's my fault. Not, as you seem to think, for being myself. I see nothing wrong with being the best I can and embracing my strengths. But I must have gone wrong somewhere if you're so afraid of life that you have to blame me."

Guilt was so bitter on Pandora's tongue she couldn't get any words past it. Just as well, since she had no idea what the words would be.

"I'm going home," her mother declared. "When you're ready to talk…if you're ready to talk, I'll be there for you."

Pandora didn't know if she wanted to call her back, to try to fix the mess they'd left splattered between them. Or if she wanted a little time and distance, at least until she figured out what she wanted to say.

But, as usual, it wasn't up to her. Her mother swept from the room, taking all the choices with her.

"So what's the deal? You're finally willing to talk? Or are you just stopping by to check out the bikes?"

Hands shoved in the front pockets of his jeans,

Caleb grimaced at his father's words. He looked around the showroom of the bike shop, noting the gleaming chrome of the custom hogs and a few Indians, and shrugged. "They are pretty sweet-looking bikes."

"Yeah, they are," Tobias agreed. He patted the diamond-tucked leather of one seat and nodded. "Best game in town, too. I get the parts dirt cheap, Lucas puts them together for a song and I sell them at a profit of about one, one-fifty percent."

"Sounds like a legit business to me."

"I told you, son. I've gone straight."

"Why do I find that hard to believe?" He wanted to. He'd spent most of his childhood wishing and hoping to hear his dad say those words. Hell, the last thing he'd told his old man before he'd left for college was that he wasn't coming home until the guy was clean. But when Tobias had called two years back with that same claim, Caleb hadn't bought it.

And now?

"There's plenty of challenge in making this place turn a profit. Between figuring out how to lure in the gullible and get them to open their wallets for a custom bike, special maintenance plans, yearly trade-ins and upgrades, I'm finding plenty to do."

"As challenging as scamming the head of a national bank out of five hundred large? How does customer service stack against selling bridge investments?" Caleb looked around the shop, noting that like everything his father owned, it was pristine, upscale and just a little edgy. "Does monthly inventory give you the same thrill as selling a fake Renoir to a reclusive art buff?"

Tobias's grin, so much like Caleb's own, flashed as he dropped onto a long, glittery red Naugahyde bench that spanned the center of the showroom. "Those were good times, I have to admit. But these are, too. The key to anything in life is to have fun with it, Caleb. If you're enjoying what you do, you'll live a happy, fulfilled life."

One of the pearls of wisdom Tobias had shared many a time with his children over the years. And frustratingly enough, the one that had been ricocheting around Caleb's head for the least year as he'd fought burnout and disenchantment.

"So tell me the truth, son. Why are you really here?"

"To see your shop." Caleb sidestepped. Then he shoved his hands into his pockets and sighed. Or to figure out who he really was, or some stupid touchy-feely thing like that.

Pulling his face in consideration, Tobias gave a slow nod. He got to his feet and walked over, patting Caleb on the shoulder before stepping around him and heading toward the back room.

Since that's the part of the shop Caleb really wanted to see, he followed.

The room was huge, with a mechanic's bench against one wall, toolboxes and an air compressor along another. He noted an open door leading to a bathroom.

"Here, have a cookie," Tobias invited, gesturing to a tray as he sat down at a small table. "The pretty little gal across the alley made them. Supposed to do wonders for your sex drive."

"I hear yours is doing wonders on its own. Isn't

dating a woman your daughter's age something of a cliché?"

Tobias's grin was wide and wicked. He tilted his chair back, balancing on two spindle legs and considered the cookie in his hand as if he'd find the answer in one of the chocolate chips.

"Now, why are you really here? You're ready to quit that misguided cop job?"

Caleb realized that he didn't even feel surprise at Tobias's insight. The man was an expert. At reading people, at twisting situations, at understanding human nature. And as much as Caleb might have wished otherwise over the past thirty years, the old guy was his father.

"I think I'm done," he heard himself admit. Grimacing, he took a cookie. Maybe chewing would give him time to censor his mouth.

"I followed your career, son. You did yourself, and me, proud. Whatever you do next, I'm sure you'll be just as good."

Overcome with an emotion he couldn't quite identify, Caleb looked away. How odd was it that he'd just realized that no matter what his choices, no matter what he'd done in his life, his father had always believed in him.

He didn't know what the hell to do with that.

Before he could figure it out, something outside the small, barred window overlooking the alley caught his eye. Caleb ambled over, looking out just in time to watch two dirtbags exchange a fat wad of cash for several large pill bottles. He'd been right. This was the main drop spot. But why here?

"Do you have storage in the back?" he asked over his shoulder.

Tobias took his time selecting another cookie before he met Caleb's eyes. "Nope. But the pretty little gal does."

Son of a bitch. Pain, fury and disappointment all pounded through Caleb. Son of a freaking bitch.

How could it be Pandora? He felt like scum just thinking of her and drugs in the same thought. But this? They were using her storage unit, her store. Did she have a clue? Whether she did or not, this was going to be a major problem for her.

Caleb dropped his head against the window and closed his eyes, fury and despair ripping through him.

He'd reluctantly come home to clear his father's dubious name. But he didn't want to do it at the expense of the woman he loved.

CHAPTER ELEVEN

CALEB CLICKED OPEN the file of mug shots Hunter had emailed. Impressed, despite himself, he had to admit the FBI had better toys than he'd had access to with the DEA. Within an hour of calling Hunter with a report of what he'd seen, a laptop had been delivered to his hotel, access codes had been texted to his cell phone and he'd had the files of eight guys who fit the description of both dudes he'd seen selling behind Pandora's store.

Throw in Russ, whose identity didn't match the info on his job application, and Caleb figured he'd nailed down the drug ring's middle-management team.

What he didn't have yet was the person calling the shots.

He took a drink of coffee, letting the flavor mingle with the rest of the bitterness he'd been tasting since he realized that the woman he was crazy for might be a criminal.

He'd been so sure she was clean. Just as he'd been sure Tobias was clean. He'd only dug into her computer files so he could tell Hunter that he'd done a thorough job.

Then he'd read the files Hunter had emailed detailing the illegal activities of her drug-dispensing ex and her part in his little prescription ring. And the note Hunter had attached warning Caleb not to do anything stupid.

What a pal.

Caleb considered pounding his head on the wall a few times, but figured he couldn't afford the possible loss of more brain cells.

Instead, he was going to ID the two guys, round them up and scare the crap out of them. Sooner or later, someone would spill a name. Or the boss would come looking for them.

Just as he started scrolling through the faces, there was a knock on his door.

He considered ignoring it. He wanted to ID this guy while the face was still fresh in his head. Then, he wanted to hit something—anything—hard, until it broke into a million pieces and left his knuckles bloody and raw.

But whoever was at the door might have another package from Hunter. And Caleb was definitely curious to see what other toys his old friend had to offer.

As a precaution, he closed the file, shut down the program and turned off the laptop. It was a secure machine, requiring two passwords, his own and the one Hunter had provided, to start it or pull it out of the hibernation it'd enter if left idle for more than thirty seconds. But still, it paid to be cautious.

He strode over and pulled the door open.

Well, well.

Not a toy from Hunter, but a toy all the same.

"Pandora," he greeted with a stiff smile.

For a brief second, he missed the old days when he'd

opened the door to gun-toting, drugged-out, murdering dealers looking to take him out.

At least he knew what to do with them.

"Hey," she greeted with a shaky smile. Eyes narrowing, Caleb saw the strain on her face. Her makeup was all smudged and drippy, as if she'd been crying.

Yeah, a strung-out dude pointing a loaded .45 at his face would definitely be easier.

But not as important, he admitted to himself, heaving a heavy sigh.

"What's wrong?" he asked.

"Do you mind if I come in?"

Yes.

He stepped aside anyway.

And tortured himself by breathing deep as she walked past, inhaling her spicy fragrance and wishing he could bury his face in the curve of her neck and see if she tasted as good as she smelled.

Stupid.

Totally freaking stupid.

Because he knew damn well she tasted delicious.

"Are you okay?" he asked after a few seconds of indulging himself by staring at her as she wandered the room. She shouldn't be here. But he couldn't kick her out. Whatever her part in this, even if it wasn't purely innocent, he wanted—needed—this time with her.

"I'm..." She stopped by the window, giving him a pained look over her shoulder. "I had a blowup with my mother. Now I guess I'm confused."

"Parents have that effect," he observed. Finally giving in to the fact that running down the hall to avoid confronting her would be blatantly chickenshit, Caleb shut the door. He didn't cross the room, though. Instead, he leaned his hip against the dresser and watched.

"I know you're probably busy. You're not expecting me. But, well, I thought about going by Kathy's, but her family is in town and it'll be really crowded and loud there. And I just wanted to see if, you know, maybe…"

She trailed off, offering a wincing sort of shrug as she wandered the room nervously.

What was he going to do? Kick her out? Grill her when she was already upset? Yes, he knew that both were perfectly solid methods to deal with a potential drug-dealing mastermind. But, dammit, this was Pandora. And she was upset.

So he'd stay and comfort her. After all, he could be a chickenshit here in his room, too.

"What happened?"

"Confrontations and ugly words and painful truths," she confessed, trailing her fingers over the glossy knotty pine of one of the four posts of the large, quilt-covered bed.

"Sounds like a family reunion to me." Although he and his father had skipped over that part of reunioning. Instead, the old man had watched with laser-sharp eyes as Caleb had stepped to the side of the window so as not to be seen while the drug deal went down. Tobias hadn't said a word, though. He'd just arched one brow and given a jaunty salute when it was over and Caleb had said he had to go.

All that cordial silence had creeped him out.

"Not my family," Pandora said with a stiff smile.

"Usually my mother is dramatic, I'm quiet and we both pretend everything is peachy keen."

She needed to talk. He could see it on her face, hear it in her tone. The previous night she'd needed sex, a little laughter and a chance to forget about everything else.

Caleb sighed, feeling the weight of the world pressing down on him all of a sudden. The sex was probably off-limits while she was a suspect, and the laughter was beyond him.

Dammit, that left talking.

He sucked at talking.

As Pandora poked a finger between the balcony curtains, closed against the night, he sighed again.

Fine.

"Want to have a seat?" he invited.

Her face brightening, she looked around. The choices were the bed or one of two club chairs next to the small table holding the laptop.

He really didn't want her near, either.

"I would, thanks," she said, taking a second to shrug off her thick white coat, laying it and her purse and scarf over one of the chairs. She hesitated, glancing at the bed, then back at his face. Then she squished into the chair alongside her coat.

Caleb walked over, picked up the laptop and moved it to the dresser, then sat across from her.

"So why's it a big deal that you tossed a few truths at your mother?"

"Because she tossed a few right back at me," she said with a wince.

He grinned for the first time in hours. "Don't you hate it when that happens?"

"I do. I had no idea the truth could be so painful. I think it was easier when she blithely pretended to go along with my claims that I was happy with my life."

"Pretending is never good."

"Sure, that's easy for you to say. You're confident enough to say screw you to everyone who doesn't accept you exactly as you are," she said with a rueful sort of laugh.

Cringing, Caleb's gaze shifted toward the door.

Was he? He didn't even know who he was, so how could he expect anyone to accept him at face value? For his entire adult life, hell, most of his life as a whole, he'd played a part.

"I admire that," she continued. She gave him a shy sort of smile and traced designs on her scarf with her finger. "I wish I were more like you. Only, not, you know. Because I really, really like being a girl with you."

He wasn't an expert on this talking thing, but he knew when someone was trying to sidestep to get out of delving into the deeper emotional stuff. And he shouldn't let her get away with it. She was hurting, and she probably should get it all out, talk and vent and spew and whatever the hell else women did to heal.

Miserably uncomfortable now, Caleb wished he'd paid more attention to Maya when she'd done this kind of thing growing up. That girl had always been talking.

"I guess you have a pretty good handle on your life, hmm?" she said, still sidestepping, though now poking her toes into his business. "You and your dad made up, you're free to come and go as you please. Or, you know, stay if you wanted."

Hey, now. Sidestepping was one thing. Poking into his life? Totally not cool. This was about her problems. Not his.

He leaned forward to tell her just that.

"We didn't make up," he heard himself saying, instead.

"But you went to the party?"

"Yeah."

"And didn't you hang out at his shop earlier?"

Caleb's eyes narrowed. Had she seen him while he was watching the drug deal go down? Was this a setup?

"He stopped by for lunch and mentioned what a great visit the two of you had," she continued, now watching her fingers poke through the scarf's fringe instead of meeting his eyes. "He was sweet. Teased me a little about the two of us, and said he liked me."

A hint of color warming her cheeks, she finally glanced up and gave Caleb a tiny smile. The kind that made him think of shy little girls sitting on Santa's lap, feeling like the most special princess in the world for those two minutes.

"He does like you," Caleb said absently, trying to figure out what Tobias was doing. That the old man was up to something was a no-brainer. But why did it involve Pandora? An inkling, a tiny germ of a hint, started poking at the back of Caleb's brain. He couldn't see it clearly yet, but the same instincts that had saved him from multiple bullets told him it was there.

"He's a good guy," she said quietly. Then she wrinkled her nose and asked, "Am I not supposed to say that? I mean, if you guys didn't make up, you probably don't want to hear someone singing his praises, huh?"

"No," Caleb realized. "I don't mind. I mean, he's easy to like."

"He really is," she agreed, reaching over to brush her hand over his. He turned his fingers to capture hers, making her smile. "So is my mother. If you can get past her larger-than-life perfection."

"Is that a bad thing?" he asked, using a method straight out of Witness Grilling 101. Ask open-ended questions that kept the other person guessing as to what you wanted to hear. They were more likely to go with an unscripted gut response.

"Not totally bad. I mean, she's fun and always makes people laugh. She's got flare and talent and, well, she's just so exuberant and alive. She walks in a room and everyone automatically gravitates to her."

"So why are you so unhappy with her?"

She sighed, staring blankly across the room as she considered that question. He noticed that there was now an actual hole in the knitted scarf from her digging at the yarn.

"Because of all those same reasons." Her smile was a little shaky. "I mean, that's a lot to live up to, you know? She's larger than life. People all around the world know who she is. Then they look at me with this puzzled stare, like they are trying to figure out where she went wrong."

Caleb gave a shake of his head.

"What?" she asked.

"You just described me and my dad."

Her laugh was more a puff of air than amusement.

She shook her head. "What are we supposed to do about it?"

He threw his hands in the air. "I don't know. I mean, they do a great job of being who they are."

"I think you do a great job of being who you are, too. So why is not being like them a problem? I don't know about you, but I'm tired of being measured by my mother."

Thin ice. Caleb hesitated before going with his gut. "But I think the only one measuring you by that is, well, you."

There went the sweet look off her face. She pulled back, her eyes narrowed and her lips tight. She looked as if she was seriously considering smacking him with that scarf.

"Me?" she asked in a tone so arch it was worthy of a queen.

"I guess I have an outsider's perspective," he mused. "I see a town that likes you, one that's actually a little defensive of you, if all the warnings I got not to hurt you are anything to go by. I see an intriguing, attractive woman trying her hand at something new and succeeding. A woman who loves cats, cooks like a dream and always has a smile and a warm word for people. Maybe you're not flamboyant and wild, like your mother. But you're just as interesting, and even more beautiful."

Her smile was bright enough to light the room. Caleb shifted uncomfortably in his chair, wanting to duck out until she stopped beaming at him. This gallant thing was more Gabriel's style than his. But he hadn't been able to stand seeing that dejected look on her face.

"So, I didn't bring any treats," Pandora said out of

the blue, nibbling on her lip in a way that made him want to beg for a taste.

"Treats?"

"Yeah. Cookies or chocolate sauce or, well, you know. Aphrodisiacs." She shrugged again, knotting together the frayed pieces of yarn to repair her scarf. "I really didn't intend to come over. I was upset when I left the store and instead of walking home, my feet brought me here. To room seventeen."

Her words ended in a wistful tone he didn't understand. What he did understand was the look in her eyes. Sexy and appreciative. Warm and sweet. God, she was incredible.

Unable to resist, Caleb leaned forward and brushed his lips over hers. She tasted so freaking good. His tongue traced the full pillow of her lower lip, then he nipped lightly.

Her gasp was followed by a low moan of approval. She skimmed the tips of her fingers over his jaw, whisper-soft and so gentle. It was all he could do not to grab her by the waist and carry her over to the bed.

Caleb pulled away and jumped to his feet. Pacing, he shoved one hand through his hair.

What was he doing? She was the prime suspect in an FBI drug case. He should at least settle a few questions before he settled himself between her thighs.

"I can go," she said quietly, her hand dropping away from the buttons of her silk top.

It killed him to see that hurt on her face. To hear the self-protective distance in her tone.

It really all came down to faith.

He'd told Hunter he was sure his old man was innocent. But a part of him, the part that knew that there was a potential criminal in everyone, had wondered.

But Pandora? At the moment, all evidence pointed toward her. With what he'd seen, what he knew and what he'd heard, he'd have felt solid making an arrest.

But his instincts said otherwise. They said she was everything he'd ever wanted in a woman. Sweet and hot and adventurous. And, dammit, innocent.

So while he might be suffering from plenty of burnout and his instincts were raw nerves at this point, he had to listen to them. Because without that, he was nothing.

He'd just have to prove the evidence wrong.

PANDORA WOKE THE NEXT morning with a feeling of absolute contentment. Eyes still closed, she stretched on the lavender-scented sheets and gave a deep sigh of satisfaction.

Yum. What a delicious night.

Shifting to the pillow next to her, she smiled and slowly opened her eyes. Caleb stared back at her, his gold eyes intense and, if she read him right, concerned. Why?

"Hi," she murmured, shifting back a little to get a better look at him. Stiff shoulders, jaw tight. He seemed distant, as if a part of him wasn't even here in bed with her.

Pandora shivered a little, then ran her tongue over her lower lip. What was going on?

But before she could ask, someone knocked on the door.

"Company?" she asked quietly, suddenly realizing

she was naked except for the soft rays of morning light. She grabbed the sheet and quilt and pulled them higher.

"Probably Mrs. Mac with another delivery. Or muffins. She thinks I'm going to starve if I don't start each day with a half-dozen blueberry crumbles."

He sounded normal. But he still looked…fake.

"Hang on," he said, shifting out of bed and pulling on jeans, commando-style. He zipped them, but didn't bother with the snap.

Pandora's mouth watered. God, he was gorgeous. Sleek, tanned skin. That wolf tattoo crawling down his shoulder to growl from the gorgeous muscles of his upper arms. She wanted to nibble her way down the small of his back, then bite him. Right there on the butt.

Grinning to herself, she shifted to a more comfy position. Starting the day with muffins and, hopefully, morning sex was a definite positive in her books.

"I could—"

"No," he said, shaking his head as he reached for the doorknob. "Wait there. I'll get rid of her. We need to talk."

She wasn't sure how scooting off to the bathroom for a very necessary morning function, to say nothing of hiding from whoever was on the other side of the door, would stand in the way of talking. But he sounded so weird that she didn't argue.

She watched Caleb peer through the door's peephole. He instantly pulled back and whispered something that sounded like a curse. Shoulders so tense his back looked like something in one of those men's muscle magazines, she heard him suck in a breath, then release it before opening the door.

He only opened it a few inches, though. With his body shielding her view, she could only surmise that it wasn't Mrs. Mac with muffins.

"Yeah?"

Her brows drew together at Caleb's impatient tone. Then she heard a man's voice. Deep, melodious and compelling.

"Party time," the voice said.

"You have the invitations already?"

Invitations? Party?

"All but the party planner. I'm counting on you for that."

Her frown deepened as she listened to the conversation. What the hell were they talking about?

"Let me in. We have to talk."

"Later."

"Now. Time's become an issue."

Caleb glanced over his shoulder at Pandora. The look in his eyes made her shiver just a little, it was so calculating. She felt bad for the guy on the other side of the door, since she was sure he was the reason for it.

"The hall?"

"Unsecure."

"You're a pain in the ass. You know that, right?" But Caleb stepped back and let the door swing open. "The balcony. Not a word."

Pandora gulped as the second man stepped through the door. Too stunned to be embarrassed, she just stared.

Holy cow.

Pure masculine intensity. He wasn't pretty, his face was too strong for that. But still, the sculpted features, long-lashed blue eyes and full lips did make quite a picture. His black hair swept off his forehead, longer in front and short in back. He stopped just inside the door when he saw her. Those vivid eyes cut over to Caleb and he arched a brow. Pandora tried to read his body language, but he was a blank. She didn't see even a hint of surprise on his part. Like walking into his friend's hotel room and finding a naked woman in bed was the norm.

The man gave Pandora a slight nod, his eyes doing a quick scan of the room, then he stepped over and opened the sliding door to the balcony.

"This might be a while," Caleb said, grabbing his sweatshirt off the footboard before following his friend to the balcony door.

"It's okay. I have to get to the store anyway," she told him with a warm smile. "I'll see you later, right?"

He gave her a long, intense look that made her stomach swoop into her toes. Then he nodded and stepped through, closing the curtain along with the door.

It wasn't until both men were on the other side of the glass with the door firmly closed that she realized Caleb hadn't introduced his friend.

Not that it mattered. She had her man.

And she missed him already.

Grinning at her own goofiness, Pandora tugged the sheet loose from the mattress to wrap it securely around her body, then slid from the bed. She padded over to the sliding glass door that led to the balcony and peered around the curtain.

Yep. Gorgeous and sexy. Both of them.

Giggling a little to herself, she did a mangled skip-step hindered by the sheet on her way to the bathroom.

Time to start her day. She had a feeling it was going to be an excellent one.

"TACKY, BLACK."

Caleb shrugged, tugging the gray fleece over his head in a useless attempt to ward off the morning chill. California or not, winter mornings were damn cold here in the mountains.

"What broke?" he prompted. He wanted the reason for Hunter's unexpected, and untimely, arrival. He did not want to discuss Pandora, his rotten choices or what a jerk he was.

"I tugged a few more strings. Ran some numbers, looked at a few different accounts."

As if his toes weren't freezing, Caleb patiently waited.

"I know who the ringleader is," Hunter declared.

Caleb crossed his arms over his chest and arched one brow.

Hunter gave him a long look. Then, his fingers stuffed in the pockets of a very warm-looking over-coat, he nodded.

"You already know."

Even though it wasn't a question, Caleb answered anyway. "I'm pretty sure I do. Did you run the records I asked?"

"Yeah. All the names you provided had arrests that led back to the same person. Why didn't you email me with your suspicions?"

"I figured they might. These guys aren't local to

Black Oak, so they had to have connected somewhere. Jail was the easy answer. I figured that'd be a good place for a clever drug dealer to recruit his team." Which was true. But it didn't answer Hunter's question. So Caleb admitted, "I didn't let you know because I don't know if he's working alone or not."

"You're worried about your girlfriend? I couldn't clear her."

Faint though it was, layered there beneath the official tone, Caleb could hear the regret in Hunter's voice. His old friend was hard-line about the law, but he didn't enjoy hurting people. Caleb flexed his shoulders and shook his head.

"It doesn't matter. Whatever you've got, it's bullshit. Because I know Pandora. She's not involved. Not knowingly."

Hunter didn't say a word. He just offered up that enigmatic stare of his. Caleb had lost a lot of poker money to that stare over the years. He wasn't losing Pandora.

"Just wait," he said, wincing, but unable to resist the cliché. "I'll prove it."

CHAPTER TWELVE

PANDORA WAS ALMOST skipping when she stepped into Moonspun Dreams an hour later. A night of wild sex with a gorgeous man without any aphrodisiacal aid had done wonders for her attitude.

Well, that and the little pep talk from Caleb the night before had made her realize she needed to come to terms with her issues. After a night of sweet, sexy loving, she figured she was in just the right mood to try to make nice with her mother.

"Hi, Paulie," she said, bending down to rub her fingers over the silky black fur of the cat's purring head. "You having a good morning, too?"

"Hey, Pandora," Fifi greeted, coming out from the back room with an armful of fluffy handwoven blankets. "We can't keep enough of these on the sales floor. I'm blown away at how much demand there is for all this homemade, organic stuff you've brought in."

"I think it's a cyclic thing," Pandora said, straightening up and crossing over to give Bonnie's ears the same loving attention she'd offered Paulie. "Twenty years ago, holistic was all the rage. I'll bet in ten more, it'll be back to New Age glitz."

Something she'd do well to remember.

"Is my mother here?" she asked, heading back to the office to put away her purse.

"Um, no," Fifi said with a grimace.

"Something wrong?"

"I'm not sure. I mean, I know you're running the store now, but I'd thought that, you know, when Cassiopeia was back in town, she'd be involved. At least to do readings or something."

"Well, yeah," Pandora agreed slowly, turning to face her assistant. "Of course she will. That's what she does. We've had dozens of calls while she was gone, and people are going to be lining up to see her now that she's back. So what's the problem?"

"Well, you left right after your mother, so I didn't get to mention it. But I asked Cassiopeia on her way out if she wanted me to start booking readings. She said not until she found a place to do them." Fifi scrunched her nose, looking as if she might cry. "What's going on?"

Pandora shrugged a shoulder that was suddenly as heavy as lead. Like the fragile flame of a candle, her happy, upbeat morning disappeared into a puff of stress.

"What do I tell people?" Fifi prompted. "I've already had a few calls and I don't know what to say. Is she going to come back?"

Pandora almost said that Fifi should tell them to find a new psychic. Lying on the counter with her black-and-white face looking so patient, Bonnie caught her eye, making her wince. Besides being immature and spiteful, doing something like that would sink the store.

"I don't know," Pandora said, biting her bottom lip and trying to figure out how they were going to deal with this. "I guess she's upset about…" Pandora being an ungrateful brat who blamed her momma for her problems instead of pulling up her big-girl panties and facing them herself. "Something or other. I can call her later, see if we can get this fixed."

As soon as she said the words, the throbbing in her temples faded and her earlier euphoria returned. Yep, all she had to do was take charge and have a good attitude. No more hiding and running.

"I'm glad. I was telling Russ about the readings last night, how totally accurate they are." Fifi's grin made it clear that she'd been sharing a lot more than store gossip with the new guy. "He's a little scared to get one, but maybe after he sees how much people like them, he'll change his mind."

Pandora's gaze cut to her newest employee, who stood out like an awkward third wheel as he tried to help a customer choose between tumbled carnelian or a citrine spear. At least she supposed he was trying to help. It couldn't be easy with his hands hidden behind his back.

"Um, Fifi," she said with a grimace, nodding at Russ. "I know he's only been here a couple of days, but he's got to get past that skittish thing he's got going on."

Fifi scrunched her nose and gave a little sigh. "He's great with some of the customers. Younger ones, you know? He's bringing them in left and right. But with our regulars…" She winced as he held out a handkerchief to take the handful of stones the customer had chosen. "Maybe I told him too many stories about how powerful you and your mom are?"

"Sorry, what?" Pandora asked. The rest of the room faded as she stared at Fifi with wide eyes.

"Well, you know. You're the Easton women. Your gramma was a witch, right? And your mom is a famous psychic. You're so amazing with reading people, and then you made an even bigger splash with the café and all those aphrodisiacs. You always know just what to offer the customers, and how to keep them from getting all silly about it. Everyone talks about it. You're almost as big a legend now as Cassiopeia." Fifi glanced at Russ, who'd rung up the crystal purchase and was now by the books with a young guy who looked as though he should be shopping in the herbal-bath section. "I'm betting Russ is a little freaked, you know? I mean, he's a believer, so it's all kinda intimidating."

Pandora couldn't care less about Russ anymore. She was too stunned by the rest of Fifi's words. She thought Pandora was on the same level as Cassiopeia? Fifi and the customers considered her one of the gifted Easton women?

It was like being enveloped in the biggest, brightest hug in the world. Pandora's heart swelled. Her smile spread from ear to ear and tears sparkled in her eyes.

"You okay?" Fifi asked, her own eyes huge with worry.

With a shaky sigh, she forced herself to focus and pull it together. There was nothing empowering about sniveling like a baby over validation.

"Sure. Yeah," Pandora sniffed. "I'll call Cassiopeia and get this fixed. Go ahead and start taking tentative bookings, letting people know that they might change depending on her schedule."

She glanced at the café and added, "Be sure to make the bookings for after two, when the café is closed. That way she has as much time and space as she needs."

Four hours later, the store was filled with week-before-Christmas shoppers. Both locals and out-of-towners browsed, compared and purchased enough throughout the morning that Pandora was ready to do a happy dance on the sales counter. She'd barely had time to leave her mom a message, let alone worry about how she'd patch things up.

By the end of lunch, her feet hurt, her cheeks were sore from grinning and she was sure they'd just had the best sales day in Moonspun's history.

She'd just pulled up the numbers on the cash register to check, when there was a loud furor at the door.

She glanced up, but couldn't see what was going on because of the throng of bodies. Then she caught a glimpse of red curls.

Showtime.

Cassiopeia took her time crossing the room. She spoke with everyone, stopping to offer hugs and exclamations to friends and strangers alike. With Paulie draped over her shoulder like a purring fur stole, and her flowing hunter-green dress and faux-holly jewelry, she was the epitome of famous-psychic-does-holiday casual.

Pandora leaned against the counter and watched the show. She didn't realize she was grinning until Russ stepped closer and whispered, "Who is she? She's famous, right?"

Her smile faded as she looked at Moonspun's newest employee. Fifi had said she'd known him, like, forever. And hadn't his application indicated he'd lived here for years? How could he have lived in Black Oak for *any* length of time and not know who Cassiopeia was? Heck, everyone in the five neighboring towns knew her by sight.

Before she could ask, though, her mother swept close enough to catch her eye.

"Russ, will you help Fifi cover the store?" Pandora quietly asked him. "My mother and I will be in the back. Please, don't interrupt unless it's an emergency."

His pale brown eyes were huge. The guy was a basket case. He was probably afraid they were going to concoct some magic potion or poke pins in a doll.

It was kinda cute, in a silly sort of way. She just patted his arm, then walked over to her mother. She heard him sputtering behind her as she went.

"Mom, do you have a minute?" she said, interrupting her chat with Mrs. Sellers. "I'd really appreciate it."

"Oh, here I am hogging your time and you must want to see your daughter," Mrs. Sellers said with a sweep of her hand. "You probably have so much to discuss. And you must be so proud of Pandora. She's definitely a chip off the old block. Or in this case, a crystal off the sparkling quartz."

Pandora glanced at her mother's face, expecting to see at least a hint of disdain. Instead, she saw just what Mrs. Sellers indicated. Pride.

Joy, as warm and gooey as her Hot Molten Love chocolate cake, filled her. Had her mother ever looked at her like that before? Or had she always, and Pandora had ignored it since it meant she'd have to move that chip off her shoulder?

"Mom, I'm so glad you're here. People have been asking about you all day." Pandora came around the counter and held out her hand. She put as much love and apology into that move as she could. "They're hoping you'll be available for readings soon."

Her mother's smile trembled a little in the corners and her eyes filled before she blinked thickly coated lashes and tilted her head in thanks.

"I'm glad to be here as well, darling." She rubbed a bejeweled hand over Pandora's shoulder, then spoke to the room at large. "I'm going to be spending some time catching up with my daughter. But I'd love to do readings. Fifi, will you go ahead and set up appointments?"

The perky blonde nodded. Before she'd pulled out a small spiral-bound notebook, there was a line of excited customers in front of her.

"You've brought in a stellar crowd, darling. Shall we go back and celebrate with cake or something sweet?" Cassiopeia said to Pandora, twining her fingers through her daughter's in a show of both pride and solidarity.

Pandora didn't trust her voice, so she offered a smile and a nod instead. Before they got more than two steps, though, the bells chimed on the front door again. Pandora's heart raced when she glanced over and saw it was Caleb. His sexy friend was with him, and the two of them made such a sight. Pure masculine beauty, with a razor-sharp edge.

"Can we talk a little later?" she murmured to her mother.

"I'm glad to see you have your priorities straight," Cassiopeia returned quietly.

Pandora glanced over, trying to see if her mother

was being sarcastic. But her vivid green eyes were wide with appreciation. She gave Pandora an arch look and mimicked fanning herself, then tilted her head. "Go say hello, dear."

"Caleb," Pandora greeted, crossing the room. She knew at least twenty sets of eyes were locked on her, but she didn't care. Not anymore. She reached out and took his hand, then, determined to push her own comfort envelope, leaned in and brushed an only slightly shaky kiss over his cheek.

There. That'd show everyone. She was dating that bad, bad Black boy and she didn't care who knew. Or what they thought.

"Hello," she murmured. She was so caught up in her own internal convolutions that it took her a few seconds to notice his lack of a response. Chilled a little, she stepped back to get a good look at his face.

Closed. His eyes were distant and cold. There was something there, in the set of his shoulders, that carried a warning. As if he was about to tell her a loved one had died. But she glanced around, making sure her mother and the two cats were still there, all her loved ones were front and center.

Her gaze cut to Hunter, who looked even more closed and distant. Was Caleb leaving with him? Was that why he was here? To tell her goodbye?

Then he smiled and wrapped his arm around her shoulder. Confused, Pandora stiffened, trying to figure out what was going on. He didn't feel right.

"Sweetheart, I've been telling Hunter how great your cooking is. We stopped by so he could check it out."

She glanced at Hunter, dressed in jeans and a black sweater that should have been casual but wasn't. Yeah. He looked like a guy stopping by to sample cookies.

"Sure," she said, not having a clue what was happening. But it felt important, and secretive. So she'd wait until she had Caleb alone to ask. "Why don't you both come into the café. We have some pasta salad left, and sandwiches, of course. The cookies are fresh this morning and I have a wooable winterberry cobbler that's fabulous with vanilla-bean ice cream."

She babbled more menu options as she made her way through the curious onlookers, achingly aware of Caleb just a few inches behind her.

Once she and the two much-too-sexy-for-their-own-good men were in the café, though, she dropped the pretense.

"What's going on?" she asked, her gaze cutting from one to the other.

Their faces didn't calm her nerves at all. Instead, her stomach knotted and black spots danced in front of her eyes. Something bad was happening here.

"We have evidence that drugs are being run through your store. We want to use this space, today, to make the bust." The words were fast, clipped and brutal.

"Bust? Drugs?" Pandora's brain was reeling. "What? I don't understand."

Her knees weak, she grabbed on to a chair.

"Ms. Easton, there's a drug ring operating out of Black Oak. Caleb came to town to stop it. His investigation led to your store. We'd like your cooperation in apprehending the people behind the drugs, especially the ringleader."

She gaped. What the hell? Drugs? In her store? No. She'd changed the inventory, she knew every single item being sold here and unless saffron was now illegal, Moonspun Dreams was clean.

But before she could worry about that, she had to sift through the fury pouring into her system like a tidal wave. Betrayal raced behind it, adding a layer of pain to her reaction.

"Wait," she demanded, holding up one hand. She arched a brow at Caleb. "You're a cop? You're not unemployed?"

"No. I'm not a cop and I am unemployed." He was, however, as distant as the moon right now. She noted his body language, how he was leaning away from her, rolling on the balls of his feet as if he was going to run at any second.

"Actually, you're on hiatus since your captain hasn't accepted your resignation," Hunter interrupted.

Pandora pressed her fingers to her forehead, hoping the pressure would help her sort it all out.

"I don't understand," she muttered. She took a deep breath and looked at Caleb again. She could see the regret in his eyes, as if he knew he was ripping her heart to shreds and was sorry. But he was going to continue to rip anyway.

"You think I had something to do with this? The drugs?" Her voice shook and she wanted to throw up. It was like déjà vu times a thousand. The humiliation, the pain, the heartache…

"Caleb has cleared you," Hunter said when Caleb stayed silent.

Cleared her. As in, he'd found proof against her guilt. Guilt that he must have believed in at some point.

"You thought I was involved? That's why you asked me all those questions before. Why you kept coming around the store? Why you—" Why he'd made love with her? Would he go that far? They did in the movies, why not in real life?

"I'll step out," Hunter murmured.

The gentle clacking of beads indicated he'd left. But Pandora's eyes were locked on Caleb's.

"You used me?" she whispered, her throat aching as she forced the words out. "You thought I was a criminal? Was everything a lie? Or did I just convince myself that what we'd shared was special?"

"No."

"No?" she repeated, her voice hitting a few of the higher octaves. "That's it? Just no? Care to elaborate a little?"

He frowned, shoving his hands into his pockets. As he did, his jacket shifted so she could see leather straps. He was wearing a gun. The room spun. Afraid she was going to collapse, Pandora reached out to grab a chair again.

"Look, it's like this—"

Before he could tell her what this was like, a rush of cold air swept over them. Then there was a quiet snick as someone shut the door to the alley.

Who the hell was using her back door? Pandora and Caleb looked at each other, her eyes wide with curiosity. His were filled with a cold warning that scared her just a little. His hand shifted to his hip.

She gulped, her heart racing as she tried to figure out when her cute café had turned into a nightmare.

Then she realized who it was and relaxed.

"Sheriff," she greeted, her voice shaking a little. *Way too much going on today,* she thought.

"Pandora. Black," the lawman greeted. He'd looked shocked when he'd first stepped through the door, but now his face smoothed into a smile. "Am I interrupting something?"

"No," she said.

"Yes," Caleb retorted at the same time. "But I'm glad you did. C'mon over. Let's talk."

Kendall's easy grin shifted as he studied Caleb's face. He took a single step backward, glancing toward the alley door. Pandora frowned, nervously gripping her fingers together. There was way too much tension in this room. She glanced at Caleb, trying to figure out why.

Whoa. She'd have stepped back, too. Caleb's smile was just this side of vicious.

"It's good to see you both," the sheriff said after clearing his throat. "I was doing my rounds, checked up the street and the alley and figured I'd come in. I hear Cassiopeia is back in town. Is she here? We've got a lot to catch up on."

His hand on the butt of his service revolver, he gave them a wide berth as he sauntered out of the room.

Pandora slammed her fists on her hips and turned to Caleb to demand an explanation.

"Quiet," Caleb ordered.

So she hissed back, "What the hell is going on?"

"Does he do that often?" Caleb asked, his words low and even.

"Sure, once in a while. Mother gave him a key for security and such."

The grim satisfaction on his face worried her. This was all happening too fast. Caleb being a—whatever he was—questionably employed in some form of law enforcement? Drugs, in her store. The sexy, intriguing man she'd fallen for and shared her body with now acting like something out of a crime novel. Too much!

"Let's go," he said, his large hand wrapping around hers.

"Go?" She dug in her heels. "No, I want to know what's going on. I'm not going anywhere until I do."

"C'mon," he said, gently but firmly moving her toward the beaded doorway with him.

When they reached it, though, he stopped and looked at her. His eyes softened and he gave a barely perceptible sigh. "Just trust me. Please."

With that, and a quick kiss brushed over the top of her head, he pulled her through the beads.

It was like walking onto the set of a crime show, with Hunter playing the part of the sexy agent in charge. He stood behind Russ, one hand on the younger man's back as he faced down Kendall. There were a dozen or more shoppers milling around, whispering and jockeying for the best viewing positions.

"Damn right I'm questioning your jurisdiction," the sheriff snapped. "What the hell do you think you're doing, coming into my town and trying to arrest one of my people?"

"What?" Pandora gasped. She was halfway across

the room—whether she was going to Russ's rescue or to smack him, she didn't know—when Caleb grabbed her arm.

Confused and angry, she shot him a glare.

"What'd you find?" Caleb asked, ignoring her, the sheriff and the rest of the crowd to speak directly to Hunter.

"He had the key and the dope in his jacket pocket."

Caleb gave a sigh that probably only Pandora noted. Then he nodded and after giving Pandora a look that said *stay put,* he approached Russ. He stopped a couple feet from the young man.

"So let's hear it," Caleb said. "Who are you working with and what's this store's connection?"

This store? Working with? Oh, God. He really did think she was involved. And now the entire town would, too. Pandora felt woozy as the room spun again. Dope. Drugs. Déjà vu. She was so grateful when her mother hurried over and took her hand.

"You might as well confess. It'll go easier on you," Caleb promised.

Why was he doing this here in the store? Was he trying to ruin her? Pandora gulped as tears filled her eyes again.

Along with the rest of the crowd, she watched Caleb take a step closer. Hunter moved to the front door to block it. Russ shifted away, backing down along the sales counter as if he could escape through the cash register.

He bumped into Bonnie, who was sitting on the counter, watching the show. She gave a low, throaty meow and butted him with her head.

"Git." Russ looked spooked, pushing the cat away.

But Bonnie meowed again, her head tilted to one side.

"What's she doing?" he muttered, a tinge of hysteria in his tone.

"She can read minds," Cassiopeia intoned melodiously.

"Nuh-uh." But Russ inched away from the black-and-white cat like he wasn't so sure.

"You might want to confess before she shares any of your secrets," Cassiopeia continued, sweeping her arm in an arc so the filmy fabric of her caftan flowed, wispy and ghostlike.

Bonnie meowed again.

Russ jumped. His gaze shot from person to person, locking for a long moment on the sheriff before he stepped closer to Caleb.

"I want a guarantee," he said, his voice shaking.

"Let's talk about this in my office," Kendall demanded. The guy looked totally stressed out and pissed, Pandora noted. His face was tense, and if she wasn't mistaken, that was fear in his eyes.

"We'll settle it here," Caleb said quietly. Pandora thought she saw an apology in the quick glance he threw her way, but then he was focused on Russ again. "Now."

"The guarantee?" Russ prodded.

His face impassive, Caleb walked across the room. Everyone held their breath, not sure what he was going to do to the young man. But he passed right by him and stopped next to the cat. Without taking his eyes off Russ, he swept his hand down Bonnie's head.

All eyes cut to Russ. The kid looked as if he was going to puke all over Pandora's imported astrology rug. He tugged at the hem of his T-shirt, his eyes nervously darting from Caleb to the sheriff.

"Who's your boss?" Caleb asked. "Your real boss."

Russ didn't even glance toward Pandora. Instead, he closed his eyes for a second, took a deep breath, then whispered, "Sheriff Kendall."

The chorus of gasps around the room was deafening.

Pandora pressed her hand against her stomach, afraid she might be the one to ruin the rug.

"Did he just accuse…?"

"He can't be saying that the sheriff…"

"Drugs? The sheriff? No…"

"I always knew he was shifty—"

"Enough," Caleb said. He didn't raise his voice or take his eyes off Russ, but the room immediately silenced.

"That's a major accusation."

"It's the truth."

"It's bullshit," Kendall said from the other side of the room. Furious, he looked as if he wanted to pull the gun from his hip and shoot someone. Tension expanded in the room like an overstretched rubber band, ready to snap at any second. Finally, thankfully, he slammed his arms over his chest instead, glaring at one and all.

Pandora met her mother's eyes, though, and tilted her head to indicate his stance. Shoulders rounded, chin low. He was lying. Her mother nodded in agreement.

"Who else?" Caleb asked quietly.

Pandora's heart raced. She glanced at Fifi, who had

tears pouring down her face and had already chewed off three fingernails.

"Nobody. I mean, nobody I know."

She noted the set of his chin, the way his fingers were clenched together. She figured he was telling the truth. Her own shoulders relaxed.

"Why here? Why Moonspun Dreams?"

"I don't know. I mean, he, the sheriff, he said it was the most convenient place. That with all the changes going on, the customers being a little weird and all, it'd fly under the radar."

Offended, the "weird" customers muttered among themselves.

"You used the storage out back. How did the store owner not catch on?"

Russ shot Pandora a guilty look, his face miserable and just a little green. "Um, well, I used to come in and hang out. I pretended I wanted to learn about all this stuff. Cards and magic and all that. I flirted a little, convinced Fifi that I could help out. That's it. The ladies, they didn't know anything."

"As far as he knows," the sheriff interjected smoothly. He'd gone from sounding pissed to looking like a lawyer trying to convince his jury. "But I've been watching this place for weeks. Pandora's made a name for herself selling more than just those sandwiches and cookies she's always pushing. Everyone on the street knows to come to her for their pills. Her reputation precedes her. Just check."

Pandora's outraged gasp was drowned out by her mother's furious roar. But neither of them had even inhaled again before Caleb moved. He strode over, and without a word or warning, plowed his fist into Kendall's face with a loud, bloody crack.

His hand grabbing his nose, the sheriff stumbled backward. He glanced, wild-eyed, at the crowd, then ran toward the beaded curtain leading to the café.

He didn't make it, though. As usual, Paulie had plopped himself in the doorway to sleep. Pandora didn't know if the cat sensed the drama, or if all the noise bothered him, but he jumped up on all fours and scurried between the sheriff's feet, sending the man flying into the far wall with another loud crack to his face.

Cheers rang out, but Caleb didn't smile as he strode over and grabbed the guy, hauling him off the floor. He started reciting something, probably the Miranda Rights, but Pandora couldn't hear anything through the buzzing in her head.

She, along with what seemed to be half the town, watched the tall, dark and mysterious Hunter slap handcuffs on her newest employee while Caleb did the same to Sheriff Kendall. Her gut roiled with horror.

"Darling?"

She shook her head at her mother. She couldn't talk about it. Not now. Not here, in front of all the gawking eyes. It had been bad enough last time, when she'd come home to hide from her relationship with a failed criminal and everyone in town had whispered about her stupidity.

Now they were all here to watch, live and up close, as she confirmed it.

"Darling, come on. Let's go home. We'll have a nice pot of tea and some chocolate cake."

"No," Pandora said, sniffing as a single tear rolled

down her cheek. She watched Caleb, one hand on the sheriff's back and the other on the gun holstered at his hip, stride out the door. He never looked back. "No. I don't think I ever want chocolate cake again."

CHAPTER THIRTEEN

"MORE TEA?" CASSIOPEIA asked, holding up her prized Hummel teapot she used for tea-leaf readings.

Her hands wrapped around her almost-empty cup, Pandora shook her head. "I should get back to the store. Or just go home."

Fifi had been a mess, blubbering and bawling as if she'd been the one arrested. Finally, calling it an executive decision, Cassiopeia had declared that the store be closed for the day.

"You need to go talk to Caleb, is what you need to do."

Pandora cringed, taking a sip instead of answering. The still-warm tea soothed her tear-ravaged throat. Then she stared into her cup, wishing she could find answers in the floating dregs.

"You've proven that you're a strong woman who knows what she wants and can make it happen," her mother continued, her voice both soothing and commanding. "Are you going to just let him go?"

"He lied to me. Worse, he made me look like a fool in front of everyone." Just remembering sent a hot flush of horrified embarrassment rushing through her. The whispers, the stares. It had been terrible.

"Dear, do you really think people care about that?

They're so busy talking about Kendall that you're not even going to enter their heads. I'd imagine that's why Caleb played that scene out the way he did."

Pandora tore her eyes off her murky tea leaves to frown at her mother. "What do you mean?"

"He could have asked all those questions at the sheriff's office. Much easier, too, I'd imagine. He did that, made that big scene, just to make sure that people knew the drugs had nothing to do with you. That they had plenty of other things to talk about instead."

Pandora stared, first in shock, then in dawning hope. Her heart raced and she bit her lip. "Do you really think so?"

"What I think is that you need to go ask Caleb."

She was scared to. Pandora dropped her gaze back to her cup and took a shaky breath. She was afraid to hear that this had all been a scam on his part. That he'd used her.

Her mother gently laid her hand over hers and squeezed. "Darling, you have to face this. You can't move forward until you do."

"Is this why your clients all love you so much?" Pandora asked with a teary laugh. "Because you're so good at telling them what they need to do in a way that makes them feel great about themselves?"

"You mean because I'm a nice bully? Of course. Now listen to your mother and go get the answers you need."

Ten minutes later, her face washed and makeup reapplied, Pandora stood at the door of the sheriff's office. Her hand shook as she reached for the handle, so she pulled it back. Maybe she should wait. Come back later. Or better yet, take the week off from the store and wait to see what people really thought about the situation.

Then she realized that none of that mattered. All she cared about was what Caleb thought of her. So she took a deep breath of the cold night air and forced herself to grab the handle. Her knees were just as shaky as her hands, but she stepped through the entry.

Caleb wasn't there. She looked around the sterile, tan room, with its two desks and a few chairs scattered about. The walls and floor were bare, and the place smelled like burned microwave popcorn.

"Wow, Kendall is a sneaky liar *and* a lousy decorator," she muttered.

"Don't forget power abuser and drug pusher."

She jumped, her gaze flying across the room. Framed in the door leading to what she assumed must be the cells was Mr. Tall, Dark and Mysterious.

"Um, hi," she said to Hunter, shuffling nervously from her right foot to her left. "I came to see Caleb…?"

"He's finishing up the interrogation. He'll be out in a few minutes."

She nodded, then looked back at the door. Should she leave? She'd definitely rather, but something about Hunter's stare made it hard to run away.

She glanced back at him, then away again. Twining her trembling fingers together, she stared aimlessly around the ugly space.

"Would you like to sit?" Hunter asked, now leaning against the door frame in what she supposed was a casual pose. Except that he still looked as if he could kill a person with his pinkie.

"Um, no. I'll just… Um, maybe I should come back later?"

"Stay."

Command or request? Did it matter? Pandora bit her lip, then stepped farther into the room so she could set her purse on one of the desks.

"I've heard about your store. Intriguing. I didn't realize your cat was psychic, too, though." His tone was conversational, but his blue eyes danced with laughter.

A giggle escaped, and with it, some of Pandora's tension. Who knew, superhottie had a sense of humor. It was hard to look at him for too long, though. He was so intense. If she wasn't in love with Caleb, she'd be stuttering and blushing and weaving all sorts of sexual fantasies.

"Bonnie's not psychic. She tilts her head because she had a series of ear infections when she was younger," Pandora replied, finally relaxing enough to lean against the desk. Then she paused, thinking back to both the cats' unnatural behavior toward Russ and Kendall. "I mean, as far as I know, she doesn't actually read minds."

His face impassive but his eyes still laughing, Hunter nodded and walked over to a small refrigerator and took out a bottle of water. He handed it to her with a small smile.

Wow. Maybe he wasn't that scary.

Pandora bit her lip, then unable to help herself, she blurted out, "What does Caleb do for you? He's…what? A cop? DEA agent? Why does everyone think he's an unemployed no-good drifter?"

"Because I am an unemployed, no-good drifter."

Pandora only jumped a little before turning to see Caleb standing in the doorway. Hunter just slanted his gaze toward the other man, then nodded and headed out the front door.

His hand on the knob, he turned back and told Pandora, "It was good to meet you. We'll talk again."

Her heart slamming against her chest, Pandora gave a jerky nod. She waited for the door to close before asking, "What's going on?"

"Russ Turnbaugh and Jeff Kendall are under federal arrest. We've commandeered the sheriff's holding cells until a team arrives to take them in."

"Federal?"

"Hunter's with the FBI."

"And you?"

"I was with the DEA, but I quit a while ago. Right now I'm exactly what I've said. Unemployed and clueless about what I'm going to do next." His words were as guarded as his expression. He looked as if he wasn't sure if she was there to talk or to beat the living hell out of him.

Pandora nodded, then looked away. A part of her wanted to beg him to make sure whatever it was, he did it with her. Another part, burned one too many times, warned her to hold back until she had the truth. All the truth.

"Are you working for the FBI, though?" Her chin high, she crossed her arms over her chest and tried to look in control, instead of on the verge of being a blubbering mess again.

"Hunter was my college roommate." He sounded less cold, more like himself now. She could actually see him starting to defrost. Whether it was because she wasn't hitting him, or he was shedding his inter-rogation-cop attitude, she wasn't sure. "We're friends. I was doing him a favor."

"I didn't realize the FBI looked into small-town drug problems."

"Not usually." He shrugged. "But there were extenuating circumstances in this case, and the drugs are a new blend. Something they wanted to stop before they gained a foothold."

"And you offered to help out of the goodness of your heart? Because you were bored being all unemployed and clueless?" Pandora winced, not sure where the anger was coming from.

"Don't blow this out of proportion. The bad guys are caught and they won't be using you or your store any longer. You're cleared and everyone knows it."

Cassiopeia was right. He had staged that little scene for her benefit. Pandora's heart pounded, emotions flying about so fast she didn't know if she should be thrilled, grateful or simply furious.

She settled on a combination of all three.

"Oh, no. No blowing things out of proportion. I should be relieved I won't have to go through weeks of grilling questions, false accusations and the loss of my computer and privacy this time." She was yelling by the last word. Apparently she'd glommed on to the fury more than all the other emotions.

Needing to get a handle on herself, Pandora held up both hands, took a deep breath. *Calm, center and collect yourself,* she chanted in her head.

Calm.

Centered.

Another breath, and she was pretty much collected.

"Look—" he said.

"No," she interrupted with a snap, whatever she'd collected scattering again. "I'm not finished. You came on to me. You poked through my computer, you made yourself at home in my house. You slept with me, over and over and over. And the whole time, you were investigating me?"

"I told you, you were cleared. I never suspected you, not really. Hell, you're not even the person I came to town to investigate." His jaw snapped shut. For the first time, Pandora saw Caleb angry. Not the stoic hard-ass thing he did so well, but really, truly angry.

Smoldering heat flared deep in her belly. It was kind of a turn-on.

"Look. You know the truth now. What's the big deal? Can't we just move forward from here?"

Move forward? Where? How? Wasn't this where he mounted his big black hog and rode off into the sunset?

The idea of that, of saying goodbye to him forever, was like a knife in her gut.

"The big deal is that I was falling for you and you were investigating me," she shouted. Horrified, she clapped both hands over her mouth. That was so not the way to dial back the drama.

CALEB FELT LIKE SHIT.

The rush of the bust, with its extra dollop of happy that he'd been able to take a schmuck like Kendall down, was gone. Now he was faced with the reality of what he'd done. With how he'd hurt Pandora.

"I didn't mean to hurt you," he said, knowing the words were totally inadequate, but having no idea what else to say. Pissed, he shoved his hands through his hair. He hated this. Hated not having a clue how to fix things with her.

"You lied to me," she said, her chin wobbling a little. *Oh, God, no. Please, don't let her cry.* Caleb wanted to grab her tight and kiss her until she forgot everything. Especially how he'd hurt her.

But he knew she wouldn't let him until he'd cleared up this mess.

"Not lied," he corrected scrupulously. "Just…with-held information."

"If not me, then who did you come to town to investigate?"

Caleb hesitated. Not only was it an open investigation, which meant the information was still confidential, but this was his father. Sure, the FBI had an entire database dedicated to cons they suspected him of. But most people, especially here in Black Oak, were clueless.

"Look, I'm not at liberty to divulge the details," he started to say. Her eyes chilled and her expression closed up.

"Because, what? You might lose your job? Oh, wait…"

"No. Because Hunter trusts me."

The ice in her eyes melted a little, but she still looked hurt. Then she nodded. "Okay, I get that. It's not fair to ask you to break a confidence."

But it was fair of him to ask her to take him at face value? After everything she'd been through, unless he told her who it really was, she'd never believe it wasn't her. Caleb scrubbed his hands over his eyes, then blew out a breath. "Okay, you have to promise that this stays between us. You can't even tell those psychic cats of yours."

She nodded, a tiny smile playing over her lips.

"The FBI had tips that there is more going on than just the drugs. That someone with a lot of influence was using the town as their own crime ring."

She nodded, then gestured toward the door in the back that led to the jail cells.

"The sheriff, right?"

"Higher."

"The mayor?" she asked, sounding appalled. Then Pandora slapped both hands over her mouth and grimaced. "I'm sorry. I'm so sorry. I forgot she's your aunt. But, I mean, who is higher than the sheriff?"

Caleb gave her a steady look.

It didn't take her long. Her eyes widened and she shook her head in denial.

"Noooo," she breathed.

"Yeah."

"No way. I mean, I don't know what kind of evidence they have, but it's wrong. There's just no way."

"That's what I said."

"So you came home to prove your father's innocence?" she asked. Then her eyes rounded again. "And what? You had to prove mine, as well?"

"It's been an interesting month," he said with a laugh.

"No kidding," she agreed. "You must have been so worried. So scared of what you'd find."

Her brow creased in empathy, she took those two mile-long steps and gave him a hug.

And just like that, everything was okay.

Caleb's shoulders sagged as he returned her hug. He let out the breath he'd been holding and gave a half shrug. She understood. Totally got it. Instead of running disgusted from the room because his father was the kind of guy who triggered a major FBI investigation, she offered comfort and understanding.

He was so freaking in love with her, it was scary.

Tension and a fear he hadn't even realized was eating at his guts faded as Caleb tightened his arms around her, never wanting to let go.

Needing to taste her, desperate for more, he swept his hands down to the delicate curve of the small of her back, pressing her tight against him. Lifting her head from his shoulder, she arched a brow. Whether she was shocked or impressed by his burgeoning hard-on, he wasn't sure.

He took her mouth in a deep, desperate kiss. Tongue and lips slid together, tasting. She was warm and delicious. Everything he needed. Everything he wanted. Everything he hoped to keep, forever.

Then she kissed him back. Her lips moved against his in welcome, then in passion. Their tongues wrapped together in a familiar dance. Caleb groaned, feeling as if it'd been years since they'd been together instead of twenty-or-so hours.

They needed to get this all settled so he could have her again.

Gently, slowly, he pulled his mouth from hers. He couldn't stop touching her, though. His hands stroked up her back, down to her butt, then made the trip again. A part of him was worried that if he let go, she'd walk out and not come back. He had this one chance with her.

And he'd damn well better not blow it.

"So what now?" she asked, her hands loose around his waist as she stared up at him.

She probably wasn't referring to the investigation.

Time to put up or shut up. Nerves jumped in his stomach, but Caleb was ready for this.

"This is a pretty nice office," he noted dryly, looking around at the barren two-desk setup. "And now it's empty."

"I'm not doing it with you in here," she warned. "There's not enough Foreplay Chocolate Cake in the world to get me to, either."

He snorted a laugh. Grinning, he tucked a strand of hair behind her ear and pressed a kiss to her forehead. Had he ever been as happy as he was with her? Had he ever felt as good about himself as he did when he was with her? Was he ever going to find anyone who made him want to share himself, his life and his heart, the way he wanted to with Pandora?

The answer to all of those was no.

Still grinning, Caleb looked around the office again. Maybe it was time to stop bullshitting around.

"No, I didn't mean sex. At least," he corrected as he pulled her tighter between his thighs, "I didn't mean now or here. I meant…"

Pandora reached up to frame his face in both of her soft hands. Smiling, she arched a brow and asked, "Meant?"

"I meant, the position as sheriff will be open. I've got an in with the mayor, could probably snag an interim appointment until the next election."

Her eyes lit up and her smile was huge. Then she gave a little wince.

"What about Tobias?"

"He's not interested in the position. He runs the town just fine without all the crap that goes with an elected job."

She smirked. "No. I meant, can you live here, in the same town as your father? Does he know you were investigating him? Will you be able to handle being his son *and* the sheriff in his town? That's a pretty big challenge."

A huge one. Because rather than clearing Tobias's name, this bust had only pulled him deeper into things. Kendall had claimed he answered to one person, and one person only. Then he'd invoked the Fifth and refused to say another word. Clearly, the first official job of the new sheriff would be to find out who was trying to turn Black Oak into their own little crime den.

But Caleb wasn't worried about handling the investigation. His old man was a lot of things, but he wasn't involved in this mess.

"Can you live here, Caleb? In the same town as your dad?"

"When I was a kid I guess I thought I had to leave, get as far away from him as I could so I could be myself. And those are just about the most touchy-feely words I ever want to say," he added, making her laugh. "But, really, he was always there. He's a big part of who I am. He's shaped my choices and my strengths. So living in the same town? That just means he's talking to my face instead of being a nagging voice in my head. As for the rest? It'll all work out fine. I have faith that he's innocent in this, and I have faith that the law will prove it."

And wasn't he all freaking grown-up and stuff. Caleb noticed the look in Pandora's eyes. Sweet acceptance mixed with pride and just a tiny bit of lust.

Just as soon as someone showed up to watch the prisoners, he'd get her back to her place to do something about that lust.

"You're really going to stay?"

He hesitated, then put it all on the line.

"Do you want me to?"

Caleb had faced a lot of scary shit in his life, but he'd never been as nervous as he was at this very second.

And, dammit, Pandora wasn't making it any easier. Instead of wrapping her arms around him and declaring her undying love and gratitude that he'd be around, she pulled away.

She removed his hands from her waist, then leaned in to kiss his cheek before stepping back and around to the other side of the desk. What? She thought he'd get violent if she didn't declare her love?

He realized he'd clenched his now-empty fists and had to admit, she just might be right.

"This is hard for me," she said quietly, lacing and unlacing her fingers together. "I don't want to make a mistake."

Caleb's gut churned, but he kept his face clear. He

was a big boy. He'd been shot at, called filthy names and once even been thrown from a helicopter—albeit a low-flying one. He could handle whatever she had to say.

"Don't try to sugarcoat things. Just say what you feel."

"What I feel? I love you," she said, the words coming out in a rush. Caleb grinned, barely holding back a fist pump. But apparently he didn't hide his triumph that well because she shook her head and held up one hand. "But…"

"No, let's skip the buts."

"But," she continued, smiling a little, "I've got a question. Or, more like a confession."

Caleb's triumph fled and his stomach went back to clenching. Shit.

"Are you sure you're not attracted to me because of the aphrodisiacs?" she asked, her words so whisper-soft he barely heard them. "I mean, every time we were together, they were involved."

"What? You're kidding, right?" She stared at him, big eyes filled with worry. "You're not kidding."

He moved to step around the desk, but she shook her head. "No, please. I get confused when you touch me. I need you over there while we talk."

Caleb cringed. Damn. He'd hoped a few kisses would suffice. Now he had to express what he felt with words?

"Pandora, I told you yesterday, you underestimate yourself. I'm crazy about you. I'd be crazy about you if we ate fast food, or if we ate nuts and berries, or if we keep eating all that delicious stuff you make. The food, that's just nutrition. Aphrodisiacs are all in the head. You said so yourself, remember?"

He cringed, knowing he wasn't good with the romantic speeches, but needing her to know how much he cared about her. How special she was.

"You're crazy about me?" she asked, looking at him through her lashes and smiling.

Needing to touch her for this confession, he took a chance and came around the desk. When she didn't order him back, he reached out for her hands, lifting them to his lips.

"I'm crazy about you," he confirmed. He looked into the hazel depths of her beautiful eyes and pressed little kisses to her knuckles. "I'm wild for you. I want you for you. You make me laugh, you make me feel good inside. You make me believe."

Her gasp was tiny, but he could feel her pulse racing as she bit her lip.

"I love you, Pandora. I really, seriously love you. And I want to give us a chance."

Her smile was brighter than the overhead lights. His heart filled with a joy he'd never imagined.

"I love you, too," she said softly. She shifted her hands so they framed his face, then stood on tiptoe to brush her mouth over his. "I really, seriously love you."

"And together," he promised, "the two of us are going to build a life. Our life, here, in Black Oak. I'm sure it'll have its irritants, given that our parents are always going to be larger than life. But it's going to be amazing, too. Love, laughter and a whole lot of that sexy chocolate cake."

"I have a large slice waiting back at my place," she admitted as she curled her fingers into his hair.

"With whipped cream? And hot-fudge sauce?"

Her smile flashed, as wickedly sweet as her cake.

"Always," she promised him right back.

* * * * *

JOANNE ROCK

Three-time RITA® Award nominee Joanne
Rock never met a romance subgenre she didn't
enjoy. The author of over sixty romances from
contemporary to medieval historical, Joanne
dreams of one day penning a book for every
Harlequin series. A former Golden Heart Award
recipient, she has won numerous awards for her
stories. Learn more about Joanne's
imaginative muse by visiting her website,
www.joannerock.com, or @JoanneRock6 on
Twitter.

Be sure to look for other books by Joanne Rock
in Harlequin Blaze—the ultimate destination for
red-hot romance! There are four new Harlequin
Blaze titles available every month. Check one
out today!

UNDER WRAPS
Joanne Rock

For the beautifully talented Winnie Griggs, who calls and checks in on me, who cheers me on, who always makes me feel like a success! Thank you for many years of friendship and wise advice.

PROLOGUE

NORMALLY, THE LAST PLACE Jake Brennan would want to
be the week before Christmas was sitting on a stakeout.

He'd promised his mom he'd come home for the holidays this year, a pledge, which made him a liar three
years running. Instead, he sat in his SUV across the
street from a suspect's business in downtown Miami,
where neon palmetto trees made a tropical substitute
for white lights in the snow back in Illinois.

But when the stakeout involved Marnie Wainwright, there were perks involved. Enough perks that
Jake didn't mind watching the storefront for her business, Lose Yourself, from inside his vehicle on a Friday
night. It didn't matter that the rest of the world went
to holiday parties right now. He had Marnie for entertainment, and two months of surveillance on the en-
trepreneur behind Lose Yourself had taught him that
was more than enough.

His hand hovered over the screen of his BlackBerry
where an internet connection allowed him access to
the camera he'd installed in her place eight weeks ago.
Soft holiday music and Marnie's warm, sexy laugh
greeted his ears even before the picture on the video
feed came into focus.

Thanks to the wonders of technology, he could sit

two car lengths up the street and still see exactly what went on inside her high-end adventure company that specialized in exotic fantasy escapes.

And as long as Marnie was there, he always got an eyeful.

"If you'll just give me your credit card, you can pay the balance on the trip and I'll mail you a detailed itinerary next week," she was currently saying to an attractive middle-aged couple in front of her desk.

Marnie had a pen tucked in the swoop of cinnamon-colored hair piled at the back of her head. He knew from hours of watching her that she sometimes stuck as many as three pens back there at a time, occasionally losing all writing implements to her hairdo. His camera was hidden inside a bookcase he'd built for her two months back, when he'd posed as a carpenter and helped remodel the front office. The carpentry skills, a long-ago gift from his dad, had been fun to brush off after his years in the military and the Miami P.D., and they'd certainly come in handy for concealing the surveillance camera at Marnie's business.

At that time, she'd been a prime suspect in a white-collar crime at Premiere Properties, her former employer. Vincent Galway, the CEO of Premiere, had fired her right after discovering embezzlement that had cost the company $2.5 million.

Vincent only had very circumstantial evidence pointing to Marnie. The missing funds had been funneled through her department, and there had been a rise in client complaints about double billing. Coupled with her frequent overtime, easy access to the accounts and constant work outside the office, Vincent had let her go for superficial reasons—easy enough to do since Florida was an "at-will" state for employee termination. Then, with Marnie out of the company and none the wiser as to why, Vince had asked Jake to quietly investigate a few key remaining employees and to keep his eye on Marnie, too. While Jake hadn't found the missing money yet, he had leads.

Today, he had the distinct pleasure of taking Marnie off the list of primary suspects thanks to the ridiculously stripped-down lifestyle she'd led for the past two months. Marnie had demonstrated obvious financial hardship while funds continued to disappear from Premiere's accounts. But Jake couldn't even share with her since she'd never known she was a suspect. Still, Jake thought of today as a damn happy occasion because clearing Marnie meant he could do more than just watch her from afar.

His eyes locked on her luscious curves as she came out from behind the desk to shake hands with her clients. Yes, the time approached when he could return to her life—as the carpenter she hadn't seen in two months—and ask her out. He could remove the surveillance equipment easily enough if she left the front office for even a minute.

There'd been a definite attraction between them when he'd first met her, an attraction he would have never acted on while she remained a suspect. But now, the path was clear to explore the fireworks he'd felt when he'd been in her office building that bookcase for her. If anything, he admired her all the more after watching her pull her life together in the wake of losing a job and getting dumped by the waste of space she'd been dating up until she'd been terminated. Marnie had defied the odds and opened her own business in a crap economy, using her travel smarts to her advantage in the new gig.

Smart. Sexy. And she'd be all alone inside in another minute once her customers left. Would he knock on the door as soon as they were gone? Or, knowing that she was prone to stripping off a few layers of clothes as soon as she flipped the Closed sign on her storefront, would he tune in to the BlackBerry a few minutes longer?

Heat crawled up his back at the thought. The need to be honorable warred with the urge to look his fill.

As she ushered her clients to the door, Jake figured he'd split the difference. He'd only watch for a minute and then he'd flip off the feed.

And this time, he wouldn't settle for just fantasizing about Marnie. He'd follow it up with a house call, because damn it, he wanted to see the show in person one of these days.

Yes, a very Merry Christmas to him....

CHAPTER ONE

A DETAIL-ORIENTED, TYPE A personality, Marnie Wainwright took all necessary precautions. So she checked and double-checked the lock on the street-level door to her business. She closed all the blinds. She flipped the sign on Lose Yourself from Open to Closed.

Only then, in the privacy of the small storefront where she'd converted the back offices into a living space, did she pump her fist in victory and break out her best Michael Jackson move.

"Yesss!" She shouted her triumph, letting down her hair with one hand and switching the satellite radio tuner to dance grooves with the other.

Two months of hard work at Lose Yourself had paid off with her biggest profit yet now that she'd booked an African safari followed up by a beach getaway to Seychelles for a wealthy local couple. Two months of nonstop trolling for clients. Sixty-one days of researching unique trip ideas to appeal to an increasingly competitive travel market full of selective buyers who could easily book online. But her idea to pitch one-of-a-kind fantasy escapes was working.

"How do you like me now?" She sang a tune of her own making, rump-shaking her way into the back to retrieve a bottle of champagne she'd been saving from the days when her paycheck had been fat and the perks of working in promotions for a luxury global resort conglomerate, Premiere Properties, had been numerous.

She hadn't salvaged much financially from that time, thanks to the bad investments she'd foolishly let her financial adviser boyfriend oversee. Little did she know then that he'd been even more clueless than he'd been charming, losing her hard-earned money almost as soon as she'd entrusted it to him. She'd been royally ticked off about that, but that had only been the prelude to *him* dumping *her*. On Facebook, no less. Apparently he hadn't been interested in her once she lost her cushy benefits at Premiere. At least she understood Alec's reasons. She never had figured out why Premiere had let her go or how her department had been losing as much money as her boss had claimed. But while getting laid off had hurt, it hadn't broken her.

Tonight's sale proved as much. She'd taken her travel smarts from all those years crisscrossing the globe for Premiere and used them to match up adventure seekers with just the right unique escape to suit them, whether that meant a spa trip to Bali or backpacking around the Indus Valley. The inspiration for Lose Yourself had come from her need to do just that. Since she hadn't been able to take a vacation from her own problems, she enjoyed helping other people to do so.

Ditching her suit in a celebratory striptease for the benefit of a life-size cutout of a Hawaiian guy offering a lei to her, she tugged on a long black silk robe for her private after-party. The Hawaiian dude had been a promotional item from a hotel and not quite in keeping with the upscale, personalized appeal of Lose Yourself. But he was cute company in the copier room that doubled as a galley kitchen until she got on her feet enough to afford a real house again.

"Cheers to me!" She raised the proverbial roof with one hand while she twisted off the wire restraint from the champagne cork with the other.

Pop!

The happy sound of that cork flying across the room pleased her as much as the taste of the bubbly would. It had been so long since she'd had reason to celebrate anything. About the only other victory that came close was curing herself of the need to throw darts at the ex-boyfriend who'd helped her lose a job and her savings. She used to regularly wing a silver-tipped missile at a photograph taped to the dartboard she kept on an office wall, but she'd torched that picture a month ago in an effort to take ownership of her mistakes.

She'd almost taken a cute guy's head off with one of those darts a couple of months ago, she recalled. Handsome contractor Jake Brennan had been hand-crafting a display case for her storefront and had unwittingly opened a door into one of her tiny arrows. It hadn't been her finest moment. Although Jake Brennan himself had been very fine indeed. Memories of his strong arms coated with a light sheen of sweat and sawdust as he'd sculpted the wood into shape had returned to her often ever since.

Pouring the top-shelf champagne into substandard stemware, Marnie lifted one side of her robe like a cha-cha girl before testing out a high kick. A little champagne sloshed out of the cheap glass, but the bubbles felt like an electric kiss sliding down her arm as she lifted the glass in a toast.

No doubt it had been thoughts of Jake Brennan that had her thinking of electric kisses.

"To me!" she cheered, then took a drink.

Rinnng! A call on her cell phone interrupted her celebration and she scrambled to grab it just in case it was a potential client. Seeing her former colleague's name on caller ID didn't mean it was a casual call. She'd been pitching her fantasy adventures to all her overworked, overstressed friends these past two months.

"Hello, Sarah." Marnie turned the music down just enough to hear her friend on the other end of the phone.

"Hi, Marnie." Sarah Anders's voice was low, her tone oddly serious next to Marnie's good mood. "Have a minute?"

"Sure." Marnie sashayed her way toward the display case the sexy contractor had built, still dancing as she savored the taste of her drink on her tongue. "I'm just having a little toast to rich world travelers who aren't afraid to take a chance on a new business."

"You made another sale?" Sarah asked.

"An African safari. Not exactly the most original trip, but it's long and involved and will keep me in business well into the New Year. Between that and a little holiday escape I booked for a couple who wanted to check out an ice hotel in Quebec City, I've had my best week yet."

"That's great." Sarah's voice didn't match the words.

"What's wrong?" Feeling the groove vibrate the floor through her bare feet, Marnie set her glass on one of the shelves of the bookcase.

"I just wondered if you'd heard any rumors about misappropriation of funds or big losses at Premiere Properties before you left."

"Embezzlement?" Marnie told herself she shouldn't care what happened over at Premiere Properties after she'd been terminated six months ago for bogus reasons. Her boss, Vince Galway, had told her some B.S. about cutting back on promotions, but the company spent money hand over fist to promote its luxury resorts. Still, she had to admit she was curious. "What makes you think that?"

"Nothing concrete." Sarah sighed, a world of stress in one eloquent huff of air over the mouthpiece. "But there's been a guy asking questions this week. He's been discreet enough, saying he's part of some forensic accounting team that Vince hired to double-check the books, but I think something's up."

For the first time in six months, Marnie almost felt lucky to have lost the job she loved at Premiere. Her business was taking off, and she didn't have any worries about corporate scams or office politics.

"I'll keep an ear out since I still do business with a lot of Premiere's hotels." In fact, Marnie had sent more than one client to the properties she used to promote. Although she didn't think it had been fair that she'd been axed with no warning, she still recognized Premiere ran first-class resorts.

"Thanks, Marnie. I'd appreciate any word."

Disconnecting the call, Marnie cranked the tunes back up, ready to get back into celebrating her successes. She'd dealt with enough crap these past six months to know that she damn well needed to toast the good stuff when it came along since life didn't give you happy days like this all that often.

Standing in front of the custom-made bookcase that displayed miniature buildings, crafts and other souvenirs from destinations all over the world, she placed her palms where Jake Brennan's broad hands had once been and ran her fingertips over a smooth edge. He'd done a beautiful job on the piece and he'd done it for a song, all things considered. She'd really needed that financial break since she'd been trying to get the doors open for her business on a budget.

Between the memories of the man, the champagne and the swish of silk around her bare legs, she experienced a rush of longing. Jake had been big-time attractive. Too bad she hadn't been in a better place emotionally when they'd met or she might have invited him to stick around after the job was done. Maybe asked him out for a drink.

Or—in her wilder fantasies—simply peeled off all her clothes and plastered herself to that gorgeous body of his.

Walking her fingers across a shelf, Marnie blew a kiss to a model of the Egyptian sphinx on one side of the case and winked at a tiny replica of Michelangelo's David. She had to freshen her flirting skills sometime, didn't she? One day, she'd get back out in the dating world again.

Retrieving her champagne glass, she knocked over an iron Statue of Liberty nearby. As she moved to straighten it, she noticed a smear on the back of the case—a dark spot that didn't belong. Unwilling to suffer a smudge in an otherwise perfect display, she reached past the travel guides and mementos meant to entice her clients.

But the spot felt smooth as glass—different than the rest of the wooden cabinet.

"That's odd." Shoving aside a few more famous buildings for a better look, Marnie peered into a small circle of smoky glass.

Her champagne flute fell from her fingers and shattered on the floor. The electric thrill pulsing through her over her good payday fizzled to nothing, even though the bass from an old club tune still pumped through the speakers.

Because at the center of that smoky glass rested a tiny camera lens. Someone had been watching her.

And given the way the gadgetry had been so perfectly incorporated into her custom-built cabinet, she only had one guess as to who that might be. After what she'd gone through with her ex-boyfriend, the next guy who crossed her would be wise to run for cover.

And right now, it looked like that man was none other than her sexy contractor.

Jake Brennan.

Music pulsed from inside the Lose Yourself storefront facade until it sounded more like a raucous bar than a ritzy travel agency specializing in exotic adventures. If Jake Brennan hadn't known Marnie so well, he might have turned around and come back another day, thinking she had company.

But weeks' worth of video surveillance on her fledgling business had not only taken her off his primary suspect list in a major white-collar crime. It had also taught Jake that Marnie liked to dance. And damn, but her shimmy-shake routine while stripping off her jacket and blouse hadn't disappointed.

He would have closed his eyes if she'd ditched more than that. Honestly, he would have. But he'd wanted to be sure she was alone before he went to the door. Could he help it if she had a habit of peeling off work clothes in favor of a silk lounging robe the second she shut her door for the day?

Rapping on the door through the hole in the middle of a fat green holiday wreath, he grinned at the memory of old surveillance footage and the brief, two-minute snippet he'd allowed himself back in the car—just enough to see her whip off the clothes and grab the champagne. He'd made sure to only point the cameras toward her work space for legal reasons, even though she'd had plans to live in the back offices. That had eased his conscience somewhat since he hated the idea of spying on anyone who was innocent—especially in their most private moments. But at the time he'd installed the camera he now sought to remove, Jake had very good reason to think she was anything but innocent.

Inside Lose Yourself, the volume of the music decreased. The quiet of the business district on a Friday night surrounded him and he couldn't help a rush of anticipation at seeing Marnie now that he'd all but cleared her.

"Who is it?" came her voice, sweetly familiar to him after scanning hours of video for evidence in his case.

Yes, he'd gotten to know Marnie Wainwright so damn well that just hearing her voice had him salivating like Pavlov's dog. And that happened even though he'd forced himself to shut off the video feed on those few occasions where she'd started to strip off a little more than a stranger had the right to see.

"It's Jake Brennan," he called through the door. "I did some work on your office a couple of months ago and I think I might have left one of my tools behind."

He knew she'd remember him from his brief stint working there. He'd given her a steal on his labor, mostly because his work was entirely self-serving.

Plus, she'd eyeballed him enough that day to make him think she hadn't been oblivious to his presence in her office. If it hadn't been for his suspicions of her back then, he would have asked her out.

Now that he was going to retrieve the surveillance equipment and declare this part of his case finished, Jake looked forward to seeing her again without his work as a barrier.

Inside, he could hear her slide a dead bolt and flip one other lock open. He could picture it perfectly since he knew the inside of that office like the back of his hand from watching Marnie run her business day in and day out. Other than the brief view he'd allowed himself in the car, however, he hadn't reviewed any tapes in a while. Not since his case had led him in another direction.

Slowly, the door creaked open.

A whisper of black silk fluttered through the crack. She'd left the final latch on the door—a long hook like the kind used on hotel rooms—so she could see into the street without leaving herself vulnerable.

Recognizing the black silk as the calf-length, sexy

number she liked to wear around the place before bed,
he swallowed hard, knowing damn well she wasn't
wearing much else.

"Sorry to bother you so late—"

The expression on her face froze him in his shoes.
Pursed lips, a clamped-tight jaw and gray eyes staring
daggers at him all suggested he'd interrupted something. Had she been arguing with someone on the
phone? Protective instincts flared to life.

"Is everything okay in there?" He stepped closer,
trying to look past her into the familiar office interior
that he'd seen often enough on his surveillance tapes.
Framed prints of the Egyptian pyramids hung next to
a map of London highlighting historic pubs.

"Everything is fine." She spoke the words oddly,
like a marionette where the mouth's movement didn't
quite match up with the sounds. "Especially now that
you're here."

"I don't get it." He didn't like the brittle set of her
shoulders or the flushed color in her cheeks. Was she
not feeling well?

Before he could ask, she raised a silver-tipped dart
that he remembered well from an earlier meeting.

"You're just in time for target practice while we wait
for the cops to arrive."

"What?"

His confusion only lasted until she arced back her
arm and let the missile fly, aiming for his eye.

Oh, shit.

Belatedly, he realized her assortment of symptoms
pointed to stone-cold fury. All directed at him.

Luckily she was so angry, that her release point was

late and the dart clattered harmlessly to the concrete pavement at his feet.

"How could you?" she yelled through the narrow opening. Disappearing for a moment, she returned with a whole handful of darts. "You pervert!"

The darts started flying in earnest now and he took cover against the door.

Ace detective work told him she'd found his hidden camera.

"Marnie?" He tried leaning into her line of sight between rounds of incoming fire. "Did you really call the cops?"

That was going to be a nightmare. He had as many enemies on the force as he had friends. With his luck, one of the former would answer the call and gladly lock his ass up for the night until he could straighten away the paperwork.

"Of course." Another dart.

He ducked.

"You can wait with me while the local police bring you a pair of handcuffs and an orange jumpsuit." A painted pink stone that he happened to know was her paperweight came hurtling through the opening now, joining the darts on the pavement.

He heard the stomp of furious footsteps away from the door. Leaning into the vacated space, he used the time to make his case.

"Marnie, wait." He pulled out his wallet and tossed it inside her storefront where it skidded across the gray commercial carpet and thudded against her ankle. "There's my ID. I'm a licensed private investigator."

She slowed her battle with the buttons on the desk

phone. Apparently, she'd been making more calls. To a friend or neighbor? Backup to be sure he stuck around long enough for his own arrest?

"If that's true, that sounds only marginally less smarmy than being a complete and total perv." She cradled the phone against her shoulder and started punching buttons again, this time with slow deliberation.

"Premiere Properties didn't terminate you because they couldn't fund your department. They terminated you because of a major embezzlement scam that originated in your sector of the company. You were a prime suspect."

She shook her head. Confused. Shocked. He'd seen that expression on people's faces when he'd worked in homicide and he'd had to face grieving family members to question them. Hell, he still saw that expression as a P.I. when a wife learned her husband had been cheating. He didn't take jobs like that often, but sometimes he could be persuaded. Having been on the clueless end of an unfaithful relationship made him empathize.

Marnie's face mirrored that kind of disillusionment now.

"Who are you?" She seemed to see him for the first time that night, her brows furrowed in concentration as if she could guess his motives if she stared hard enough.

Relieved, he pointed to her feet.

"My ID is right there. Just hang up the phone long enough to let me talk to you."

With a jerky nod, she replaced the receiver and retrieved his wallet. Seeing his Florida private investigator's license inside, she met his gaze again.

"I didn't really call the cops yet. I only just found that camera a minute before you arrived."

Thank God. He didn't want to deal with that drama tonight.

"I'm going to collect the darts out here," he told her, scooping up the littered sidewalk. "If you want to meet me somewhere you'll feel safe, we can talk."

By the time he straightened, she was already back at the partially opened door. The stiff set to her shoulders had vanished.

Her caramel-colored hair slid loose from a messy twist on one side, the freed strands grazing her shoulder where her satin robe drooped enough to show she wore a black cotton tank top underneath it. Her gray eyes locked on his, searching his face for answers.

"I don't want to go anywhere. Not when my thoughts are so scattered and my head is spinning like this." Over her shoulder, he could see the mess in her office. It looked as if she'd cleared everything off the display case he'd built, probably searching for other cameras. "I'm suddenly very, very tired."

Without warning, she closed the door in his face and he thought she'd ended the conversation. Then, he heard the safety latch unhook and she reopened the door, silently inviting him inside.

"Are you sure you're okay with this?" He didn't like the idea of setting foot in there if she thought for a second he could still be some random lecher taking video for fun.

She nodded. "A real perv would have put the camera in the bedroom or over the shower, not pointing at where I do business. Besides, a colleague from Premiere called tonight and mentioned something about rumors of a financial loss. I know you're not making it up about possible embezzlement. Are you the guy Vince hired to ask discreet questions around the office?"

He nodded.

"Then you might as well come in." Her words lacked the red-hot fury of the flying darts, but there was a new level of iciness that didn't feel like a big improvement.

Accepting the grudging invitation, he stepped inside the storefront and closed the door behind him.

"I'll just set these down." He piled the darts on her desk, an elegant antique piece out of place with the rest of the utilitarian furniture. Kind of like her. Her silk bathrobe probably cost as much as the old beater she drove to work lately.

Marnie Wainwright had fallen on some hard times, but he admired her grit in not letting them get the best of her.

"I refuse to apologize for the darts." She produced an open bottle of champagne along with two glasses, then dropped onto the love seat in her office's waiting area. "Even if you were conducting an investigation, a hidden camera is still a disturbing way to go about obtaining information."

But legal for an investigation of this magnitude, as long as the device wasn't inside her private residence. He took the chair at a right angle to her, observing the way she recovered herself. Her fingers shook with the leftover churning of emotions as she handed him a glass of bubbly. He hated that his investigation had freaked her out. Hated that she'd found the damn camera in the first place. He'd been banking on hitting on her, not having her glare at him as if he were evil incarnate.

"Granted. But it was also the fastest way of proving your innocence. If my client had gone to the cops, you could have been stuck trying to clear your name from inside a cell, since the evidence they had on you was pretty damning." He set the glass she'd given him on the coffee table.

She seemed to think that one over as she poured her own glass and held the cool drink against her forehead like a compress.

"Why didn't they go the police?" she asked softly, her hands shaking just a little as she lowered the flute and took a sip.

He tried not to envy the glass for its chance to press against her lips. She was dealing with a crisis, after all. But he'd been battling an attraction to this woman ever since the week he'd built the custom-made cabinet to house his spy equipment. He couldn't help subtly ogle a bit now that he was finally free to act on that attraction. Her dark robe slipped away from her calf enough to reveal the delineation of the long, lean muscle in her leg. A gold toe ring winked from her bare foot, a small row of pearls catching the light as she shifted.

Jake had a sudden vision of that long, bare leg in his hands, his body planted between her thighs. And wouldn't that fantasy be helpful in explaining why he'd been spying on her? Cursing the wayward thoughts, he forced himself to talk about the case.

"The CEO of Premiere doesn't trust the local police

ever since they misplaced key evidence that would have convicted some crooks involved in his last company."

The case still pissed off Jake, too, even though it had been two years ago.

"Brennan. You were the investigator on that crime." She snapped her fingers in recognition. "I thought your name sounded familiar when we met. I did a little research on it because I worked for Premiere when they hired Vincent Galway to take over as CEO."

Great. Jake didn't want to be associated with an investigation that screamed police corruption. He'd left the force because a couple of the cops appeared to be flunkies for some bigwigs who didn't want that particular corporate fraud case prosecuted. To keep his eyes off Marnie's legs, he diverted his attention to a nearby painting of the Anasazi cliff dwellings, decorated for the holidays with a few balsam sprigs on the top of the frame.

"I quit when the system screwed over Vince. He talked to the cops and the Feds to try to throw some light on dirty dealings in his last company, and he was the one with mud on his face after the evidence was misplaced." Jake swiped the champagne glass off the table. "But I know Vince from way back. He served in Vietnam with my dad. Because Vince trusts me, he hired my services to help him wade through the embezzlement scandal that could have hurt his company if news about it leaked."

Marnie swirled her glass and watched the bubbles chase each other.

"So you got onto the work crew when I had the office overhauled and you installed a camera." Her bathrobe slipped off her knee, unveiling bare skin for as far as the wandering eye could see up her leg.

A slice of creamy thigh proved too much competition for the picture of the damn cliff dwellings. His gaze tracked up her skin as he calculated how quickly he could have her naked…

"Yes." His throat went dry. "It was a fast way to either clear you or confirm your guilt, and it's a tool the cops rarely use because—"

"—because it's highly unethical and borderline illegal?"

"Because it takes a lot of reviews to obtain permission for it." He'd be damned if he'd let her call his honor into question. "Technology is saving a lot of manpower hours at your local cop shop, so I can guarantee you it's not illegal when there is just cause—for me, or for them."

"But I've been cleared of any wrongdoing, thanks to having my life put under a microscope?"

"You're no longer a prime suspect." He watched her retuck the bathrobe around her legs, possibly feeling the heat of his stare despite his best effort to rein himself in. "In fact, I was hoping to remove the equipment tonight."

Right before he hit on her. He planned to get very close to Marnie Wainwright in the near future. Now? Who knew how long it would take for him to rebuild some trust?

"You thought you'd just saunter in here tonight after I hadn't seen you in two months?" The precariously lopsided twist in her hair finally gave up the ghost, spilling caramel-colored strands and spitting out a pencil that had been holding it all together.

"I figured you wouldn't want to have that equipment running any longer than necessary," he told her reasonably as he retrieved the fallen pencil and placed it on the coffee table.

"Of course not, but since I didn't know I'd been under surveillance for the past two months, might I inquire why you thought I'd even let you in?"

Animal attraction.

But he knew better than to say as much.

"I figured I'd look into a fantasy escape." Heavy on the fantasy. God knew, she'd been occupying enough of his lately.

The woman had compromised his investigation every time she sashayed past that surveillance camera, her confident feminine strut one hell of a distraction.

"At this hour?" Her gaze narrowed. Suspicion mounted.

And with damn good reason.

He hadn't even come close to laying his cards on the table with her yet.

"I work late." He shrugged, not sure what else to offer in his defense. "Do you want me to take the equipment now?"

"No." She leaned forward on the love seat, invading his personal space in a way that would have been damn pleasant if she hadn't fixed him with a stony glare. "I know how to take a sledgehammer to the cabinet, but thanks anyway. Right now, I'm more interested in two things."

"Shoot." He breathed in the warm, spicy scent of an

exotic perfume he wouldn't have noticed if they hadn't been this close.

"First, you didn't say I was cleared of suspicion. You carefully distinguished that I'm no longer a prime suspect. Care to explain what that means?"

Her silk-covered knee was only inches from his. One bare foot sat so close to his loafers that he'd have to be careful of her toes if he stood. The nails had been manicured with glittery white polish except for the big toe on each foot, which featured a carefully painted holly berry leaf.

Lifting his gaze to meet hers, he wondered if he was the only one fantasizing about peeling off her robe.

"It means that there's an outside chance you could still be a conspirator, but we don't think that's likely and we are one hundred percent sure you are not the primary force behind the embezzlement."

"How reassuring." She tucked a strand of hair behind one ear, frowning as she seemed to consider the implications of that.

"You said you were interested in two things?" He saw the dartboard behind the love seat no longer contained a picture of her ex-boyfriend, something he hadn't known from the video feeds since his camera didn't give him enough of a wide angle on the room.

Good for her for not caring anymore. Jake's investigations had dug up more than a little dirt on him.

"Right." She fixed him with her gaze. "I'd also like to know just how much of me you've seen with that camera lens of yours."

CHAPTER TWO

MARNIE HAD HER ANSWER in a nanosecond.

The heat that flared in the private investigator's eyes practically singed her skin before he said one word.

Hell, he didn't have to say a word.

"Oh, my God." She buried her face in her hands to escape Jake's gaze. Or maybe to hide from the answering heat inside her that she had no business feeling for a man who had spied on her.

Damn him.

"Please believe it was never my intent to see more than the business transactions." He had that cool, authority-figure voice down pat and she wondered how she ever could have believed he was a carpenter, let alone a good guy.

Jake Brennan had *dangerous* tattooed all over his big, imposing bod, a wedge of powerful muscle that looked fit to take care of business in a back alley. The brooding, hot expression in his eyes communicated something altogether inappropriate, as if he knew exactly what she looked like naked and had devoted a fair amount of thought to seeing her that way again.

Was she reading into that enigmatic look of his? Maybe. But his presence made her twitch in her seat.

"But you did see more than business transactions,"

she snapped, frazzled by sexual thoughts. She lifted her head and quickly realized she'd sat far too near to him for this little tête-à-tête.

His knee was so close she could feel the warmth of him through the thin silk of her robe. He sat forward in his seat, his sculpted shoulders leaning toward her as if he debated offering comfort. A worn gray Henley shirt stretched over the taut muscles of his arms, the sleeves shoved up to his elbows past a heavy silver watch that rested on one wrist. Wavy dark hair brushed his collar; his jaw was bristly with a five-o'clock shadow.

She wondered what it would feel like against her skin. And damn it, why did she care? It had to be because she'd spent the past weeks thinking about Jake the Carpenter in a romantic way, building him up to be someone he wasn't based purely on attractiveness. A stupid habit, that. Hadn't she been burned oh so recently by a guy who was all flash and no substance?

Although comparing Alec to Jake was sort of like weighing a cheap copy of a famous painting against the original. One was nice to look at. The other took your breath away it was so freaking magnificent.

"When I installed the camera, I had no idea you would make yourself so comfortable in your office space. How many people work in their pajamas? Um, legally, anyway."

He said it without a trace of a smile, but she could swear she saw a glint of amusement in his flinty gaze.

Defensiveness steeled her spine.

"I thought I was alone so I refuse to be embarrassed." Could she help it if she'd gotten in the habit of peeling off a layer as soon as she flipped the Closed sign on the business?

It had been a damn difficult year between losing her job, losing her savings due to her ex's crappy financial management and finding out the ex himself was the kind of superficial jerk who only cared about her worth as his personal sugar moma.

Oh, and that was all before she found out she'd also been under suspicion for embezzlement.

"You definitely don't have any reason to be embarrassed." He cracked a smile that time—the barest hint of a grin that revealed an unexpected dimple. "I thought your dance moves were great."

In different circumstances, she would have been totally charmed.

But flirting with the P.I. who'd surely seen her mostly naked and who, by the way, hadn't fully crossed her off his suspect list didn't strike her as a particularly wise move.

"Thanks. But on that note, maybe I should let you take the camera and get back to your investigation." She stood, feeling awkward and too aware of him.

"I appreciate that." He stood, too, topping her by several inches and filling her vision with more than his fair share of studliness. "I'd hate to lose expensive equipment to a sledgehammer."

He didn't move, however. At least not right away.

Her heartbeat quickened.

"Jake." Saying his name aloud felt foreign and familiar at the same time. She'd thought about him often enough since their first meeting.

Strange that all the while he'd been feeding her daydreams, she might have been playing a role in his, too. The thought stirred desire so palpable it made her breath catch.

"Yes?" He'd been waiting. Watching.

Still not moving.

"Who else has seen those surveillance tapes?" She had to know. Because while she might be able to write off Jake's eyes following her in her most private moments, she didn't think she could handle knowing her former employer had been reviewing the footage.

"No one but me has seen the actual footage. I just pulled off a few stills to show some of your transactions in progress. I would never compromise your privacy any more than absolutely necessary."

She nodded, believing him.

"Thank you for that, at least." Warmth swirled through her, although why she should feel so comforted that he would keep her amateur stripteases to himself, she wasn't quite sure. "Do you need any tools to remove the camera? I have a screwdriver somewhere."

Turning, she moved to retrieve it.

"Marnie, wait." His hand clamped lightly around her shoulder and she froze. Not that he was holding her in place. Far from it. She could have easily kept on walking.

But it was the first time that he'd touched her for real and not just in passing—or in fantasies. The contact made her mouth turn dry and her legs felt a little shaky.

"What is it?" Her words were breathless.

She hoped he would interpret that as nervousness from finding out she'd been suspected of a major felony and under surveillance all in one evening. And honestly, that was part of it.

His hand slid away now that he had her attention, but the memory of it continued to warm her shoulder like a phantom touch.

"Would you consider answering a few questions about your work with Premiere Properties?"

"Of course." She resisted the urge to fan herself. Obviously, if she was so desperate for male companionship that she would continue to think about someone who had spied on her in an, er, romantic way, she needed to get out more often.

"I've eliminated a lot of people." He reached into the back pocket of his jeans and emerged with a paper. "My focus has narrowed to people involved with this place."

He handed her the folded sticky note with a half-dozen luxury resorts listed, along with highly placed individuals within those properties. Although a handful of names were still legible, only one resort wasn't crossed out.

"The Marquis." She knew the property well. "You've got your work cut out for you."

Returning the paper to him, she took a step back in every way possible. He might as well have indicated a nest of rattlesnakes.

"Why do you say that?" He frowned, looking at the paper again.

"You haven't done much homework for a guy who's been on the case for two months, have you?" She thought about pouring herself another sip or two of champagne, then figured she'd be better off just finding the damn screwdriver so he could take his camera and go.

She slid out from behind the coffee table to hunt through her desk.

"On the contrary, I've worked my ass off. White-collar crimes like this can be filtered through so many different accounts electronically that it makes it damn difficult to trace." He followed her to the desk, sidestepping a few items on the floor from when she'd cleared the shelves in a frightened fury. "After hiring a forensic accountant, I spent most of my time investigating you since, on first look, the money appeared to have been leaking wherever you traveled last year."

Her frantic culling through pens and paperclips paused.

"You think someone wanted it to *look* like I was responsible?" A new fear gripped her, superceding her outrage at being secretly videotaped.

"Yes. And when you opened this business, I wondered if you'd just found a new way to skim money from the same properties you worked with at Premiere since you continued to book trips to a lot of the same resorts."

"Because they're great destinations and I know them inside and out."

"Including the Marquis?"

Slamming the door shut with her knee, she rubbed her temple where a stress headache wanted to take root.

"No. That one isn't really—" Sighing, she began again. "It's a unique place. Well off the beaten path just outside of scenic Saratoga, New York. Strictly for adults."

"It didn't come up in my early searches, but I just figured it was one of those high-end places that doesn't advertise."

"It is." Just thinking about the things she'd seen there the last time she visited made heat crawl up her cheeks and take up residence. "Technically, Premiere doesn't own it, but they are a partner of the eccentric owner and they take care of the food service and a few other basics. It's a complicated relationship and it's important that it remains under the radar since the guests are guaranteed a highly—" she cleared her throat "—sensual experience."

Was it just her, or was sex coming to mind way too much during this conversation? While she'd like to believe it was just the buzz of good champagne in her veins that made her feel so pleasurably warm inside, she knew it had more to do with Jake Brennan being in the room with her. He would make any woman take notice.

"Sounds like the perfect place to hide an embezzlement crime." His jaw flexed, and she could almost see the wheels turning in his head, fitting this new piece of evidence into the puzzle.

"Actually, precious little is hidden in the rooms of the Marquis." She studiously avoided looking at him while thinking about what went on in that private resort. Her eyes locked on the screwdriver in a silver cup holder on her desk. "Here."

She passed him the tool and eased past him to clear a path to the bookcase so he could take his equipment— and his questions—and go.

He took the screwdriver, following more slowly.

"It also sounds like the perfect place to lose yourself."

"Excuse me?" She pulled the belt tighter on her bathrobe.

No matter that she wore a tank top and comfy pair of girly boxer shorts underneath it. The more layers the better during a conversation about a sex-drenched playground with a droolworthy stud who'd not only seen her mostly naked, but seemed to enjoy the view.

Ah, who was she kidding? She was enjoying checking him out just as much. Too bad he had already pulled a fast one on her or she might have considered acting on the sizzling connection between them.

"I want to avail myself of your services through Lose Yourself. I need you to book me a trip to this place as soon as possible."

The image that presented—Jake Brennan stalking the secret lairs of the sexually adventurous—gave her heart palpitations. And, oddly, inspired a ridiculous surge of jealousy for all the women who would dole out their best tricks to attract his notice.

"No." She folded her arms. Shook her head. "You don't want to go there. There's a strict policy about hidden cameras anyway. Definitely not your kind of place."

"Don't you want to find out who tried to pin about ten different federal crimes on you?"

"Yes, but—"

"Good. That's why you're going with me."

CHAPTER THREE

"FORGET IT."

Marnie wrenched the screwdriver out of his hand and turned toward the display case that held his camera as if to remove it by herself.

"I need you there." He slid his arm between her and the bookcase to stop her. The fact that his knuckles brushed against her flat stomach and his shoulder rubbed along hers was a pleasurable bonus.

"Don't be ridiculous." She stepped back, her face flushed and her pulse twitching visibly at the base of her throat.

Agitated because of his touch? Or his proposition?

He couldn't deny a bit of agitation of his own at the thought of spending time with her at some trumped-up luxury love shack. While he'd had every intention of getting close to her sooner or later, he hadn't intended for the circumstances to be quite so intense.

But then, he hadn't considered what an asset she'd be in an investigation at a hyperexclusive resort. She knew the place. And if the real embezzler had set Marnie up to take the fall for the crime, she might be able to finger the enemy faster than he could on his own.

"You said it yourself." Sliding the screwdriver from her grip, he set it aside, not needing it to free his sur-

veillance equipment. "You visited dozens of properties all over the globe for Premiere, so you know these
resorts well. You've been to the Marquis and you've
dealt with the people who work there. Why let the trail
turn even colder while I waste time trying to get the lay
of the land when you know the place inside and out?"

She gaped at him as if he'd just suggested she sign
on for a suicide mission. Was the thought of spending
a few days with him that bad? He forced his attention
to the camera equipment as he extracted a tiny wireless transmitter.

"Even if I wanted to do that—and I don't—I can't
just take off at the drop of a hat. I have a business to
run." She held out her hand to take the transmitter from
him while he pried out the camera itself.

"Everyone deserves a getaway," he parroted back
her business's pitch line, knowing he was onto something. He had to convince her to do this—and not just
because he wanted to get to know her better. Her input
could be the key. "Besides, maybe you can't afford
not to go."

Straightening, he tucked the small camera in his
back pocket, then took the transmitter from her and
did the same.

"What do you mean?" Frowning and distracted, she
didn't seem to notice when he put his hands on her
shoulders to turn her around so they could converse
somewhere besides the narrow space in front of the
shelves.

How easy would it be to slide his hands lower, to
graze her chest just above the rise of her breasts? The

fragrance of her temptress perfume wafted along his senses as he guided her toward the desk.

With more than a little regret, he released her.

For now.

"Someone went to considerable effort to make it appear as though you were behind a highly lucrative crime. That suggests you've got an enemy you don't know about. What if this enemy raises the stakes next time?"

Her gray eyes searched his and he could see the moment she wondered if he could be the guilty party.

"Here." He took out his cell phone. "Vincent is on speed dial. Call your old boss at Premiere Properties and check out my story. He can tell you how seriously he's taking this investigation."

And although it stung a little to see how fast she reached for the phone and dialed, Jake knew the line separating the criminals from the cops—or P.I.'s—could be razor-thin sometimes. He'd left the force just because there was too much crossover in his opinion. He could hardly blame her if she found it difficult to know who to trust.

Still, he didn't care for the lack of color in her face by the time she disconnected her call and handed him the phone in silence.

"You okay?" He didn't want to crowd her when she'd had one hell of a night, but she sure looked as if she could use a shoulder.

"You're right. He says 2.5 million dollars is missing. That's a lot of money." Her bleak tone was a far cry from her normal Friday-after-five voice. Usually she spent a good hour belting out tunes along with her radio.

And while he regretted bursting her bubble of ignorant bliss, she was better off knowing the truth. He had to consider her safety.

"Someone's taking great pains not to get caught. That raises the chances they could resort to violence if they think we're on his or her trail."

This would have been a whole lot simpler if he hadn't investigated her. Hadn't lied to her and spied on her. If none of that had happened, he'd be dusting off seduction skills he hadn't used in too damn long. Instead, he needed to tread carefully to convince Marnie to help him nab Vincent Galway's embezzler. But it was the least he could do after all the ways Vince had been screwed by the justice system. Jake had always hated that one of the most honorable guys he knew—after his own dad—had had his integrity questioned. His life put under a microscope because he'd tried to do the right thing.

And yeah, he couldn't deny an unexpected need to protect Marnie. His case had taken on a new slant after talking to her and he wanted to be sure the embezzler didn't try something more drastic to point suspicion her way.

"I agree that it would be in my best interest to figure out who this person is before he targets me all over again." Marnie stalked toward her work computer and sat down at the screen. At first, she simply squeezed her temples, as if she wanted to rub out all the worries in her head. Then, she peered up at him with new determination in her eyes. "Since I have this bastard to thank for putting me under suspicion and exposing me to a stranger, it would be worth the time off if I could help put him behind bars."

Surprise, surprise.

She was going to agree to this without a fight. But she didn't look happy about it. Figuring it would be in poor form to break out the victory dance while she was so clearly upset, he concentrated on all the plans he needed to make for this new strategy to work.

Jake watched her click through some keys to pull up a web page for a genteel-looking inn with wide white columns and a long veranda. Four stone chimneys dotted the roof. It could have been out of *Gone with the Wind* except for the fact that the place was surrounded by snow and decked with holiday evergreens. A cobalt-colored front door was the only feature of the building that didn't fit with the classic Georgian architecture.

"You'll get us into the Marquis?"

"Damn straight," she muttered, clicking a code into the system that activated a reservation form he assumed wasn't available to the general public. The photo of the Marquis didn't even have a sign out front, though a caption under the photo gave an address in upstate New York. "I've gone through hell the past six months because of this. I had to move out of my house and into a room in the back of the business to protect my credit after I lost my job. My savings. All this time, I thought I'd done something wrong to make Vince question my capabilities, when in fact I just had an enemy I didn't know about. An enemy who made me look like a criminal."

He heard the hurt in her voice. Felt for her situation.

"Can you be ready to leave tomorrow?"

"Are you kidding?" She turned frosty eyes on him. "Someone wants me behind bars. And whoever it is, I have that person to thank for losing a great job at the worst possible time. So I can have my car gassed up and ready to head north in an hour."

Surprised at her new level of commitment to the plan, he wondered if she had any idea how close they'd have to be throughout this trip.

"Are you sure you don't want to wait for a flight out in the morning?"

"Tomorrow is a Saturday. We'll be lucky to find an afternoon flight, let alone something in the morning." She went back to her computer keys and started filling out information for the exclusive resort. "Besides, I won't be able to get any sleep with this hanging over my head."

Twenty-plus hours on the road with Marnie? His agenda shifted to accommodate the prospect.

"Fine, but you need to give an assumed name for check-in purposes, just in case the embezzler is someone who works on-site. We can pick up a wig or something on the way up."

She nodded, lips pursed in a tight line.

"Plus, I want to take my SUV and we can spot each other in the driver's seat so we can go straight through the night and into the day tomorrow." Before she could protest, he added, "I've got four-wheel drive and it looks like we'll need it where we're going."

"Fair enough." She frowned as she paused her typing. "You can fill me in on how you think it's going to be any safer for me there than here since—assuming you're correct about where the embezzlement originated—we'll be walking right into enemy terrain."

"Easy." He dug his keys out of his pocket. "You'll be in disguise and hidden away in the room as much as possible. More important, you'll be with me."

She bit her lip but kept right on with the data entry thing, flipping to a new screen.

"And don't forget," he reminded her as he headed for the door. "We'll need to stick together both for appearance's sake and for safety purposes, so—only one room."

At last, her typing fingers slowed. Stopped. He hadn't expected to get that one past her.

"Is your client springing for the expense of this trip?" she asked, her eyes narrowing shrewdly.

"Yes. But while I'm sure he could afford two rooms—"

"That's not necessary." She went back to the keyboard, a golden brown lock of her hair sliding off her shoulder to frame her cheek. "I'll get one room, but it's going to be the biggest damn suite in the place. Vincent Galway and Premiere Properties owe me that much."

It wasn't exactly the kind of fantasy escape she tried to sell to her upscale clientele.

Even reclining in the leather passenger seat of Jake's full-size SUV, Marnie didn't think a twenty-five-hour car ride counted as decadent and indulgent. But at least—twelve hours into it—they were making excellent headway. Jake had shaved off some serious time overnight by tearing through Georgia and the Carolinas like a bat out of hell. Easy to do when traffic was so light. No one wanted to head north in the winter, except for a few die-hard skiers.

"You don't think you could sleep if you leaned back the rest of the way?" Jake peered over at her from the driver's side, his shades hiding his eyes now that the morning sun was well over the horizon.

He'd turned out to be a decent travel companion. He'd stocked up on bottled water prior to the trip and kept her cup holder stocked. Periodically, he pointed out rest areas and asked if she wanted to stop. Best of all, he'd given her control of the radio stations. Considering he had spied on her and played her for a fool by pretending he was a cute contractor instead of a dangerously deceptive P.I., Jake was turning out to be an okay guy.

She would have felt more comfortable around him, however, if she wasn't still highly attracted.

"I can't sleep when I'm wound up," she told him finally. "Doesn't matter if I've got the world's best accommodations and total silence. If I'm upset, nothing short of an animal tranquilizer would help me close my eyes."

"That explains a few late-night dart-throwing sessions." He changed lanes to avoid a semitruck trying to merge into traffic.

All around them, the lush greenery had faded, leaving them in a brown and gray barren part of the country. No snow yet, but the temperature had dropped a good twenty-five degrees.

"You know, I don't think it's fair that you've got all kinds of inside dirt on me and I don't know much of anything about you."

Maybe her attraction would lessen as she got to know him better. Real life had a way of dousing the best fantasies. Besides, talking about his world would keep her from picturing him watching her dance around her office in her skivvies at midnight when she realized she'd left some notes out front that she wanted to work on.

The thought of him keeping tabs on her all that time sent a fresh wave of awareness through her. She so could not let herself start thinking he was an okay guy, damn it. She needed to help him with his investigation—find out who wanted to frame her—and get back to rebuilding her life.

"You want the life story?" He drummed his fingers on the steering wheel with a staccato beat that smacked of impatience.

Too bad. She was only too happy to turn the tables on him. Let him see how it felt to be the one under the microscope.

"A few highlights would be nice."

"I'm a Midwestern farm boy turned Marine. I liked it a little too well. After my last tour was up, I figured I'd put the skills to use and became a cop."

The life story was decidedly condensed.

"What brought you to Miami?" It seemed more appropriate than asking him how many women he'd spied on while they undressed.

"More varied and interesting crime."

"Oh." She wasn't quite sure what that said about his psyche, but she could respect the desire to utilize his skills.

"I'm good at my job. Rather, I *was* good at the job

before I quit the force. At the time I figured I might as well challenge myself." He downshifted for construction work ahead and then tapped the windshield lightly; on the other side, snow had begun to fall. "And you can't beat the weather."

"Tell me about it. I have a coat from my trips to ski destinations, but since I usually scheduled those in the off season, I've hardly ever worn it." She shifted uncomfortably in her seat as the topic of wardrobes came up. "The resort we're headed to has extensive shopping facilities if you need anything, by the way. We'll have to buy some clothes for the parties."

Up ahead, traffic condensed into three lanes as they left Washington, D.C., in the distance. The snow was falling faster and Jake switched on the wipers.

"I brought a suit," he assured her, clicking a button for the defrosters. "I should be fine."

"Actually—" She adjusted a fleece blanket on her lap that he'd brought in case either of them wanted to sleep on the way. But even if she could have talked herself into sleeping, she was a little afraid that the man was so much on her mind she might end up moaning his name during a sexy dream or something equally embarrassing. Between Jake and their unconventional destination, she was having a hard time keeping her thoughts on the straight and narrow. "This resort caters to a very particular clientele. The name Marquis is a nod to the underground gentlemen's clubs that served British aristocrats in the latter half of the nineteenth century. Guests are expected to uphold the fantasy element of the experience, so we'll have no choice but to dress like the natives."

He cut a quick glance her way, eyes full of skepticism.

"I hope you're messing with me."

"I wholeheartedly wish that I was," she answered, envisioning herself stuck in layers of petticoats with a bustle and corset.

"What kind of hotel imposes a dress code?"

"First of all, this is not your normal hotel. It's a privately owned club—more like an elegant country house that offers exclusive invitations. Second, the period costumes aren't mandatory. But if we don't play the game, it would be like wandering around a nudist colony in a tux. You don't want to stick out at the resort if you're there to question people and track down information."

"I'm not wearing a sissy-boy collar up to my chin with a two-mile necktie."

"I'm pretty sure it's called a cravat." And it would be a far cry from the blue dress shirt he wore with a worn-in white T-shirt underneath.

Though she was pretty sure he would look as mouthwatering in one as the other. Her gaze darted over his broad shoulders. Everything about him broadcast power. Strength. Hotness.

"Whatever."

"The good news is that I recall a lot of functions that call for masks of one sort or another. That will help me mingle more since there will be very little chance of being recognized that way."

In the pocket of her trench coat, her cell phone vibrated with an incoming message. Checking it, she saw a note from the management at their destination.

"It's a confirmation for our reservation. They want us to know that we'll miss the main seating for dinner and that they'll serve us in our room." She scrolled down the screen, not ready to think about sharing a bedroom with the man in the driver's seat. The suite contained a queen-size bed plus a trundle; apparently pullout sofas weren't period-accurate for their furnishings. The trundle thing had always struck her as amusing since they so obviously weren't meant for people bringing kids to the hotel. Apparently a trundle was the Marquis's comfortable answer to a threesome sleeping arrangement.

But in their case, it meant Jake would be sleeping only a few feet away from her, even in the biggest room available.

How awkward would that be to go from throwing darts at him to bedding down with him in a thirty-hour span? A quick shiver chased down her spine.

"Sounds good. I won't be ready to face a bunch of role-playing swingers the moment we step into the place anyhow."

"Although—" her thumb hovered over the scroll key on her phone "—we are invited to the evening entertainment that starts at eleven."

"Should I be afraid to ask?" He cruised past signs for Baltimore as the snow coated the landscape.

A few cars with Christmas trees tied to their roofs passed, the sight a little surreal during this conversation about private sex clubs and role-playing naughty aristocrats.

"Apparently it's a vignette called The French Maid." Jamming the phone into an open compartment on the door of the SUV, Marnie didn't want to think about it anymore, let alone discuss the nature of the club with Jake.

"You've been there before. What are the entertainments like?"

"I—" Her cheeks heated at an old memory. "I don't consider myself overly uptight, but I couldn't sit through the only one I ever started to watch."

"You're blushing?" He sounded far too amused.

"How would you possibly know that if your eyes were on the road?" The air in the SUV's interior felt warm and heavy—too intimate by half.

She shoved the blanket from her lap and tossed it in the backseat.

"Details, please."

Retrieving her bottle of water from the cup holder, she took a long swig, partially to delay. Partially to cool off.

"It was that good?" he prodded, all too aware of her discomfort.

"No. I don't know." It would be important to prepare for their stay, to steel herself against whatever wayward thoughts the place inspired. "It was more elegant than I imagined it would be. More of a peep show exhibition than anything overt."

"You ran because it was a turn-on."

"I didn't run. I left because it felt icky to share a steamy moment with a room full of strangers."

"How was it any different than watching a movie at the theater?"

She pointed toward the sign for 95 North where the interstate divided.

"There's more anonymity in a theater somehow with the chairs all facing one direction. Plus, that's a movie. This had real live people acting it out in front of us and the show was nowhere near PG-13. The entertainment at the Marquis felt more…communal."

Now Jake reached for his water bottle and chugged it faster than she had.

"Maybe this isn't the best topic for someone who needs to drive for ten more hours, after all." He replaced the water and cracked the window.

Had she been aware of him before? Now she could practically feel the warmth of his exhalations across the console between them.

"You asked," she reminded him.

"And with good reason. The more I know about this place, the better." He tugged at the collar of his dress shirt even though the neck was open. "But for now, maybe we shouldn't dwell on the gratuitous nudity."

"I never said anything about nudity."

"And you see where my mind went anyhow? Moving on." He cleared his throat and straightened a pant leg at the knee. "Did you bring anyone to that show with you? A work colleague, friend, boyfriend?"

"As a rule, I don't mix business with pleasure and I always traveled alone in my work for Premiere."

"You should make a list of everyone you remember from that last trip—anyone from management to waitstaff who stands out in your memory, anyone you came in contact with who worked there."

"Okay." Grabbing her phone, she slid open the keypad to type some notes.

"I'll have you email it to my office and we'll run

some background checks to see if anything unusual comes up."

"We should do that before we arrive. Did I mention there's no wireless on-site? Or phones, either. Well, you can have a phone, but if they see you with one in any of the common rooms, they hold it until your departure date. You have to agree to that in a waiver when you check in."

"For a luxury resort, it's damn restrictive, isn't it? Although I'm sure that's what makes it all the easier to commit a crime from a place like that. Less eyes watching your every move."

"On the contrary, there are eyes everywhere. They're just more focused on erogenous zones than technology."

He slid another sideways glance at her and she felt it shiver over her skin as surely as if he'd touched her.

"I'm beginning to think the surroundings are going to prove a hell of a distraction."

No. The biggest distraction would be Jake himself— but she didn't want to put that into words when she needed to be building barriers against him instead of demolishing them.

"As long as we focus on finding a crook, we'll be fine." Some anonymous scumbag had cost her a lucrative living and tried to have her jailed for a crime she hadn't committed. The sooner she found out who, the easier she'd sleep.

"Or…" He rubbed a hand over his jaw like a man in deep thought. "Instead of ignoring the obvious, we could act on it."

She blinked, not sure she'd understood.

"Excuse me?"

"Part of the problem is not knowing how we're going to deal with the inevitable sexual chemistry once we're bumping up against each other day and night in a small space." He got into the left lane and slowed down as an exit approached.

"I think it's imperative we ignore that in a working relationship." She hadn't been kidding about not mixing business with pleasure.

"It'd be easier to ignore if we confronted the chemistry, tested the wattage and found out it was just some idle urge, wouldn't it?" Getting off the exit, he darted into a coffee shop parking lot.

Next thing she knew, the SUV was in Park and Jake Brennan had his seat belt off. He reached over to pop hers open with a click, as well.

When his knuckles grazed her hip, she knew this wasn't a routine java run. He'd pulled the car over with a clear purpose that he communicated through a hot perusal of her body, from thighs to hips, belly to breasts.

"That's a ludicrous idea." Mostly because she had the feeling that "testing" any chemistry would uncover a wellspring so hot it would take days to tamp it back down.

"Is it?" He reached across the console to smooth a strand of her hair behind one ear, inciting a path of gooseflesh up her arm directly underneath his hand.

The words *hell yes* never made it to her lips, even though she darted her tongue along them to prime the path for the utterance.

His eyes followed the movement like a tracking device, his pupils dilating so that his green eyes turned almost completely dark. Her heart hammered against her chest. Her brain trotted out every misplaced fantasy she'd ever had about Jake since first laying eyes on him that day he'd built her cabinet.

Each of those sexy daydreams came back to her now, conspiring against all her best intentions.

Just one kiss.

The thought crossed her mind long enough to propel her forward a scant inch—past the point of no return.

CHAPTER FOUR

TWO MONTHS' WORTH of waiting for Marnie paid off.

Big-time.

He knew the moment she'd consented to the kiss and he sealed the deal an instant later, capturing her mouth with his for that first experimental taste. The bubble gum scent of her lips and the subtle hint of a surrendering sigh drew him closer. He wrapped an arm around her back, anchoring her to him.

Hands coming to rest on his shoulders, she twisted her fingers in the fabric, her nails scraping lightly over the pressed cotton. He'd waited so damn long to feel that sensation of her arching against him. How many times had he watched her in his surveillance footage, only to war with his conscience about wanting her? Now, her lips slid sweetly over his, her whole body melting into his like hot butter.

The gearshift pressing in his side didn't matter. Nor did the water bottles rolling on the floor as he knocked things off the console. Marnie's breathy hum sang in his ears like a victory tune.

If only he could have a little more of her...

He hooked a finger in the V of her trench coat and tugged her nearer. She responded by wrapping her arms around his neck, ratcheting up the heat. The soft swell of her breasts grazed his chest and his blood surged south so fast he could have taken her then and there.

If it had been dark outside, he would have been able to pull her onto his lap without anyone around them being the wiser. But in the middle of a parking lot in broad daylight?

Damn it.

He broke away from her with a truckload of regret, his breathing harsh. Her eyes opened slowly as she seemed to process the break in the action. Her pupils were dilated, her lips slightly open as if awaiting another kiss. Finally, her fingers unfurled from his shirt, freeing him.

"Bad idea." She pronounced the verdict even as her cheeks remained flushed and she ran her tongue over her lips as if to seek a final taste of him.

"The kiss wasn't to your satisfaction?" He swiped his thumb along her jaw, unable to release her totally.

"You know perfectly well that's not the problem." She slid away from him, settling back into her own seat until his hand fell away. "Testing the chemistry was the bad idea since all we did was prove how combustible it could be if we touched each other."

Frowning, she tightened the belt on her trench coat and tucked the lapels closer together. Did she think a frail cloth barrier could stifle the sensations that surely raced over her skin the same way they sizzled along his?

The hell of it was, all she accomplished by cinching that belt was to accentuate show-stopping curves he wanted to thoroughly explore.

"Wrong." His fingers itched to undress her since he

knew better than anyone how much she liked to wear silky slips under her buttoned-up business attire.

Not that it would help his cause to remind her of that particular fact.

"Excuse me?" She glared at him across the console, her golden brown hair trapped in the collar of her coat until she flipped it free with a flick of her wrist. "Have you forgotten we need to work together this week? Don't you think this kind of distraction complicates a working relationship?"

"Maybe. But that doesn't make the kiss a bad idea." He put the car into Reverse, trying to turn his focus toward getting them safely to their destination as quickly as possible. He sure hoped he could shave some time off the twelve hours his maps suggested it would take. "It's always better to know what you're dealing with than to wait and wonder."

"And now we know." She didn't sound too happy about the fact. "We're not only stuck in a hedonistic sensual haven together, we're also susceptible to sexual temptation. Don't you think that's a problem when we need to concentrate on finding a thief before he bankrupts your client or me, or both of us?"

When she put it that way, it did sound like a problem.

"Nothing will interfere with my job," he assured her. "I guarantee you that much." He owed Vincent Galway a quick resolution to this mess.

Without the handful of investigative jobs from Premiere during the year since he'd left the force— and the contacts Vince had shared to help land Jake some lucrative work—Jake would have never grown his thriving business so quickly.

"Good." She settled into the corner of her seat farthest from him and closed her eyes as if she would finally sleep. Or at least, pretend to. "Then we're agreed we'll never let that happen again."

Never?

That was a long time in Jake's book and he didn't plan to agree or disagree. As far as he was concerned, strong sensual chemistry would lend their cover more authenticity.

And after one electric taste of Marnie Wainwright, Jake knew there wasn't a chance in hell they'd resist the lure of that attraction for long.

"Names, please?"

The request was issued by the sleek and incredibly sexy brunette behind the desk of the Marquis that night.

Marnie half hid behind Jake as they checked into the resort to ensure no one recognized her. She had never seen this woman who greeted them before, though, not unusual since the Marquis didn't employ many regular staff members, preferring to run the place more like an ashram than a business. Guests who lingered there for more than a week took turns as greeters and hosts, welcoming other guests. Guests could even sign up for waitstaff and housekeeping duties, jobs that frequently filled role-playing fantasies. No doubt tonight's greeter was a hotel guest looking to meet new people if she'd volunteered for desk duty.

With that in mind, Marnie didn't worry quite so

much about being recognized. Besides, she'd purchased temporary hair color when they hit the New York border and was now a redhead. She'd also braided a plait around the crown of her head so that she fit in with the historically themed Marquis. A small, cosmetic change, but it gave her a very different look.

"Jack and Marie Barnes," Jake lied, signing the old-fashioned register with fake names while the hostess ran a credit card.

Marnie had been interested to see if the transaction would work, but Jake had assured her that the card was tied to a false business that could not be traced back to him.

Apparently, no one knew their way around the law quite as well as an ex-cop.

"Welcome, Jack and Marie. I'm Lianna." The dark-haired siren handed Jake a room card imprinted with a photo of an old-fashioned iron key. "Is this your first time with us at the Marquis?"

The woman looked as if she could have walked right out of a late nineteenth-century painting. Everything from her loosely upswept curls to her pink gown fit in with the elegant surroundings. Exotic Persian carpets in an array of patterns dotted the highly polished wooden floors. Wrought-iron sconces hung at regular intervals along the walls of the reception parlor, the flames flickering with the regularity of gas fixtures. Softly worn tapestries depicting maidens in varying states of undress were the only indication that the Marquis might not be your average historic hotel.

The sensual works on the walls made for an interesting contrast with the holiday decor. Every inch of the place was decked in greenery and holly berries. Evergreen boughs had been struck through the spindles on the wide main staircase as they entered. Bowls of fruit with gold ornaments dotted tables and stands.

"We've never been here before," Jake told the woman, taking the key. "It's my understanding we can have dinner brought to our suite?"

"If you wish, but we encourage all our guests to become acquainted with the layout of the rooms and the other residents as soon as possible to make the most of every moment here." Lianna came out from behind the secretary desk that served as guest reception, her bustled pink skirts swishing softly with her movements. "Ideally, your first night under our roof should give you a taste of all the delights to come."

She paused so close to them that Marnie could smell the woman's perfume. Her long, dark lashes fell to half-mast as she sent a look of blatant invitation in a glance that darted from Marnie to Jake and back again.

Marnie had known she and Jake would face temptations at the Marquis—from each other as well as from third-party invitations. She just hadn't expected them to start arriving so damn quickly. Possessiveness made her thread her arm through Jake's, even though she had no idea if Lianna was flirting with him or her.

"I'm sure the meal will taste just as delightful in our room as it does in the dining hall." Marnie tugged on Jake's elbow, away from the bombshell in pink satin.

"Lianna." Jake remained in place. "We'd like to observe some of the evening's activities without joining anyone else. Is that possible?"

Lianna's dark eyes lit with approval.

"We welcome voyeurs, of course." She turned back to her desk and, bending forward over it to search for something, she presented them with a close-up view of her ruffle-swathed rump and a hint of seamed stocking.

Marnie suddenly hoped the woman proved guilty of the crimes they were investigating so that Marnie could see the flirtatious temptress behind bars.

Jake wrapped his arm around her, at least, assuring Marnie he hadn't forgotten she was alive. Not that she wanted to embark on some torrid affair with the P.I. herself. But somehow it would have bothered her to have him ogle another woman while he pretended to be her husband.

At least, she wished that was the only reason for the surge of jealousy.

"Here you go." Lianna turned around in triumph, holding another key card in her hand. This one had a picture of a wooden door with a cutout slit, sort of like the flip-open slots used in a prison to serve a confined inmate his meals. "Just slip this key into any of the peepholes that look like this around the hotel."

She tapped the card to indicate the image of the wooden slot.

Marnie recalled seeing those slots around the Marquis the one other time she'd visited in her promotional efforts for Premiere Properties, but she hadn't had the slightest notion of their purpose. Consensual voyeurism was one thing. Being spied on unaware was something totally different. Had she been watched on her last trip here without ever being the wiser?

"Do any of the private rooms have peepholes that we won't know about?" Marnie was horrified to think some unseen guest might be able to spy on her and Jake in their suite.

The thought reminded her all over again that Jake had watched her for two months without her knowledge. She couldn't help another surge of anger at his violation of her privacy.

"Of course not." Lianna leaned closer to give Marnie's arm a reassuring squeeze as if they were close friends. "The only guests who have ones in their rooms request it specifically at check-in."

"Exhibitionists," Jake clarified, pocketing the key.

"A voyeur's best friend," Lianna added with a wink. She settled her hand on her hip in a pose worthy of Mae West, her curves displayed at a suggestive, pinup girl angle. "Let me know if there's anything else either of you need. I'll be at the desk all night."

"Thank you." With a nod, Jake turned away from her and tucked Marnie under his arm to lead her through the hotel.

Ducking her head, she allowed Jake to guide her toward an antique-looking elevator with the old-fashioned gold gate that pulled across the doors. They had agreed in advance to let Jake be the public face of their couple since there was a chance Marnie could be recognized even in disguise.

"We can take the elevator to our room on the third floor." Marnie knew she should be exhausted, even though she'd slept a little on the trip. Still, adrenaline coursed through her after the run-in with Lianna and being inundated by talk of voyeurs and images of half-naked women on the larger-than-life tapestries. She'd seen those same wall hangings the last time she'd visited, but somehow they packed more punch with Jake standing next to her. Her senses seemed to have become hyperacute ever since that kiss in the SUV on the way up here.

Now she wondered how she could have ever visited this place without thinking about sex every second.

"No." Jake kept walking past the elevator. "Let's see the clothing store first. We're going to want to get straight to work tomorrow and apparently we'll need the right duds."

They passed a woman—clearly a guest—dressed in a red velvet maid's uniform with a Santa hat and stilettos. The volunteer worker pushed her cart full of scented soaps and complimentary bottles of edible massage oil as if it were all in a day's work, but her eyes cut to Jake with even more obvious intent than Lianna had shown.

Marnie had seen enough. Her senses couldn't take another moment of nonstop sensual bombardment.

"I can't do this." She lowered her voice until the maid disappeared around the end of the hall where a seventeen-foot-high Christmas tree welcomed visitors.

"What do you mean, you can't do this?" He turned to face her in the now-deserted corridor. Only a few sconces lit the long stretch of hallway. Somewhere nearby, she could hear hints of chamber music and laughter. A party of some sort, or dinner perhaps.

Jake's green eyes narrowed, all his attention on her, his arm still wrapped about her waist. He let go of the rolling suitcase behind him.

"I think I'm just overwhelmed. It's been such a long couple of days. I went from a normal life to finding a hidden camera and then starting on this thousand-mile…odyssey to seek vindication."

With a dark look, he covered her mouth with his hand.

"Not here."

The feel of his fingers on her lips sent a surge of longing through her. She had the strangest impulse to flick her tongue along the inside of his palm but she forced herself to be sensible.

Of course, he was right. She was just overtired and muddleheaded. Someone could be listening. Or watching. Hadn't they just discovered there were peepholes for private spying everywhere? But she was so keyed-up she couldn't think straight.

She wanted to tell him that she needed to find their room and get her bearings, but before he released her, a door sprang open about ten yards away. Light and sound spilled into the corridor from a large gathering where the string music originated. A young blonde in a white linen gown raced from the room, laughing and trailing blue ribbons from a silk scrap of lace she hugged to her chest. With a squeal, she lifted her long skirt with her other hand, picking up her pace to run past Marnie and Jake. Seconds behind her, two men emerged from the same door. With broad, muscular shoulders housed in matching dinner jackets, the guys resembled one another in every aspect from their long, dark hair to otherworldly tawny eyes that could only come from colored contacts. The twins set off in pursuit of the blonde, though the one who trailed a step behind his brother bumped Marnie as he passed.

"Excuse me." He halted immediately. Tawny cat's-eyes sought hers as he reached to straighten her. "So very sorry."

He bowed over her hand and kissed it, eliciting a low, possessive growl from Jake.

"Move. On." Jake leaned toward the other man without ever releasing Marnie's waist.

Nodding serenely, the other man let go of Marnie's hand and jogged in the direction where the other two had gone.

"Come on." Jake pulled her away from the open door and back toward the elevator.

And while Marnie's hormones remained stirred by her private eye companion and not the he-man twin playing dress-up with his eyewear, she appreciated that the incident had caused Jake to feel the same jealousy that Lianna had inspired in her. The possessiveness in his voice and in his grip stirred a warmth low in her belly.

"It is not as fun when the shoe is on the other foot, is it?" She tipped her head onto Jake's shoulder, seeking comfort from a source she couldn't afford to resist any longer.

They needed to present a united front while they were in this place full of potential land mines.

"No one else touches you while we're here." He punched the elevator button and the doors opened to reveal a silk settee resting in front of an Indian-printed length of gold fabric.

A thrill ran through her that she had no business feeling as he ushered her in. How could she be so turned-on by a guy who'd investigated her and spied on her for weeks without her knowing? A guy she needed to work with? She tried to work up a surge of anger and failed. She was too tired. Overwhelmed.

And still turned-on in spite of everything.

Her pulse spiked at his obvious interest.

"Does that exclusivity work both ways?"

"Would you like that?" He turned her toward him while the lift took them up two floors. "Would you like knowing you're the only woman who touches me this week?"

She knew he asked her so much more than what the surface question revealed. Mostly—did she want him as much as he wanted her?

And while she hadn't been prepared to take that plunge before, now that she'd experienced the way this place was going to get under their skin, she needed to be a little more realistic.

"Yes. I want to be the only one." She couldn't deny how much she wanted that assurance of exclusivity when it came to Jake.

Her blood stirred at the thought of the kiss he'd given her.

No matter how awkwardly their relationship had been forged—her on one end of a camera lens and him on the other—she couldn't deny that he'd peopled her fantasies even before then.

The elevator door chimed but they remained still a long moment before Jake reached to open the outer gate on their floor. The scent of spicy incense from a nearby censer wafted toward them while her heart-beat sped faster.

She'd just committed to far more than an investigation this week.

CHAPTER FIVE

WOULD SHE REMEMBER what she'd said the night before?

Jake watched Marnie sleep the next morning from his spot in an armchair a few feet away. Pale northern sunlight filtered through drapes on the French doors to dot her face and shoulders while the sheet wound around her midsection and thigh like a snake.

She'd slept fitfully most of the night. He knew because he was highly aware of this woman at every moment. Being with her almost nonstop for the past forty hours had given him new insights about her that he hadn't been able to glean through his surveillance of her.

For one thing, she was in constant motion. He'd known she had an energetic personality from her penchant for dancing around the office and belting out rap tunes for her own entertainment. But he hadn't realized that part of that was because she was tightly wound and driven to succeed. She had a tough time sitting still and letting life happen. Even in sleep, she waged battles, taking on Egyptian cotton until she had it in a choke hold.

His gaze dipped to where the creamy fabric pulled her yellow nightshirt up over a heart-shaped bottom.

She wore pink panties covered in tiny hearts and he didn't stand a chance of pulling his eyes away.

Which accounted for his need to keep his ass firmly planted in the armchair. Once he lay anywhere on that bed with her—trundle or otherwise—there would be no turning back.

As it was, he'd been plagued by erotic dreams every time he slept for more than ten minutes at a stretch. Every last one of them had starred Marnie—sometimes with her natural caramel-colored hair, sometimes as a redhead. Dressed in black silk, a trench coat or nothing at all. He didn't have a clue how he'd move forward with this investigation until he had her. The wanting was going to kill him.

"You're still watching me, aren't you?" Marnie's sleep-husky voice acted like a caress down his spine.

She hadn't moved a muscle for a long moment, which perhaps should have tipped him off to her wakeful state.

"At least I've gone from spying on you to looking out for you." He reached for a crystal carafe of orange juice a maid had brought in on a breakfast tray half an hour before.

Pouring her a glass, he tried like hell to rein in his thoughts.

"Is that what you call it?" Marnie yanked up the down comforter she'd kicked to the bottom of the bed hours ago and covered everything from the neck down. "Looking out for me?"

"Hey, I'm not the one who chose to sleep without pants." He leaned forward enough to hand her the glass and something the maid called a crumpet, but that he felt sure was a doughnut. "You damn near blistered my eyeballs."

She took both the offerings and settled back against the carved headboard of the four-poster bed to eat.

"Will you get a load of this place?" She peered around their suite with appreciative eyes and he didn't know if she'd changed the subject to distract him or because she was genuinely impressed. "I stayed in a smaller room last time and the decor in here is completely different. My last room was a nod to ancient Rome with lots of baskets of grapes and silk cushions on the floor. There were even complimentary togas instead of bathrobes. To me, that's the mark of a really interesting property, when the rooms are all unique."

He hadn't taken much note of the suite beyond the extravagant gilt mirrors dotting the walls and even on the ceiling. Somehow the heavy carved frames featuring intertwined Celtic designs made all the mirrors feel a little more upscale.

"Guess I'm not much of a world traveler. As long as there is good water pressure, I'm content." He would rather study the way her newly red hair slid out of the braid she'd fastened it in last night.

She'd accomplished the whole dye job in the bathroom of a fast-food restaurant, the operation as quick and efficient as any superspy would have managed. No wonder the woman had recovered from a job loss by opening her own business seemingly days later. She was a detail person—a planner who took charge and got things done.

"Spoken like a man. I would have thought you'd

have at least been curious about the carved positions from the *Kama Sutra* around all the mirrors."

"Kama Sutra?" He couldn't help but look at those damn mirror frames again. And sure enough, they weren't decorated with Celtic symbols at all, but intertwined couples. Threesomes. Moresomes. "Is that one even possible?"

He stood to take a closer look at a pretzel-twister of a position on the mirror closest to him.

"Doesn't it make you wonder where they got all this stuff? Pervy Antiques R Us?" She turned a brass alarm clock toward her and seemed surprised at the time. "So what's on tap for today? Shadowing suspects? Setting up a stakeout?"

"Hardly." He passed her another pastry but she nixed it. "I stayed up late last night to contact my office and run some preliminary workups on names from the guest book. It turns out most of the guest names are aliases, just like ours."

"How did you get a copy of the guest book?" She frowned and set aside the empty juice glass.

"I took a picture of it with my phone while Lianna ran the credit card."

"Lianna." Marnie's lower lip curled in evident disapproval. "Could that woman have wriggled her butt any more for your benefit?"

Jake grinned. "It didn't compete with the show you gave me before you pulled the blanket up."

Tugging a pillow from behind her back, she hurled it across the bed to hit him, but he deflected it easily so that it landed onto the floor.

"You can't blame me for honoring our agreement." His cell phone vibrated with an incoming text message.

"What agreement?"

"We're not going to let anyone else touch us besides each other this week, remember?" He didn't move any closer, but he could feel the spark of awareness arc across the bed between them. Oh, yeah, he liked that. "Which I interpret to mean that I won't be demonstrating interest in anyone else, either."

"I—" She nodded. "I remember. This place has a way of rousing emotions."

He suppressed another grin. It aroused something, that was for damn sure. And since he'd known that he'd wanted Marnie for months, he was grateful that a little competition for his attention had made her realize maybe she wasn't as immune to him as she'd like after all.

"I'll check my messages while you shower." He'd already taken a cold one around 3:00 a.m. after a vivid-as-hell dream. Though the cold water hadn't helped much when he saw the big claw-foot tub built for two, surrounded by showerheads at convenient angles for maximizing the feel-good effect. "Then we can secure some clothes downstairs and check out the lay of the land. The sooner we get to work, the sooner we figure out who could have moved the Premiere Properties money around and tried to frame you in the process."

Although it was going to be a challenge since he'd be picturing Marnie in that shower the whole time.

"Right." She nodded, causing more hair to slide out of the braid circling her head. Rising from the bed, she tugged the blanket off with her to throw around her shoulders like a robe. "Let the charade begin."

WAVING OFF THE dressing-room attendants later that morning, Marnie had found four semiauthentic late nineteenth-century gowns to wear during her stay at the Marquis. Well, they were probably authentic for late nineteenth-century prostitutes. The low necklines warred with the major push-up effect of the foundation garments, making her breasts the objects of continually opposing forces.

Successfully picking out the clothes was no easy feat, considering all she had on her mind between the unsettling attraction for her P.I. roommate and the uneasy news he'd received from his Miami office this morning.

Then again, picking out the dresses themselves was a cakewalk next to picking out all the assorted undergarments she needed. And while she would have liked to have blown off that portion of the shopping spree, the underwear of yesteryear served important functions for making the clothes fall properly. It wasn't as simple as substituting a cotton bra for an elaborate corset. The gowns needed the straps and hooks, the stays and the wiring provided by the foundation pieces in order to stay up. Of course, they came complete with openings in the most interesting places. Ease of access was apparently a high priority in clothing provided by the hotel's boutique.

Now, Marnie checked out her reflection in the full-length dressing-room mirror, ensuring her bustle had been properly pinned and her dress covered the corset around the low bodice and down the back. The boutique didn't just sell period costume—they specialized in the most scandalous of historical dress so that Marnie's gown gave way to a surprise lace-up inset that plunged to the top of her bottom. If she'd been sporting a tramp stamp back there, it would be perfectly framed by white muslin.

"Marie." Jake's voice called to her through the thin pink taffeta curtain separating their dressing rooms.

They'd been given the couples' fitting room in a far corner of the establishment, providing them privacy from the staff with a locked door while separated from each other only by the diaphanous piece of fabric. Despite the supposed privacy from the outside world, however, she noticed he called her by her assumed name.

"Yes, Jack?" She responded in kind, hoping she could remember to use the alias today as they began their investigation of the property.

"Are you ready?" He sounded tense. Irritated.

She wasn't sure if it was because of the news he'd received this morning that all five employees Marnie remembered from her last trip here two years ago were no longer working on the property, or if he was simply frustrated about the elaborate menswear he needed to wear if he had any hope of "blending in."

Marnie took a deep breath, remembering the glimpses she had stolen through the curtain while he tried on his clothes. She'd told herself not to look, knowing he'd be even more tempting without a shirt. Or pants. It turned out he was a boxers man. She'd gotten a peek at blue plaid shorts before she'd forced herself to turn around.

"Yes, I—"

No sooner had she answered then he wrenched the curtain open.

He stood in the other half of the dressing area looking as if he could have set sail on the *Titanic* with the upper crust, although she knew the clothes dated from about forty years before then. Still, the long charcoal cutaway coat revealed slim-cut pants that showed off strong, muscular thighs and narrow hips. A starched white shirt with tiny crystal fastenings didn't begin to take away from the broad masculine appeal of his chest. The half-tied cravat loose around his neck made him look like—what did they call it back in the day?

A rake.

Yes, he looked as roguish as Rhett Butler right before he carried Scarlett up to bed to prove sex was best left to men who knew their way around a woman.

Her pulse rate spiked. Fluttered wildly.

"I didn't spend this much time dressing when I wore a flak jacket and enough combat equipment to take out a city block." He tugged impatiently at the tie. "I'm going to burn this when the week is up."

"I think it's…" Gorgeous. Delectable. Enough to make her weak-kneed. "…nice." She stepped closer, her jeweled, high-heeled satin slippers surprisingly comfortable.

Untwining the knot he'd made, she slid the silk free to try again, the feel of delicate material an appealing contrast to the hot, tense body beneath it.

"You have to admit it's excessive." His eyes took

on a dangerous gleam as he looked at her. "Although when I look at what you're wearing, I begin to see the appeal."

His gaze tracked downward in a long, thorough sweep of her body. She wasn't immune to the words or the low, confidential voice in which they were uttered. Her skin heated in response.

"Thank you." Lifting her arms to wrap the silk around his neck again, she couldn't help but notice the way the movement raised her breasts to rub tantalizingly against the stiff confinement of the corset.

Apparently, he noticed, too, since his gaze dipped to the swell of cleavage at the neckline of her white muslin day dress.

"Wow." His second compliment struck her as even more eloquent than the first since his breath sounded more labored.

She eased back, satisfied with the new knot she'd tied around his neck.

"You look good, too," she acknowledged, her fingers itching to slide between the crystal buttons on his shirt to test the warmth of the skin beneath. "I think that's the lure of so much clothing. It makes you all the more aware of your body, and the restrictiveness adds a layer of difficulty to touching or fulfilling any…urges."

Sure a miniskirt could be sexy. But sometimes keeping the body under wraps created an eagerness and delayed gratification that only heightened awareness. It was a theory she'd developed while watching *The Tudors*.

"Interesting." He ran a fingertip over a silk rosette on one shoulder of her dress before following a line of pale blue piping along the top of the neck. "But I like thinking about you half-naked in the sheets this morning, too."

His finger hovered over the plump curve of one breast, his touch almost straying onto her bare skin, but not quite. Her breath caught at the gossamer-light contact, a pang of desire bolting straight to her womb.

"Shouldn't we—" She knew they had something else they should do but it was difficult just now to recall what. Hypnotized by his green eyes turning darker by the second, she never finished the thought.

"In a minute." He dropped his hand to span her waist, steadying her as he bent to kiss that tingling patch of skin a mere inch from her aching nipple.

Tongue darting along the cup of the corset, Jake tasted a path that made her knees weak. She might have twisted an ankle in her jeweled heels as she fell into him, but he held her upright against the hard length of his body.

A moan slipped free from her throat, the sound a wordless plea for more when she had no business making such a demand. Still, sensations ran through her at light speed, her thoughts swimming. The hypnotic swirl of his tongue along her flesh sent an answering thrill to her most private places.

Debating how to ease off her dress, she rolled her hips and shoulders in the hope some fabric would fall away. But the motion only heightened the sweet torment of her situation since it brought her in delicious contact with the hot, hard length of his arousal.

Knock, knock.

A rap at the door startled her, halting her hungry hip

shimmy. Jake peered up at her from where he'd started to peel down the corset with his teeth.

"Can I get you anything?" A woman's voice drifted through the door that separated the couples' dressing area from the rest of the store.

"No." Jake's tone brooked no argument.

Yet the female dressing-room attendant pressed on.

"We have some very sultry pieces for private moments." Her breathless voice suggested the woman was intimately acquainted with just such encounters. "Or not-so-private moments."

Her rich laughter on the other side of the door made Marnie wonder if their dressing room might be one of the places where outsiders could peek in.

Apparently, Jake had the same idea since he returned her dress firmly to her shoulder and eased back a step. Not until that moment did she notice the complimentary basket of condoms on a table nearby. She'd seen the grooming items lined up under a pewter lamp and had thought the hairspray and scented antiseptic hand sanitizers were thoughtful additions to the dressing area. But apparently, other couples had gotten even more carried away while trying on clothes.

"Come on." His breathing was as ragged as hers and she found herself wondering when they'd be able to continue this moment in private. "We'll pay for these things and have them sent upstairs while we check out the place."

She nodded her assent, since she hadn't fully recovered her capacity for speech. While she'd felt a draw toward Jake from the moment he'd switched on his jigsaw to craft her display cabinet with an artisan's skill and a laborer's muscle. But he'd become so much more in the past two days. More complicated. More appealing. And far more apt to lead her straight into danger, no matter what he said about keeping her safe.

With her heart pounding wildly and her senses still reeling from his kisses, she trusted him to protect her from the rest of the world. But who would protect her heart from him?

CHAPTER SIX

LIANNA CLOSSON DUCKED behind a wall of drawers containing silk hosiery and naughty underthings as Jack and Marie Barnes emerged from the couples' dressing room. She could practically taste the pheromones rolling off the two of them as Jack pulled the beautiful redhead through the store. Their flushed cheeks and tousled hair suggested they'd had some fun in the dressing room—the kind of fun Lianna wouldn't have minded indulging in herself if her new romantic interest had arrived at the resort this week like he was supposed to.

Dang it.

Not attracting so much as a second glance from either of them, she toyed with the crystal knobs on the tall cabinet full of exotic undergarments and wished her lover would show up at the Marquis soon.

Well, her soon-to-be lover.

Lianna had met Alex McMahon at the Marquis a year ago, back when they'd each been involved with other people—Lianna with her husband, who'd introduced her to a swinging, couple-swapping existence that had seemed fun until he dumped her for his best friend's wife. Alex had been a guest at the Marquis with a girlfriend who hadn't worked out for him, either, and he'd contacted Lianna out of the blue a month ago. They'd gotten better acquainted online until he'd asked her to meet him here.

And while Lianna looked forward to reigniting a love life for herself, she wasn't in a hurry to have her heart broken again. As fun as it might be to play sexy games with friends and strangers, she had new respect for protecting the deeper ties that bound a couple together.

Tugging open a drawer marked Holiday, Lianna discovered a wealth of seamed stockings, each set bearing different embroidered or studded icons around the ankle. She pulled out a white pair with red poinsettias to wear for tonight's entertainment.

She wanted to look special for Alex if he finally showed up. He'd made excuses about getting caught in a snowstorm the past two days, but if he didn't appear tonight, Lianna planned to keep an eye out for other entertainment. After all, Alex hadn't made her any promises. What if he was a total player?

He might be charming, but she wouldn't wait around for him forever. Besides, the fact that he wanted her to keep an eye on any new visitors to the Marquis had made her wary of his intentions.

Was he a swinger like her ex?

The thought had her worried as she paid a trim little blonde dressed as a courtesan for the stockings. No way would Lianna tread down that path again. But why else would Alex be interested in new hotel guests unless he was on the lookout for potential playthings?

She'd quizzed him about it on the phone the night before when he'd expressed such interest in the newcomers from Miami. He'd tried to reassure her, saying he was only curious because he used to live in Miami. As if he thought he'd know Jack and Marie Barnes—surely not their real names—from a city with half a million people? He'd asked her to find out more to feed his "curiosity."

Well, she could tell him quite honestly that the new couple only had eyes for each other. The sight of them together filled Lianna with envy since her ex had never looked at her that way. Perversely, she'd flirted lightly with the couple, half hoping they'd ignore her and prove that love and loyalty existed within a passionate romance.

She'd been oddly gratified when they'd done just that.

So if Alex McMahon didn't bother to show tonight—and if he was only interested in having her scope out fresh prospects for him—Lianna would cut her losses. All the books she'd read on divorce counseled not to get involved with anyone before the one-year mark anyhow, and she'd only just reached that. Maybe she'd jumped into something too fast with Alex.

If he wanted to spy on Jack and Marie, he'd have to come to the Marquis to do it himself because that wasn't her style.

For her part, she planned to keep her eyes open for the kind of chemistry that pinged between the couple. She'd settled for a relationship based on shared interests last time. That had resulted in a lukewarm marriage that sent her husband out looking for adventure.

So when she got involved again, she wouldn't settle for anything less than, hot, sexy, all-consuming passion.

SETTLING INTO A LOVE SEAT across from a floor-to-ceiling window that looked out on the property's grounds, Jake kept Marnie close to his side. They'd explored the hotel this morning after the incident in the dressing room, attempting to get acquainted with the place before it became crowded in the evening. Now, they watched out the window as a party of five braved the falling snow to enter a horse-drawn carriage complete with sleigh bells and fur blankets.

A driver in his mid-twenties wore a top hat with a sprig of holly at the band, and he peered back into the sleigh full of women with open eagerness. Did the kid really stand a chance with five women?

Jake was just damn glad to have a chance with this one. But he wanted to keep her under wraps here as much as possible, which meant he needed to get her back to their suite now that more guests were waking up.

"We should get back to the room." He checked his watch, thinking he should be able to get another update from his office regarding patrons of the Marquis over the past year.

If the embezzler had targeted Marnie to take the fall for the crime purposely, chances were good he was keeping tabs on her. Would he—or she—know by now that the scheme to frame her hadn't worked? Would the embezzler take enough interest in Marnie as to know she'd closed up her shop in Miami and had left town?

"Don't you think we should divide and conquer to cover more ground first?" Marnie kept her voice low and had gotten in the habit of leaning close to him to speak so that if they were observed, it looked as if she was whispering lusty suggestions in his ear.

He had the feeling she did it simply because she was a detail person who didn't overlook the small stuff. But he liked to think she got a charge out of being next to him. God knew he enjoyed the soft huff of her breath on his skin, the brush of her shoulder against his as she moved in close. It was all he could do not to press her down to the bench and see how fast he could unfasten all those clothes she was wearing. No matter how many ties, bows and buttons between them, he knew he'd set a land speed record getting her naked and hot underneath him.

"I don't want anyone to recognize you," he spoke softly in return, her neck within tempting reach of his mouth.

Memories of what had happened in the dressing room had never been far from his mind this morning. Every now and then, he'd catch a hint of her exotic floral scent and he'd be transported right back to that moment behind the curtain, tugging off her gown with his teeth like a damn ravenous beast.

"I bought a mask, remember?" From her drawstring purse, she withdrew the white scrap of satin. The fabric had been decorated with green sequins patterned to look like pine boughs.

She wrapped the pliable satin about her eyes and tied the white ribbons behind her hair. And wow, she was a knockout with the red hair spilling onto her shoulders, her plump lips the only feature of her face that remained visible.

"If I was looking for you," he confided, letting his

breath warm the skin around her collarbone, "I would know that mouth anywhere."

The lips in question parted slightly. She licked the top one.

"Lucky for me, no one else is going to take such an interest."

"That's lucky for *them,* actually, because if I caught anyone checking out your mouth, I'd have to hurt them." He'd seen plenty of men notice her already, even though the resort was fairly quiet at this time of day. She had a natural confidence that drew the eye, a way of moving through the world that said she knew what she was doing. Maybe traveling the globe for her job had given her that ease.

"Violence will attract far more attention than any facial feature, so let's hope you can behave." She nuzzled his cheek as another couple walked by them, effectively hiding from view while driving Jake out of his ever-loving mind.

A lock of silky red hair slipped forward, teasing along his jaw. He struggled with the urge to plunge both hands into the auburn strands, to hold her still for a kiss that wouldn't stop until tomorrow....

Focus, damn it.

He needed to think about his investigation and not personal pleasure. His first responsibility was to protect her from whoever had made her a target.

"Maybe we can find some of the rooms with secret viewing." He passed her the security card bearing a picture of a peephole. "As long as we don't mingle, we can circulate a little while longer. I'd like to meet whoever runs the place on a day-to-day basis."

Something that had been tough to do with a resort run like a private club. Everyone he'd talked to so far— from a doorman to a waiter—was working in order to accumulate points that would help them to book rooms in the future. Marnie had explained that most of the guests volunteered for the jobs, but he'd thought they were just enjoying the fantasy of being a maid or a lusty waiter. But apparently the Marquis had a whole elaborate system in place to fill the gaps in the staff by offering guests incentives to work extra hours.

Jake had to hand it to the operation. It was a clever piece of business.

"That's very admirable of you to work so hard. Doesn't the atmosphere ever distract you?" Marnie nodded meaningfully to a white marble statue on a nearby end table.

The piece hadn't caught his eye before since the style was more impressionistic than realistic. But now that she'd pointed it out, the lines became clear. Like carvings he'd once seen in an historic Indian temple, the statue featured a woman lying on her back with knees parted to accommodate a man's shoulders. Clearly, his mouth was aligned with her sex.

And oh man, he'd like to think Marnie had pointed out that piece for a reason. He couldn't imagine anywhere he'd rather be than in their suite re-creating that moment for her. A growl rumbled up the back of his throat, and he had to fist his hands to keep them off her.

"Hell, yes, it's a distraction." But then, you couldn't look anywhere in this place without seeing something erotic.

And unlike some girlie magazine, this stuff was

subtle. It crept up on you and settled into your consciousness before you could think about changing the mental channel.

Taking her hand, he pulled Marnie to her feet. She stood willingly enough, but he noticed she spared a small, backward glance for the statue on the end table.

And didn't that just torch his focus in a heartbeat? Bad enough to conduct an investigation while being tormented with carnal temptation on all sides. But it was even worse trying to think about the case knowing the woman beside him was every bit as turned-on.

"I'm losing my mind here." He had to touch her soon or he'd jump out of his skin. "Go back to the room and I'll meet you there in an hour. I need to check around for any accessible hotel computers where the embezzlement could have originated, but after that…"

He couldn't begin to articulate what he needed. The urge was deep and primal. He didn't just want to touch her. He wanted to possess her.

Thankfully, she spared him the effort of translating his need into words fit for her ears.

Nodding, she gripped her key to her chest. "Hurry."

BACK IN THE SUITE, Marnie fought off the sexual edginess by flipping through a few electronic documents that Jake had sent to her phone after receiving an update from his office. They hadn't been apart for long—forty-nine minutes, according to the clock on the nightstand—but every moment away from him only stirred a hunger she couldn't deny any longer.

She'd never felt sexual chemistry like this. It was so strong, so palpable, she didn't know what to do about it. Did other people feel like this about sex? Whoa, had she been missing out for her whole adult life?

Fanning herself, she tried to concentrate on the notes from Jake. He'd sent her a list of visitors to the Marquis in the past year, even though they'd already established that most of the names would be fake. Still, Jake had asked her to look at it since most people didn't vary the names much. Just like Jake and Marnie became Jack and Marie, apparently most people using an alias chose something close to their real names.

She tucked her toes beneath a blanket as she lounged in an oversize club chair. The moment Jake had left, she'd ditched the restrictive gown she'd been wearing along with the underskirts that made the train puff up. She'd kept the corset on, unwilling to have to wrestle with it again before dinner. But at least this way, her dress would remain wrinkle-free. She didn't know exactly how things would go with Jake when he returned, but she had the feeling clothes would only get in the way.

Fifty minutes.

With her finger hovering on the wheel to advance the screen, Marnie surreptitiously listened for footsteps in the hall. Her heartbeat danced a crazy rhythm in her chest. Odd how even the blood in her veins wanted Jake. It was elemental. Undeniable. The kiss he'd given her in the dressing room that morning had ripped away any illusion she had of keeping him at arm's length during their stay here.

In a space of time, Jake had become more than a hot contractor who'd flirted with her or an intrusive P.I. who filmed her without her knowledge. She could easily be in jail right now if it hadn't been for his determination to find out the truth of Premiere's missing money. Her ex-boss had assured her of as much in their brief phone conversation before she left Miami.

His fierce intelligence and sense of justice had made him invaluable to Vince Galway—a man Marnie respected. And his smoldering sensuality—well, that flat out left her breathless.

Forcing herself to finish combing through the documents now saved on her phone, Marnie clicked to the next screen, where her eyes alighted on a surprise name.

Alex McMahon.

She read it twice, knowing it wasn't her ex's name, but seeing a similarity between that and Alec Mason.

Double-checking the date of his visit, she saw that it had been a year ago, during the time that they'd been dating. And that Alex McMahon had checked in with a woman who'd shared his last name. Of course, it was entirely possible that Alex McMahon hadn't been married to Tracy McMahon. Plenty of dating couples signed hotel registers as married just for kicks.

Besides, Alec had been a crappy manager of money but that didn't necessarily make him a cheater, did it?

Her mind racing, she clicked out of that screen and opened the calendar function on her phone. As a true type A, Marnie could call up her activities electronically for every day of her life going back five years.

More if she consulted a paper file back home.

And while yes, that made her nerdy as all hell, it had proven useful a few times. Like now. When the calendar for last December showed that she'd been on the road during the time in question. Specifically, she'd been evaluating promo angles for a restored villa in Tuscany. Which meant that—while she'd assumed Alec had been back in Miami—he could have been anywhere in the world and as long as he'd called from his cell phone, she wouldn't have known the difference.

A knock at the door interrupted that troubling realization.

"Room service," a masculine voice announced, reminding her she'd ordered hot tea to help shake off the cold of December in upstate New York.

"Coming!" she called, dropping the phone and blanket to slide into a white spa robe provided by the Marquis.

Hurrying across the hardwood floor covered with a smattering of rich Oriental carpets, she unlocked the door to admit a waiter with a silver tea cart followed by a sexy brunette in a maid's costume complete with little apron.

Lianna.

Did the woman work at every conceivable job on the property? Marnie stood back to admit them, and as they passed her with the tea, she realized that Lianna had found a new man to capture her attention since all her focus was on the young waiter. Not just any waiter, either. The guy setting up the tea tray by the fireplace was one half of the tawny-eyed twins who'd brushed past her in the corridor downstairs the night before. Instead of his dress attire, he wore tight breeches with—wow—everything readily displayed. His tunic was half-buttoned as if he'd just rolled out of bed or as if he were inviting the touch of every stray woman who passed.

"Would you like me to pour it for you?" the behemoth asked, his muscles testing the strength of those close-fitting pants and his voice taking on the tone of bedroom confidences.

Lianna all but drooled as she posed invitingly against the cart, her eyes glued to her cohort's bicep, visible through the thin linen tunic.

"Yes, please." Marnie waved him along to expedite the process. She wanted the pair of them out of her room before they got busy on her love seat.

Still, the guy took his time arranging the china teacup, lighting a single white taper and adjusting a pink poinsettia bloom in a pewter holder on the tray. Lianna watched every move in rapt fascination, it seemed, until she suddenly turned to catch Marnie staring at her.

The other woman smiled warmly, making Marnie feel small inside for thinking cranky thoughts about her. Beautiful women couldn't help being beautiful.

"Do you come here often?" Marnie kicked herself as soon as she brought out the well-worn barroom conversation staple. But it had occurred to her that if Lianna volunteered for so many jobs at the Marquis she must have seen a lot around the resort. Maybe it wouldn't hurt to cultivate her goodwill.

"It's my third time here," Lianna admitted. "It's fun to play dress-up, isn't it? Although I notice you seem to have lost your dress."

Lianna winked and the tawny-eyed waiter grinned. Marnie reminded herself that they weren't trying to be obnoxious because most people visited this hotel for just this kind of thing.

Hence the trundle bed.

Clearing her throat, she took a step back from the odd dynamics of the moment.

"The bustle and I weren't getting along," she confided. Then, forging ahead to firm up the new contact, she continued, "It's my first time here, actually. If you have time tomorrow, I'd be interested to find out all the inside scoop on the best things to do here."

It was another loaded comment, and both Lianna and Golden Eyes laughed.

"Um." Marnie tried again. "Beyond the obvious."

"Sure," Lianna agreed easily, crooking her finger toward her friend and leading him toward the door. "I'm up early. Meet you at noon for breakfast?"

That was early? Apparently that was the prevailing sentiment around the resort since it had been so quiet today before midafternoon.

"Sure. Sounds good." Marnie didn't know what she'd ask the woman, but while Jake conducted the supersleuthing, Marnie could at least offer up one skill to the mix. She knew how to listen. And sometimes women observed things that men never noticed.

As the two of them opened the door to leave, Jake stood in the entrance, key in hand as if he'd been about to enter. He took one look at who'd been visiting and Marnie was pretty sure he flexed his muscles in predatory display. There was some silent message passed between the men, of that much she was certain. Lianna had to haul her friend away by the undone laces on his tunic to break the staring contest.

As the door closed behind them, leaving Jake facing Marnie in a robe and corset and nothing more, she could feel the awareness in the room simmer.

"Hi," she said needlessly, wanting only to break the silence.

Jake dropped his key and yanked off his jacket, letting both fall to the floor while he stalked closer. Green eyes fixing her in his sights, he tore off the neckwear he hated and wrenched open the top fastening of his crisp white shirt.

Her heartbeat tripped before it picked up speed. She sensed her fight-or-flight moment at hand. She would need to get out of his path right now if she didn't want this.

Him.

Licking her lips since her mouth had gone dry, she kept her feet rooted to the spot.

She wanted whatever he had in mind.

CHAPTER SEVEN

HEAT ROARED THROUGH HIM like a furnace, the atmosphere in the room growing taut with need.

"This place is making me crazy." Jake stopped himself a hairbreadth from Marnie to give her fair warning of his mood.

His intent to have her naked in the next ten seconds.

"Me, too," she admitted. Breathless.

"When I first saw them in here—"

"Nothing happened," she said quickly.

"I know." Of course he knew. "But this place messes with your head until all you think about—all the time—"

He gave her an extra second to let it sink in, his hands flexing at his sides from the effort to hold back. He needn't have bothered though, because she launched herself at him.

Thank You, God.

Relief and desire damn near took out his knees, but he held strong for her, his arms full of soft, warm woman. The clean scent of her skin and hair teased his senses. Gathering her close, he held her tight, her soft curves encased in too much stiff lace beneath her thick white robe. He lifted her higher, sliding his arms under her thighs so she had no choice but to wrap her legs around his waist.

Oh, yeah. She followed him willingly. Eagerly. Soft, urgent sounds hummed in the back of her throat as he maneuvered her right where he wanted her, the hot core of her positioned over his erection, their bodies separated by too many clothes. That connection soothed the hunger in him enough to slow things down just a little, to appreciate her the way she deserved to be. The moment was so damn charged, and he didn't want to miss out on a second of pleasure because they were so damn hungry for this.

She pressed urgent kisses along his jaw and down his neck as he held her. He took deep breaths, willing his heart rate to slow down, his body to put her needs first. Then, slowly, he lifted his hands to explore the soft skin between the tops of her stockings and the bottom of the corset. She was soft. More silky than the fabric of her expensive underthings.

He forced his eyes open, to see her and savor her. Her gray eyes were at half-mast, lashes fluttering as he touched her. Behind her, the silver tea cart glinted in the firelight, steam wafting up from the brewing pot.

"You had clothes on when I left you last time," he observed, tracing a pattern along the back of her bare thigh. "You can't blame me for wondering when I come back to find you mostly undressed and entertaining guests."

"My dress was highly uncomfortable." She worked the fastenings on his shirt, as nimble dispensing of his clothes as she was with her own. "So you can imagine how fast I ditched it after you left the room."

His shirt slid to the floor. Her cool hands raked down his chest, his muscles twitching in the wake of her touch. He'd wanted this for so long.

"And I didn't even get it on tape." He could only imagine how much he would have enjoyed that show. "Was there any dancing involved, like when you closed up your shop on Friday night?"

"You enjoy your job a little too well." She gave his shoulder a gentle bite in retaliation, her teeth scraping lightly along his skin. "All that time, I thought you were concerned with protecting my privacy."

He flicked open one garter behind her thigh and then the other. She shivered. He couldn't wait to see what else would elicit that response.

"Guess I'm more concerned with protecting it from anyone else *besides* me." Lowering her to the floor in front of the fireplace, he nudged the black robe off her shoulders and his breath caught at the sight she made.

Firelight warmed her skin to spun gold next to the ivory-white corset. The rigid stays in the garment made her look like a naughty fifties pinup queen with no waist to speak of and breasts at eye-popping proportions. The curve of her hips was exaggerated in the back by a knot of gathered lace that helped the bustled gown sit high when she was dressed. At her legs, her stockings sagged a little in back where he'd unfastened them, but the fronts remained hooked. The white straps framed the juncture of her thighs, right where he wanted to be.

"Intimidated?" she asked, cocking a hip to the side, a hand at her waist.

"By you?" He grinned at the thought. "It seems to me like I have you completely at my mercy right now."

And he really, really liked the thought of that. They weren't leaving this room for a long time.

"Not by me. By this contraption I'm wearing." She gestured to the corset. "I'll bet you have no clue how to spring me loose."

"I think I'll manage." He reached for the remaining garter straps and plucked them free, eliciting another shiver from her. "Besides, if I touch you just right—" he stroked a knuckle up the inside of her thigh for emphasis "—you might melt right out of it."

The soft sound she made in the back of her throat pleased him to no end. Her hands found his waist. Fingers spanning his sides, she glided a light touch up his chest, her hips swaying closer as if she danced to a song only she could hear.

"Promises, promises," she whispered over his chest as she bent to kiss him there.

She was as sexy and sensual in real life as she'd appeared in hours of secret surveillance. And right now, she seemed as keyed-up and ready for this as him.

"Never let it be said I don't deliver." Stripping off his shirt, he tossed it on the ground behind her. Then, scooping her off her feet, he laid her on the rug in front of the hearth, carefully spreading the shirt out beneath her.

He stayed on his feet long enough to remove his pants and retrieve a condom. Marnie watched his every move, lifting one leg to slide off her stocking with all the finesse of a showgirl. When she had it free, she wound the silk around her wrists and extended her bound hands to him.

"Want to take me into custody?"

He carefully raised her arms over her head and held them there while he stretched over her.

"Not yet, but there's no telling what might happen if I find a strange man in our room again." He slid a hand down her back where a row of endless hooks kept her delectable body captive. One by one, he began easing them free.

"He only poured my tea," she assured him, wrapping her bare leg around his and massaging the back of his calf with the ball of her foot.

"I don't care about the tea." He loosened the corset enough to expose the plump swell of her breasts and he flicked his tongue over one taut nipple. Then, leaving the remaining hooks for the moment, he palmed the warmth between her thighs. "As long as you leave the cream and honey for me."

Her body quivered as soon as he touched her. Impatiently, he brushed aside her panties and sought the slick center of her. Circling the tight core with his finger, he mirrored the movement with his tongue along her nipple. Her breath grew short, her back arching under him as she sought more.

Drawing hard, he took the tight peak deep in his mouth as he slid two fingers inside her. She bucked and cried out, her release coming fast. The spasms went on and on as he coaxed out every sweet response.

Freeing her wrists from the slippery stocking bondage, she looped her arms about his neck and whispered a new demand.

"Come inside me."

Marnie willed Jake to comply with her request, her whole body crying out for his. She'd never peaked so fast or so easily, but then she'd been on fire for this man for days. The steamy atmosphere of the Marquis had only made it worse.

He stared down into her eyes, his strong features cast in stark shadows from the fire. The red light illuminated his sculpted muscles in deep bronze, every sinew visible as he positioned himself between her legs.

Tracing the outline of his hard flesh with her hands, she absorbed his heat and his strength as he rolled on a condom. The aftershocks from her release intensified as he entered her, sending her hips into motion as she rode them out. Jake stilled, splaying one hand on her waist to hold her in place.

When he moved again, it was to roll her on top of him. With both his hands now free, he unfastened the last of the hooks on her confining corset and slid it off. Then, taking her hips in his hands, he guided her where he wanted, pulling her close as he thrust deep inside.

The slow, satisfying rhythm made her rain kisses all over his chest and his face, the bliss of being with him so overwhelming she didn't know what to do with it all. Too soon, the steady, delicious dance built a new ache inside her; she could hardly stand the discipline of each measured thrust. Seizing his shoulders, she arched back to take her pleasure in her own hands and give her hips unrestricted access to every inch of him.

He called her name as she spiraled over the edge of the abyss again, her heart galloping wildly as the moment had its way with her. Jake wrapped his arms around her, anchoring her tight to him, and amid the haze of her own release she could feel his pulse through her, too.

Collapsing on him in a boneless heap, she couldn't catch her breath for long moments afterward. When she finally became aware of herself again, she realized he'd shifted her to lie beside him on his shirt, his arm tucked beneath her ear like a warm, muscular pillow.

He was more than a skilled lover. He was a thoughtful, considerate man. A watchful partner who would protect her no matter what. She saw all that clearly now as he came into focus for her.

He watched her just as closely, his eyes missing nothing, and she wondered what he saw. A strong woman who took her fate in her own hands by traveling to the other end of the country with a stranger for the sake of justice?

Or a woman who simply needed to lose herself, just like the name of her start-up company suggested?

She wasn't certain herself. And for a woman who'd always been so sure of herself, a woman who'd carefully marked out every path she would take so there would be no missed turns, that rattled her almost as much as having an unknown enemy lurking in the shadows.

The thought reminded her of the discovery she'd made before her tea arrived.

"Jake?"

"You look worried." He rubbed a finger over her forehead, making her realize she'd had her eyebrows scrunched together. "You aren't allowed to have any regrets about what just happened."

She relaxed against him. With nothing but the fire to light the room as dusk fell, the moon outside illuminated a few snowflakes swirling against the French doors nearby. The aroma of the ginger tea she hadn't touched mingled with the scent of burning wood.

"I don't. I've known that was bound to happen since you kissed me in the car on the way up here." She'd also told herself she wouldn't let it happen, but that had been before she'd experienced the full impact of the man and the Marquis. "I just hope it doesn't make working together awkward."

"It can't be more tense than it was to start with." He threaded his fingers through her hair and stroked the strands away from her face. "If anything, maybe this will make the rest of the week more productive now that we're not so preoccupied all the time."

This would make them *not* preoccupied? She was already thinking about when they'd be together again.

For that matter, her planner personality wanted to know what would happen to them when they returned to Miami. Would they return to being strangers and write this trip off as an intense getaway where emotions had flared out of control, never to be repeated?

Would her private investigator walk away from her as easily as the contractor had two months ago?

She hated not knowing.

Sensing the moment had come to protect herself from just such possibilities she retreated first, pulling a crocheted afghan off a footstool and wrapping it around her naked body.

"Actually, now that we're not preoccupied—" she used his term to show him she could be as easy with this as him "—I should tell you that I spotted an interesting name on the Marquis guest list for last year."

"Someone you know?" He tensed, instantly alert, and she half regretted bringing this up now.

Part of her had been hoping for a more romantic end to their time together.

"Not necessarily. But there was an Alex McMahon here last year and—"

"Sounds a lot like Alec Mason."

"That's what I was thinking."

He rolled to his side, still naked and amazing looking in the firelight in front of the hearth. He didn't need tight breeches or any other costume to make him completely mouthwatering.

"I looked into him early on in the investigation." He frowned. "I didn't think he could have pulled this off at the time, based on his lack of access to the Premiere accounts, but that was before I knew the crime involved a lot of cyber decoys..."

He trailed off as he jumped to his feet to retrieve a laptop. She watched the flex of muscles in his thighs as he walked and wished she could feel him against her all over again.

"You investigated Alec?" She felt adrift suddenly, both because Jake had bolted so fast after telling her they wouldn't be preoccupied now that they'd—essentially—gotten the sex impulses out of their system, and because she was at such a major disadvantage in a relationship where he knew far more about her than she knew about him.

"He made a few investments for you," Jake explained, not even sparing her a glance as he fired up the computer and connected it to his phone for internet access since the hotel didn't have wireless. "That gave him a certain financial savvy. And I knew you ended things acrimoniously based on the fact that you nearly took my eye out in an attempt to throw darts at a picture of his face."

"But you cleared him." Marnie tried not to let it sting that Jake had reverted to his supersleuthing. That was, of course, why they were here. "So you must have had some evidence to toss him aside as a suspect. When you cleared me, you needed video proof."

"You were a far more likely candidate for this. You're smarter, for one thing." Jake slid on a pair of boxers and a T-shirt before bringing the laptop back near the fireplace.

Near her.

Her heart beat faster, and for once, it wasn't simply because of his proximity. New worries crawled up her spine as she began to grasp the implications of Alec's possible guilt. She gripped the afghan tighter to her chest to ward off a sudden chill.

"Alec is a Princeton graduate," she reminded Jake. Not that she wanted to defend her ex-boyfriend, per se. But she wanted Jake to know she hadn't chosen a total loser.

"Actually, he lied about that." Jake flipped his screen around for her to see, showing her a brief background sheet on Alec Mason. "He doesn't have a criminal background, but it looks like he's bluffed his way into most of his jobs with padded résumés."

Marnie scanned the highlights of Alec's career as Jake spoke, trying to absorb the fact that her ex had betrayed her on even more levels. The ground shifted under her feet, and this time it didn't have anything to do with Jake or Alec. Instead, she simply felt like the world's biggest fool for trusting men in the first place.

"I used to think it was a good quality to see the best in people." How many times had she counseled friends to look on the bright side? How often had she told herself that life's obstacles were merely road signs to take a new and more exciting path? "I had no idea it made me so—"

She couldn't decide on any one word that would describe how she felt right now. Alec's face grinned at her almost as if he knew he could take her heart for a ride and get away with it.

"Hey." Jake set the laptop aside as he reached for her. Putting an arm around her waist, he pulled her close. "It is a good quality to see the best in people. I tend to see the worst, and I can tell you that has bitten me in the ass more times than I can count."

Her eyes burned, but she refused to feel sorry for herself.

"At least no one ever takes you for a sucker." That was the word she'd been looking for. She'd been a total sucker where Alec had been concerned. "You've never been taken in by someone who wants to use you."

"No. But I've been roped in by ideas and institutions, believing in the police force or the military only to be disillusioned when there's corruption." He planted a kiss on her hair, a gentle comfort that twined around her heart in spite of the dark cloud that had settled on her mood. "If everybody chose to see the downside of those places, they wouldn't be half as effective as they are."

"I just need to have more realistic expectations." Starting right now. Instead of baring her soul along with her body, she should be retreating. Building boundaries and erecting defenses so she didn't get sucked into thinking her time with Jake meant anything more than…sex.

Standing, she knew it would be safer for her heart not to accept comforting kisses from this man, who had a cynical side a mile wide.

Jake stared up at her in the firelight. The room had turned fully dark otherwise.

"I'll just finish up here and then we can figure out a game plan for dinner." He grabbed the laptop again, appearing to focus on the task at hand.

Just like she needed to.

"Good." Wrapping the afghan more securely around herself, she headed for the shower to wash away the tantalizing scent of him that clung to her skin. "The sooner we can find out who's trying to frame me the better."

Finding out who did it—and sending his or her ass to jail—would be her first chance to prove she wasn't the sucker they'd taken her for.

CHAPTER EIGHT

ALEX WOULD BE FURIOUS if he showed up now.

Lianna thought as much, but could not find the will to push Rico away since his hands were finally on her. She'd noticed him in the dining hall the night before. Had flirted with him when Alex—once again—hadn't bothered to show up for their rendezvous. She knew now that Alex must be a player. Maybe he got off on the idea that a woman was waiting for him at a sexy hotel. Well, not anymore. She'd captured another man's attention. A man who seemed so vivid, real and sexy that she had trouble recalling what Alex McMahon even looked like.

No more waiting around for a man who shared her interests. She would follow her passions.

"You kiss like an angel." Rico came up for air long enough to whisper soft words in her ear.

He was a sight to see as he hovered over her, his dark Latin looks and tawny eyes enough to make her melt. But he also listened when she spoke. Made eye contact instead of lingering over her breasts the way men on the prowl did.

The warmth of his caress on her hip soothed the bite of the hardware poking into her back as she leaned against a huge apothecary cabinet tucked into an alcove down a quiet little corridor outside the billiard room. She'd played Rico for a kiss to be administered wherever the winner chose, and while she'd heard some of those games had turned wild in a hurry when other guests played, Rico's request after winning had been for a traditional lip-lock.

Lianna hadn't decided if that was because he was a gentleman, or if he knew his persuasive powers of kissing would win him whatever he wanted in the long run. But was she really ready for more with a man she'd only just met?

Cold feet shouldn't happen when the rest of her body burned so hot, but there it was. She felt nervous. Vulnerable.

For a lawyer with a reputation as a shark in the courtroom, the feelings were uncomfortable.

"I shouldn't have played that game with you," she blurted loud enough that her raging hormones would hear her over the rush of her heartbeat.

Edging back a fraction, she gazed up at him by the flickering flame of a gaslight sconce on the wall to her right.

He loomed over her, broad-chested and infinitely appealing in his servant's tunic and breeches that revealed a—um—great deal of manhood. It was difficult to gauge his expression through the colored contacts he wore that made him indistinguishable from his brother. Apparently the two of them enjoyed being totally identical when they came here. Lianna had learned that, under the contacts, Raul's eyes were brown and Rico's were blue.

"You regret a kiss?" He frowned, his hands disappearing from her body even though his hips remained a mere inch from hers. "From the way you followed me around today, I had every reason to believe—"

"I know." She didn't want to think about the way she'd flung herself at him. Or flirted shamelessly with any number of guys since showing up here. "The kiss was great. It's just that I had told someone I'd meet them here and when he didn't show tonight, I figured I deserved to have fun anyway."

Rico's hips closed that last inch, his hands returning to her waist.

"You do," he agreed. "And I'll bet I can make you forget all about him by morning."

The rush of longing came at her so hard she had to swallow the urge to rub up against him like a cat and forget all about her niggling conscience.

In the background, she could hear a woman's shriek of laugher emanating from the billiard room and wondered if the stakes had gone up in the gaming area. Usually they waited to play games for articles of clothing until after dinner had been served, but some folks got rowdy early. It wasn't uncommon to spot a man coming from the hall minus garments that he'd lost in a game.

Or a woman as she streaked by in a corset. Or less.

"But I'm on the rebound from a divorce." Lianna had no idea what had come over her to pour her heart out to the hottest guy she'd ever been fortunate enough to kiss. But there it was. Apparently she wasn't too jaded for an attack of scruples. "So I can't trust my emotions so well where men are concerned. And for that matter, my ex cheated on me at the end of the marriage. I hate to do to someone else what he did to me, even if I don't know this guy that I planned to meet here very well."

Rico blinked, his long lashes sweeping low to fan over his burnished bronze skin as the light from the flickering sconce cast stark shadows on his strong features. In the narrow alcove, he blocked her view of all else besides him.

"Lianna." His thumb smoothed a gently teasing caress along the bottom of her corset where it rested on her hip. With a little pressure, he could have slid it underneath that seam, even though her gown still would have been in the way. There was something endlessly tantalizing about a man navigating his way through that many layers to unveil you.

"Hmm?" She tried not to sway with the hypnotic power of his touch. She had noble intentions for once, damn it.

"Most everyone here is on a rebound of some sort or another." Perhaps he spied her confusion because he explained himself. "How many people would come to places like this just for the hookups? A few. But the Marquis packs the rooms every week because most of the guests need a complete escape. Here, you can forget about your job that's going poorly or your ex who cheated, or a wife who didn't want any part of a noisy, cantankerous clan of six brothers and decided she'd rather go out for groceries and never come back."

"There are six of you?" The mind reeled at the vision of so many studly males in one family.

"Who said I was talking about me?" He winked and something about the gesture made her realize he was the more outgoing of the twins—the one who liked to party. The hell-raiser. "It was Raul's wife who took off, but yes, I have five brothers. My point is that there is nothing wrong with getting caught up in the moment when you are not married. This man who did not show up to meet you does not have any right to claim you."

Persuasive fingers trailed lightly over her hip, the heat of his touch penetrating the rose-colored taffeta and two layers of underskirts. He'd taken such care to ease her conscience. If he was so considerate of her needs now, what might he be like in bed when her needs would be more obvious and far easier to address?

A little breathless gasp robbed her of speech for a moment. Purposely, she leaned more heavily into the apothecary cabinet behind her, allowing the hardware of the drawers to poke against her uncomfortably and remind her that she couldn't just slide into his arms for the night.

"In theory, I agree," she admitted. "But in practice, I'll feel better if I send him a note and let him know my intentions before we, er, kiss again."

"I have a phone," Rico admitted softly, leaning close to nip her ear with a gentle bite. "You can call him from my room."

"Doesn't that seem a bit wicked?" Her eyelids fell to half-mast as she swayed against him.

"It's Christmastime, Lianna. And you've been a very, very good girl." Rico rubbed a path up her ribs to the underside of her breast as he kissed her neck. "Don't deny yourself the reward you deserve."

She felt her resolve slipping along with her red velvet maid's uniform that borrowed liberally from the wardrobes of Mrs. Claus and a Victoria's Secret catalog. The low-cut, fur-lined bodice inched down until it barely covered her breasts. Her nipples peaked against the fluffy white trim of her outfit.

"I wasn't *always* a good girl," she confessed, wanton heat swirling along her skin as he tugged the costume down a fraction of an inch more, exposing her to his waiting tongue.

Desire pooled in her womb as he drew one stiff peak into his mouth and flicked it again and again. By the time he relinquished her breast and tugged her dress back up to cover her, she was such a trembling mass of nerve endings, she couldn't have denied him if she tried.

"I bet I'll enjoy hearing about the times you were naughty just as much as the times you were nice," he assured her in a low growl. "But you're going to have to sit on my lap the whole time."

He palmed her bottom in his hands and gave each cheek a little spank. He caught her squeal of surprise in a kiss, silencing her as he passed her his cell phone.

Fully, deliciously committed to the plan, Lianna tucked the phone into her cuff and told herself everything would be all right. Rico was a once-in-a-lifetime man, and she deserved this night.

Alex had proven his lack of loyalty by ignoring her this week, showing more interest in having her spy on Jack and Marie than in coming up here to be with her himself.

For all she cared, the three of them could play their voyeur games without her. If Alex ever showed tonight, he could watch the redhead all by himself.

Jake watched Marnie from across the dining area, her green bustle twitching restlessly with every move of her hips as she walked toward the card parlor for the evening's entertainment.

The mood in the dining area had been raucous and bawdy, with guests flirting and dancing between courses. Now, as the tables were cleared away, some people lingered by the bar area to be close to the musicians, who were dressed like holiday court jesters in red and green velvet jackets. Other guests moved toward the billiards lounge and card room to wait for the evening entertainment. Jake and Marnie had agreed to split up after the evening meal, hoping to find out more about the staff behind the scenes at the Marquis. The embezzlement of 2.5 million dollars had originated on a Marquis computer; of that much his people were certain. So as long as Marnie wore her mask around the hotel, he didn't mind her searching out leads on where staff offices were located and who had access to them. For his part, he would do the same. But all the while he wove his way toward the library, he brooded over missing signs that Alec Mason might be more deeply involved in this mess.

"Looking for company?" a petite blonde in a vampy black dress asked him as he passed her in an archway between rooms.

Her gown was floor-length, but the insets down the sides were lace-up panels with nothing underneath, so you could see about an inch-and-a-half swath of naked flesh from knee to breast on either side of her.

"No." The word came out sharper than he'd intended for a guy who needed to schmooze if he ever wanted answers. "Actually," he said, changing tactics mid-stream, "do you know where I go to sign up for work here? Is there an office or do I just go to the front desk?"

"What kind of work are you looking for?" she asked, tossing her hair over one shoulder and angling a hip closer as she looked him up and down. "I've got a few jobs you'd be perfect for."

How could he ever check out this place when flirtatious women put themselves in his path at every opportunity? His case came first, and his carnal thoughts were all for Marnie.

And even worse than this woman flirting with him was the fact that guys would swarm Marnie the second he wasn't attached to her side. Like right now in the card room.

"Sorry, I don't hire out to individuals, but thanks anyway."

The vampy blonde crossed her arms over her chest and glared at him.

"I'll keep that in mind when you end up as my waiter or my manservant tomorrow. Because the second you take on work for the Marquis, I will find you and make you do just what I want." With another toss of her stick-straight hair, she stalked off on sky-high heels, full of dominatrix attitude.

Who were these people? Jake had seen some strip joints in his day and a few sleazy cathouses when he'd been stationed overseas, but he'd never run into an operation like this one. It had to be tough to keep it from turning into an all-out orgy on any given night, which would definitely make the place lose a lot of its character. But the people who stayed here seemed hip to the game—to push the boundaries of public displays without sliding into vulgarity.

In the billiards room, Jake saw a waiter serving drinks and figured he'd ask the guy where the offices were. Until he got closer and realized it wasn't just any waiter but the behemoth pretty boy who'd hit on Marnie earlier.

He'd just decided to get his information elsewhere when the guy turned around and saw him, his expression surprisingly blank considering they'd had a stand-off just a couple of hours ago.

"Dude, I know that look and I can guarantee you've got me confused with my brother," the guy said, easing past him with a tray full of empty glasses.

Jake did not appreciate the brush-off.

"Does that angle work on everyone? The old 'I didn't do it and it must have been someone else' bit?"

He kept step with the waiter, figuring that if nothing else, he'd follow him wherever he was going until he located the offices for the Marquis.

"No. Usually we just end up making twice as many enemies. But whatever Rico did to piss you off, just keep in mind he's my twin, not my responsibility." The guy hardly noticed an exotic-looking brunette dressed in a gown that—no lie—appeared to made entirely of whipped cream. "So no need to follow me, okay? I'm Raul, and you've got the wrong brother. I'm mostly here under duress anyway, so I don't need trouble."

Something about Raul's obliviousness to the whipped cream woman gave authenticity to his claims.

Jake had a feeling that Rico's head would have been on a swivel if that walking dessert had just passed him.

"I'll take it up with your brother, then. But yes, I'm following you because I need to know where the offices for this place are located and shaking a straight answer out of this crowd is like pulling teeth."

Raul grinned. "It's an affliction I call sex on the brain." He nodded toward a back wall behind a fifteen-foot-high Christmas tree. "This way."

Peace made with the guy, Jake appreciated the heads-up. He'd checked out most of the hotel on his own earlier that day, but he'd only succeeded in locating kitchens, storage and laundry rooms—no real base for operations. He'd begun to think the administrative area must be somewhere well hidden, a fact that would really limit computer access for his suspect.

Tonight, he wouldn't give up searching until he'd found the offices he sought and checked out the computers. His sixth sense had been itching all day that whoever was trying to frame Marnie could show up here at any time now—especially with an Alex McMahon on an old guest list. If Jake had overlooked something in the guy's past—some connection to this case he hadn't seen the first time—he didn't want Marnie to pay for that mistake.

The sooner he retrieved the necessary intelligence, the sooner he could pack up their stuff and get Marnie out of harm's way for good.

THE ATMOSPHERE IN THE card room made Marnie uncomfortable.

Still wearing her mask to protect her identity from

anyone who might recognize her, she stuck to the outskirts of the room to avoid attention from the drunken revelers playing what amounted to strip poker in the center of the room. The game involved six players in varying states of undress while a crowd of onlookers obstructed her view of most of the table. Apparently the chips they used were not worth money but sexual favors, with the winner claiming whatever he or she wished from the players who'd lost.

Partially hidden behind an old-fashioned cigar store Indian, Marnie decided she would leave long before that moment arrived. The mood here was far more sexually aggressive than the vibe she'd felt earlier in the hotel. But before she departed, she hoped to catch a better glimpse of one of the men who observed the game. There was something familiar about his face and if only she could see him better, she felt as if she might be able to identify him. Did she know him? Or was he simply employed by the Marquis and she'd seen him here the last time she visited the property?

Ducking out from behind the carved wooden figure, she scanned the faces again, trying to see over a tall woman wearing an elaborate headpiece that made her look more like a Vegas showgirl than a nineteenth-century actress.

Before she could find the man in the crowd, however, two hands clamped over her mouth while two strong arms wrapped around her waist.

Panic coursed through her. She screamed behind the tight hold on her mouth, but any sound was lost in the laughter around the poker table. Without attracting any attention whatsoever, two tuxedoed men wearing black eye masks hauled her sideways into an opening in the wall where a bookcase hid a paneled door.

"Mmph!" she cried behind one hard hand, kicking at her captors' legs as they dragged her into the darkened space no bigger than a closet and then shut the paneled door behind them, locking the three of them in the dark.

"Damn, she's feisty," muttered one of the men, a smelly, stocky man whose strong cologne mingled with even stronger scents of alcohol and tobacco. "Are you sure this is the right girl?"

Her blood chilled as she wondered who they were and what they wanted with her. Were these the men who'd tried to frame her? She squinted in the darkness to try to make them out.

Just then, the one who'd been holding her—a shorter man built like a bull—released her mouth.

Whatever his answer was, the words were lost in her scream for help.

Over and over she screamed until one of the men struck a match and lit a sconce behind her head. The two of them had lifted their masks to sit on their sweaty foreheads, and they stared at her as if she'd grown horns and a tail right before their eyes.

"What the hell?" one of them asked, scratching his chest as he watched her with a worried frown.

They were no longer restraining her, but they'd locked her in here with them and she could not see the way out, even though she knew where the door should be. Her eyes could not make out any kind of knob or handle at all.

"She's wearing a mask," the other one observed. "Aren't you playing the game?"

Their conversation sounded far away because her ears were ringing from the panic alarms clanging relentlessly in her head. She fought to catch her breath while her unanswered cries for help seemed to echo eerily in the unmoving air of the closet.

"What game?" she asked finally, guessing the hidden space had been soundproofed since she couldn't hear anything from the card room she knew rested on just the other side of the wall.

The short man leaned closer and she arched away from his groping hand. Still, he succeeded in ripping off her white silk eye mask.

"The masquerade," the tall man answered, pulling a yellowed sheet of old-fashioned parchment from a pocket of his trousers. "Our clue said the next wench would be wearing a white mask with poinsettias."

He waved the silk in his hand like a pennant won in battle before making a lunge toward her.

Leaping backward out of his grip, she banged into a wall behind her. Nowhere to run.

"I assure you, I am not the next wench." She gave them a moment to let the words sink in since the two of them appeared to have imbibed early and often. She prayed they were just drunk and not complete bastards. "It is a simple coincidence that I'm wearing this mask, because I didn't sign up for any masquerade game."

Her heart rate slowed by a tiny fraction as the men who'd jumped her seemed to weigh that newsflash. She hoped they would do the right thing and release her. Heaven knew, it seemed like a good sign they weren't restraining her. But plastered, sexed-up males couldn't be trusted to behave like gentlemen. They exchanged inscrutable glances now, and her fear factor spiked again.

What if they were too lazy to go find the woman who wanted to play this awful game of theirs?

In the wake of that worry came a dull thumping on the other side of the paneled door.

"Marie! Marie, are you okay?" a faint feminine voice called to her in time with the knocking.

Hope surged through her.

"That's me." She moved toward the door, shoving past the manhandling creeps who'd grabbed her. "My friends are looking for me."

She could not imagine who would know she was in here, in fact, but the voice could have been shouting for Penelope, and she would have pretended it was her dearest and most protective friend in the world.

"But we're playing a game," the taller, more sloshed man explained patiently. He appeared confused and more than a little dismayed at the prospect of her leaving.

Marnie started banging on the door in response to whoever was on the other side.

"I'm in here!" she shouted for all she was worth. "Help!"

Swearing, the shorter, smarter man appeared to understand the potential consequences of holding a woman against her will as he moved away from her and toward a button now visible on the far wall. Jabbing at the small device with one chubby finger, he must have tripped the hidden door. All of the sudden, light spilled into the tiny closet.

There, centered in front of the door, stood Lianna with a worried frown.

"Marie!" she cried, wrapping Marnie in a hug that felt really, really welcome right now. "Are you okay?"

Marnie became aware of many faces swarming around behind Lianna. It seemed the whole card room, including the half-naked players who'd been involved in strip poker, had circled around the bookcase to find out what was happening behind the hidden wall.

As her eyes met their curious gazes, she realized she no longer wore her mask. Anyone here might recognize her. Anyone here could be the one who'd tried to set her up.

Ducking her forehead onto Lianna's shoulder, she kept an arm locked around the other woman's waist.

"I'm okay. I just want to go back to my room," she whispered, wishing Jake was there. "I—don't want to be alone yet."

She'd said it mostly so Lianna would walk with her and help keep her at least partially hidden from the room full of prying eyes. But it was probably truer than she'd first realized, since her knees were still shaking from being grabbed and dragged out of sight faster than she could blink.

"Of course," Lianna murmured soothingly, tucking Marnie close with one arm while she cleared a path with the other. "Coming through! Make way! Coming through, for crying out loud. Give the woman some room."

Shoving her way through the crowd, Lianna

blocked like a lineman while Marnie hurried along half a step back.

"How did you know I was in there?" Marnie asked once they'd cleared the thick of the crowd.

Closing in on the elevators, Lianna loosened her hold.

"I've been—" She seemed to hesitate and Marnie couldn't imagine why. Unless, of course, the other woman felt bad about flirting shamelessly with Jake the night before.

"You're my new hero," Marnie assured her. "I really appreciate you knocking when you did because those guys really had me scared."

She shivered again, thinking about what could have happened.

"Usually the girls who sign up for the masquerade games like that sort of thing," Lianna murmured distractedly, peering around the main foyer of the resort as if she were looking for someone. "They really ought to have a sign near the masks in the costume shop so people don't pick them up without knowing what they mean around here."

"No kidding," Marnie agreed, her whole body buzzing with the adrenaline letdown.

Damn it, where was Jake? More than anything right now, she wanted to feel his arms around her.

She moved to hit the button to call the elevator and realized Lianna was staring at her with an inscrutable expression. Despite the red sexpot gown falling artfully off one shoulder and the sprig of holly leaves tucked in her dark hair, she had a shrewd intelligence in her gaze.

"Although," she began slowly, "why else would anyone purchase a mask?"

The question contained a note of assessment that made Marnie a bit uneasy.

"For fun." She shrugged off the question. "The masks are beautiful."

"Or some people wear masks to stay hidden," Lianna mused. "But that would mean they know they're being watched."

Did Lianna know something about her purpose here? Could she know who was trying to frame her?

Confused and more than a little worried, Marnie didn't want to step into the elevator cabin with Lianna, even though the lift had arrived and the doors had swooshed open in silence.

Lianna took a step closer to her.

"Did you know someone has been watching you?" she asked, her voice low.

Threatening?

Marnie clenched her fists. She'd been ready to take on two full-grown men if they touched her tonight. There was no doubt in her mind she'd do some serious damage to the woman in front of her now.

"Marie," a familiar voice called to her from the other end of the hall.

Both women turned to see Jake jogging toward them in his dinner clothes, the formal attire an enticing contrast to his raw masculinity. Marnie's knees went weak with gratitude and relief.

"Thank God," she murmured, not knowing who to trust and feeling as if she'd been ripped raw tonight.

"Don't go anywhere near her," he warned, though

at first Marnie wasn't sure which one of them he was speaking to.

As he stopped short between them, though, he grabbed her by the arm and pulled her away. Turning to Lianna, he spoke through gritted teeth.

"You've got some explaining to do."

She shook her head so hard the holly berry sprig that had been perched in her hair fell to the carpeted floor of the main foyer.

"I didn't do anything," she protested, her voice sounding panicked.

But, oddly, she didn't sound all that surprised by the accusation.

"I don't understand." Marnie squeezed Jake's arm, feeling a strange twinge of empathy for the other woman, who, after all, had just saved her from possibly being assaulted.

"She's the one who's been moving money around." Releasing Marnie's arm, he pulled a sheaf of papers that looked like computer spreadsheets from his jacket pocket. "She's the one who breached the Premiere accounts and tried to frame you."

CHAPTER NINE

"YOU CAN'T BE SERIOUS." Marnie bit her lip as she looked from Jake to Lianna and back again. "I'd never even met Lianna until yesterday."

Jake kept his eyes on Lianna, who'd turned pale but hadn't run. The elevator doors closed again, leaving the three of them together on the main floor.

"Well, Lianna?" he prodded, evidence in hand thanks to the hotel's computer database.

"I don't know what you're talking about." She shook her head, as if she could make the accusations go away.

"But you just said something about me being watched." Marnie lowered her voice as a young couple came through the resort's front doors into the foyer.

Sensing the need for privacy, Jake pushed the button for the elevator again.

"You're coming with us until we get to the bottom of this," he warned, knowing he'd never get away with that kind of intimidation as a cop. But as a P.I. operating out of state? He figured the rules were open for interpretation. Especially if it meant keeping Marnie safe.

"In the interest of privacy, perhaps that would be best." Lifting her chin, Lianna was the first one to step inside the elevator when it arrived again.

Jake knew a seasoned criminal would have never

gotten into the elevator with him. He also knew that
whoever had tried to frame Marnie had laid too much
groundwork to pull off this crime to make mistakes
now. So between this small tip-off and the fact that Lianna Closson was willing to face his accusations, he
had a pretty good idea she wasn't the one who'd engi-
neered the 2.5-million-dollar swindle.

But her vaguely guilty behavior told him she knew
something, and he would damn well find out what.

Bringing her for questioning to the suite he shared
with Marnie, he held the elevator door for the women
as they arrived at their floor. Unlocking the door to
the room, he tried to process Lianna's behavior while
Marnie spoke quietly in his ear, insisting that Lianna
had saved her from—

"What?" He stopped cold inside the door to their
accommodations as Marnie's words finally penetrated
the high-speed swirl of thoughts in his head. "Someone grabbed you?"

He tensed everywhere, already furious with himself for letting her out of the room. Out of his sight.
Quickly, she recounted the ordeal along with Lianna's
role in saving her.

"I will find them," he assured her. *And gut them,* he
assured himself. "You're certain you're unharmed?"

His eyes roamed over every inch of her, looking for
bruises on her arms or any signs of her dress being
askew. The whole time he took his inventory, he had
to swallow back fury by the gallon.

He flipped on more lights in the suite as he maneuvered her under the chandelier in the living area so he
could examine her better.

Throughout it all, Lianna paced nearby. And though she appeared worried, she didn't have the shifty look of a woman who was about to run. Despite the rumpled and well-used tissue in one hand, she seemed resigned to get to the bottom of this.

"I'm fine," Marnie began, then stopped herself. "Actually, I'm still a little shaken up."

As if to prove the point, she held up a hand to the light. He could see her fingers tremble before she tucked them back into the folds of her dress.

This time, he swallowed back curses along with his anger. She didn't need to hear it.

"I'm sorry I wasn't there." Hauling her into his arms, he held her. Absorbed the quivers vibrating through her. "Have a seat, okay?"

He shoved aside some needlepoint pillows in keeping with the elegant Victorian-style room, clearing a place for her. Lianna pulled a small lap blanket off the back of a chair near the fireplace and put it around Marnie's shoulders.

And while that move won the other woman some points, it wouldn't let her off the hook if she'd had anything to do with his case.

Turning to her, he gestured for her to take a seat on a nearby ottoman.

"How did you know she was in that room?" He'd get to the other stuff in a minute. Right now, he wanted to find out everything he could about the men who'd grabbed Marnie.

"I was in the gaming area waiting to—that is, I had a phone call to make before I could meet Rico tonight." She peered over at the grandfather clock near the entryway. "Another guy stood me up this week and I wanted to tell him that I was going to see someone else before I, you know, started hanging out with him."

"How noble of you," Jake remarked. "So you're in the gaming room and you saw the men grab Marnie?"

"Marnie?" Her brow furrowed.

"Marie," he clarified.

"Oh." Her expression cleared; she was probably used to fake names being used by the guests of the Marquis. "No, I didn't see them take her or I would have reacted faster. But I noticed her in the room one moment and when I looked for her the next moment, she was gone. And I just had a bad feeling about it since the whole place was so rowdy tonight."

"You were looking for me?" Marnie asked, leaning forward on the sofa.

She seemed steadier now, though Jake noticed she hadn't taken her hands off him since they'd returned to the room.

"I—" Lianna shifted on the ottoman, her velvet dress pooling around her high heels. "I'd been keeping an eye on you because I knew it was your first time here and this place can be a trip for newbies."

Marnie appeared satisfied with the answer, but Jake sensed more to that story. Still, he left it alone for the moment in his rush to confront her with what he'd discovered earlier.

"Can you explain these?" He tossed the sheaf of computer printouts on the table and let her leaf through the spreadsheets, which showed her guest user account for the Marquis had been used to access the Premiere Properties account.

"I don't even know what they are, so I'm sure I'm the last person who could explain—" Frowning, she ran her finger over the lists of numbers dates and accounts. "Wait. This is my user information and pass code for the resort's guest volunteer system. I use this to sign up for work around the hotel."

Marnie moved to sit beside Lianna. Whatever dislike Marnie might have had for Lianna at one time seemed to have vanished when the woman rescued her tonight. Was that part of Lianna's plan? Had she sought to gain Marnie's trust? Jake tried not to think the worst of Lianna, but his tendency to see those darker motivations were what had made him a good cop, and a good P.I. now.

"It looks like her user name masqueraded as mine to hack into the Premiere Properties accounts." Marnie saw the implications immediately as she read over the sheets. Straightening, she gave Lianna a level look. "These papers suggest you used your access to the Marquis computers to frame me."

"Frame you?" She shook her head, uncomprehending or doing a damn good job of looking clueless. "For what? I don't even use a computer when I come here because there's no access. I have to sign up for jobs before I arrive or else use the main computer downstairs, which I only did once and—"

"You brought your phone with you," Jake pointed out, knowing she could connect through that if she wanted. "You said you were going to call that guy who stood you up."

"Everyone smuggles in a phone here," she argued, her voice rising to a higher pitch as she became noticeably agitated. "That doesn't mean I brought a computer."

"You could have internet access on the phone." Jake watched as the woman's eyes darted around the room, her pulse thrumming visibly in her neck. She was hiding something and she was scared.

"Are you a cop?" She looked back and forth between him and Marnie. "I want to know what this is about. You have no right to keep me here."

Jake held up his hands, waiting for her to break. "No one is holding you here."

Marnie, unaccustomed to interrogation, didn't wait for the breakdown.

"You've been everywhere I've turned since I got here," she told Lianna, still hugging the dark wool lap blanket around her shoulders. "As much as I appreciate you helping me get out of that hidden room tonight, I don't believe you were keeping an eye on me just because I'm new to the Marquis."

At first, Jake feared the comment would distract Lianna from her fears and delay a confession of whatever she knew. But then she pulled one of the needlepoint pillows into her lap and hugged it to her like a security blanket.

Shoulders tense, she seemed to collect herself.

"Look. I haven't done anything wrong. If I've been close to you the past two days it's because this guy I was supposed to meet here—the one who stood me up—wanted to know about any new people who checked in this week." She shrugged as if that was no big deal. "The Marquis is all about meeting new people, right? So I figured he just wanted to find out if there were any exciting strangers to, um, have fun with."

She had Jake's full attention now. And he had a damn good idea where the story was going. This was the missing piece.

"Right. You thought your boyfriend was on the lookout for new playthings, and being fairly liberal-minded yourself, that didn't bother you in the least."

Lianna frowned. "First of all, Alex is not my boyfriend. Second, I wouldn't say—"

"Who?" Marnie interjected, her gray eyes locked on Lianna's face. "Who did you say is not your boyfriend?"

"Alex," Lianna repeated clearly. "Alex McMahon. He's just some guy I met here last year. He got in touch with me after my divorce and wanted to see me this week—" Lianna stopped in mid-sentence. "Are you okay?"

Marnie folded her arms more tightly around herself. Her lips moved though no words came out for a long moment.

"Alex McMahon," she finally repeated.

It was a name Jake wasn't surprised to hear. A name that his investigation kept coming back to. But at least now, he had a solid connection to a guy with a lot more criminal smarts than Jake had given him credit for.

"We need to know everything about this guy," Jake explained. "I'm a private investigator and I think he could be a threat to you as well as Marnie."

He passed the woman his Florida P.I. license, even though it wasn't worth all that much in a different state. Chances were good she wouldn't know that.

Lianna looked over the license while Jake studied Marnie. Some color had returned to her cheeks by now, but her lips were drawn tight as her mouth flattened with worry.

"Okay," Lianna said, situating herself more comfortably on the seat now that she didn't seem to fear getting in trouble. "For starters, Alex was very interested in your arrival. He asked me to follow you."

Two HOURS LATER, Marnie had her bags packed.

She'd offered no protest when Jake announced they had enough evidence in his case to vacate the Marquis. Between Lianna's lead about Alec Mason—who she recognized from the photograph in Jake's online files—and the paper trail Jake had obtained from the hotel's database, he had enough to turn over to the police and ensure Marnie wouldn't be a suspect. And while she was relieved beyond words about that, she was even more glad to leave the hotel because of the uneasiness that had settled over her ever since those men had grabbed her. Although she'd stopped shaking long ago, she still felt a chill deep in her bones that no amount of layers had taken away.

Now, she tossed her bag in the back of the SUV, her leather boots crunching in the snow as the exhaust warmed her legs. White Christmas candles glowed in every window of the resort, imbuing the place with a magical allure in spite of the scary night she'd had.

"I don't want to leave," Lianna protested a few yards away as Jake hustled her out a side entrance.

They weren't running out on the bill since the place had their credit cards, but they weren't exactly following checkout procedures. Jake had thought it safest to leave as fast as possible without anyone in the resort being any wiser. That way if Alec came looking for them—and Jake felt certain he would—they would buy themselves a little time.

"Do you really want to be there when your boyfriend shows up now that you know what a rat bastard he is?" Jake asked her as they got closer to Marnie.

He carried his bag and a dark plum leather suitcase that must belong to Lianna.

The other woman hadn't even bothered to change into street clothes yet, her red velvet gown visible between the gap in her long winter coat as she walked.

"He's not my boyfriend," Lianna reminded Jake. "Remember? I haven't seen him in person in a year."

Marnie didn't want to think about the fact that Alec had been at the Marquis with another woman while flirting with Lianna *and* pretending to have a relationship with her back in Miami.

She hopped up front in the passenger seat while the other two settled in. Marnie watched Jake as he came around the SUV, a fresh snowfall dotting his shoulders and lingering in his dark hair.

He'd certainly worked quickly and efficiently here, flushing out evidence against Alec faster than she'd envisioned. But while she was grateful to him for finding out who wanted to frame her, she couldn't help but regret their time together was coming to an end quicker than she'd imagined.

While her rational side told her maybe it was best that they part before she fell for him—a possibility that felt all too real even after knowing him a short while—her heart longed for just a few more days.

A few more toe-curling nights.

"All set?" he asked as he fastened his seat belt.

Not by a long shot.

"Yes." Marnie nodded, trying to ignore the lump in her throat. "But where are we going?"

She knew Jake wanted to keep her and Lianna safe. But she didn't know what keeping them safe involved.

"We can go to my house," Lianna offered, leaning forward from the backseat. "I live just north of here."

"No." Jake put the vehicle in gear and pulled out onto the access road in the same direction they'd come from. "He'll know where you live. Don't you get it? He tried to ruin Marnie financially and then frame her to boot. You have no idea what he's capable of."

When Lianna remained silent, Marnie mulled over the fact that Alec had turned out so much worse than even she'd pictured. And she'd spent a lot of time winging darts at his mug.

"Why do you think he wanted to implicate me in his crime?" Marnie stared out into the snow rushing at the windshield as Jake's tires spun around a wide turn. "I don't understand why he had so much ill will against me. It's one thing to fleece me out of my savings, but it seems sort of excessive to make it look like I stole millions."

In fact, she was royally pissed off, and not just at Alec, either. How could she have dated someone so manipulative and heartless?

"One of the best ways to get away with a crime is to make it look like someone else did it." Jake said it so matter-of-factly that she realized he'd probably seen scenarios like this a hundred times in his line of work.

As far as he was concerned, she was just another gullible mark. And man, that knowledge didn't settle well.

"I'm going to sue his butt ten ways to Sunday," she muttered, out of sorts and angry with herself.

"I'll represent you," offered Lianna. She popped up from the backseat, a business card in hand.

Reading it, Marnie saw she'd used her real name at the Marquis. Lianna Closson, Attorney At Law.

"You're a lawyer?" She turned around in her seat to see the sexpot in the Mrs. Claus-Gone-Wild dress.

"Defense against medical malpractice mostly, but I've been thinking about taking on some flashier clients to make ends meet in this economy. And I'm no longer using Wells by the way." She tucked a silver card case back into her purse. "You can be my first flashy client. And we'll whip the pants off this guy in court. Because while I may not always get my man in my personal life, I can guarantee you I'm a shark in court."

She smiled and Marnie had to laugh, seeing Lianna in a whole new light.

"Somehow, I can picture that."

Jake turned the wheel hard all of the sudden.

"Hold on," he warned as they ducked in between some trees and he switched off his headlights. "Someone's following us."

CHAPTER TEN

TAKING HIS 9 MM from the glove compartment just in case, Jake sat in the darkness as snow piled on the windshield.

Inside the SUV, he could hear the women breathing as they all waited. Watched.

After a long minute, the car that had been following them finally approached, the headlights cutting a dim swath through the snowy trees. Maybe it was nothing—just someone else who'd checked out late. But Jake's sixth sense twitched something fierce.

Then the car's headlights spun wildly, the car careened out of control on the snowy road and it landed—hissing steam—in a ravine nearby.

"Oh, no!" Marnie peered over at him, worried.

Crap.

Did he dare play Good Samaritan? What if the person in the other car had followed them on purpose? On the other hand, how could he *not* check when someone could be seriously injured in the other vehicle? At these temperatures, they could freeze to death in a hurry.

"I'm going out." Jake met Marnie's gaze in the dim interior lit only by moonlight. He checked the rearview mirror. "Lock the doors and do not leave the vehicle for any reason. I'll be back."

He clenched his hands tight around the gun and the steering wheel to resist the temptation to kiss her, touch her, reassure her. Then, levering the door open, he braced himself against the blast of cold air.

"Hey!" a man's voice shouted in the distance, echoing through ice-laden trees.

Alec Mason?

One of the men who'd grabbed Marnie earlier?

Both possibilities made him grip the 9 mm tighter as he dodged toward a frosty tree for cover. He moved silently through the soft cushion of snow that stifled sounds.

"Lianna?" the man shouted again, the voice closer this time. "Is that you?"

Jake pressed his spine to the tree, frozen bark rough against the back of his head, trying to see into the whiteout before the guy was on him. Who the hell would be looking for Lianna? Could she be working with Alec Mason after all?

Had he left Marnie locked inside the SUV with a dangerous criminal? He spun to check the vehicle.

From inside the cab nearby, Jake could hear scuffling noises. What the hell?

The rear door of Jake's SUV popped open just as he made out a shape jogging through the trees.

"Rico?" Lianna's high-pitched voice blurted into the night. Her white coat blended with the falling flakes as she leaped from the vehicle. She took big, awkward steps through the snow. "Rico, I'm here!"

A tall figure emerged from the shadows. Garbed in a long man's dress coat and leather riding boots that could have only been purchased at the Marquis's exclusive boutique, the guy who'd pissed Jake off on more than one occasion burst through the tree line. This was the twin he didn't like—Raul's brother, Rico, who'd eyed Marnie one too many times.

"Easy there, bud. She's not alone." Jake stepped forward enough to be seen. He didn't raise his weapon, but he didn't ease his grip in case anyone else came out of the woods. Then again, his fingers were pretty much frozen in place. "Is anyone with you? Were you followed?"

"No." Rico seemed to assess the situation, looking from the women in the vehicle to Jake. "Is that a gun? What the hell is going on here?"

"Were you following me?" Jake took another step forward.

He needed to find out who'd been behind them on the road before he relaxed his stance.

Rico lifted his hands about waist high.

"Take it easy, dude. I came after Lianna when I saw her leaving the Marquis. I couldn't tell who she was with and I wanted to make sure she was okay." He leaned sideways to see past Jake. "Is everything all right, Lianna?"

"I'm fine," she called back. "For crying out loud, can't you put the gun away, Jake?"

"Was anyone else with you in the car?" Jake pressed, unwilling to relax his guard until he was damn certain no harm would come to Marnie.

Hearing that she'd been manhandled tonight had awoken dark protective instincts that still had him on edge.

"No. I tried picking up speed when I couldn't see

your taillights anymore, but then I started fishtailing and—boom. I live in Southern California. We don't get weather like this."

He studied the guy, weighing his words. In the end, he trusted his gut. Raul had been a stand-up guy helping him out earlier. Could his brother be that different? Besides, Jake had solid evidence implicating Alec Mason, and he had no reason to believe Rico was involved in his case.

Finally, Jake slid the safety back into place on the weapon and tucked it inside his jacket.

"You can ride with us." He motioned the guy toward the rear door where Lianna still peeked out into the snow. "But we're not going back to the Marquis."

The other guy nodded, but he kept a wary eye on Jake.

"Sure thing. My brother can retrieve the car in the morning." He moved toward the SUV and Lianna, whose arms were already outstretched. "I just hope someone clues me in on why we're on the run with a handgun in the middle of the night."

Jake figured he'd leave that up to Lianna. He wasn't in the mood to talk considering all that had happened tonight. He would be on the phone to the cops as soon as he got Marnie somewhere safe.

Stepping up into the driver's seat, he punched in the request for lodging on the GPS and steered the vehicle back onto the main road. The faster he got checked in and handed off the dirty work to the authorities, the quicker he'd have Marnie all to himself. And with a hunger driven by that edginess that had gnawed at him all day long, that moment couldn't come soon enough.

"THERE IT IS." Lianna pointed out a blaze of red and green Christmas lights from the backseat.

Marnie smiled at the sight, her mood more relaxed now that they'd left the Marquis behind. It had taken almost an hour to drive twenty-five miles in the wretched weather, but they'd found the bed-and-breakfast. Or at least according to Lianna's pointing finger they had.

Marnie had the sense that Lianna was not a woman accustomed to the backseat. A moment later, the GPS confirmed they'd arrived at their destination, the All Tucked Inn.

It was hardly the Marquis—no elegant candles in the windows or stately chimneys at regular intervals. The All Tucked Inn was more of a country farmhouse that had spawned as many additions as it had survived generations. The original building looked to be a large white clapboard affair in the Federal style, but the add-ons were an assortment of oddities that had a collective charm. Draped with evergreens at every window and red and green miniature lights around all the porch posts, the bed-and-breakfast gave the impression of being a safe hideaway from embezzlers—and overzealous sexual thrill seekers.

Pulling into a parking space to one side of the door, Jake switched off the lights while everyone piled out of the SUV. Marnie noticed he hadn't said much in the car ride, letting Lianna and Marnie do the talking as they filled in Rico on Alex McMahon aka Alec Mason. Even now, as Jake carried in their bags, his jaw remained set like granite.

Marnie liked Rico well enough. He couldn't take his eyes off Lianna. And for her part, the formerly flirtatious Lianna seemed utterly smitten. There was a definite connection there that went beyond the obvious. They cared about each other.

Or maybe that was just her optimistic side talking. Jake probably saw something totally different when he looked at the couple.

She wanted to say something to break the tension as they walked in silence toward the inn, but before she could, an older woman with long silver hair tied in a festive red bow met them at the door.

"Welcome!" She held the door wide, making room for the four of them as they trooped inside. "I felt so bad for you being out in this weather. I worried ever since you called for your reservations an hour ago. I'm so glad you made it safe and sound."

The interior of the farmhouse glowed with holiday warmth. A fire crackled in a huge stone hearth while two sleeping black Labs slept on a braid rug in front of it. A tall fir tree packed with ornaments loomed in the far corner of the room. White lights twinkled above piles of brightly wrapped presents. Clearly, their hostess had lots of loved ones in her life. A family. Children and grandchildren. Seeing all those cheery decorations reminded Marnie that she would be the only one of her siblings at Christmas dinner without a significant other, let alone a spouse and kids. As much as she loved her family, there was a certain loneliness in being surrounded by so many couples. Even her friends were pairing off at an alarming rate. In the past months, two of them had found The One—the guy they wanted to spend their lives with.

The thought sent Marnie's eyes toward Jake. Would

he want to be with her tonight, or would he be all about the investigation? The need to be with him warmed her blood, melting the chill she'd carried in from outside.

Fifteen minutes later, rooms were assigned, keys were distributed and Marnie found herself in a back wing of the house with Jake. Jake had liked that he could see three sides of the property from their room. Apparently, former cops appreciated a wide range view. He'd asked that Lianna and Rico take the rooms nearby so he could hear if there were any disturbances.

For their part, Rico and his lady lawyer seemed oddly polite with one another—a real switch from all the overt flirting they'd done earlier in the week. Marnie wondered what the night would bring for them behind closed doors. She knew the confusion that came when you didn't know where you stood with a guy.

Like her. Now.

She unpacked the bulky gowns she'd bought at the Marquis and shoved them in an antique, painted wardrobe just so they would be out of the way. The room could have been an advertisement for shabby chic, the vintage cabbage rose wallpaper broken up by big, airy windows dressed with white lace curtains. Sturdy farmhouse furniture kept the room from feeling too precious, the oversize bed and stuffed chairs swathed in simple, crisp white fabrics. As a nod to the holiday season, a pewter urn of fresh spruce boughs stood tall in one corner, a handful of wooden ornaments dangling off some branches.

While she found her nightgown and switched on the gas fireplace, Jake used the inn's wireless connection to email his evidence to the local cop shop. He balanced a phone in one hand while he hovered over his laptop perched on the pullout stand of an old-fashioned secretary desk. He'd shoved aside the wooden rolling chair with his foot, all restless energy and intensity.

She had the feeling she was seeing the most authentic version of him, a man she wasn't entirely sure she'd understood before now. When they first met that day he'd handcrafted molding around her furniture to make the cheap stuff look like beautiful pieces, he'd flirted with her quietly—a nice, normal guy.

Then, she'd peeled away that laid-back veneer when she'd discovered he was a P.I. who'd been watching her. Later, his urgent kiss in the car and his unrestrained lovemaking in the hotel had shown her a man of deep passions.

Now, seeing him work at the job he was so clearly meant for, she began to understand who he was underneath all that—someone intensely driven in his quest for justice. Someone who wasn't afraid to walk away from a job—or a woman?—if they didn't conform to his high standards.

The realization made her wonder how they'd ever ended up together in the first place. What did he see in someone who'd been under suspicion for a felony?

As he finished his call and turned toward her, she felt as if she'd been caught staring. Clutching her flowered bag of shampoo and toothpaste, she nodded toward the bathroom off to one side of the homey accommodations.

"I was going to shower." She backpedaled toward the bathroom, her socks gliding over a section of the varnished hardwood that wasn't covered by a throw rug. She felt awkward around him tonight, unsure what it meant that they were sharing a room. "What did the police say?"

He stripped off his coat, cueing her into the fact that he'd done nothing else since he'd walked in the room other than take care of business. Apparently she was the only one thinking about peeling his clothes off.

"They whined about jurisdiction until they received my files. Once they saw how much I've got on Alec, they started paying more attention."

"But since we don't know where he is—"

"They'll get a warrant and post his picture, but they can't make an arrest until they know where he is. He could be out of the country or back in Florida." He stalked closer, his blue-and-white Oxford button-down back in place now that he'd ditched the clothes from the Marquis. A worn gray T-shirt lurked underneath.

"Or he could be on his way to the resort, like he told Lianna." Marnie's heart beat faster, but only because of Jake's proximity. She didn't worry about Alec when she was with Jake.

He might have spied on her without her knowledge, but he'd also made sure her name was cleared. His sense of right and wrong had demanded it. And she really, really liked that about him.

"Alec won't touch you." Jake plucked her bag of shampoo and toiletries from her hand. "I promised you that no one else would touch you but me, and I broke that vow when those bastards grabbed you tonight."

Anger blazed in his eyes, but his hand was gentle when he slid his fingers beneath her hair along the back of her neck.

"I think the promise was that we wouldn't let other people touch us," she clarified, remembering well those words they'd spoken that first night at the Marquis when she'd been exhausted and acting on pure instinct.

She'd wanted him then for reasons she hadn't fully understood. She wanted him more now, even knowing he could stride out of her life without a backward glance once they returned to Miami.

"Semantics." He stood so close that she had to look up to meet his eyes. "I let you down tonight and I'm so damn sorry I didn't protect you."

Green eyes probed hers, asking for forgiveness she would have never guessed he needed. And, oh God, she wanted to give him that and so much more.

"Jake, I never would have sat quietly in our suite at the Marquis while you did all the investigating. So if you think it's your fault for not locking me up in the room, I can assure you I only would have left to contribute to your case in any way possible. Remember, it was my good name and reputation on the line." She smoothed a hand over the unrelenting wall of his chest where his heart thudded a steady beat. "I didn't ride shotgun with you for over twenty hours on the way up here so that you could put me in the backseat once we arrived."

He tucked both hands under her hair, his thumbs remaining on her cheeks to skim small circles on her skin. She could catch hints of his aftershave when she leaned close enough, and the spicy scent lured her nearer with vivid memories of the last time they'd been wrapped around each other.

"But I never would have involved you if I had

thought there was any real danger." He shook his head, brows furrowed together in worry. "Embezzlement is a white-collar crime. The chance of violence is—"

"It wasn't Alec we had to worry about." She tipped her forehead toward his neck, absorbing the warmth of his skin. "I didn't know the guests of the Marquis could turn so aggressive, and since it's my job to be very well acquainted with all the properties I recommend to my clients, I assure you I won't advise anyone else to stay there."

"I'll call Vincent and make him aware of that, too." Jake rubbed his cheek over hers, the light abrasion of his stubble sending a sweet thrill of longing through her. "He needs to know that place is a lawsuit waiting to happen so he can disassociate with it before someone gets hurt."

His arms banded around her tighter as he spoke, his hands sliding down her back to span her waist. Her hips.

"I was just about to take a shower so I could wash away the feel of strange hands on me," she confessed, shuddering at the memory of being grabbed. Shoved. Held against her will. "Maybe you could help."

She hoped it didn't sound like a desperate come-on. But she needed him. Wanted him. Knowing that her last relationship had been a lie from the start had made her feel more than a little empty inside. And all the in-your-face holiday reminders urged her to take what happiness she could now.

He edged back from her enough to see her face, and perhaps to gauge her expression for himself.

"I'd like that," he said finally, picking up her bag

and untwining himself from her enough to lead her toward the shower.

Marnie thanked her lucky stars.

Once inside the bathroom, he leaned over the tub to crank the hot water on high. Then, setting her bag down on the edge of the vanity, he pulled her into his arms. Kissed her.

Marnie had a vague impression of clean white tile everywhere and a crisp linen shower curtain surrounding a huge claw-foot tub, but after that, her senses were only attuned to the man and the moment. Jake's mouth covered hers, molding her against him to fit just the way he wanted. She seemed to melt everywhere, her knees going boneless and her insides swirling hot and liquid.

He filled her senses, obliterating everything but him and a vague sense of heat from steam filling the room. His tongue stroked hers with seductive skill, reminding her subtly of all the sensual tricks he could perform.

A moan reverberated deep in her throat and he answered it by sliding his hands under her T-shirt and skimming the cotton up and off.

"I fantasized about you in the shower at the Marquis," he admitted between kisses rained along her exposed collarbone. "I wanted to point all those showerheads at you." He palmed the cup of her corset where it pushed up one breast.

She'd been in too much of a hurry when they left the Marquis to change out of all the complicated underwear, settling for exchanging the gown for jeans and a T-shirt.

"I fantasized about you in the shower, too." It was

impossible not to have sexy imaginings under the powerful water pressure at the Marquis, where the spray
nozzles were strategically positioned to hit the erogenous zones. "Except I thought about focusing all that
jet power here."

She palmed the hard length of him through his
jeans, stroking upward while he sucked in a gasp between clenched teeth.

"But after the day you had, I'm going to make sure
tonight is all about you." He turned her around so that
he stood behind her, his one arm still wrapped around
her waist. "Look."

Blinking her eyes open, she saw their reflection in
a mirror above the double vanity. Any moment, steam
would cover the image since it crawled up the glass already. But for the moment, she saw herself with flushed
cheeks and eyes dark with desire, her red hair tousled
and clinging to Jake's shirt. His muscular arm dwarfed
her, the thick bicep making her look small and delicate
against him while his tanned hand roamed the white
satin corset.

"This is what I will remember from tonight." In a
million years, she would not forget the sight of herself,
wanton and all but writhing against Jake.

"You look so good. I can't wait for a taste." He un-
hooked the first few fastenings on the corset and bent
to place a kiss on her back. In the meantime, the steam
covered up their reflection in the mirror.

All at once, he wrenched apart the sides of the corset, undoing the hooks in one move.

"Come on." He tugged the garment down, unfastening the garters holding her stockings as he went.

Soon, all she wore was a pair of pearl-gray lace bikini panties—something of her own underneath the layer of under things she'd bought at the Marquis.

She trembled everywhere as Jake hooked a finger in the lace and dragged the panties down her thighs. He didn't pause except for a single kiss on her stomach, right beside her navel. Toes curling against the tile floor, she didn't protest when he lifted her off her feet and stood her in the tub.

He shielded her from the water, taking the handheld sprayer off the hook to shoot down into the tub before he peeled off his wet shirt. When he reached for his belt, however, she couldn't simply watch any longer.

"Let me." Nudging his hands aside, she worked the buckle herself. "I want to taste you."

Jake couldn't have refused her on a good day. But tonight? After the scare she'd had back at the Marquis? He would have let her string him up by his toes if she wanted.

And this was so much better.

Her skin felt softer than silk against him, a sleek, gliding warmth that peeled his clothes away until he was bare-ass naked and rock-hard in her hands. Leaving a condom on the sink, he stepped into the tub with her.

Steam drifted up from the water around her so she looked like a slow-motion beauty shot in some film, her red hair curling around her neck with the heat. Her lips perfectly matched the tight peaks of her breasts, the deep pink flesh puckered and ready for his kiss.

Except then she was down on her knees in front of him. Kissing. Licking. Savoring every inch of him with a slow thoroughness that made his blood rush and all his muscles clench.

He longed to hold back, to let her take the lead in every way. But his release pounded in the base of his shaft already, coaxed on by the feel of her fingernails scraping lightly up his thighs.

"Marnie." He stroked her hair, blocking out everything from the day but this. Her.

A slick trick of her tongue all but did him in, and he had to pull back. When she blinked up at him, she moved as if to kiss him again, and he had to hold himself away for a second to pull it together.

"I want to be inside you when I finish." He dropped to his knees with her in the hot water rising slowly up the sides of the deep tub. "I want to be everywhere at once."

In fact, it seemed imperative to make her feel good all over. To erase every fear and unpleasant sensation and replace it with pleasure. Wrapping her in his arms, he bent his head to her breast.

"Like here." He flicked his tongue along her creamy flesh as he cupped her. "I've been thinking about doing this ever since I kissed you here in the dressing room yesterday."

Taking his time, he lingered over his feast, scarcely coming up for air until she whimpered and dragged his hand down her body, almost to the water level. Right to the juncture of her thighs.

He drew back enough to take in the full-body flush of her skin, the parted lips and half-closed eyes.

"You're so beautiful right now." He anchored her waist with one arm while he sifted through the damp curls that shielded her sex. "When I first saw you take off your dress at closing time in one of those surveillance videos, I imagined you just like this. Passionate. Demanding."

He'd fantasized about her all the time after that. Not because she'd been wearing the sexiest black-and-red bra imaginable, or because she possessed curves any man would love to touch. No, he'd been fascinated by her uninhibited dance and her obvious joy in life.

That was sexy as hell.

"Really?" She opened her eyes fully, the gray flecked with gold as she arched her back and rubbed against him like a cat. "Then touch me. Now."

By the time he stroked along her silky center, she was so ready for him that she cried out at the contact, her body convulsing in a heated shudder. He throbbed to be inside her, the need to take her so sharp that he couldn't possibly play around in the tub just for the sensual thrill of it. The time for playing had come and gone, leaving them both on fire and shaking.

He leaned away just long enough to retrieve the condom and roll it on. Then, leaning her against the back of the tub, he stretched over her. Hips immersed in the water, he edged her thighs wide to make room for him. When he slid inside her, she cradled his jaw in her palm, wet fingers trailing down his cheek as their gazes locked.

He'd never felt so connected to a woman. Not during sex. Not ever. There was a fire in her eyes that called to him. Challenged him. Made him want to join her in all those unrestrained dances of hers.

Jake responded by thrusting deep. He touched every

part of her, possessing her for however long she would have him.

Her eyes slid closed and he focused on the building pleasure, the keen tension already so taut he thought he'd snap with it. Heat flooded his back as water swirled around his legs and sloshed over the sides of the tub.

Marnie's fingers clenched the porcelain rim to hold herself up. He thrust over and over, finding a rhythm that tightened the knot inside him to until it became sweetly excruciating. Her feet wrapped around the backs of his calves, holding him in place. She cried out as her release hit her, racking her body with shudders.

He followed an instant afterward, unable to hold back another second. Their shouts mingled as seamlessly as their bodies, the sound echoing through the tile bathroom and off the churning water as they moved.

Long minutes later, when he stopped seeing stars, Jake heard the sound of running water and remembered why they were there in the first place. Toeing off the nozzle, he shifted so that Marnie lay beside him in the bath. He would take care of her. Watch over her every second until they returned to Miami.

He couldn't risk her being hurt again, something that awakened a dark realization. Would she *ever* be safe with a guy like him? He'd been so certain when they first met that he would have made a move on her if she hadn't been a suspect. He'd wanted her badly. But now that he'd spent time with her, he recognized she wasn't the kind of woman he normally dated. She might seem easygoing and fun-loving on the outside with her impromptu stripteases and dancing around her office while belting out her favorite songs. Beneath that, however, she was as intense and passionate as him.

She could mean so much more to him than anyone ever had before. Which was exactly why he needed to be careful not to get any more caught up in her world. He didn't want her hurt, and that meant he had to protect her—from himself, from the dark world that he moved in and from anything else that might threaten the most warm-hearted woman he'd ever met.

CHAPTER ELEVEN

AN HOUR AFTER they arrived at the All Tucked Inn, Lianna still couldn't stop shivering.

She hid it well enough, she thought, keeping her coat on while she unpacked her clothes, then trading it in for a soft chenille lap blanket while she prowled around the room she would share with Rico. But the chill that had set in back at the Marquis wouldn't go away.

If anything, she'd only gotten more nervous on the ride here, seeing the connection that shimmered between Marnie and Jake. It was obvious they had strong feelings for each other and it had made Lianna wish she could step back in time for a do-over with Rico. She'd thrown herself at him shamelessly, treating him like any other guy at the Marquis who only went to the resort to practice their seduction skills. But she didn't want a relationship like that with Rico. He was more than just a fantasy man. He'd come after her when he thought she was in trouble. Surely that meant he must care despite the superficial way they'd related to each other at the start?

Peering over at him now as he shoved around a few logs in a cast-iron woodstove, she felt a fresh wave of nervousness.

"I'm glad you followed me," she told him, still surprised that he'd come after her in a snowstorm.

"Yes? You've been so quiet since we arrived, I was beginning to wonder." He set down the poker on the hearth and watched her thoughtfully.

Maybe she hadn't hidden her worries as well as she'd hoped.

"I'm just shaken up, I guess." It felt strange to admit the weakness. To talk about something that mattered with a man she'd once viewed as simply another player—like her. Or at least, like she used to be. She wasn't so sure she wanted to play the games going on at the Marquis anymore. "I'm a lawyer. I defend those accused of crimes. I'm not used to being on the receiving end of accusations. Having Jack—I mean, Jake— think that I could be a criminal…"

She trailed off, still processing the emotions of the night. She felt like she'd been on a roller coaster with all the highs and lows, beginning with Rico's kisses in the hallway outside the dining room and ending with taking to the road to elude a devious liar who'd fooled her from the beginning.

Rico rose and crossed the floor. As he drew near, she clutched the chenille throw tighter, not sure what she wanted from him just yet. Being with him here felt different than at the Marquis. She felt more naked here—under the layer of nubby chenille—than she ever had at the Marquis in her revealing costumes.

"This Alec Mason is a heartless bastard to incriminate the people he gets close to. But you are not the only one he deceived. How long did Marnie say that she knew him before she discovered his true character?" A trace of his accent came through the words as he touched her shoulders, warming her through the soft fabric of the throw.

"They dated for months, apparently." Lianna had been too upset to recall all the details of Marnie's story, which she'd shared with Lianna and Rico in the car on the way over. Normally, she had a clever mind for remembering nuances of information, an asset in her work as an attorney. But apparently all bets were off when she was the one under the microscope.

"And Marnie is a smart, successful businesswoman, right?" His fingers drifted up her arm and landed on her cheek, gently encouraging her gaze. "So that tells you that Alec is a skilled liar."

She noticed that he had removed the contacts that made him indistinguishable from his twin. Sea-blue eyes replaced the predatory tawny gaze. Another layer stripped away between them.

"Con artist, more like it." She sifted through her troubled feelings and tried to define what upset her most. "But I guess we are all playing games when we visit the Marquis. How can we trust what anyone says, when all of us are purposely pretending the whole time?"

"The idea behind the Marquis is a good one, but some people take it too far. In theory, it is nice to throw off the conventions of everyday society and play games for a few days. But we all have to be careful not to take the fantasy too far."

"Like the scumbags who grabbed Marnie."

"Yes. Or like Alec, who uses the anonymity of the place to slip into one character after another. Who knows how many other women he has taken advantage of in this way?"

The thought made Lianna want to jump into the nearest tub and scrub away every vestige of the place.

"I'm glad we're here now," she admitted, not sure how to proceed. How to tell him she wanted a do-over. "I don't know if I'll ever have fun playing those kinds of reckless games again."

"Maybe it isn't reckless when you stick to playing with someone…special." Rico trailed his fingers down the side of her neck and back up again, landing in the half-fallen mass of her hair that drooped just above her shoulder.

"What do you mean?" Her heartbeat sped up and she hoped she hadn't misunderstood.

Could he want a do-over with her, too?

"I mean, maybe we don't need sexy games to entertain us when we've found something better." His fingers did wicked things to the back of her scalp, massaging lightly as he reeled her closer. "Something deeper and far more compelling."

By now, her heart just about jumped out of her chest. There could be no mistaking those words. She wanted that—something better. Deeper. More compelling. Rico was all of those things.

Her skin humming pleasurably while her heart warmed with new hope, Lianna let herself be drawn in by the magnetism of the man and the moment. She wanted nothing more than him.

"I would like that more than you can imagine."

At her acquiescence, he unfastened two pins and her thick hair tumbled down, releasing the fruity scent of her salon shampoo. Since she always wore her hair up at the Marquis, she already felt she had one foot in reality.

"I'm so glad, Lianna." He traced a lock with the back of his knuckle, following it down her shoulder. "When I heard you left the resort tonight, I realized you were the only reason I wanted to be there."

His fingers sifted through her hair to graze the skin beneath, inciting the sweetest possible shiver.

"The Marquis has been like a summer camp vacation from my real life for the past two years. I love the waltzing and the glamorous gowns." Most of all, she loved the kisses in the hallway she'd shared with Rico.

He grinned with wicked knowing as he trailed a knuckle down her chest to the top of her cleavage.

"You have an open-ended invitation to indulge in those things with me." He wrapped an arm around her waist, pulling her hips close to his. With his other hand, he wove their fingers together, positioning them for an impromptu dance. "Waltzing is a specialty of mine."

He whirled her around, the quick spin making her skirts billow and sending a breeze around her ankles. At the same time the cool air drifted around her legs, the heat of his body pinned against hers shot a wave of erotic longing through her. There was no mistaking his interest in her.

For a moment, she could not speak. Sensations came alive, chasing away her anxieties with the reminder that her vacation was not over yet.

"You know what they say about men who can dance." Easily, she followed his lead around the smooth planked floor. He was a strong partner, guiding her without dominating her. Yet she knew she could give over the reins completely and he would still take them where they needed to go.

"My father is a steelworker," Rico confided, never missing a step. "I will refrain from sharing with you what he thinks about men who can dance."

The self-deprecating smile surprised her, along with the insight into his family life. She felt a surprising surge of protectiveness toward this man, who dwarfed her in size.

"The wisdom among women is that men who can dance are good in bed." Her cheeks heated just a little, which was strange for a woman who had flirted so shamelessly all week. It must be another by-product of being away from the resort. She wasn't just another anonymous guest here.

Rico wasn't just another man.

"Ah." His sea-blue eyes darkened as he watched her in the firelight. "This I would be happy to prove to you in no uncertain terms. But only when you're ready."

The unspoken half of his message burned in his eyes. *Are you sure you're ready?*

He pulled her hand over his heart, folding it inside his palm. Silently, he waited for her direction.

"A few hours ago, back at the Marquis, I would have vaulted into your arms and ripped off your clothes with that kind of prompting." She wondered if she used her vacations at the Marquis to ratchet up the heat in her romantic encounters so that she wouldn't feel the emptiness inside her afterward. So she wouldn't dwell on the fact that she was missing out on a whole lot more intimacy than physical joining alone could provide.

"And now?" He massaged her fingers, one by one, working them from the base to the tip until he kissed each in turn. The last one he lingered over, flicking his tongue over her knuckle in an electric stroke while she watched.

Hypnotized.

"What would you like to do instead, Lianna?" he prompted her, since her brain has shut down.

Her only thought was for his mouth and how it felt over her skin.

As he watched her, she could almost feel that languid, fiery stroke in other places on her body. Her breath caught. Held. Fire licked over her skin. Erotic images of her entwined with him rolled, slow-motion style, through her brain.

"I don't want to make another mistake. And I think that place messes with my judgment."

She'd nearly rendezvoused with Alec, for crying out loud. Apparently when she let down her guard to flirt and have fun, all her lawyerly instincts went out the window.

Rico took a step back, though he kept hold of her hands.

"Look at me," he commanded, even though her eyes had been tracking him every second. "You said yourself that coming here exposes us, right? No more hiding behind costumes and parlor games."

She nodded, reminded by his aquamarine gaze that he had made an effort to peel away the pretense. "But you went to the Marquis to have fun. To play."

"Right. I figured a few days up here would help Raul forget about his runaway wife, and I planned on having a good time as a reward for being a stand-up brother. But maybe I found someone who interests me on a whole different level. Someone who could mean a hell of a lot more to me than a vacation distraction. Why would I say no to that?"

In that moment, with his brow furrowed and his shoulders tense, Lianna realized it was the first time he hadn't sounded at all like her fantasy Latin lover. Another hint that she could see beyond the exterior to the person beneath.

And wow, did his words ever make her feel special. More than that, she believed them.

Mind made up, she took a deep breath.

"Did I mention how great it was of you to follow me after I left the Marquis?" She splayed a hand on his chest, eager to feel the warmth and strength there. To return to that place of hot, lingering kisses and tantalizing touches.

"If what was between us was just a game to me, I would have opted for brandy by the fireplace rather than freeze my ass off in the snow to follow you." He twined his finger around a strand of her dark hair and used the end like a paintbrush to tickle along her bare shoulder. "So you can be sure there's nowhere I'd rather be right now than here with you."

Tingles skittered along her skin where he teased her. But when he trailed lower, following the line of her breastbone down into the valley of her cleavage, the humming sensation gathered and concentrated. Vibrated all the right places as thoroughly as any sex toy, when all he did was play with her hair.

"I'm right where I want to be, too," she said, her

voice breathless. Excited. When his knuckle grazed the side of her breast in his quest to unfasten the front laces of her red velvet gown, she shuddered with pleasure. "I don't know what you're doing to me, but—wow."

"I'm seducing you," he whispered in her ear, relinquishing the lock of her hair to untwine laces in earnest. "Is it working?"

"That would be affirmative." Her knees turned liquid as he peeled away fabric, exposing the candy cane–striped corset beneath.

He whistled softly.

"You're the gift that keeps on giving, aren't you?"

"I like dressing up." Especially for Rico, since he rewarded her efforts with gratifying looks.

And a new urgency in his hands as he sought clasps and hooks to free her.

"I damn well like seeing you this way, too. But right now, I've only got eyes for what's beneath."

Which was just fine with her. She couldn't wait to feel his hands on her bare skin.

Arching up on her toes, she wrapped her arms around his neck, silently giving herself over to him. To whatever he wanted.

He groaned with approval as she pressed her breasts to his chest, her hips cradling his erection.

"Kiss me," he demanded, bending close to brush his mouth over hers.

She'd known that he was a great kisser from those stolen moments in the alcove outside the Marquis's dining hall. But the contact then had been skill and persuasion, restrained heat and tantalizing potential. Now, the bold sweep of his tongue was all about passion and possession, a seductive mirror of the mating they both wanted.

But even that wasn't nearly enough when she was ready to crawl out of her skin to be with him. Her hands were shaking and awkward as she shoved off his jacket and freed a few buttons on his shirt.

Rico made far better progress on her corset, flicking open the fastenings that held her stockings in place. The brush of silk sliding down her legs teased a fresh wave of want along her thighs, the contact too gentle for what she wanted.

He backed her against a closet door near the fireplace, his weight pinning her there.

"Another night, I will give you the fantasy," Rico promised, his breathing as unsteady as hers while he raked away the last restraints on her corset and sent the garment sliding to the floor. "Tonight, we strip it all away."

Lianna remembered how easily he fell into a role from their time playing servants together at the Marquis. She had no doubt there would be sexy games in their future.

"Yes." She reached between their bodies to palm the hard ridge she wanted inside her. "The more stripping, the better."

He dispatched her panties on cue, dragging the imported silk down as he dropped to his knees in front of her.

Um…if this was his idea of delaying her fantasies, she couldn't imagine what fulfilling them might look like.

Then he spread her thighs to make room for himself and kissed the pulsing center of her. She would have fallen if not for the door behind her and Rico's hands bracing her legs where he wanted them. Liquid heat pooled inside her, gathering, swelling. Her fingers trailed helplessly along his shoulders as each stroke of his tongue propelled her higher.

When the release hit her, the pleasure swept through her so fast and so hard she twisted mindlessly against the door. Wave after wave of lush sweetness had her calling out his name, her fingers twisting in his dark, silky hair.

She'd only just barely come back to reality when he lifted her in his arms and carried her to the couch. Aftershocks still hummed through her when he sheathed himself with a condom. He loomed over her, gloriously naked. Deliciously hungry for her.

She reached out to him, trailing her fingers down the chiseled muscles of his chest. Down to the rigid length of his arousal, He sucked in a breath between his teeth as he followed her down to the couch, bracing his weight on one arm.

He came inside her slowly, allowing her to get used to him as he moved deeper. Deeper. He parted her thighs farther before he claimed her completely. His chest met her breasts. His teeth nipped her ear.

And then he started to move. The hot glide of his body inside hers sent ribbons of pleasure through her, making her shiver in delight. She ran her hands through his dark hair and over his broad shoulders, wanting to touch him everywhere. He treated her like a woman he wanted to take care of. A woman he wanted to please.

And *oooh,* did he please her. No man had ever tried

to give her just what she wanted before. Just what she needed.

Rico anticipated her every desire. The thought sent her hurtling over the edge as surely as the drive of his hips into hers. She clutched him close, holding on tight as her release rocked her whole body.

He came with her, surging impossibly deep. She wrapped her legs around his waist, holding him right where she wanted him, her ankles locked.

There were no barriers. No masks. No games. Just a gorgeous, generous lover who made her feel special. Blissed-out. Sexy.

As she lay beneath him in the firelight, trying to catch her breath, Lianna knew another woman might have been simply counting her blessings in the wake of incredible sex. But she had never been particularly lucky in life, and fairy tales didn't happen to her.

So she squeezed Rico tight and soaked up the scent of his aftershave, hoping she'd remember this moment forever. Because her lawyer instincts were up and running again, and they told her that anything this good couldn't last for long. A smooth-talking criminal had tried to frame her as surely as he'd tried to frame Marnie.

And she didn't doubt for a second that Alec Mason would be back when she least expected it.

CHAPTER TWELVE

MARNIE COULDN'T SLEEP.

After her trip to the bathtub with Jake, he'd carried her back to bed and held her while she dozed off. But she'd become immediately alert when Jake moved away from her; it seemed he had no intention of sleeping himself while Alec was still on the loose and possibly looking for them.

He'd only gone to work on his laptop in a chair a few feet away from the bed, but just knowing that he wouldn't relax made her restless. Worried.

Well, that coupled with the sensation that the closer she got to Jake, the further he slipped away from her. She felt herself falling for him—knew she wanted more from him. Yet he retreated each time they touched, no matter how earth-shattering the sex was or how much he shared with her in bed. The thought of returning to Miami only to get dumped scared her. But the optimist in her told her he was a man worth fighting for. So she would try to walk that line between getting closer to him and not totally losing her heart to him.

Finally, she snagged her own laptop and cracked it open, figuring she'd at least catch up with her friends or check her work email.

"Am I keeping you awake?" Jake asked, peering

at her over the blue glow of the electronic screen in front of him.

"The idea that you think you shouldn't sleep is what's keeping me awake, if that makes sense." After firing up the machine, she waited for it to boot up. "It makes me nervous to think there's a possibility—well, actually, I don't know what there's a possibility of at this point. I thought we agreed Alec was more of a white-collar criminal."

Or had that just been what she wanted to believe?

"As the stakes get higher, people stop thinking rationally and start getting desperate." Jake punched a few keys with excess force before he met her gaze again. "Too many good people have been hurt by this guy for me to rest until he's behind bars."

Marnie was reminded of his friendship with Vincent Galway and the fact that Jake had resigned from the force when he had gotten screwed by corrupt cops and "missing" evidence.

"You're really determined to settle this score for Vince, aren't you?" While she admired Jake for being the kind of man who championed his friends, she was reminded of yet another reason that Jake might find it easy to walk away. He hadn't started pursuing Alec to avenge her. When it came right down to it, he had Vince's interests to protect, not hers.

Jake punched a few more keys, but she had the feeling he was mostly avoiding her question.

He wasn't exactly the type of guy to spill his guts.

"Will you ever go back to being a cop?"

He dropped all pretense of working and met her gaze head-on.

"Why? Does it matter that I'm a P.I.?"

He couldn't have broadcast *raw nerve* any more clearly.

"Just curious. I wondered if making things right for Vincent would allow you to go back to a job you traveled halfway across the country to take."

"I don't know," he admitted, the electronic glow casting shadows on his face as he frowned. "Working alone has its benefits."

Did he prefer to be alone in his personal life, too?

Marnie mulled over his statement while she opened her email and read a worried note from her mother asking why she hadn't been at the local community center's pancake breakfast with Santa, an event she normally worked every year. Shoot. She clicked on Reply to explain her whereabouts.

"Doesn't it get lonely?" she asked, wondering suddenly about more than his job. Who would take him out for pancake breakfasts with Santa?

"I'm not the most social guy." He reached for a glass of water by the bed, his bare chest lit by the screen as he leaned.

Right now, she'd like to teach him to be a lot more social. With her. Preferably involving a scenario where she tasted her way down his pecs to his taut, defined abs…

"What about outside work?" She cleared her throat to try to banish her sudden case of hoarseness. "Do you have plans for the holidays?"

"I don't think I'll make it back to Illinois this year since this case isn't closed and we're looking at—" he flipped his wrist so he could see the face of his watch "—December twentieth."

"I can't imagine spending the holidays apart from the people I love." Even if they would all show up for dinner with their happy families while she would be alone. She paused before sending her mom the email. "Although, I do wish I could convince some of them to leave Miami and take a Christmas holiday somewhere up north. The snow is so...pretty."

She'd been about to say romantic, but she could almost picture Jake being allergic to words like that. And she had the feeling all her talk about loved ones and the holidays was scaring him off anyhow. He stared at her from his spot in the armchair, his expression thoughtful.

Foreboding.

"What are you working on?" he asked. The question was so irrelevant to what she'd been saying that she would bet he hadn't listened to a word.

Frowning down at the laptop, she smacked the Send button and tried to keep the hurt out of her voice.

"Just emailing my mom so she doesn't worry about me."

"Wait." He half threw himself over the bed to grab her computer.

"What are you doing?" She didn't mind giving up the laptop, but he yanked the cord out of the back of it, turning the screen black. "That can't be good for it."

"He could have access to your computer." Jake sat on the bed beside her, his bare chest temptingly close.

"Alec?" She stilled as her brain sifted through the

implications. "What do you mean? That he could have grabbed it when I wasn't looking? Or—"

"He's got to be great with computers to have pulled off the embezzlement and to frame both you and Lianna." He kept the laptop closed, his grip tight on the case. "So it's very plausible he'd know how to set up remote access to your computer. In fact, he probably did it before the two of you even broke up so that he could keep tabs on you afterward. He certainly knew that you were headed to the Marquis fast enough, right?"

A chill shivered down her spine. Could Alec have been watching her this whole time?

"I let him use my computer on several occasions." She'd never thought twice about it. "You think he… did something to it? Installed spyware?"

"My guess is he did much worse than that. Did you already contact your family tonight?"

"I had just sent an email when you unplugged it."

"Did you tell them where you are right now?" He covered her hand with his, a gesture of comfort that didn't soothe her in the least.

"Yes." She'd written all of three lines, but she'd mentioned the All Tucked Inn by name. "I've traveled alone for my work for years and that's a habit I got into long ago. I always let my family know where I'll be and when to expect to hear from me again."

She'd always thought the system helped protect her safety. But in this case, she had the feeling she'd endangered Jake, Rico and Lianna along with herself.

"We can't stay here." Standing, he shoved her laptop in the case he kept his in, then jammed his alongside it.

"But what about the snowstorm?" She didn't look

out the window since Jake had already briefed her earlier on the importance of not making herself a target to anyone watching the building from outside. But she didn't need to look out to know the snow still fell with blizzard force. "We barely made it here and the GPS didn't show another hotel for miles."

The drawback of romantic, snowy mountain regions was that there wasn't a hotel and a Starbucks on every corner. She wasn't in Miami anymore.

"We don't know what he's capable of, Marnie." Jake pulled on his pants over his boxers. "So I'd rather take my chances in the snowstorm than play sitting duck for this guy."

Fear clogged her throat as she began to appreciate how serious this could be. Guilt compounded the sick feeling since it would be her fault if Alec found them.

"I'm sorry about this." She hated that she still hadn't learned enough caution, that Jake was forced to clean up her mistakes.

"I should have thought about the computer before." He shook his head, and the dark expression on his face made it clear he blamed himself. "I'll go next door and explain to Rico and Lianna that we need to leave. Don't use the phone, okay?"

She nodded as she rose from the bed, grateful to him for taking care of her. For looking out for all of them. If not for Jake Brennan, she could easily be behind bars tonight instead of here, falling for a hardened P.I. who might never love her back.

"Thank you," she blurted before he left. "For everything."

Marnie got the full impact of his undivided attention for a long moment, his green eyes inscrutably dark in the firelight.

"I want to keep you safe." He spoke the words like a declaration, with the kind of vehemence you'd expect for a more personal sentiment.

She had an odd, disheartening premonition that this might be as much of a commitment as she ever received from Jake Brennan. She thought about calling him back when he tugged a shirt on and headed for the door, but his name died on her lips when a woman's scream pierced the night.

Jake sprinted through the dark hall of the bed and breakfast.

The scream had faded by the time he tried the handle on Rico and Lianna's room.

Locked.

Pounding on the paneled door, he heard voices from inside. Behind him, he detected Marnie's soft, fast footsteps running toward him in the corridor.

"Go back to the room," he ordered, needing her out of the equation so he could focus on whatever was happening here. "Lock yourself in and don't open it until you're sure it's me."

A quick glance back revealed her worried face as she nodded and backed away. The rest of the floor remained quiet; it appeared they were the only ones renting rooms tonight.

He hated that this was scaring the hell out of her. He'd freaked her out before when he'd run around the blizzard with a weapon in hand, and again when he'd snatched her computer out of her hands. But at this point, it would be better if she was frightened and hiding out than around when trouble erupted.

"Rico, open up." He kept pounding. "It's Jake."

The lock clicked and the door gave way. Rico stood inside with an ashen Lianna under his arm.

"We're okay," the other man assured him. "She saw a man's shadow at the window, I guess."

Jake did a visual sweep of the room, taking in the open suitcase and the still-made bed. Clothes were scattered around the living area. Parted curtains against one window looked out into a darkness lit only by a security light in the front yard, half obscured by the storm.

"We're on the third floor." He propped the door open so he could keep one ear trained for sounds in the hallway. "You sure you saw a person and not just swirling snow or something?"

"I know what I saw," Lianna insisted, still pale, but her voice remained steady. "It was the outline of a man's upper body—from the hips up—as he moved past the window."

"There's a catwalk outside that leads to a fire escape," Rico explained, pointing toward the window in question. "I looked out, but I couldn't see anyone."

Jake crossed the room to check, lifting the shade carefully so as not to give away his position. The light was dim behind him, the glow from the fireplace the only illumination in the room, just like it had been back in the suite he shared with Marnie.

Marnie.

Damn, but this was when not being with a cop sucked. There wasn't a chance in hell he'd be able to

obtain police protection for her, especially when they
had piss-poor little to go on other than a few strange
coincidences. But he felt in his gut that Marnie's former boyfriend wasn't going to just take his money and
run. The fact that he'd been angling to meet with Lianna—to spy on Marnie through her—told Jake the
guy wasn't done making trouble. Although what exactly he wanted and why remained a mystery.

"I don't see anyone." Peering through the casement,
Jake sought signs of movement at the edge of the woods
nearby, the backyard lit by a couple of security lights
around the perimeter and the glow of red and green
decor along the roofline. "But I think that snow on the
catwalk might have been disturbed."

Tough to tell with the snow falling thick and heavy.
The walkway was a wrought-iron construction with
lots of open grates so the snow didn't gather there
much.

The phone rang while Jake wedged open the window for a better look out into the frigid night.

"Hello?" Lianna answered while Rico opened another window a few feet away from him, the second
cold blast pushing back the flames in the fireplace.

Jake kept one ear tuned into the conversation while
he searched the iron path for signs of a footprint. Lianna must have been speaking with the owner of the
bed-and-breakfast because she was explaining that
she'd seen someone's face at the window and went on
to ask if anyone would be working outside their room
at this hour.

"Jake, check this out." Rico called to him from the

other window, his face barely visible through the falling blanket of white.

Closing his window, Jake moved to the next one, where Rico looked out into the night.

And there, he could see the framework for the fire escape extended beyond the window, around the corner of the building. Leading anyone right to Jake and Marnie's room.

Shit.

Marnie.

Jake pushed away from the sill and plowed over a duffel bag to get out the door. Back to his room.

His feet jackhammered down the hall as hard and loud as his heart, dread pumping through him. He didn't bother knocking, instead using his key card to open the door. When the slide bolt caught—proof she'd double-locked it from the inside—he kicked the thing down. It cracked easily, since the old home didn't contain the steel doors used in big hotels.

"Marnie," he shouted, not seeing her right away. He called again, louder, as he burst into the bathroom.

There, cold wind blew across the empty claw-foot tub. An open window had curtains whipping in the breeze as snow gathered and melted in a pool on the tile floor.

She was gone.

CHAPTER THIRTEEN

"Be very, very quiet."

Alec Mason's voice whispered against Marnie's hair as he hauled her across the side lawn of the inn through the blinding snow. The pistol barrel wedged under her jaw and the duct tape strapped across her mouth were far more persuasive than his lowly growled words, however.

She hadn't found one chance to tip off Jake about Alec's return. She'd been so worried about Lianna after the scream that she'd sealed her ear to the exterior door to hear what went on in the room down the hall; Marnie had never heard her ex-boyfriend steal in through the window and right into the suite. God, she hated that she'd let him take her so easily after all the warnings Jake had issued about being vigilant. To think she'd double-locked the door—but who would ever expect someone to climb in a third-story window?

Now, after wrestling her down the narrow fire escape and out into the bitter cold, Alec led her through knee-high snow to the woods. Her slippers had rubber soles, but didn't begin to keep the chill at bay. She shivered in a pink sleep shirt and pajama pants. Behind them, she thought she heard Jake and Rico at the windows, but that might have been wishful thinking. Her heart beat so loudly in her ears she could hear little else.

"Here we go." Alec spoke softly as they arrived at his transportation, his voice puffing clouds in the air. His wiry frame was surprisingly strong, his expensive cologne pungent in her nose. How could she have ever thought for one moment this man was date material?

She stumbled, her slippers not gaining much traction in the snow, and the gun barrel nudged scarily deep. As he yanked her to her feet, she saw where they were headed.

There in the woods, behind a potting shed, sat the horse-drawn sleigh from the Marquis. She recognized the elaborately scrolled tack and the stacks of furs. Except the driver wasn't an inn employee with a sprig of holly in his top hat. It was one of the guys who'd grabbed her and forced her into the tiny hidden room back at the resort. Alec wasn't some lone bad guy. He had backup. An operation.

Marnie had the swelling sense that she was in far deeper than she'd ever imagined. With his knack for adopting aliases, Alec had probably committed more crimes than they'd begun to ferret out.

"Up we go." Alec continued to give her directions as if he were her date instead of her abductor. Still, his ironclad hold on her never wavered while he handed her up into the sleigh.

As soon as he had her inside, lying sideways on the pile of furs and blankets, he kicked the back of the driver's seat. Fur tickled her nose, but at least the heavy weight of the blankets cut the wind. The creep with the reins in his hand urged the horses forward. As they moved into the forest, they made very little noise, especially with the fresh snow muffling all sound, and there were no lights on the conveyance. Maybe a horse-drawn sleigh wasn't such a crazy choice for a getaway vehicle in a blizzard.

How would Jake ever follow her?

Alec removed the gun from under her chin, but he looped a rope of some kind around her leg, tying her securely to the sleigh with a painful cinch of the cord. Where was he taking her?

New fear set in faster than the cold. What could he possibly gain by hurting her? Then again, what else could he want from a woman he'd set up to take the blame for a felony? His plan for her to be in jail had failed, so maybe he wanted to ensure she never implicated him.

For once, she needed to think like Jake and see all the possible ways this could end badly. Maybe that would help save her somehow.

Beside her, Alec moved up into the bench seat while keeping an eye on her on the floor. Snowflakes gathered on her face, but he covered the rest of her with the excess furs. Her foot remained tied to the sleigh, and her toes were numb through her slippers from the walk through the snow. As her body warmed, her skin burned with the ache of nearly frostbitten skin returning to life.

With the gun resting on his knee, Alec's guard was a bit more relaxed now that they'd put some distance between them and the inn. Her captor pulled out a cell phone and started tapping keys, the electronic glow illuminating his unshaven face. And as she lay there staring up at this man who'd deceived her in more ways than she could count, she tried to imagine what Jake would suggest she do in this situation.

Buy time.

The answer was there so quickly and with such certainty, she would swear she caught the message on a wave of ESP direct from the source. Jake would come for her—she knew that. But she needed to make sure she remained in one piece long enough for him to catch up.

"Mmpf." She braved a small noise behind the duct tape now that his firearm wasn't jammed against an artery.

Alec looked down at her almost as if he'd forgotten she was there, his watery blue eyes visible until he snapped his cell phone shut and cast them in total darkness again.

"Mmpf!" she tried again, pointing to the duct tape and hoping she wasn't pissing him off by reminding him of her existence. But maybe if she could talk to him, she could find out his plans and delay him somehow.

"The lady wishes to speak," he mused, cocking his head sideways so he could look at her more directly in her awkward position on the floor. "I hope if I allow you the freedom of speech you will be kind. You look like a Christmas angel there, wrapped in your furs with that lovely skin. And I hate to lose that image of you with ugly words."

The odd comment made her wonder if Alec might be losing some of his grip on reality. He'd always been charming, but his attempt at gallantry now seemed downright ludicrous.

He must have decided to risk the outburst as he gave a brief nod, indicating she was free to speak.

Gently, she pried up the edges of the tape with one hand, carefully removing the restraint.

"Thank you." Her skin burned from the sticky glue and she didn't feel one bit grateful, but she tried to stay calm so as not to rile him. "Alec, I'm frightened. Where are you taking me?"

She hoped to appeal to his human nature, assuming he still had one underneath his mask of clean-cut, all-American good-guy looks. With his J.Crew clothes and trimmed dark blond hair, he appeared boy-next-door trustworthy when everything about him was a lie.

"We're making a brief stop at the Marquis to change vehicles, then we're lifting off at dawn by plane." He smiled as he spoke, a lock of dark blond hair slipping loose from the navy-blue wool cap on his head. "I know how you like to know your travel particulars. I've missed you, Marnie."

The handgun to her throat was a funny way of showing it. But she tried to keep the conversation more focused on relevant information and less focused on his personal delusions.

She closed her eyes and conjured up a vision of Jake's face. He would find her before Alec did anything crazy. She trusted in that and as far as she was concerned, that wasn't optimistic thinking. That was a logical fact based on everything she knew about Jake Brennan. He'd promised to keep her safe and he would do anything and everything in his power to do so.

She was lucky that he was so committed to his work. Lucky that he didn't just clear her off his suspect list, but also make sure she didn't get framed for someone else's bad deeds. She loved that he put so much of himself and his honorable nature into his work. Hell, she just flat out loved him.

She loved him.

That knowledge was there as sure as her faith in him and the realization of that love gave her the courage to maintain her cool with a desperate criminal.

"You've missed me?" She tried to sound only slightly surprised and not at all accusatory. Finding the right tone, in fact, required one hell of an acting job. "But you broke up with me."

On Facebook, no less. But Christmas angels didn't remind crazy men of things like that when their lives were on the line.

She twisted away from a bough full of snow that dropped suddenly into the sleigh and noticed a little give in the rope around her ankle. Under the cover of her fur blanket, she hitched at the rope with her other foot.

"I needed to distract attention from me for a while until I could hide the movement of the money." He shook his head while he brushed some of the fallen snow from his lap. "It was like a shell game trying to hopscotch the money from one account to the next, creating diversions and dead ends all the time. You know I'm not as organized as you, so it wasn't easy to keep track of it all in my head."

That was why normal people took jobs to make money instead of stealing it! But she stifled that thought, too, and strained for any sign of other sounds in the night besides the dull clop of hooves through the soft snow and the swish of the sleigh runners.

Would Jake return to the Marquis? Or would he try to follow their path through the woods?

She wished she could communicate with him now, to warn him that Alec seemed to have grown a little mad and that a calm, quiet approach might work better so as not to startle him into violence. The thought of anything happening to Jake sent a dark, panicky chill through her, jabbing at a heart still tender from the newfound realization of how much he meant to her. How much she'd lose by never seeing his face again, never feeling his strong, muscled arms around her.

"How did you find me tonight?" She couldn't understand how he came to be lurking around the All Tucked Inn so soon after she'd sent her email. He had to have another way of knowing her movements besides tracking her computer.

"Luckily, the lady lawyer is even more dutiful about reporting in to friends and family than you are. She sent a text message from her phone a couple of hours ago, letting her sister know she was at the charming All Tucked Inn. As luck would have it, I'd been staying there myself this week, keeping an eye on things at the Marquis until a couple of more deals came through for me, so I was very familiar with the layout of the place." He winked at her as he pulled his wool hat down more securely over his ears. "That part worked out so well, you couldn't have planned it better yourself."

Marnie ignored his self-congratulations to focus on what else he'd said. A couple of deals? How many people had he been swindling? She tried not to let her distaste show as she chose her words carefully.

"I'm worried there are a lot of people looking for you," she confided, keeping her voice low so the driver didn't hear her. She couldn't be certain how involved he was in Alec's plans, but she knew from experience that he didn't much care if he hurt her. "You might attract less attention if you put away the gun once we arrive at the hotel."

"Innocent Marnie." Alec tucked the weapon into a holster beneath his wool pea coat. "It's precisely *because* so many people are looking for me that I need to have the piece within easy reach. Your P.I. friend has run me ragged the past two months trying to cover my tracks, but he's not going to win in the end. One bullet keeps him quiet forever."

He patted his coat where the gun rested beneath, and a thick dread rose like bile in her throat. Alec had every intention of killing Jake. A vision of Jake lying cold and lifeless in the snow pierced her heart and chilled her blood in a way no snowstorm could.

The sleigh began to slow as the driver pulled back on the reins.

"Looks like we're nearing our destination." Alec reached down to replace the duct tape on her mouth and haul her up to the seat beside him as the sleigh halted in the woods near the Marquis. The driver jumped to the ground and disappeared into the dark. "You're coming with me until I'm safely out of the country. Your new boyfriend isn't the only one looking for me now."

Marnie's heart dropped at the realization that he'd only taken her to be a hostage.

She might never see Jake again.

Click.

The unmistakable hitch of a weapon being cocked for fire sounded inches behind them.

"I'm the only guy looking for you who counts."

Jake. He stood inches behind the sleigh, his 9 mm pointed at the back of Alec's head. She had no idea where he came from as he'd arrived in total silence, but somehow he was there.

Marnie wanted to warn Jake that Alec had a gun and that there was another guy with him, but Alec held her arms so she couldn't remove the duct tape.

"Let her go," Jake warned. "I've got backup and we've already got your driver and his friend. It's all over."

In the distance, Marnie heard the wail of a siren. Headlights entered the resort parking lot nearby, ringing the sleigh with light.

Thank God. Thank you, Jake.

She sat very still until she felt Alec make a sudden move. Her captor released her to go for his gun, but Jake was in the sleigh and on him in a nanosecond. Three slugs from Jake's fist and he was out cold, slumped and bleeding on the furs.

All at once, the woods were filled with light and sound and people. Rico and his brother arrived. The brother—Raul—had a pair of handcuffs and he took care of dragging Alec out of the sleigh. His ease with the job made her guess he was probably one of the people who had been hunting for Alec.

"Hold still." Jake's arm went around her as he took the seat beside her, his other hand gently peeling the tape away from her mouth. "Are you okay? Did he hurt you?"

"I'm okay." She swallowed hard, still trying to take in what had happened. She wanted to find out how he knew where to find her, how he'd arrived at the Marquis before them. But right now she was just so grateful to see him safe that she flung her arms around his neck and buried her head in his shoulder. "You found me."

TWO HOURS LATER, Marnie still looked spooked.

Jake watched her as the local detective finished taking her statement in the lobby of the Marquis at dawn. He'd talked to a half-dozen different departments and task forces that had been investigating crimes linked to Alec Mason. Or at least, it seemed like there had been that many. The cop work was a blur because he hadn't given a damn about closing out an investigation. His one concern was getting Marnie out of here and back home safely as soon as possible.

She wavered on her feet, still wrapped in a fur from the sleigh that bastard had used to abduct her. The damage Jake had done with his fists hadn't come close to satisfying his need to tear the guy apart. When he'd first heard her tell the police that Mason had held a gun to her head, Rico had to keep Jake from hunting down the cop car the scumbag sat in so he could finish him off.

For now, he tried to put that out of his mind to be the kind of man Marnie needed. The kind of man she deserved.

"We're free to go," he told her, sliding an arm around her waist to lead her out of the lobby. "And we've got a safe, quiet room we can stay in here. The police contacted the owner of the Marquis and he's canceling the entertainments for a few days while the cops check out the computer systems. They're assigning a guard to your room to be sure no one bothers you."

Jake had personally made sure of that. He wished he could take her far from here, but the road crews hadn't made much of a dent in clearing the snowfall.

Marnie nodded, allowing him to lead her toward the back of the resort where a handful of rooms overlooked a paddock containing the owner's horses. Jake had checked out the accommodations ahead of time to be sure the windows locked. Logic told him everyone involved with the embezzlement was now in police custody, including the two goons who'd grabbed her in the card room. But for his peace of mind, he'd need windows that locked—preferably, the kind that had bars across them, too.

"How did you find me?" she asked as he opened the door to a suite decked out in Tudor decor.

A marble fireplace rested across the room from a four-poster bed draped in quilted burgundy-colored satin. The tea cart held pewter goblets and silver-domed dishes that likely contained the breakfast he'd requested for her.

"Rico's twin was working undercover here. And actually their names aren't Rico and Raul. They're Rick and Rafe." Jake locked the suite door and bolted it, then sat her on the edge of the bed before he pushed the tea cart close so she could eat. "Apparently Rafe had been tracking a perp named A. J. Marks."

Marnie ignored the food and the juice goblets to pour herself a cup of hot tea.

"Another alias for Alec." Her dark eyes searched his.

"Right. And he had intel that said Marks was meeting up with his crew here, so he called Rick to let him know he might be following a suspect tonight. The other guy from the closet. And wouldn't you know, Rick and I were just trying to figure out where Alec would have taken you, so we banked on the fact that Alec and A.J. were one and the same."

"But how did you get here faster than the horses?"

"Turns out our bed-and-breakfast hostess keeps some kick-ass snowmobiles in her shed. There's a wide-open trail that follows the power lines between the inn and the resort, so I took off after you on a more direct route to the hotel, closer to the highway. Rick followed with Lianna and they got here about five minutes after me. We made a lot faster time on the sleds in the open fields, not having to guide a horse through the trees."

They'd met up with Rafe, who had already taken care of the other goon after trailing him to the meeting point. Marnie hadn't arrived for about five minutes more after that. The time had stretched so impossibly long that Jake thought he'd lose his mind. He'd second-guessed his decision to head them off here a hundred times in those frigid cold moments while he waited in the snow and the dark.

The kicker was that he wouldn't have even known where to find her if not for Rick's twin working the case from another angle. More proof that he'd failed Marnie.

Something he couldn't afford to do again.

"I wasn't careful enough," Marnie confessed between sips of tea. She must have warmed up a little because the fur blanket fell to the bed, unheeded. "I stayed by the door to listen to what was happening in Lianna's room and because of that, I never heard Alec coming."

"It wasn't your job to be careful." Shaking his head, he buttered a slice of toast and offered it to her. "That's what I was getting paid for."

She accepted the bread, but didn't take a bite.

"No. You were trying to find the embezzler. Protecting me was never part of your responsibility."

"It damn well should have been." He couldn't begin to explain the sick feeling eating away at him because he hadn't kept her safe.

His gaze tracked the delicate curve of her jaw, the fall of her tousled red hair starting to show its warm, natural caramel color at the roots. She wore a pink T-shirt and blue pajama pants with pink hearts. Hell, she'd been dragged through the mountains in those clothes.

"Jake, you were here." Setting down the toast, she reached for him. Brushed a hand along his bicep until his muscle twitched with awareness. "I knew you would find me. The whole time, the only thing that really scared me was the fear that something would happen to you when you came for me."

Her concern melted a warm spot in his chest. The sensation was so strong, so damn real, he had to touch the spot for himself to see if he was still holding together there.

"I'm an ex-Marine. A former cop. And enough of a general badass that people don't tend to worry about me." His forehead tipped to hers of its own accord, his need to be with her so tangible he didn't know how he'd ever be able to walk away from her once they got back home.

"I'm not just anyone," she reminded him, her dark eyes shining. "I care about you, Jake. So much."

Maybe if he'd been better at relationships—or more wise in the way of women—he would have known what to say. But her soft admission caught him off guard.

And scared him far more than any crook with a gun.

Straightening, he tried to find the words that would keep the situation from getting any more awkward.

"Marnie, I—"

Her fingertips brushed his lips, quieting him.

"I need to say this," she assured him. "I know we started out kind of rocky between you thinking I was a felon and all the spying on me without me knowing. But you chose the most efficient means to clear me, and I'm glad now that you did."

Jake's mouth was dry as dust, so interrupting her now wasn't an option. Besides, maybe part of him couldn't believe where she might be headed with all this.

"But something changed for me this week. You made me realize what I felt for Alec—even before we broke up—was just a shadow of how much I could care about someone."

By now, his brain blared with code red sirens and somehow he got his tongue engaged before this situation careened any more out of control.

"Marnie, I can't—that is—I care about you, too." He mirrored her gesture, swiping a finger across her lips. "My lifestyle has always been dangerous. And I like it that way. But this week? When you were at risk? I didn't like that one bit."

He'd never been so freaking scared. And he'd worked some hairy situations in his day.

"I don't understand." She shook her head, her brow furrowed in confusion. "Alec's going to jail. We can go back home—"

"Exactly. We can go back to our lives before all this happened. You'll be safe at your business and you can spend Christmas with your family. And I'll be grateful as hell knowing you're okay."

Far removed from firearms and violence—basically, all the things that had become staples in his life over the past ten years. This was what he was good at. Too bad the job didn't allow him to rope off his personal life and keep it safe from his professional world.

"You want to go back to the way things were before." The softness in her voice was gone. With her shoulders straight and her fingers laced together, she reminded him of the way she looked when she was behind the counter at Lose Yourself. Professional. In control.

And yeah, distant.

Hard to believe that was what he'd been going for. With regret, he kissed her forehead and nudged her breakfast tray closer.

"Yes. I think that would be—" painful "—for the best."

CHAPTER FOURTEEN

"You're a cop?"

Lianna tried to remind herself this wasn't a cross-examination and that Rick had been instrumental in helping nab a bad guy.

She paced the floor of a freebie suite assigned to her by the owner of the Marquis as a thank-you for her role in capturing a criminal who'd bilked the hotel. Lianna found it frustrating to think that Rick had still been hiding behind a mask the night before when they'd been together.

Her heart had been totally engaged, some long-buried romantic side of her thrilling to the idea that Rick wanted to peel away the pretense and touch the woman beneath. All the while, he'd kept a big part of himself secret.

She'd slept alone for a few hours after they gave their statements to the local police. Rick had told her he needed to help his brother tie up a few loose ends and she'd been so exhausted she hadn't argued. But when he'd knocked at her door a few minutes ago, she'd been ready for answers.

"Technically, yes." Rick sat on the small sofa in her room with its Victorian-gone-deviant decor. Crushed red velvet wallpaper covered the walls between framed

ink drawings of antique sex toys. A life-size manne-
quin of a Victorian nobleman sported a codpiece that
would have made for one heck of a conversation starter
if she'd been in the mood to discuss that sort of thing.
Which she absolutely was not.

Right now, with the realization that Rick had been
lying to her all along, her heart ached in a way no li-
bido ever could.

"Meaning?" She had been questioned in a separate
room from Rick, so she'd heard only sketchy bits of
his statement to local police, and even that had been
filtered through the chatter of half a dozen other witnesses to the showdown just before dawn.

"Meaning, that while I happen to be a cop in San
Diego, I'm not here in a work capacity. I took a vacation week to help Rafe out. This was personal for him,
since Alec swindled his wife out of her savings and
duped her into thinking they'd elope." Rick lowered an
arm across the back of the small sofa, the heavy rope
of muscles drawing her eye and reminding her what it
felt like to have his arms around her.

She wanted to know his touch again, to feel the
things only he could make her feel. Yet how could she
be with someone who withheld the truth from her?
Who might have only been with her for the sake of an
investigation?

"So Rafe is a police officer, as well." She tried to
search for what had been true in the things Rick had
told her. "And what you said about coming here with
him to forget about the wife who left him was at least
partially accurate."

"Well, I thought he'd get over her faster if he found

the bastard who'd led her astray so we could send the guy's ass to jail. Yes. True enough." His chin jutted forward, defensive. His jeans and T-shirt were rumpled as if he'd caught a few hours of sleep in a chair in the lobby.

Unfortunately for her, that didn't come close to dimming his appeal. Whereas Alec had been charming and slick, Rick was earthy and real. His dark good looks made it tough to even recall what Alec looked like.

She smoothed her hands over the simple lines of a long, forest-green dress she'd purchased in the boutique that morning since her suitcase remained back at the All Tucked Inn. The ankle-length outfit she wore now could have passed for a modern holiday dress if not for the laced-up cutout all down her back. But since she'd bought a white cashmere pashmina to wear like a sweater, no one could see the hint of skin beneath the laces.

"Then why didn't you tell me the truth last night after you learned Jake was a private investigator?" This was the part she kept coming back to, the idea that upset her most. Alec had used her. And while the two men were different in a fundamental way—one was a cop and one was a crook—she still worried they both saw her as nothing more than a pawn. Her fingers wove through the cashmere, clutching it in her clenched fists. "You must have known that Alec was the same guy you sought."

Rick shook his head.

"Lianna, I wanted to explain everything. But I'd promised Rafe I'd keep cover until we found our guy, and my brother wasn't answering his phone last night for me to clear it with him." He sat forward on the couch, his beautiful sea-blue eyes locked on her. "Besides, maybe I wanted to believe that outside stuff didn't matter. That you and I were already seeing what was real and important in each other. Did it change anything that you're a lawyer and that you live three thousand miles away from me? Or that I'm a Mexican-Irish cop who will drop everything if my family needs me?"

Rising, he closed the distance between them. Did he know how persuasive he was close up? Ah, who was she kidding? He'd done a damn good job of persuading her from across the room. She had the feeling he'd be equally compelling on a phone call from the west coast, too.

"I don't know." She wasn't sure what to think anymore. "Maybe I'm just scared about getting involved with someone when I don't know them well. I spent half the week waiting to meet up with a guy who turned out to be a total fake."

But Alec had lied to her for months, whereas Rick had only needed a couple of days before being up front with her. And bottom line, Rick moved her in a way Alec never had.

"He didn't tell you who he was because he wanted to take advantage of you." Rick brushed his hands over her shoulders, sweeping them under the pashmina to grip her arms. "I didn't tell you who I was to keep you safe. Now you know everything and my life is an open book for you."

The sincerity in his eyes couldn't be faked. She'd evaluated enough witnesses for trial appearances to know that. But what appealed to her most was the fact that he was still here, and he still wanted to be with her. Much of her worry had stemmed from the fear that his undercover work meant his time with her had all been a lie. That he'd only been with her as part of a job. But obviously, that wasn't the case.

Hope bloomed in her chest.

"Do you really have five brothers?" she asked, curious about the real Rick.

"Yes. My twin and four others, each one a bigger pain in the ass than the next." The affection in his voice was clear no matter what he said, warmth lighting his gaze as he talked about them.

His touch skimmed down her back, loosening the cashmere around her shoulders as he drew her closer. Her heart rate stepped up a beat, the pace quickening at his nearness.

"Was your dad really a steelworker?"

"Straight from Pittsburgh before he moved out west and settled down. Why would I lie about that?" His strong fingers dipped lower, finding the laces over her spine that exposed bare skin. "And yes, he thinks dancing is for sissies. His words, not mine. Although I think I caught him watching *Dancing with the Stars* once when one of his football heroes competed."

Lianna smiled, wondering about the family that had raised such a warm, wonderful man. A man who didn't care one bit about her past, but seemed—she hoped—interested in her future.

As his touch threaded between the laces down her spine, her skin heated in anticipation.

"My family is scattered all over." Slightly breathless

from their talk as much as his touch, she thought a little exchange of information was only fair. "My parents divorced when my sister and I were in college. They both left town to travel and pursue their own dreams and they don't keep in touch more than once a year. My sister is a nurse in Arizona."

He lingered at the small of her back, sketching light circles until her skin hummed with awareness.

"Maybe you could schedule a visit with her when I succeed in bringing you to San Diego for a visit."

"You want to see me again?" she clarified, determined there would be no more misunderstandings or false pretenses between them.

"I want to spend every second of your vacation with you since you still have a few days off. Then, after we both go back to work and miss each other like crazy, I'll fly you out to Southern California and make you fall in love with warm weather and sunshine."

Just hearing him say it made her realize he was absolutely correct. She would miss him dearly if they were separated. Wrapping her arms around his neck, she let her shawl fall to the ground while she held him close, eyes burning with unshed emotion.

"You want me to fall for the *weather?*"

He grinned, his teeth brilliantly white against his deeply tanned skin.

"Put it this way—I want to be sure you find some reason to keep coming back." He dropped a kiss to her neck, his lips branding a hot reminder into her skin. "Maybe you'll love it so much, you won't be able to leave. They need good lawyers in San Diego, too, you know."

He must have taken her breath away because she couldn't catch it for a long moment. Tenderness unfurled inside her along with a deep desire for that kind of life—that kind of love.

With him.

"I'd really like that." She nodded and the motion jarred a happy tear from her eye.

He caught it with his thumb.

"Are you sure?" He kissed her ear before he whispered in it. "I warned you, I come from a pushy family. If I'm moving too fast for you, I can slow down. I just don't want to leave here without telling you what I'm hoping for."

Stretching up on her toes, she squeezed him tight, savoring his strength and so much more.

"I'm hoping for the same things," she whispered back, her chin brushing his shoulder. "And considering that I'm a trial attorney, I think I'm going to hold my own with you."

This time, she would have a confidence in her personal relationships to match the self-assurance she'd always had in the courtroom. No more being drawn to guys who were bad for her.

He chuckled softly as he rained kisses down her neck. Her skin was on fire by the time a knock vibrated the door to the hotel room.

Rick's soft oath echoed her thoughts, but he came up for air long enough to shout, "Who is it?"

"Jake."

The sharp bark didn't sound pleased.

Lianna leaned down to retrieve her shawl so she

could cover up the back of her dress while Rick moved to open the door.

The tension that had marked their early interactions had vanished, she noted. The two of them no longer glared warning signals at each other constantly and they exchanged brief nods before Jake stepped just inside the threshold so Rick could close the door.

"I'm headed back to Miami," he said without prelude. "Just wanted to thank you and Rafe for the help."

"I'm sure Rafe is going to want to thank you, man." Rick clapped him on the shoulder. "He's been itching to can this guy for months."

"Where's Marnie?" Lianna asked, wanting to say goodbye to her. After an awkward beginning, she'd come to respect the way that Marnie had no need for the games and charades that used to entertain Lianna. She seemed to know who she was and what she wanted.

"She…" Jake's jaw tensed "…left about an hour ago."

A long, awkward paused ensued.

"Did she want to fly home?" Lianna knew it wasn't truly her business, but the gritty P.I. who'd scared her half to death when he accused her of embezzling funds now looked so brittle he was ready to break.

Something had gone terribly wrong.

"She decided to take a vacation to recover from her vacation, I guess."

Without him. Lianna tried to put the pieces together in her head, to offer up some words of wisdom for a man who was obviously stinging from whatever had happened between them.

Rick, it seemed, didn't waste time searching for the right words. He forged directly into the breach.

"Dude, don't let her get away." Rick shook his head in obvious disapproval, frowning the whole time. "That woman's crazy about you. And you should be smart enough to know when a good thing comes along."

Lianna was prepared for a sharp retort, but Jake surprised her with a slow shrug of his wide shoulders.

"Seeing her in danger…" He shook his head like the memory was too real. "I couldn't handle that again. And the work—you know how it is. You don't leave it at the office. Some of those cases follow you home."

Was that the life of a police officer? Lianna wondered.

"Hey, don't scare my girl." Rick winked at her as if he'd read her thoughts. "So you get a place outside the city and a big freaking dog. But you can't let that rule you."

"A big dog?" Jake turned toward the door. "That's your answer?"

"Hey." Lianna stepped in, feeling the tension ratchet up in the room. "Jake, I think Rick means that you're a smart guy and you'll figure out how to keep her safe. Because the other alternative isn't an option. If you push someone away because you're afraid you'll lose them, you end up losing them anyway. Even though I don't know Marnie that well, I saw how she cared about you, and I'd bet everything I have that she's hurt like hell. No woman wants a man to let her go like she's… inconsequential."

The way Alec had treated her when it suited him. Rick, on the other hand, came after her when she was scared and alone. One of many reasons she knew this was right. *He* was right.

Jake seemed to take a moment, weighing that statement. And a twitch in his right eye told Lianna he didn't like the idea of hurting Marnie one bit.

He swore softly under his breath, cursing himself, before leaning in to give Lianna a quick thanks and a kiss on the cheek.

Rick growled possessively, pulling her closer to his side. Jake offered him a terse nod before he turned on his heel and left, slamming the door behind him.

As if he had a woman to pursue.

Lianna broke the silence in the aftermath by clearing her throat.

"You weren't kidding about the pushy thing, were you?"

"Hey, I was doing him a favor by pointing out what he can't see. With five brothers, I've learned to recognize when a guy is being pigheaded." Rick stalked back across the room to be close to her. "You watch, he'll thank me one day for that pep talk."

He unwound her shawl from her shoulders and tossed it on the couch. Then, he gathered her hair on one side of her head and tucked it in front of her shoulder, exposing the laces on the back of her dress.

"You think he'll thank you? I think it was me that put a finer point on it than 'Get a big dog.' And if that was a pep talk, by the way, I sure hope you never try to cheer me up."

Spinning her around, Rick halted her so that her back faced him. He slid one finger under the knot that held the ties together.

"I've got an entirely different approach to take when I want to make you feel better." His breath warmed the back of her neck as he leaned close. "Would you care for a demonstration?"

Knees melting beneath her, Lianna couldn't wait.

MARNIE DIDN'T REGRET flying out of Saratoga late that afternoon.

She'd sprung for a flight to get her away from the man who'd broken her heart as fast as possible. Jake had protested, arguing that he could return her to Miami so she could spend the holidays with her family. But he couldn't keep her where she didn't want to be.

And she damn well didn't want to travel anywhere with a man who didn't recognize her right to choose what kind of life she led and who she spent her time with. She couldn't bear one more round of his refrain about her safety.

Did he think she was made of glass?

Now, strapping on a pair of ice skates in the moonlight a day later, Marnie gazed up at her hotel in northern Vermont. More of a ski lodge than a hotel, the Three Chimneys Inn sat on a quiet mountain side with access to cross-country skiing, sledding and a big pond for skating. She'd rented a one-room bungalow outside the main building, unable to return home to all the happy members of her family seated around the holiday table in pairs while she sat alone.

Again.

Inhaling the clean, cold air, she stood on her skates and hoped she remembered how to do this. As it turned out, she needed to lose herself now far more than when she'd been under suspicion for a felony and on the run from the man who framed her. A broken heart trumped all else when it came to reasons for booking a fantasy escape.

She needed this time to figure out how to go on without Jake.

Pushing off on one toe, she leaned forward on the other foot, feeling the blade cut into the bumpy, un-groomed ice. No one else was using the pond tonight, so she had it all to herself. Then again, most people were at home celebrating the holidays with family. Loved ones.

Banishing the thoughts of Jake for the umpteenth time in the past hour, Marnie launched into an upbeat Christmas carol, hoping to sing herself happy.

"It's great to hear you sing."

The deep, familiar voice cut right through her cho-rus about holly boughs and candles on the tree.

"Jake." She spun to see him standing in the moon-light at the pond's edge and her heart raced as if it were in triple overtime, even though she willed herself to be calm. Composed. "How did you find me?"

Her breath fogged the air in front of her. She was so not ready to revisit the heartache she'd experienced at his hands earlier this week.

"Don't worry." He remained at the edge of the ice, one boot hiked up on the log where she'd sat to lace up her skates. "It didn't involve any hidden cameras or anything. I just called your mom."

Oh. She could just imagine how that conversation went. Her mother had probably bombarded him with nosy questions before assuming he'd be present for

Christmas dinner. She was like that with every boy-friend and male acquaintance Marnie had from the time she was thirteen.

"You could have just called me." She tried not to pay attention to the fast trip of her heartbeat. He'd made an impression on her the first time they'd met when he'd built the cabinet for her display at Lose Yourself. And she'd been drawn to him ever since, even when that wasn't wise. Now was no different.

Forcing herself into a small spin on her skates, she hoped the activity would serve as a distraction so she didn't gape at him like a starving woman drooling over Christmas dinner.

"I wasn't sure what kind of reception I'd get and I didn't want to risk you telling me to go take a flying leap or anything like that."

Moonlight spilled over him, his breath huffing white and rising quickly in the cold.

She didn't argue since she wasn't sure what she would have said to him. She still didn't know.

"So why did you want to find me?" Slowing her spin, she took some pleasure in discovering the skating lessons she'd taken as a teen were still stored somewhere in her muscle memory.

Besides, thinking about skating seemed more prudent than letting her imagination run away when it came to Jake.

"For one thing, I wanted to return your laptop." He shoved his hands in his pockets, the snow and the moon surrounding him in white and silhouetting his big, powerful body. "I removed the spyware and cleaned it up for you. It's at the front desk of your hotel."

Stepping out onto the ice, he stalked toward her. She couldn't spin or skate now. All she could do was watch him come closer. And hope that he had far better reasons for trolling around the dark Vermont hillside than to deliver electronics.

"That was thoughtful of you." She kept her cool outwardly, her voice even despite being so unsteady inside. But the closer he came, the more certain she was that he could see how much she missed him. Wanted him.

When only a few inches separated them, he stopped. She was almost eye to eye with him while she wore her skates. His body blocked the wind, sheltering her in a way that made her warmer, yet gave her a shiver, too.

"I figured it was the least I could do to make it up to you for pulling the freak-out show yesterday." His voice, all low and growly and private, sent a jolt of pleasure through her, reminding her of other conversations that had been for her ears only.

She liked the idea that this intense, focused man could have a side he saved just for her. Not that she was getting her hopes up, damn it.

"I'm not sure what you mean." And she wanted to be one hundred percent clear. No more assuming the best because of her optimistic nature.

"Marnie, I'm sorry I went caveman on you yesterday. I kept waiting for you to go into shock after what you'd been through, but I think it was me who went a little crazy afterward." His expression was so serious. Tiny lines fanned around the outside of his eyes as he frowned. "I had no business dictating that we shouldn't be together because I got scared by this case.

Rick pretty much called me a candy ass to my face for acting like that."

"Really?" She tried to picture Jake standing still long enough to take that kind of criticism, and couldn't.

"Yeah." He shook his head, an odd smile lifting one side of his mouth. "He's not such a bad guy. And he was right."

Marnie's skates nearly slid right out from under her.

Apparently, Jake saw her surprise as he reached to steady her, but he kept right on talking.

"I've really put relationships on the back burner for a long time. I had a girlfriend mess around on me while I was on a tour overseas and it sort of cured the itch to have any kind of lasting commitment for a while. I just kept up the happy bachelor thing and devoted the best of myself to the job. Until you."

The night was so still and silent except for his voice. Smoke from some nearby cabins drifted on the breeze. All around them, the fresh fallen snow twinkled in the moonlight. And Marnie had the feeling she would always remember every tiny impression of this moment when Jake had cared about her enough to share something of himself. To open his heart, if only a little.

"I'm sorry some wretched woman cheated on you." She couldn't imagine stabbing a guy in the back like that while he was half a world away, and she knew firsthand what it felt like to be deceived.

"She wasn't The One." Jake took her hands in his, sliding his fingers inside her mittens to touch her skin. Her heart fluttered like a teenager's. "Apparently she was a bump in the road on the way to something better. And I'm not going to be too blind to see the best thing that ever happened to me when she's standing right before my eyes."

Marnie tipped her forehead to his, a profound sense of peace and rightness wrapping around her.

"Jake Brennan, you brought a much better gift than a laptop." She couldn't ask for anything nicer for Christmas than to have him here with her. Tunneling her arms inside his jacket, she wrapped herself around him.

"There's more."

"You're going to stay with me through Christmas?" she guessed, already picturing the fun she'd have unwrapping that particular present.

"I'm very on board with that, if you'll have me." He bent to kiss the top of her head, the rough edge of his unshaven jaw catching in her hair. "But I also had an early Christmas present to give you."

He reached inside a jacket pocket and pulled out an envelope that he handed to her.

"A present?"

"You'd better check it out and see if you like it."

Glancing at his face, she tried to guess and came up blank. Opening the envelope, she saw…

"MapQuest directions?" A route had been highlighted from Vermont back to Miami, with stops in between. "Philadelphia? Savannah?"

"I felt bad you didn't get to have much of a vacation so I talked to Vincent Galway, and he helped me figure out some of the Premiere Properties resorts you liked best. I figured you haven't gotten to travel much since you started your own business and while this isn't exactly Paris and Rome—"

Happy sparks showered through her as bright as the Northern Lights. She all but tackled him, squeezing him and her gift tight.

"You gave me a road trip." She'd been envious of the ones she'd booked for her clients, needing a getaway herself. "It's the best gift."

"Vincent says you can have your job back any time you want it, but at the least, he wanted to give you some comp rooms to apologize for terminating your position with Premiere."

"I'm really happy running my own business." She looked up into his eyes, feeling as if she were still spinning—no, floating—even though her skates remained in place. "But I'll gladly take the comp rooms as long as you're sharing them with me."

Jake nodded as he took the papers back and shoved them back in his pocket.

"I'm part of the deal." He wound an arm around her waist, his hand curving possessively over her hip. "And I'd be glad to take you back to your cabin and show you what an asset I'm going to be during this vacation of yours."

A light, swirling snow started to fall around them, the flakes as fat and glittery as the kind that came in a snow globe.

"Mmm," was all Marnie could manage, happiness and pleasure making her dizzy with wanting him.

"I want you in my life, Marnie. Thank you for giving me another chance."

"Thank you for coming for me." She kissed his cheek, so glad to have the promise of this night with him. This week. A future. "And thanks for making this the best Christmas ever."

Slanting his lips over hers, he met her mouth in a kiss that promised many, many more.

EPILOGUE

Nine days later

"SMILE FOR THE CAMERA." Marnie stalked her quarry barefoot across the carpet in the hotel room they shared at a historic property on Jekyll Island off the coast of Georgia. They'd spent Christmas together in Vermont before starting their road trip south, straying from the course when the mood suited them.

Now, on New Year's Eve, they'd decided to return to their hotel room, ditching the small champagne party in the dining club downstairs before the clock struck the zero hour. Shortly before midnight, with the sounds of the dance band wafting right through the closed balcony doors, Marnie sashayed around the room in her emerald-green satin cocktail dress, counting her blessings for the year.

Starting with the man in the middle of her zoom lens.

"Not more video." Jake shook his head as he unwound a black silk tie that he'd paired with one of the dinner jackets he'd bought during their stay at the Marquis. With the undone tie looped around his neck, he went for the buttons on his crisp white dress shirt. "Are you still trying to get payback for that hidden camera of mine? I don't think you can possibly capture as much footage of me as I've got of you."

His wicked grin teased her, but she deliberately panned lower on his strong, muscular bod to take in his exposed chest. The taut abs she could start to see as his fingers kept up the work on the buttons.

Would she ever get enough of this man?

They'd spent every moment together since the night he'd followed her to the Vermont skating pond, but she still got breathless when he got close to her. Not just because of the phenomenal heat that sparked between them. She just flat out liked to be with him. To hear about how he'd caught various bad guys. To understand how committed he was to his work. To be a part of his world. Yeah, she had it bad for him. And she couldn't be happier about that.

Especially now that two more witnesses had come forward to make statements about Alec's various schemes. According to Jake, they already had enough evidence to put him away for at least twenty-five years.

And that hadn't been all the good news they'd gotten on their winding road trip south. Lianna had called her two days ago, asking her to book a trip to the California coast for her to see the sights and take in a few neighborhoods for prospective house hunting. Marnie had been only too happy to oblige, spending an afternoon researching fun places for her and Rick to stay.

Right now, she was glad to think about her own future, however. It seemed to be turning out just right with this hot stud of a man in her viewfinder.

"I'm dispensing with the boring bits," she explained

"and getting only the juicy parts on tape. So my video archives are going to be way hotter than yours."

Jake stripped off the shirt and her mouth went dry.

"All flash and no substance?" He went for his belt buckle and she had the feeling her gasp of anticipation would be well documented in the audio. "Where's your artistic integrity as a filmmaker?"

Downstairs, she could hear the sudden blare of horns from the dance band and a chorus of shouts. Setting down the video camera, she checked the clock and saw the time.

"It's a new year." Her eyes went to his without the filter of the lens between them.

"To new beginnings." He spoke the words like a toast, but instead of lifting a glass, he stepped toward her. Clamping his hands around her waist, his fingers warmed her skin right through the silky green satin of her dress.

He bent close, the heat of his body kicking up her pulse. She licked her lips in anticipation. Nudged the strap of her slim sheath toward the edge of her shoulder and down. Off.

"Cheers to that," she agreed, her heart and her body so very ready for him.

As she shimmied her way out of her dress, Marnie was glad she'd turned off the camera for what she knew would come next. She had the feeling it would be a New Year's neither of them would ever forget.

* * * * *

New York Times bestselling author
Tawny Weber delivers a sexy new SEAL story.
Here's a sneak peek at

Christmas
with a SEAL

The Las Vegas penthouse was a kaleidoscope of sensations. Neon lights glinted off sparkling chandeliers, sending colorful sparkles off the crowd of partiers. Dressed in everything from sequins to plastic, denim to silk, bodies filled the room, covering the leather couches, perching on chrome stools around the bar and flowing onto the dance floor.

Accenting it all were intense music, free-flowing drinks and men. So, so many men.

And, oh, baby, they were gorgeous.

It wasn't just knowing that most of these muscular, sexy men were navy SEALs that made Frankie Silvera's insides dance. It was knowing that somewhere among them was her dream hottie and the answer to all of her problems.

She just had to find him.

"See anything you like?" Lara asked, stepping up beside her.

A room full of sexy guys with smoking-hot bodies?

What wasn't to like?

"I'm here to celebrate your wedding," Frankie said. "Not to hook up."

HBEXP79823

"You're in Las Vegas, Frankie. Go wild. Have fun." Lara laughed as she turned to leave. "Don't forget, what happens in Vegas stays in Vegas."

"Tempting, but I'm not the wild Vegas type," Frankie demurred, keeping her secret dream just that—secret. Frankie wasn't about to share her hope of finding a guy she'd only seen infrequently over the past ten years and seducing him.

Especially not when the guy was Lara's brother.

Taking a second glass of liquid courage that tasted like champagne, she decided it was time to get to work on the best weekend of her life.

Not an easy task. She looked around. There were at least two hundred people here. Figuring it was a gift that all the guys were hot and sexy and made searching fun, she moved through the bodies to cross the room.

Whoa. Frankie narrowed her eyes.

Was that him?

Sitting alone in one booth and looking as if he wanted to be anywhere else, the man was nursing a drink. Mahogany hair, shorn with military precision. A navy blue sweater covered his broad shoulders, emphasizing his perfect posture and, from what she could see, a gorgeous chest.

Lieutenant Phillip Banks.

He was even better looking now. And, oh, my, he was hot.

Nerves danced in her stomach. Frankie bounced in her beribboned heels, wondering if this was what Cinderella had felt like when she'd spotted the prince at the ball.

Half delighted, half terrified.

And totally turned on.

Pick up CHRISTMAS WITH A SEAL by Tawny Weber in November 2014 wherever you buy Harlequin® Blaze® books!

HBEXP79823

When it snows, things get really steamy...

Wild Holiday Nights
from Harlequin Blaze offers something sweet, something unexpected and something naughty!

Holiday Rush by *Samantha Hunter*

Cake guru Calla Michaels is canceling Christmas to deal with fondant, batter and an attempted robbery. Then Gideon Stone shows up at her door. Apparently, Calla's kitchen isn't hot enough without having her longtime crush in her bakery...*and* in her bed!

Playing Games by *Meg Maguire*

When her plane is grounded on Christmas eve, Carrie Baxter is desperate enough to share a rental car with her secret high-school crush. Sure, Daniel Barber is much, *much* hotter, but he's still just as prickly as ever. It's gonna be one *looong* drive...and an unforgettably X-rated night!

All Night Long by *Debbi Rawlins*

The only way overworked paralegal Carly Watts gets her Christmas vacation is by flying to Chicago to get Jack Carrington's signature. But Jack's in no rush to sell his grandfather's company. In fact, he'll do whatever it takes to buy more time. Even if it takes one naughty night before Christmas...

Available December 2014 wherever you buy Harlequin Blaze books.

HARLEQUIN®
™

Blaze®

Red-Hot Reads

www.Harlequin.com

HTHMS1014-5